J. LEIGH

WAY WALKERS:
TAINTED TALENT

Way Walkers: Tainted Talent
The Tazu Saga™: Book 3
Red Adept Publishing, LLC
104 Bugenfield Court
Garner, NC 27529
http://RedAdeptPublishing.com/

For Pop-pop and my Father,

both of which probably never imagined they'd share a dedication.

Pop taught me the right thing was always worth doing, and Dad taught me that sometimes you can do all the right things and still lose.

You two couldn't be more different, but you shaped me all the same.

Thank you, love you forever.

Prologue: Plans

"**A**nnesi, there's news."

Her shoulders tightened only slightly at the title. No matter how long she'd been called *Mother*, the label always played strangely in her ears. *Sister* had always been the moniker she preferred despite having fallen out long before with those who'd bestowed the name. Perhaps that was why she'd adjusted it a touch with her apprentices. *Older Sister* always had such a more youthful ring to it than *Mother*.

And my womb shall be mother to no one. That choice was made long ago, and not by me.

Putting down a pen held by a dark hand that looked far too aged and frail, she turned to face Sal'mar, adjusting her hood slightly to keep her eyes in shadow—a subtle effect, but still effective even when used on a follower employed as long as Sal'mar. *One should never forget the nuances of theater.* One could hold more sway over the masses than many could comprehend by using subtle plays and pretending at power. Nobody really needed power to do anything, only the perception of it.

Fear is the strangling coils of the Red and holds enemies and followers alike at bay.

"News of what precisely, Sal'mar?"

"The Grand Artifact. And the boy."

Unseen chills racked her body. She measured Sal'mar's stern black eyes and red face—the color of the Middle Lands clay from which the Annarite got his name—for a few heartbeats. She had always been patient, always able to see the long game, but the well she'd maintained for this thirty-year saga had gone bone dry, making her turn her back to it in pursuit of other founts. The idea that the silly moot prince had survived in Mikkal's clutches to surface again staggered even her.

"Where?" she asked.

"In Tar'citadel. One of our spies amid the Balori reports he's exposed both himself and the Artifact to the general populace."

"Himself? So the brat *is* a nontraditional Talent, then?" *Ishane, you were wrong about so much. How could you have been right about this?* "Do we know the type?"

Sal'mar tapped the ring and middle fingers of his right hand upon the line of the weighted chain wrapped around his chest while the stumps of his index finger and thumb twitched as if longing to pull back the bowstring they no longer could. That did not matter since he was as efficient with his *kusarigama* as he'd ever been with arrows. "I'm not familiar, Annesi, but the spy said something about a Negater."

A bubbling akin to that of her alchemical potions boiled in her stomach, then a flush warmed her cheeks. Her realization and craving were so deep and broad that they bordered upon sexual excitement. "A Negater." *The Grand Artifact must have been using the boy as a vessel.* She nearly giggled but held her tongue. "Thank you, Sal'mar," she said, turning back to the desk. The stump that was once her left arm twitched, the phantom fingers of the lost hand flexing eagerly, even without her prosthetic. Right-handed, she retrieved her pen and fresh paper. "You may go. But send up Matamir. I've need of him."

"Yes, Annesi."

Beneath her hood, Older Sister cracked a smile she knew made people weep in fear for their very souls. *I've plans to make.*

Chapter 1
Negater

A'ron De'contes laughed.

Rocking back and forth on the ground like an upturned turtle, the leader of the Balori and supposedly reformed Red Mage guffawed like a child having heard a joke about flatulence. "A Negater!" He gasped, choking on heaving giggles. Tears formed at the edges of his garnet-colored eyes, and he didn't look as though he would soon be rising from where Jathen had pushed him to safety from Master Arika's attack.

Concerned, Jathen turned away from the strange spurs of earth that had formed when Master Arika had unleashed her fire spiral. Her intended target had, of course, been A'ron, likely because she'd wrongfully assumed that the Red Mage had attacked her. The Rosinic Way Walker still had her arms up from the casting, though her delicate features belied shock, not dismissal. Nearby, Seren and the blue-clad Turinic Walker, Utför, wore similar expressions of alarm and awe. The Pearl Paladin, Master Mağrur, ignored all of them except De'contes, throwing an unveiled expression of disgust at the giggling leader of the Balori.

Inside Jathen's chest once again, the Grand Artifact of Bree and Bron buzzed lightly as Master Arika took a tentative step toward him. Her purple robes caught in the snow, wetting them at the edges.

"Was that truly an Artifact?" she asked.

"Oh, Spirit, yes," A'ron confirmed, wiping his face. His red-and-black robes were becoming spattered with snow and soil stains. "That has to be Yvette Ashton's work! Not sure which, but Spirit in Heaven, this is a lark—ruddy Children are sending Negaters toting Grand Artifacts to save me. I must be doing something right!"

Alarm suddenly shot through Jathen as he recalled the assassin he'd been protecting A'ron from. He whipped his head about but saw no sign of the dark-skinned Annarite. "Where did Nannazen go?"

His only answers were blank stares from the Way Walkers and the gradually quieting chuckles of De'contes. Never before had he longed so hard to punch a wall. *But there are no walls left—just two neat piles of rubble that were once townhouses.* "Three Way Walkers and a ruddy *Red Mage*, and no one saw where she went?"

"Child, an Artifact just *merged* with you." Master Utför's voice somehow managed to mix worry and disapproval. He was the eldest of the three Walkers A'ron had called to meet, and the frown on his tan face made him look like he'd been carved from an old boot. "And you're concerned about an assassin?"

"I *knew* about the Artifact, but she had a soul-sever blade! Or are you of the mind to let random teenagers run around with something that can kill High Mages and Avatars?"

One hand pressed against her chest and the fingers of the other tangled in her auburn hair, Master Arika turned to her fellow Walkers. "Who *is* this boy?"

"Take a glimpse at his eyes, Arika." Walking past the dirt spurs and Jathen, the Pearl Paladin gazed through the shell of a house and out across the perimeter of the block. "Ten to one, that's the missing moot prince everyone's been talking about." He drummed his fingers across the hilt of his sheathed sword.

Ignoring the scheming glint suddenly shining in the Rosinic's light eyes, Jathen asked Master Mağrur, "Do you sense Nannazen?"

Seren walked up beside Jathen then, her sapphire-colored scales paled to a cerulean blue. A cursory glance showed that the half-blood Chertith was unharmed—confused, clutching at her coat with shaking hands and missing one of her gloves, but well.

"No, not the assassin." The Angani Master shook his head then pointed his chin toward one of the few sheds backing the property. "Someone is in that, though, and not happy about it."

"I've found the soul-sever blade!" Finally up and liberated from his giggling fit, De'contes wiggled the silver hilt between two fingers as if the deadliest master-charm in existence were a carnival prize to be proud of. "But Jathen is right." Calling over their heads, he addressed the small crowd of curious Balori members who'd started to creep back toward the house's shell. "Everyone, please spread out and see if you can catch a trace of where Nannazen limped off to. I doubt she had enough energy to teleport, with the hit she took—the fire clipped her fairly hard. And do please dig out the shed—someone seems to have taken refuge in there and is now trapped by snow on the door."

"I'll summon the tar'ka-besh." Master Utför offered then looked poignantly at Jathen. "We need to keep all the major witnesses nearby."

"There was a Balori girl, a human teenager that Nannazen knocked over when she ran back into the house." Jathen rubbed his backside, the ache there reminding him of his own collision with the porch. "She might have seen something more than I did."

"Yes, yes, we all must comply properly," De'contes agreed, calling again to his followers. "Anyone who saw anything, please stay and speak to the tar'ka-besh."

The Balori scattered like rats fleeing a sinking ship.

Seren's mouth fell open. "Are they coming back?"

"Hopefully." De'contes sighed softly. "Trusting the other Ways, and especially the tar'ka-besh, is a slow process."

"Those with nothing to hide have nothing to fear," Master Mağrur said bitterly.

"Being Red alone is something to hide, my dear paladin," De'contes replied. "Even to believe as a Balori can bring death outside Tar'citadel."

"You wouldn't know, Red Mage, for fear of stepping out of the city and losing your sanctuary. Tell me, which of the Originals do you think would kill you first, Orrick Ashton or Erin Manna?"

"Hostilities later, please." Master Utför stepped up to the Red Mage, hand held out. "Though Mağrur makes a point. The blade, De'contes. Such a thing should not be in questionable hands."

"Are yours considered unquestionable then, Utför?" A'ron grinned, his fangs out with a slightly feral glint. "With all due respect, this was just used to try to kill me. I think I'd feel more secure with it in the only set of hands I know *won't* try to repeat the act."

Five tar'ka-besh in white robes teleported into the yard before Master Utför could protest, along with a human man wearing a set of silver pants and over-robe. Cut similar to the tar'ka-besh's but trimmed in gold, not a wrinkle or spot was on them. Of Lubreean heritage, the man appeared to be in his midforties, though he could have been older, as Lubreean humans tended not to show their age until their sixties. His thick black hair was cut tight in the back and long in the front, giving him a disjointedly disheveled appearance compared to the neatness of the rest of him.

"A'ron, the blade, please," the newcomer said, sounding mildly bored as the tar'ka-besh fanned out. A braid of gold chain and small diamonds on his shoulder winked in the winter sun as he extended his hand. "I'll not ask again."

"But of course." De'contes relinquished it with a flourish. "Unquestionable hands, as Master Utför so eloquently suggested."

The man's dark, almond-shaped eyes belied no amusement as he placed the deadly weapon in an inner pocket of his robe.

Jathen leaned in toward Seren. "Who is this?"

"I am Dàshī Jidoja," the man himself replied. "High Chancellor of Tar'citadel."

"He's also a High Mage," Seren whispered back.

Jathen swallowed, instantly intimidated. Only a handful of High Mages lived on the continent, energy manipulators who'd fused with an elemental source of energy to give them an unlimited source to cast from. The process also made them immortals. Even the lowly moot prince knew Dàshī Jidoja was the most powerful of them, save for Orrick Ashton—not because he wielded greater Ability than the others but because he essentially governed Tar'citadel.

High Air Mage, I think—or was he water? There's another High Mage who is of Tazu Nation origins, but I could never remember which was which. Jathen measured the man again, wondering briefly if he would give a Red Mage reason to hesitate to enter a fight. *Would explain De'contes's compliance.*

The High Mage stood stoic, hands clasped behind his back as he watched the tar'ka-besh. Three teleported out, while another removed the snow covering the shack's door with slow waves of his hand. "That has more snow on it than what Arika could have blown over there," Dàshī Jidoja said after a moment. "The tar'ka-besh should focus on the investigation for now, so I shall leave their uncovering to your people, A'ron."

"Fair enough, Chancellor. So long as whoever is inside isn't in any danger."

"The Balori are citizens, A'ron, and you know I do not play favorites based on what Way someone follows."

The snow-shoveling tar'ka-besh stopped and teleported out as well. Jathen bit his lip uncertainly now that the danger had truly passed. As much as he wanted to ask De'contes about having been named a Negater, broaching the subject in front of tar'ka-besh and the High Chancellor seemed contrary to his desire to keep his identity a secret. *Though I have a feeling that might be a useless venture at this point.* The gazes from the three Way Walkers made him more nervous with each passing moment. *It's like they want to eat me.*

Seren's voice popped into his head. *More like you're some prized antique just placed up for auction.*

She slipped her gloveless hand into his, giving Jathen another wave of those odd little energy zaps. It wasn't unpleasant this time, but like her capacity to speak in his mind and his sudden ability to hear her, it was another mystery to add to the list.

Are you all right? she asked.

Well enough for the wear. Champing at the bit to find out what De'contes was laughing so hard about. Hoping they find Nannazen and really hoping they don't arrest me for something.

Seren smirked. *I doubt the last part, truly.*

Do you recall what a Negater is, from your books?

Not enough—only that it was on the list of possible nontraditional Talents that I'd eliminated for one reason or another, thanks to your contradicting attributes. It was one of the more complicated ones, with many variants and arguments about what they are capable of. She frowned, pushing her long blond bangs away from her right eye with her free hand. *I'm sorry.*

Jathen squeezed her hand then let go. Suddenly feeling very tired, he watched the tar'ka-besh trying to corral Balori a few streets down.

The wayward Balori followers did saunter back shortly thereafter, including the girl who'd taken a fall on the porch with Jathen. Skinny, she seemed to be drowning under her long brown hair, the mess of waves cascading over her shoulders and down well past her waist. Biting her bottom lip, she shivered visibly as she talked, her eyes darting back and forth among the Balori members slowly shoveling out the door for the mystery person in the shack, De'contes, and the Chancellor. She also shied as far away from Master Mağrur and his shiny white plate mail as physically possible.

"Nan's been actin' odd," she finally explained. "Ignorin' me."

The Chancellor glanced at De'contes. "They are friends?"

"As far as I know."

He nodded then returned his attention to the girl. "How long has she been out of sorts?"

"Two days? Maybe three? She didn't want to sit with me anymore. Always followin' the Proph... er, Master De'contes around." She shifted her weight from foot to foot. "But she'd never hurt him, really."

"You and I both saw her try to stab him," Jathen replied.

"I saw her face when she turned back around to, yes." She bit her lip again then locked eyes with the Chancellor. "It was all calm and... practiced. Nan has fits. She gets angry, fumin' and spittin'. Even some kickin'. But she's no assassin, to look calm before killin' a man."

The High Chancellor exchanged long glances with both De'contes and Master Mağrur before nodding. "You may go," he told her.

Ruddy telepathy, Jathen grumbled to himself as the girl practically fled. "Wait!" he called, suddenly remembering. "Did you see the flash?"

She stood in the snow, brow furrowed and lips twisted as if she suspected he was entrapping her. "What flash?"

"When I grabbed her arm, there was a flash."

"No."

Jathen sighed then turned back to the others with a shrug. "When she thrust the blade at him, I grabbed her arm," he explained. "There was a glimmer of light, and her skin... changed. That's what distracted me, so she was able to knock me over before running back into the house."

While Master Mağrur scowled, Dàshī Jidoja pursed his lips, thoughtful. "You might be correct," he told De'contes.

"As I said, I do not think she'd willingly harm me."

Master Maǧrur gazed suspiciously at Jathen. "It still does not explain what you'd gone back there for, nor why you were here in the first place, missing prince." Jathen didn't need telepathic Ability to sense the unspoken question the Pearl Paladin was indubitably thinking: *Nor why I can't read your mind or how you could move through my stasis spell.*

Before Jathen could reply, two of the tar'ka-besh teleported into their midst, practically elbowing Jathen and Seren out of the circle of Way Walkers.

"We found this two alleys over, sir," one said. She was the tar'ka-besh that'd been on guard duty with Ass'shiri's brother, Burjiro, the day Jathen had taken the crossbow back to the kasior order. An older woman with silver-streaked black hair, Dredona handed an elaborate necklace made of gold and precious stones to the Chancellor with a formal flair. "We think it was damaged during Master Arika's attack and discarded by the assassin. Unfortunately, there's no emotional imprinting left on it."

He cradled the broken bauble in his hands, looking thoughtful. "A master-charm, and a fine one at that." He clicked the crystals together. "I'd even venture to say this was Yvette Ashton's work. A'ron?"

The Red Mage took the piece from him and held it up to the light. "Yes, the signature is here, embossed into the gold."

Dàshī Jidoja turned back to Dredona and the other tar'ka-besh. "Search the grounds for the *real* Nannazen, and quickly. Start with that ruddy shed. She may have been hurt by whoever used this to take on her appearance."

Both tar'ka-besh jumped to obey, practically elbowing the shoveling Balori aside.

"A glamour charm?" Master Utför asked, eyes wide. He huffed slightly. "I didn't think anyone could make one elaborate enough to impersonate a specific person."

"Not to mention not see through it or notice the spell." Peering at the piece as well, Master Arika crossed her arms. "She *felt* like an innocent child—*not* an assassin."

"Do not lament your skills, Arika. As said, this is Yvette's work." A'ron's fingers closed over the remains of it, making crystals crack. "Someone is sending me a message."

"And it's a long list of possible *whos*," the Chancellor added darkly. "You're not making this easy on me, A'ron."

"And you have my deepest apologies for that, Chancellor."

"We've got her!" Dredona cried out.

Jathen felt as though he was in a strange parade, following the Red Mage, the High Mage, and a slew of Walkers over to the shed, with Seren close on his own heels.

De'contes helped the tar'ka-besh pull Nannazen out and removed a dirty gag from her mouth. "Nan, can you hear me, child?"

Her head lolled to one side as he patted her dark cheek.

"Dehydrated and hungry," Dredona said, putting two fingers on the younger girl's forehead. Her companion untied Nannazen's wrists and ankles while De'contes held her steady. Dredona shook her head. "She'll recover, but I can find no memories of her attacker in her mind."

"Fucker hit me in the head," the teenager rasped. She tried to stand but slipped, ending up completely in A'ron's arms.

"Nannazen requires medical attention. Chancellor, with your permission, I'd like to oversee that care." He shifted the girl in his arms, holding her as if she weighed nothing. "She might also be more forthcoming with myself than others."

"Of course, A'ron," Dàshī Jidoja agreed, but then his tone turned stern. "Though you're getting a tar'ka-besh escort as well. For both your protection and supervision. I'll have no vigilante investigations, De'contes. This is a Tar'citadel matter."

The Clansman pursed his lips very slightly but then nodded. "Very well."

"Chancellor, if you would," Master Arika broke in before De'contes had an opportunity to leave. "I'd prefer your permission to take the boy from here as well. De'contes has named him a Negater, and we can't just have him wandering about. He must have questions—"

Dàshī Jidoja crossed his arms, looking tired. "Arika, really, with all you've given me to deal with, a verified Negater is the least of my concerns at present."

"What *I've* given you?"

"Atop of losing an assassin, you stripped two buildings down to their studs, Arika, essentially making the Balori homeless. Do you have any idea the logistics it's going to take to gather enough energy manipulators to *remake* the ruddy things? Not to mention the costs?"

She stabbed an accusatory finger at De'contes. "I thought there was a Red Mage inside, murdering someone! Isn't that what you would have done?"

The Chancellor hooked a thumb at Seren. "I'd have taken two seconds to listen to the Tazu telling me someone was trying to assassinate the head of the Balori."

Seren blinked repeatedly, apparently unaware that he'd been privy to her memory of the day.

"She even threw her glove at you, and you still didn't listen." He pointed at Jathen. "Nor did you listen to the second person who came running at you, screaming not to attack A'ron but stop the girl instead. And you attacked while *both* of them were under a Pearl Paladin's stasis spell, completely unable to defend themselves. It's legitimate grounds for assault, and you're lucky I am taking into consideration the extenuating circumstances."

De'contes smiled snidely over Nannazen's head. "Well, she did have enough sense to turn off the water main before destroying the buildings."

Master Arika's glare was so intense that Jathen could practically see her fantasy of sinking a soul-sever blade into the Red Mage's heart. "Patronizing me is not a mark in your favor for currying mine, De'contes."

"Oh, is that still on the table? I'd assumed your attempted assault was the final death knell for my chances. But if you are still interested in hearing out my plea for Balori fairness, by all means, I'll happily switch back to verbose flattery, my dear master of matter deconstruction."

Dàshī Jidoja snapped his fingers, the sound echoing far more loudly than naturally possible, making even the half-conscious Nannazen twitch. "Discontinue before I remind the tar'ka-besh that there are equally valid cases to be made for *both* of you to be charged with at least disturbing the peace. And in all fairness, my choices are that either both or neither of you will be incarcerated for the minimum, so do not test me."

"The house was coming down anyway," Jathen intervened. "The structure was unsound, with the way they'd cut into the walls between the houses."

"Thank you." Master Arika's body language toward him softened.

"All this aside, I must point out there is also a Grand Artifact in play, Chancellor," Master Utför added tentatively. "An untrained Talent of any category cannot merely tote that around. Such things belong under the laws of cultural items of significance and therefore can be construed as property of the city-state of Tar'citadel in the absence of its corresponding Avatar to claim it."

"Not to mention he's probably our illegal teleport from a few weeks back," Master Mağrur reminded everyone. "Used it to that end, I'd wager to guess."

"I didn't exactly have a choice in the matter," Jathen protested, his body going rigid in alarm and anger. As much as he'd originally wanted to pass the responsibility of the Grand Artifact on to another, he balked at the idea of it being forcibly taken from him. *Especially by these idiots.*

"The Grand Artifact brought you here of its own accord?" Dàshī Jidoja asked.

Jathen couldn't suppress rolling his eyes. "It does everything of its own accord, including using me as a hiding spot when it pleases—or not, apparently."

"Which may mean it revealed itself now for a reason, amid those who'd recognize it and know better what to do with it," Master Utför said.

Inside Jathen's chest, the Grand Artifact whined in agitated disagreement.

"If you believe you'd know better than a Grand Artifact what to do with it, then you truly are a fool, Utför," A'ron said blandly.

The Chancellor quelled any angry responses with a wave of his hand. "Do you know which Artifact it was, Utför?"

"No," he admitted begrudgingly.

"Arika?"

"You know very well I studied matter deconstruction, not Grand Artifacts."

"A'ron?"

"I suspect one of the several Yvette disassembled during Car'son's reign. But, no, not specifically."

Saying nothing, Dàshī Jidoja just gazed at Jathen with his dark-brown eyes.

"It's the Grand Artifact of Bree and Bron," Jathen whispered. "Made by Yvette Ashton and born of both their hearts—to find what has never been found, hidden within what was never hidden."

The Chancellor smiled. "A'ron might be ineloquent in his delivery, but he is correct. I've limited dealings with Grand Artifacts, but the few I've come across pick their own guardians. In lieu of Bree or Bron to claim it, Jathen here is where it will stay. Besides, I think the prince of the blood of the Tazu Nation does qualify him to be a bit more on the responsible end of those who could be 'toting it about.'"

"Thank you." Though oddly relieved, Jathen found that having his full name used unfortunately reminded him of other troubles. "And if possible, I'd very much prefer it, sir, if you wouldn't inform the Tazu embassy of my presence here."

"I'm afraid I must do that, Highness. While I respect your free will and will certainly not force you to go to the embassy nor divulge where it is you are staying in the city, my duty to the First Law and you ends there. My second duty is to the state of Tar'citadel, and our alliance with each and every nation on this continent carries weight. I cannot—nor shall I not—show a preference for a person over that of the interests of an entire country's political future. And knowing whether or not their heir lives, I'd say, will greatly affect the political climate of the Tazu Nation." He paused. "I shall say, however, that I sense no imminent danger for you while here. My intuition on such things is strong, as is my precognition. You are safe here."

"If your precognition is so wonderful, then who tried to kill De'contes?"

While the other Walkers and Seren gawked at Jathen in mild horror, the Chancellor merely smirked. "Someone who wasn't interested in killing *you*, Highness. Which is all you need concern yourself with at this time, I should think."

With a growing foreboding in his stomach, Jathen watched A'ron De'contes, the two tar'ka-besh, and Nannazen teleport out. *I don't exactly have a good track record when it comes to spoiling evil people's plans. They do tend to try to kill me, after.*

No, but I don't think the Chancellor is interested in pursuing the matter too deeply, Jathen, Seren added to his thoughts. *And whoever tried this probably knows that and won't bother with you either.*

So he'll let an assassin go free, free to try to kill again, all because he doesn't like De'contes?

I don't think it's that simple. And I don't think he likes or dislikes A'ron. He's one of the ones who agreed to his sanctuary here. He just can't seem too sympathetic to any side. It's a tightrope this man walks. Pick your battles.

"Jathen," Master Arika tried again, her voice tentative, "truly, child, you should come with me now and meet with High Walker Jiāojīn. A Negater is very rare, and I'm certain you have questions—"

"And I still have questions for him, as should the Chancellor," Master Maǧrur said with a scoff. "Besides, since when does Rosin hold a monopoly on nontraditional Talents? The Pearls have a long tradition of training them as well. And given that the *only* reason I came today was to protect you two, I'm starting to think this whole calamity was Angani's way of making certain the boy was passed off to the *proper* hands."

Practically shaking in his robes, Master Utför broke in, "Oh! Of all the self-righteous—"

"The three of you will ruddy well *shut up.*" The air quaked when Dàshī Jidoja spoke, making everyone inhale and momentarily freeze, even Jathen. "The prince's business with the Balori is his own, but I suspect it had to do with *being* a nontraditional Talent in the first place. A'ron has forgotten more about nontraditional Talents than the Rosinics have written about them in their library. As to his intervening with an assassin..." He turned to Jathen.

After a quick breath, Jathen skirted the truth. "I had a premonition, leaving. I saw a dagger, a flash. I didn't know who it was intended for but thought if I just warned De'contes, that would be enough."

The Chancellor's eyes led Jathen to think the High Mage might be aware that he was holding back despite not being able to read his mind. For a horrible moment, he thought Dàshī Jidoja would declare him false, bringing up the story of Ra'vien's appearance and demanding to know why an Aspect who'd once been murdered by De'contes would now save him.

Instead, the Chancellor merely nodded. "That satisfactory for you, Mağrur? Because it seems reasonable enough to me."

The Pearl Paladin's blue-gray eyes narrowed sharply. "I suppose one cannot go against what the High Chancellor finds reasonable."

"Finest thing you've said all day." He folded his hands behind his back again. "Now, Master Mağrur, if you'd be so kind as to supervise my tar'ka-besh for the rest of this... escorting Balori to a temporary establishment and taking statements? I've other matters to attend to."

"Where are you putting them?"

"I was hoping I could call upon Angani's mercy and borrow some space from the penitents. I do believe they've an abundance of spare beds this time of year, with the number of pilgrims low due to snows."

Master Mağrur did not look the least bit pleased but didn't protest.

The Chancellor smiled. "Good. Master Arika, if you could organize the energy manipulators necessary to rebuild the Baloris' homes...?"

The Rosinic's mouth gaped open and closed like a fish. "But Chancellor, you yourself said the cost—"

"Will be offset by the Way of Rosin, since I do believe this was an excessive use of force on your part—perhaps not the deconstruction but certainly the assault on A'ron and, by proxy, his Highness Prince Jathen. You are *extremely* lucky he is a Negater and thus redirected your little fire column back into the earth energy you used rather than just *dying* as a normal person would have." His tone turned cold as she pursed her lips. "Believe me, if he had, I'd be cleaning up a massive international incident, and you'd be explaining to High Walker Jiāojīn why she would better accept your resignation than enter into a war between the Way of Rosin and the Tazu Nation itself. Consider this a *minor* penance."

Hope sprang up inside Jathen, and not at Master Arika's quite comical sullen expression. "You know what a Negater is," he said to the High Mage.

"Of course. Though as said, I have several other matters I must attend to." Turning, he took a few steps through the snow, away from the mess and the three sour-looking Walkers. "Walk with me, both of you."

"Walk?"

"Yes, Highness, you are a Negater. They cannot be teleported."

Can't be teleported? Jathen's heart began to race, not merely because he and Seren were chasing after the High Mage. *Mikkal told me that, at the summit—that I couldn't be teleported.*

"But Jathen *has* been teleported." Seren fell into step as well, walking with the Chancellor between her and Jathen.

The still-lingering crowd of Balori members parted quickly for them, clearly intimidated, though Jathen wasn't sure if he or the Chancellor spooked them more.

"The Grand Artifact did so," Seren continued. "This was one of the reasons why we'd eliminated a Negater as a possibility."

"A fair assessment when not taking into account the Grand Artifact's actual abilities." He nodded, turning his attention to Jathen. "I assume that each of the teleportation instances occurred immediately after you were hit with a large wave of energy. An attack spell, perhaps?"

"Yes. I'd already noticed that correlation."

"Then I believe two things may have been happening to you at once, Highness. Firstly, you are a Negater. When energy already ma-

nipulated into a spell hits you, your type of Ability reverts that energy to its original energetic state. In this case, Arika's pillar of fire she'd
made using earth energy reverted into stone—those spurs that grew
up behind you. This is an automatic, natural response of your body's
when the energy has no direction. Essentially, you unmake spells."

"Unmake?" Jathen stopped a moment, stunned. *Wards, I negate
wards!*

Memories of half a dozen instances surfaced in a rush: the time
he'd walked into the makeshift charm shop, only to have Ass'shiri
smack face-first into a ward; the incident with Shandi Miolung and
the demons that had gotten into the room somehow; when they
were running through Dodbyen and Spinnek's protective influence
didn't fully extend over him; "eating" the iungo plants' auras; even
the little charms Seren had made to disguise his eyes.

You dispelled them, she said.

It's been getting stronger.

Jogging a few steps, he caught up to them quickly. "Just now, with
the Nannazen impersonator, I grabbed her arm, and her skin faded
from black to pink. I negated the master-charm's glamour spell."

"Presumably, yes. It's probably why she panicked and ran from
you. You could be a very unexpected complication for many Talents."

"You just said that's what happens when the energy he reverts has
no direction," Seren said, furrowing her eye ridge. "Does that mean
Jathen can direct it? And if so, in what ways?"

"Sadly, I have not had the pleasure of knowing any Negaters to
give you a detailed answer to that." The Chancellor shook his head.
"However, I can reasonably assume that while you cannot absorb and
then manifest energy yourself, with focus and training, you should
be able to determine what state the energy you negate manifests *as*.
The conversion rate for a Negater would presumably be considerably
more one-sided, since you are siphoning from already-manipulated
energy, so for more complex intentions, you'd need a considerable

amount of energy to hit you. However, because you have a Grand Artifact in your keeping, when energy is reverted and you *don't* give it some sort of intention, we can assume the Grand Artifact itself has been grabbing the energy for its own use."

That explains why "be better" worked when we first got to Dodbyen, Jathen told Seren. *After the Artifact used up all the energy it needed to teleport me and Izzy, I used the rest. And later, it worked during Marcasith's field blast. His energy made me better. Interesting.* "But this last time, I asked the Artifact not to teleport me anywhere, so things reverted instead."

"That's good—you can control or at least *request* of the Grand Artifact." The Chancellor's lips twitched in a minor smile. "I'll sleep better now knowing I let you keep it."

"Jathen, that's what happened on *Charmed Wind*," Seren said, her breath coming out in excited puffs in the cold. "You hadn't put together the Artifact half yet, so when the wind energy converted from the charm-engines hit you in the face, it then reverted, thus blowing up the engines themselves."

"And this last time in Dodbyen, the same charm-engine energy hit me, and I prayed I'd end up somewhere safe—so the Grand Artifact dropped me here."

"A reasonable conclusion." Dàshī cocked his head. "I should mention this all describes what is known as a True Negater, who can negate *all* types of energy. Most Negaters tend to only negate one or perhaps two types of vibrational energy—such as sound or light. They rarely negate one of the major four: earth, air, wind, or water."

Jathen took a deep breath, running his hands through his hair. "True Negater." Putting words to it felt so strange, to have a category, a list of attributes for what he was. *And yet, I still have no idea what it really means—at least not yet.*

"You should also be aware that this is probably why a Grand Artifact chooses to reside *inside* you."

"Oh?" Jathen and Seren said at the same time.

He regarded them with a certain bemused air. "Tell me, when you originally came across this Artifact, was it in a box of sorts?"

"Yes, made of negation stone." Jathen actually laughed. "It thinks of me as another hiding box!"

The Chancellor nodded. "A Grand Artifact such as this can actually merge with anyone it chooses, but only inside a Negater would it remain hidden, unreadable within your aura."

"Find what has never been found, hidden inside what has never been hidden." He smiled at Seren, his soul liberated of so many questions even as others squirmed in the back of his mind. "I finally know."

"I am glad to have assisted," the Chancellor said, stopping. "But as said, I have a mass of other matters to attend to, so I must take my leave of you." He bowed his head, formal. "Highness."

"But, wait—" Jathen stumbled verbally, not certain how to ask what he must. Answers were well and good, but the idea of continuing to randomly flounder with his Abilities wasn't pleasant, not when he had enemies waiting in the wings. "You said you don't know much about Negaters, but do you know of anyone who *could* train me?"

The High Mage's eyebrows shot up in either surprise or amusement. "I would not presume to direct anyone in their life's choices, Prince Jathen, but respectfully, we are in Tar'citadel. Master Arika was correct—a Negater, especially a True Negater, is rare. And *incredibly* useful. Rosin's Aspect has been reborn as a Negater several times, so Rosinics have that basis, as well as what Master Mağrur said about the Pearl Paladins training nontraditional Talents. If those don't suit, then you've an entire city that is the seat of every one of the Twelve Ways. If anything, I believe you might have an abundance of teachers coming to you after today. The choice, as always, is yours."

With that, he disappeared.

Chapter 2

"You're not happy."

Walking back to the University Citadel, Jathen tried his best not to let the impact of Seren's comment show on his face. "What makes you say that?"

"You've been quiet." The pretty half-blood Tazu glanced sideways at him, her bright-blue eyes flecked with gold like two miniature star charts—not as impressive or mystical as the Drannic eyes Jathen had once seen, but still pretty. "You forget I knew you a long time back home. I learned your moods, same as Thee. A *Negater*—Jathen, do you know how many opportunities this will open up for you? You saw those Way Walkers. They'd all give their left feet to have you with them. The Chancellor practically said as much." She grinned encouragingly, but the expression waned as he raised his eyes to meet hers. "And that's the very thing you're worried about."

"It was all too public, Seren. Sister will know now, and Mikkal," he whispered. Looking up at the University Citadel looming a few blocks away, Jathen wasn't sure if the pearly white tower was a protector or a beacon for trouble. "Yes, I know what I am. But at what cost? Are Marcasith and Izzy and the rest of Dodbyen safe? Have they landed safely from that hell, only to be swept up by Sister and Mikkal in order to get at me?"

"Izzy and your uncle will be here soon, Jathen," Seren assured him. "They are surrounded by Way Walkers and my father. It is as

23

Annakki said: Tar'citadel is the safest place in the world for you and them. Those two demons can't strike at you now, lest the world know."

"But that brings up another point—Annakki." Grasping at the lump in his shirt where hung both the Monortith signet ring and Ass'shiri's crossbow bolt, he tried to quell the sick feeling building in his stomach. "I saved the life of the man who murdered her parents. What kind of reception do you think that will earn me?" *I might never see Dor'rhean again.* Jathen still mourned—indeed, would always mourn—Ass'shiri, lost once to death and a second time when his soul chose to cross to the far-side of the Veil. Losing access to his friend's son was a cut Jathen wasn't certain he could bear.

Seren sighed long, resting a hand on his back. "With any victory, there will always still be shadows. You can revel in what you've gained or wallow in the darkened recesses of the unknown."

"Another Hatori quote?"

"He was incredibly eloquent when he wanted to be." Putting her hands in her pockets, Seren turned her face skyward, silky blond hair falling back away from her cheeks. Her eyelashes caught a few flecks of a light snow that had started to fall. "I do understand, though. In the end, it's just a word, a label. Negater, moot, prince, king—they will all have their benefits and shortcomings. You worry for the living. That's an admirable trait."

Jathen stared up past the beautiful skyline of ice and light, peering deep into the foggy gray clouds. Nothing comforting was there, though the flakes felt good on his warmed cheeks. "I chose that once, on the summit with the Interpreter, to be in the world rather than to go with him and get answers."

"And now you are in the world *and* have your answers." Flicking the snow from her eyes, Seren grinned. "I still say that's a victory."

"For now," he allowed. As her dissatisfaction seemed ready to summon another point, he said instead, "Did you really fling a glove at an angry Rosinic?"

She coughed a laugh. "Oh, I know it was idiotic, but I was so frustrated! None of them even tried to listen. And I was worried about you. That woman clearly didn't care who got caught in the crossfire."

"Well, I suppose it's nice to know you'll use anything at your disposal to save me," he said, letting a small smile bloom.

Seren snickered, placated. They walked back the rest of the way in silence while Jathen mulled over the strange encounter with the Aspect of Rhean. *She told me to save him. But why? Was it just so I know what I am? Or is there something deeper, as De'contes said? Ruddy Children sending Negaters toting Grand Artifacts to save him... By Spirit, what does that mean if the Balori are correct about the Red?*

"I should probably clean myself up," he said when they were nearly to her room, having not come to any conclusions but one. "And I should head over to Annakki's as soon as possible. I really prefer she hear this from me first."

"Wise," Seren agreed, opening the door. "Though I do—" She squeaked in alarm and dropped her key, halting so quickly that Jathen nearly collided with her.

A man clad in black stood calmly in the center of the room, directly beneath the skylight. Nearly a head shorter than Jathen, he had copper-toned hair and the bright tangerine eyes of a Clansman. His heart pounding, Jathen immediately put himself between the stranger and Seren, cursing himself again for not having Hatori's sword cane or his daggers on him.

"Please, there is no need to be alarmed." The interloper spread his hands, palms out defensively, looking sheepish. "Allow me to introduce myself. I am Nevershen Supai."

Relaxing, Jathen better examined the man's clothes—another Tar'citadel-style uniform, obviously Rheanic. *Though his first name sounds more Annarite than Clan.* He crossed his arms, not amused. "You are in my room."

"Technically"—his tangerine eyes swept over to where Seren was retrieving her key from the floor—"you are in Serendibiss Chertith's room."

Jathen deepened his glare. "You are *in* my *room*."

"There is a reason for that." A smile slithered across his lips. "Discretion and the like."

"And being a ruddy purveyor of the dramatic," Seren quipped, slamming the door shut.

"Yes, and making the point that you've obviously always known where to find me but weren't interested in bothering with me until now." Jathen snorted at the man's bemused expression. "I'm also not in the mood for cloak and dagger—especially such a transparent swatch of it."

"I am here on behalf of the Way of Rhean," the man finally said.

"I can gather that." Jathen's shoulders slumped, tiredness creeping into his bones as his previous magical stunt continued weighing him down. "But couldn't you *wait*?"

The Clansman actually chuckled. "As alluring as being the first to speak to you about choosing a Way is, my choice of locale does, truly, have more to do with discretion than impatience. As this is technically not your room, I am *technically* not here."

Jathen uncrossed his arms. "As endearing as Rheanic word-weaving can be for me at times, I am exhausted. I am in a bad mood. And I need you to make your ruddy point."

"You saved the life of A'ron De'contes. The current High Walker of the Way of Rhean and a fellow Clansman, while somewhat tolerant of A'ron, cannot be seen to directly sympathize with him. However, to ignore the benefit of having a Negater in our ranks would be, well, foolish of us. So I am here in an unofficial capacity to extend an open invitation, as it were, to come to us."

Seren snorted. "So that the Rhe'don can save face, you are here to tell Jathen you'd like him to go to the Way as if it were his idea." Peeling off her remaining glove then depositing it on her dresser, she gave him another sour look. "That about right?"

"Essentially."

Tapping his foot, Jathen sensed Seren's irritation fueling his own. "And let me guess—you'd like my visit to have a certain amount of discretion?"

He smiled pleasantly. "Yes. I see you do have a Rheanic bent to your thoughts already."

"Only out of necessity," Jathen admitted. "Amid everything else that's happened to me, I'm still trying to decide if I want to try to gain my kingdom. As much as I am at home with most Rheanics, openly being one is *not* going to sit well with certain figureheads back home. I have to save face too."

Nevershen grinned as though he'd just come across a rabbit after not Feeding all day. "No one ever said it had to be 'openly.'"

Jathen actually laughed, as the whole situation suddenly felt silly. "Well, to be honest, I've already turned down an offer to be part of some secret group, so much as I appreciate the offer, I'm going to say no."

"Secret?" Nevershen eyed him quizzically for a moment then shrugged. "Understood. But keep in mind the door is always open, and Rhean will always be... watching, as it were." He grinned again, bowed, then disappeared.

Draping her coat upon her desk chair, Seren turned to Jathen, eye ridges aloft. "That was... unusual. And unsettling. You're not supposed to be able to teleport inside the school."

"That was a Rheanic." Jathen shook his head again, feeling woozy. "Let's not discuss it any further for the moment. He might still be lurking, listening."

"Ugh, no wonder Hatori was paranoid. Did you know he had me help him re-ward the entire charm shop about a dozen times a month, checking for listening charm-devices?"

"Sounds accurate." Jathen finally removed his own coat. He began to drape it over a chair and then, thinking better of it, pulled one of his throwing daggers from his pack and placed it in the coat's inner pocket before putting it down on the edge of his bed. *I need to get a belt with proper knife loops.* "Though who knows... Perhaps you had to re-ward it because *I* was somehow negating them over time."

"I... I hadn't thought of that."

"Also explains why he never asked me to help him in any large capacity." Jathen flopped down upon the extra bed, tiredness of mind and body seeping into every pore and nipping at the edges of his consciousness. *I need to find out if there's a correlation between negation and being physically drained.* He yawned so long and hard that his jaw hurt when he finished. "Ugh. I'm spent."

"Get some sleep." Seren turned down her sheets. "You can worry about overzealous Way Walkers in the morning."

I'm afraid I have other things to worry about tomorrow.

ONCE DAWN HAD CRESTED and Seren headed out to class, Jathen dressed and left, knowing Annakki, with at least one of her Clan ears placed squarely upon the ground, had probably already heard of his exploits with De'contes. He didn't really want to face her, but he did it out of respect for the woman Ass'shiri had loved, Hatori's niece and mother to Ass'shiri's child. She deserved the truth from his own lips. *I just hope I have the strength to tell her.*

His mind thrashed and crashed against different possibilities of how best to broach the conversation as he exited the elevator into the citadel's crystalline foyer. Determining anything was difficult, considering how little reference he had for Annakki's reactions—as much as they'd shared, Jathen had to admit he really didn't know the daughter of the last Incarnations of Rhean and Ra'vien very well. His stomach flip-flopped, queasy despite a lack of food. *This could go very badly.*

Conjuring, assessing, and rejecting phrases occupied his mind so thoroughly that he nearly collided with a student on the street just past the school's threshold. "Sorry," he mumbled as she slid past, narrowly missing his shoulder with an elegant smoothness akin to Clan or, more likely, Ability.

On age with Jathen, she grinned at him, friendly as she said, "Cor'mon."

Jathen barely registered her beyond her differently colored eyes—one light, one dark—merely nodding at the Tar'cil pleasantry as he shuffled past. Shoving his hands into his pockets after turning up his collar and hood, he shot through the cold and the crowd like one of Ass'shiri's bolts, single-minded in his desire to get his confrontation with Annakki over with.

Weaving through the mass of bodies going about their business in the early morning, Jathen watched the colors of the uniforms moving past—in particular a set of violet blurs that kept passing him then backing around and passing him again. They were literal *blurs,* moving through the crowd, a pair of Talents with Clan-like speed, probably using Ability to do so. Jathen stopped, just missing one of the blurs as it jetted past again. *What are they—*

"Hey, Negater!" a voice, mischievous, called out beside his ear. Shocked and confused, Jathen turned just in time to see a crackling ball of pure energy slam directly into him. His face prickled as from the pinching heat of coming into the warmth of a home after being out in the cold, and he was too startled to give the Grand Artifact a direction before it teleported him away.

THE TOE OF A SHOE PRODDED Jathen in the ribs. "Are you alive?"

Sore and mentally cursing every Child, Jathen managed to push himself out of the pile of books. More corners and scrolls poked and prodded him as he sat up. Disoriented, Jathen shook his head, trying to get his bearings. Many bookcases carved of mahogany and interlocking cherrywood lined the walls, and beneath him lay a rug adorned with a scrollwork design common in Featorian illuminations. A high ceiling of pale-blue marble spread out above him, arches and intricately carved moldings belying the private library or study of a grand manor.

"Oh, no, no, no!" Panic flooded Jathen as the previous events solidified in his mind. "Not *again!*" Shaking with rage and dread, he scrambled to get his feet back under himself, slipping and sliding on loose books for his efforts.

"Could you be a *bit* more careful? Some of those are older than the citadels," scolded the man who'd poked Jathen. Human and perhaps in his early forties, he had tanned skin framed by curly black hair that seemed to reflect rainbows in its shine. Born of perhaps Aralim or northern Zo'den, the man had dark eyes, nearly black, that had a playful glint despite the sternness in his tone.

"Where am I?" Leaning on the bookshelf behind him for support, Jathen managed to stand without trampling anymore scrolls. "Please. I need to get back to Tar'citadel."

Clutching a thick tome in crossed arms before him, the man huffed a laugh. "Calm yourself, boy, you're *still* in Tar'citadel. You just managed to stumble into a private spatial room."

Jathen ran shaking fingers through his hair. "A private spatial room?"

"Yes, there's an interconnected set of pathways across the city that lead to a variety of rooms, both first and second type of spatial anchoring. Typically, one can't get into them without knowing the proper passwords or intentions, but as this is Tar'citadel, accidents *do* happen." He flicked an imaginary fleck of dust off the front of his pale-lavender robes. "This is the restricted materials library attached to the university. There's a Temple Citadel restricted library as well, attached to the same network, and I admit I'd have preferred it if you'd popped in to destroy those shelves."

"Oh." A wave of relief cascaded over Jathen, immediately followed by one of embarrassment. "Well, my apologies for the intrusion. If you point me to the exit, I'll be on my way."

The man chuckled and held up a hand. "Very well. I'll teleport you out, then. Where to?"

As the Grand Artifact hummed pleasantly inside Jathen's chest, almost as if also chuckling, he opened and closed his mouth like a fish. "I... uh, *can't* teleport. Is there a manual exit or...?"

Dropping his hand, he narrowed his eyes. "You're the Negater, aren't you?"

Jathen stiffened. "How did you know that?"

"Well, firstly, I couldn't see your aura, hence why I asked if you were alive. And secondly, I've also been prodding you telepathically for the last few minutes, and you haven't so much as *flinched*—impressive, by the way. And thirdly, I happened to be in the room when Master Arika burst in yesterday and told Jiāojīn she'd have to pay for the Balori's new townhomes, and well, she quite frankly didn't shut up about you."

"Wonderful." Leaning his head back on the shelf, Jathen resisted the urge to groan aloud then eyed the man more suspiciously. "So you're a Rosinic."

"Oh, Spirit, no," he said between chuckles. "I'm retired."

Jathen snorted. His unexpected host might have been clad in the lavender robes worn by Second Tier University students newly inducted in the Way of Rosin, but Jathen would've bet good money that the man was no mere acolyte or simple retiree. "Well, perhaps you can at least tell me why your fellow Walkers *attacked* me this morning?"

"Attacked?" His eyes grew wide then blinked repeatedly, then he let go of whatever decorum he'd been holding onto and burst out laughing. "Oh, my poor boy—they weren't trying to attack you, they were trying to *Awaken* you."

Jathen jerked back, horrified and confused. "*What?* Why?"

Wiping away a laughter tear, he shook his head. "Because Negaters are absurdly rare and because Akira's flapping her mouth loud enough for the whole Way to hear."

"That's not what I meant."

"I'm aware." He smirked, sobering. "Rosin's Aspect rarely Incarnates, but when he does, he's *always* a nontraditional Talent and *usually* a Negater. They think you're her Aspect and are just trying to help you sort that truth."

Jathen found himself with his mouth hanging open yet again. "By throwing random waves of energy at me?"

"Much like a case of the hiccups," he said with a bit of a squeak then coughed into his fist, clearly trying to repress a larger bout of laughter.

"How did they even know I was a Negater? They could have killed some poor innocent walking down the street!"

"Sadly, my dear prince, I have to tell you that once one knows to look for one, a Negater can be terribly obvious." Clutching his book a bit more tightly, he angled his dark eyes to hold Jathen's gaze with a more controlled air. "Especially since you're in that in-between place of your powers working without you really controlling them. While you may be mistaken for either a Talentless individual walking down the street or, conversely, a *powerful* Talent who is masking their aura, the moment anyone tries to read you, they will notice, quite abruptly, that you don't feel as if you are there at all—which is, decidedly, a Negater trait."

Jathen closed his eyes, this time groaning as he tapped the back of his head on the bookcase. "So I now officially have a target on my back."

"Well, it's a mildly harmless one for the moment," he said with a shrug. "They are just trying to help you discover yourself."

"I am *not* an Aspect," Jathen declared, adamant as he glared at the man.

He arched an eyebrow. "Are you so certain of that?"

"*Yes*. A Drannic was kind enough to inform me of the fact."

The expression on the man's face was a menagerie of restrained laughter, perhaps a bit of surprise, and maybe respect. "Well then, that'd do it. Very well, let me help you find your way out. I *think* there's an old door around here somewhere."

That took a bit of time, as the physical door to the room had been covered by one of the heavy bookshelves. Luckily, the strange Rosinic was an energy manipulator, and he moved several shelves away from the wall without any difficulty while they searched. When he finally found it behind the sixth case, literally without breaking a sweat or losing a single book or scroll to the floor, Jathen had to admit he was impressed and thanked the man.

"As long as you are put back to where you need to go," he replied, gesturing into the narrow curve leading down and out. "Just follow the hallway down to the next door, and you'll find yourself in the library proper. I don't *think* there's another bookshelf blocking it."

He sighed. "And do manage to not repeat this little incident, if you would. Or if it's unavoidable, do aim *away* from the bookshelves when you land."

"I'll keep that in mind," Jathen replied, stepping down onto the curved stairway.

"Oh, and a bit of advice before you go," he said, that slight smirk still playing on his lips as he stood in the doorway. "There's a reason I am retired from the Way of Rosin and haven't gone taking up any other Way. Do not underestimate the existence of politics in any structure of persons, Prince Jathen. You are going to find yourself at the heart of a lot of ambitious individuals' interests from here on out."

Staring up at him, Jathen furrowed his brow. "I'm... not quite certain I take your meaning."

"Don't you understand?" He grinned fully, an expression that wasn't quite friendly. "Whichever Way gains the *Negater*... gains the *prize*."

With that unsettling comment, he shut the door, leaving Jathen to find his own way.

"WHY?"

The single word pierced the quiet of the drawing room, pouring acid over the wound cut across Jathen's soul since he'd saved De'contes. Annakki stood in stoic silence, staring, waiting, her silver-white dress trembling with her body.

Jathen shivered, mildly aware of Chūjitsun's presence hovering just outside the door, as if eagerly awaiting the moment Annakki would bid the master servant to eject Jathen from the home. "Because I was told to," Jathen finally whispered. He nodded in the direction of the painting of her family, to where Bolynne des Rheadani de la Ra'vien's brilliant green eyes stared out at them, superior. "Because *she* told me to."

What little stoicism Annakki had been maintaining crumpled into some demented expression of rage, fear, and disbelief. "*Never.* She would never, *ever*—"

"She did." His body shook, stomach rolling. "Do you think in a thousand years I wanted to? I reacted because she told me I must. Do I understand it? No. Did I like it? Spirit, *no.* But it's done."

Hands balled into fists held stiffly at her sides, Annakki flared her nostrils. Her tourmaline-colored eyes darted across his face—looking for what, Jathen wasn't certain. "Why were you *there* in the first place?"

"Because Hatori had been writing him letters, asking about nontraditional Talents—asking about *me.* I wanted to pick up the pieces, but I didn't want to intrude upon you in your grief." Jathen sighed, feeling as if the world were falling away with every word. "Spirit knows that man's done enough. I did not want to mention his name inside these walls. I still don't."

Annakki's pretty eyes flicked away then returned to him, the irises darting quickly back and forth as they measured his face. "Very well." She closed them a moment, and when they opened, she relaxed her hands, stoic again. She smoothed her dark hair for a moment before saying, "You won't be safe at the university now."

Jathen blinked at the sudden change in emotion. "I'm sure I'm not in any danger—"

"Not physical, no." She smirked knowingly. "But they will seek you out there. You would do better to stay here."

Considering the unceremonious arrival of his Rheanic representative last night, along with his lovely detour to a spatial room and an odd Rosinic that morning, he had to concede that Annakki had a point. "You're probably right, if only because I owe it to Seren. I've interrupted enough of her life, and with finals coming soon, it seems only fair I give her a break."

"It's settled, then. I'll have a guest room aired out for you."

Jathen bit his lip, still uncertain. Annakki had Clan mannerisms he didn't always understand, but her sudden change of heart had an odd overtone to it. "Thank you, but I'd understand if you'd rather not have the attention after what I've done—"

She waved a hand dismissively, her silver pinky ring in the shape of a dragonfly catching the light. "I don't understand it, but I do believe you did as directed. Avatars have always had their own agendas, regardless of what we perceive as right or wrong. For all either of us know, you saved the man so he might continue suffering in his guilt. Or perhaps it was the only way for you to discover what you are. Either way, I shall not condemn you for being a tool of powers beyond my ken." She sighed long, the breath suspiciously creeping toward sounding like a shudder. "Spirit knows I'd be a hypocrite if I did."

"ARE YOU CERTAIN ABOUT this move?" Seren asked after Jathen stealthily and safely managed to return to the University Citadel. "I think I might actually miss the company." Kneeling on her bed, Seren kneaded her claws slightly at her pillow as he gathered his things. "Not that I'm not grateful for you thinking of me, to lessen the distraction you've been, but, well..."

Jathen chuckled at her loss of words. "I understand, Seren. It's been oddly comforting to have someone from home to talk to. But it's also been terrible of me to impose for so long. I need to leave, if only for your comfort. Annakki is right—I'm going to have more Walkers knocking at my door before this is done."

"And I'm grateful to be spared that. Just... don't be a complete stranger, hum? I find myself actually enjoying you as a friend."

"The feeling is mutual. And I will."

He wrote down Annakki's address, and she promised to poke her head in when she could. He hesitated a moment as she showed him out, debating if hugging her would result in full-body electrocution. In the end, he risked it, drawing her close the way he'd always done with Thee. She expelled a light breath, sounding surprised, but then returned the embrace, wrapping him in a warm, humming sensation instead of agitated zaps.

"Be well," she said upon releasing him, voice slightly thick. She patted his chest. "And you two Avatar hearts better try to keep him *out* of trouble instead of getting him *into* it."

Jathen chuckled as the citrus smell of her hair lingered. "I honestly don't think they'll listen."

"Worth a try." Seren shrugged then swept her golden hair behind an ear again.

The thought of her being pretty flitted through Jathen's mind, but he snuffed it quickly, lest she hear inadvertently. Even if she hadn't been a half-blood, a chasm of differences still lay between the Chertith heir and a wayward Monortith moot, and Negater or not, Jathen wasn't willing to give unrequited fantasies free rein to dance about in his head. *Besides,* he thought as he walked out of the University Citadel. An image of Ishane, her sly smile melting into a stern mask as she stabbed Ass'shiri, briefly flitted through his mind. *Friendships are far less complicated.*

THE LETTERS DID COME, starting the second day after he'd relocated. Turin's, Kubesh's, and Feator's missives arrived in the morning, followed in the afternoon by Rosin's, Angani's, and Beleskie's. Laced with a perfume so cloyingly sweet, the last envelope, bright pink, set a scowling Annakki to covering her nose with a thick kerchief and Jathen to nearly gagging.

"That"—he handed it off to another of Annakki's manservants—"is an emphatic *no*."

He'd run into Chūjitsun only once more since having moved in, which had been awkward enough that he sensed Annakki had advised the man to leave Jathen be for a while. Jathen was immeasurably grateful. Something about Chūjitsun's disapproving eyes made Jathen absurdly uncomfortable—like being watched by a shark or the sanbarna warriors of Dodbyen.

Thank goodness for Dor'rhean. Jathen bounced the boy on his knee. Ass'shiri's child shoved bits of oatmeal into his mouth, squealing in delight as Jathen continued opening his mail during their lunch hour. *You are certainly worth the price of admission, kid.*

"I'd recommend hearing out Beleskie's High Walker, despite the poor choice in fragrances," Annakki said after putting aside her kerchief. She picked up her round, handleless teacup and resumed blowing gently over its steaming black ceramic form. "Learning a thing or two about social cues and flirtation would serve a king well—not to mention the entire scope of diplomacy."

"I've had my fill of Beleskie," Jathen insisted.

Ishane's face had begun to fade. He could no longer recall the exact curve of her cheek or the shape of her eyes, but the flick of her hand and the fall of her pale-blue hair across her forehead as she drove the knife into Ass'shiri still lingered, haunting. He softened his tone, not wishing Annakki to believe his ire directed at her. As strange as her change of heart was in taking him in, he was truly grateful.

"Besides, a Negater *negates* emotional energy, right? I don't intend to become a buffer for emissaries and diplomats to carry out their intrigues without fear of a Talent's subtle touch."

"I'm certain it's more involved than that," Annakki coolly responded. "But as you wish. You can always claim you lost the missive if needs be."

"To be honest, all of them have to wait." Jathen scanned over the one letter not from a Way. "I never got back to Seren's father about my life ladder, and he's asking I come as soon as possible. Might be prudent to see what he has to say about it now that being a Negater has been discovered—but before the Ways try and have at me."

"Wise."

Grinning at Dor'rhean, he bounced the kid a bit harder, gaining him some delighted squeals. "Guess I'll be seeing Seren again a bit sooner than anticipated."

SEREN LOOKED WELL, her blue scales blushed slightly purple at the cheeks from the cold. A scarf of Lubreean silk thrice wrapped over her head and neck served as a makeshift hood.

"Miss me yet?" Jathen jested as she walked up.

They'd met a few streets over from the Great Temple Citadel, not far from the Featorian's office.

"Yes." She smirked. "I sat up all night without the high, nasally wheeze of your snoring to lull me to sleep."

"I do not snore!"

"Only when you're stressed, which I imagine is nearly every night."

"Lovely. Thank you. I so enjoy being insulted whenever we meet."

She shot him a furtive glance. "How are you, really?"

"Uncertain," he answered honestly as they fell in step together. "Though that's not really anything new, this particular dose of ambiguity has me a bit unsteady on my feet. I've become accustomed to uncertainties of tragedy and limited options. To be suddenly thrust into a multitude of positive ones is uncharted territory."

"Well, perhaps my father's information might help focus some of that indecision."

"Maybe, but I'm unsure how. What more can he tell me, aside from the fact that I'm a Negater?"

"Well, *something*, apparently. Otherwise, he'd not still be pestering you." She shook her head. "Trust me, a good portion of the higher-up Walkers in this city know what you are now and that you're here. I don't think Daddy would ignore that fact to tell you things you're already aware of."

"I suppose I can hope." *Though I have a bad feeling I'm just going to get more questions.*

"If you keep to that attitude, then nothing my father says is going to be very helpful," Seren said. "Even if all you get is more questions, they can at least put you on a correct path to find answers."

"Maybe I can discover why the ruddy hell you can read my mind when no one else can," Jathen replied. "Spirit knows we were too frazzled to remember to ask the Chancellor or De'contes, and I certainly am not going to venture back anytime soon, lest Annakki catch wind." *Or any more Rosinics looking to prove me an Aspect of Rosin by blasting my head off.*

Seren's eyebrows shot up, and he realized she'd heard. She didn't pry, however, saying instead, "Sometimes, Jathen Monortith, I question if the reason is simply you secretly *want* me to hear you. Remember, negation is still reflexive, like any other Ability. You can control it."

Jathen shot her a thank-you-for-not-asking look then shook his head. "I tried to in Dodbyen—Marcasith had the same theory, but we still couldn't get it to work."

"Then perhaps it is practice as well as subconscious."

"Perhaps." *Or perhaps you're just weird, Seren Chertith.*

"I heard that."

The Featorian offices were modeled in Casfeildian architecture, and Jathen's eyes lit up at the sight of spade-shaped arches and beautiful scrolling woodwork.

"I never liked Casfeildian architecture." Seren surprised him as she knocked. "I know it's supposed to be uplifting, but all the lancet arches and pinnacles make everything seem so *pointy*. As if a dozen spears are always poised at my back."

"Tazu architecture has pinnacles and arches—granted, ours are more rounded, but it's essentially the same thing."

"Yes, but ours don't extend out everywhere, and Tazu make thick spikes meant for walking or landing on. Casfeild just has them there to *be* there: descending from ceilings as well as curling up off walls and spires on top of spires." She shook her head. "Then again, maybe I'm just sick of spending so much time in the university library. The whole thing is Casfeildian. Crystal, but Casfeildian."

"I always thought it was spiky like a dragon," Jathen muttered.

Then the door opened, cutting short Seren's amused smile.

A young man in a brown pageboy's uniform bade them enter. He reminded Jathen of Spinnek, but his brown hair was neatly cropped in a bowl cut. He had similar brown eyes, though, as if someone much older resided beneath. "I'm Tallo. Master is expecting you, sir, miss." He led them to a spectacular library lined in gorgeous maple paneling and built-in bookshelves with more lancet arches. Jathen sighed with delight, while Seren rolled her eyes.

Seeming out of place in the space, a huge oval mirror with a silver-and-gold frame hung opposite the door, its old and murky glass too opaque to reflect anything. Once Tallo left, Jathen strolled over to examine it. "Its frame looks like it might be fitted to house a crystal." He tapped gently at the empty niche, mindful not to inadvertently set anything off via negation or Grand Artifact. *Or emotional empathy.* He put his hands behind his back. *I might need to start wearing gloves.*

"It is a charm-device, yes."

Turning around, Jathen saw a thin man in his midsixties, holding a sleek rectangular quartz in his bony fingers. Dressed in long bronze Featorian robes, he looked the part of wizened old historian with his pointy, well-kempt salt-and-pepper beard and square, rimless spectacles.

He shuffled in past Seren and up to the mirror. "Step aside, please."

Jathen did so, and the Featorian placed the crystal in the frame. Closing his eyes and bowing his head, he held his fingers on it a moment. The murkiness of the glass seemed to ripple, then it cleared, revealing an image of Seren's father, Gwydion Trahern.

Nodding at Seren, he pushed his glasses up his nose. "Hello, dear. My apologies for not being there in person, but there are literally thousands of people here to coordinate, and I've not had the opportunity to teleport back yet."

Jathen resisted the urge to boggle over the unique charm-device. "Is everyone doing well over there? What of my uncle?"

"He is well, and it's progressing slowly. But really, I have limited time to speak in private, and this isn't what needs be discussed." He motioned to the man who'd brought in the crystal. "You've met Master Vitaescal. We can trust him to be discreet."

"I'm afraid I don't fully understand," Jathen said. "Just about everyone in the city of any importance knows I'm alive and a Negater at this point. What's there to still be so secretive about?"

"Being a Negater isn't something that's clearly defined in your life ladder, child," Vitaescal explained softly. "All we can determine is your general Ability level, which is *very* high. But I digress—no, what we need to discuss is something else. Something I've *never* seen before."

A chill ran through Jathen, and he exchanged a concerned glance with Seren. "Tell me."

Vitaescal reached up and retrieved an octagonal master-charm from a shelf. Somewhat familiar with life ladder projectors, Jathen had never seen one in person, however. Boxlike, its top was shiny and smooth—obsidian, if he remembered correctly from Hatori's ranting—and the metal sides were inlaid with crystals and gems in geometric patterns. Vitaescal placed it atop one of the nearby writing desks in view of the mirror then motioned Jathen over.

"I will need another drop of blood to show you. We didn't wish to record in any way what I had seen. Seren, child, close the door, please."

Seren obeyed while Jathen gave over his finger to be pricked. The bead of blood looked gemlike on his skin.

"Please wipe it across the top of the charm-device. Then step back."

Again, Jathen complied.

An image grew up from the obsidian surface, a twisted ladder in the same green as most crystal-readers' projections. Jathen admired it a moment while sucking on his pricked finger.

"It doesn't look particularly different," Seren said.

"You are hardly an expert, Seren," her father said through the mirror.

"I just meant with the fuss you were making, I expected something more visually dramatic." She pointed as she spoke. "Each rung on the ladder is a trait or half a trait. You have to be an expert to read the full thing, and there's a bit of Ability required to intuit portions of it as well, like how the rungs interact and how certain ones are possibilities versus actual traits." Her claw traced the line of one side's outer edge, and when she reached the base, the image moved downward, as if unrolling the bottom part of a scroll while rerolling the top half. She stopped, her claw coming to rest at a particularly shimmery rung. "This is your eyes, here. Monortith gold, the dominant rung from your mother's side. Pretty but not abnormal."

"But to a trained eye, it *is*," Vitaescal intervened. Reaching out, he manipulated the image, breaking the ladder in half vertically. The rung defining Jathen's eyes snapped in half, both sides still shimmery. "Highness, you see, your life ladder is only *half* Tazu. Every life ladder has a basis that they gain from each parent, mother and father, which then combine to create the physical life's contract for the child. Every race has a very distinctive structure, you see, and we can easily match parents to children, siblings to siblings, and even further out, using this framework." He motioned toward the portion of the ladder on his right. "Your Tazu side, your mother's half of your ladder, is very distinctive, but your father's..."

As he stared at the other half of his very life's blueprint, Jathen's heart skipped a beat. "Are you telling me I'm a half-blood? Half human?"

"No." Vitaescal squirmed a little, placing his hands inside his robe's sleeves. "Jathen, I'm telling you that I don't *know* what race your father is. The material he gave to you, while similar in portion to Tazu and human, is *not* Tazu or human. Take, for example, the eyes trait. This is golden in color, similar to Monortith gold, but at the same time, it's not. And it's also not human, not Clan or Ki'ra or Muilan or anything else I've ever seen. Your father's *entire* side is like this—bits and pieces are individually similar, but as a whole, it is distinctly not any known race."

Jathen crossed his arms, mind racing. *Skaniss had hinted that Bertrandith was my father, but he's a pure-blooded Tazu as far as I know. Furthermore, I was hatched, so how the ruddy hell could any other race couple with a tyrn? Spirit in Heaven, what does this mean?*

"I'm sorry I harassed you about more questions." Seren placed a hand on his arm, making him wonder if she'd been privy to his thoughts again.

Jathen held silent. The time had come. He'd never asked, never pressed, not once in all his twenty-some years.

He turned toward the mirror and the man beyond. "I need to speak with my mother, privately if possible. Can that be arranged somehow?"

"It can," Seren's father said. "Word has gone out to the Nation at this point that you've resurfaced. I can check in with Seren's mother to see if the queen is willing to make the arrangements to set up a charm-device such as this one in the palace as well as the embassy. Or I'm sure she'd be willing to teleport up."

"Do it."

Chapter 3

G rief lingered.

Always aware of its presence, Jathen felt its sting more sharply as he entered the Great Temple once more. *Not been here since the funeral rites.* The weight of Ass'shiri's bolt seemed to press into his chest beside his signet ring, both heavy on his heart as he crossed the massive twelve-point star inlaid in the floor. Passing by Turin's alcove, Jathen did not bother with the other tar'ka-besh, relieved to not see Ass'shiri's blustering ass of a brother, Burjiro, stationed in their ranks. Instead, he made right for Commander Na'vosh, who casually strolled the perimeter of the room, hands behind his back.

"I have an appointment with the High Walker of Rosin."

"I heard." Annakki's brother—Jathen had to admit the resemblance was far more obvious to him now—turned toward the elevators, motioning for Jathen to follow. "I can imagine there will be many other appointments for you in here."

"As a Negater, I am apparently popular," Jathen joked. Luckily, he'd not had any more incidents with Walkers hurling energy at him, but he had become aware of the eyes of other Talents following him in the streets, assessing, whispering, and making him unmercifully paranoid. *Ah, Hatori, how I wish you'd told me how you lived with this fear of monsters in the wings. Might have better prepared me.*

Na'vosh smiled slightly as they entered the elevator but then turned serious once the doors closed. "Word is also that you saved a certain A'ron De'contes."

"Not entirely by choice," Jathen replied honestly.

Na'vosh's eyebrows shot up. "Oh?"

He held his tongue a moment then decided to trust the Rheadani. "You—your mother appeared to me and told me to save him." Jathen gave him a desperate glance. "I'd have never, ever intervened otherwise. Please believe that."

"I do." Silent for a few heartbeats, he then asked bluntly, "Was my sister behind the attack in the first place?"

"*What*?" Stunned, Jathen racked his mind for some rebuttal, but all that stumbled out of his mouth was "Why in Spirit's name would you *think* that?"

"Why wouldn't you?" When Jathen simply continued staring, Na'vosh sighed long. "I will not do anything about my suspicions, young prince, if that is your concern. The attempt failed, and no one wants justice for A'ron at the moment, not even A'ron. He's of the opinion that he must be doing something correctly if people want him dead rather than in the Great Temple. If it comes up, just tell her I said *not* to try it again."

"But how can you imagine she'd do it in the first place?" Jathen whispered. "She invited me to stay under her roof after I stopped it, for Spirit's sake!"

The Clansman smirked in a way reminiscent of Rhodonith when a younger Jathen hadn't fully understood something the adults had said. "That is what made me suspect, Jathen. Having you there, when everyone knows how much she hates him... It's to stay their thoughts away from her. Who would suspect she's behind the attempt when the man who foiled the plot resides in her home?"

"I—" Jathen couldn't seem to gather his thoughts. It made logical sense, but the very idea that Annakki had been the one to impersonate Nannazen and thrust a dagger at De'contes... It just didn't seem right. "Really, Na'vosh, you don't think this is some major Rheanic paranoia here? I don't mean to be intrusive, but perhaps this is more your father's thinking than what's really going on."

Na'vosh sighed and replied gently, "Annakki hides it well, but there is a great deal of anger in her still. The poisonous regrets of a life robbed." He frowned. "I fear Ass'shiri's loss has set her healing back farther than I'd have liked, for her to strike at A'ron—and I truly do believe she is capable of it. And if so, I'm relieved our mother used you to intervene, for her sake."

"You think Ra'vien made me save De'contes for *Annakki*?"

He nodded. "Mother first, she was. If A'ron had died, he'd be a martyr, and there would have been a rallying cry around him. If a treasonous Rheadani were to be found behind it... I cannot fully explain to you the political ramifications of that. And what would have happened to Dor'rhean?" He shook his head, smiling slightly. "And our mother used the *one* person who could trump Annakki's full wrath by virtue of being close to the only man I believe she's ever really loved. No, there is no other conclusion than that our mother is still watching out for her child."

The elevator stopped.

"I hope you're wrong about Annakki," Jathen murmured.

"As do I. But that is a truth to find at another time. Come." Na'vosh stepped into a hall tiled in violet and white triangles. "This is the Rosinics' floor."

As with the Rheanics, banners hung upon the walls, violet and embroidered in gold threads. They reminded Jathen of Monortith colors, striking a minor pang of homesickness. *The marble floors and walls are too pure, too smooth, though. Tazu marble would have more inclusions, more pattern.* Na'vosh took him to the very last door, a double-wide thing of heavy walnut. It opened into a round chamber with a very high domed ceiling—architecturally impossible based on the citadel's structure.

Spatial magic, Jathen thought, his admiration mellowing his mood slightly. The Grand Artifact hummed in agreement.

"I'll leave you to it," Na'vosh said. "And I shall make certain my tar'ka-besh know your face when you're due back. No need to ask for an escort from now on. You may just come right up to whomever you're meeting with."

"Thank you," Jathen replied, slightly curt despite himself.

Na'vosh's accusations left him feeling like he was once again standing upon the bow of a ship, the ocean heaving the wood beneath his feet at a whim. However, Na'vosh seemed to take no offense, inclining his head deeply before closing the door.

High Walker Jiāojīn teleported in as soon as the door clicked shut. Silver hair hung long past her waist, perfectly trimmed and without a single split end. Like the High Chancellor, she might have been of Lubreean blood, with her skin, smooth as porcelain, not quite as perfect or pale as Clan. However, she might have had some Muilan heritage as well, given the slightly lavender hue. Otherwise unmarred by age, she had a slight showing of crow's feet at the corners of her almond-shaped eyes. *I wonder if there's some sort of vanity magic at play.*

The assessing stare of her dark-brown eyes reminded Jathen uncomfortably of Kyanith as she paced around him. "Second-level emotional empathic, first-level visual medium, first-level precognitive." She spoke in a clinical tone, the click of her heels against the ceramic-tiled floor emphasizing each word. "Telepathy is limited, of course, because of the inversion of the energy empathy Ability—that means you can, at times, receive communications and send them, but it is based entirely upon the variant of the emotional energy available—and since you cannot directly absorb emotional energy but rather *perceive* it via sensory manifestations, I'd imagine it's almost random at this point. This shall improve with time and the increased skill gained from controlling your emotional empathy. Then there is the energy manipulation."

Jiāojīn stopped, eyes tracing the outline of his head. "Bright violet aura tipped in white and magenta with a core of black. A classical True Negater, atop being an Exemplary Talent. It is almost laughable you went unrecognized for so long. It would never have happened if you'd been presented to a *proper* Rosinic." She huffed, finally meeting his eyes. "Well, come along then, and we'll get you started." She turned, strutting toward the door.

Jathen barely swallowed his sputter. "Excuse me?"

"With your Walker training." She stopped, the deep-violet hem of her robe fluttering around her ankles. "To be honest, the time you've already wasted is deplorable, and I'd prefer to get you and your Abilities much better managed as soon as possible." A single eyebrow rose. "I'd assume you'd desire the same."

"Well, you assume *wrong*," Jathen retorted, balking at her oppressive tactics. *She didn't even let me speak.* "I wish to understand my Abilities, yes, but I don't *want* to be a Rosinic—or any Way Walker."

"Child, this is where you belong," she said as if his protest were simply a minor inconvenience best explained to him as if he were a hatchling. "No one is going to teach you, train you, like we will. They aren't capable of it. The Way of Magic is the only Way that can possibly help you reach your ultimate potential. I know the Rheanics and the Kubeshians will spout some tired rhetoric about how a Negater should be used *against* a typical mage, but all their talk is useless without the proper tools. The truth is, child, there hasn't been a Talent like you in near on three thousand years. They aren't going to help you develop every aspect of all five Abilities. We are. And the best way to do that is as a Walker of the Way of Magic." She paused, her expression scrunching as if she'd bitten something bitter. "For you to be in any other Way is simply... *unfathomable*."

Jathen crossed his arms, blood simmering into a boil. He'd come with a somewhat open mind despite the rumor-sparked attack and his distaste for rigid authority, but this High Walker had gone too far. "You do realize you're basically telling me I don't have a choice."

Her mouth dropped open, breaking her snooty façade as she clearly realized the monumental hypocrisy of a Way Walker saying such a thing. "Well, of course not. I mean, it is not what I am *implying*. I mean to say... any other choice would be rather... illogical."

Jathen regarded her with a feeling shockingly close to pity. "And you really think logic is all that matters?" He held up a hand, stifling her reply. He honestly just didn't want to hear anymore. He'd had enough of being *told* what was best for him despite what he actually wanted, back in Kidwellith. "I'll consider your offer on the merits of your knowledge of Negation." Jathen strode past her toward the door. "But as you have nothing else to offer, I will have nothing more to consider."

"SO LET ME UNDERSTAND." Annakki returned her teacup to the saucer with a soft click. Despite the cold, they were taking their lunch in the solarium, surrounded by ferns while overlooking the dormant backyard gardens. "She offered you the chance to train your Abilities, and you... walked out?"

Fiddling with his spoon, Jathen tapped it a few times on the side of his own cup. Na'vosh's comments prodded him hard, but he pushed them to the back of his mind, determined. *I've been wrong about so many people. I can't be wrong about her. Not about someone Ass'shiri loved.*

"It wasn't so much what she offered," he finally replied, "as much as *how* she offered it. All the Ways will probably offer training, so that's not really a captivating argument."

He put the spoon down, clenching his jaw as he adjusted himself in the wrought-iron chair. "No, I rejected her arrogance, her blatant disregard for what *I* want. She would see to it I understood my Abilities, but she would mold me into what *she* would have me become—to hell with my desires. Annakki, she didn't even *ask*. To enroll as a Way Walker means I must train for Spirit knows how long then spend at least two years in service to Tar'citadel. I must return to Kidwellith to decide if I want to rule in less than four. What if those paths aren't compatible?" Jathen tapped his chest. "Not to mention the Grand Artifact. I'd be a fool, now, to not accept that it has its own agenda for me. And she is *not* a part of it."

"*She* isn't, no. To that I do agree. Jiāojīn holds a reputation for being... *suppressive*." Plucking up her own spoon, Annakki stirred her tea with a grace only Clan could achieve. "But what of Rosin? You cannot discount a Child because one of their Walkers isn't to your taste."

Jathen sighed. Above him, a lone bird that had wandered inside sang its glory from atop one of the imported trees. *Black with purple breast feathers. How apt.*

"I won't. The Rosinics might be the only choice I have to learn more about my Negater Abilities. I don't like it, but I'll keep the option open." He tapped the cup a few times with the spoon again. "I just wish there were an alternative." *Too bad I never bothered to get that retired Rosinic's name... though I honestly wasn't certain about him either.*

"Perhaps one shall present itself." Putting down the spoon, she retrieved an envelope from under her napkin and slid it across the table. "This came while you were out."

"Desmoulein?" Jathen raised an uncertain eyebrow at the green paper within. "Isn't the Way of the Healer on the opposite side of the Walker's star from Rosin? Last I checked, they couldn't be more different."

"Would send a very clear message to Jiāojīn, though, do you not think? You are not all bravado and are so serious about exploring legitimate options that you'll even speak to the Way seemingly furthest from your Ability's usefulness." Annakki shrugged, sipping her tea. "But as you know, you've several others to pick from. I merely am the messenger."

Though Ass'shiri no longer whispered in his ear, Jathen could all too easily imagine his words. *She's the daughter of Rhean, Jath. Even if the worst is true and even if she has her sharper side, no one is going to know politics like a Rheadani. Heed her.* "No, you're right. I have options." Picking up his cup, he raised it to her. "I might as well make use of them."

A DAY LATER, HE STOOD in the office of the High Walker of Desmoulein, a room decorated with long vertical windows and bedecked with glass shelves. A scent of spice floated in the air, the shelves lined with dozens of darkened glass jars filled with herbs and remedies. Jathen breathed deeply, the jumble of aromas warming his lungs.

"I do the same whenever I come in," someone behind him said in a dulcet voice. Bedecked in deep-green robes edged in silver, she was a Muilan, dark eyed and lavender skinned. Closing her door, she offered her hand. "Greetings, Prince Jathen. I am High Walker Zhìliáo."

Shaking it, Jathen asked, "Do I...? Have I met you before?"

"I believe we did cross paths briefly a few weeks ago." Passing around behind her white ash wood desk, she sat. "You were walking past my home, and I caught sight of your unusual aura—one that flared and then dwindled to nothing. I debated pulling you aside, but it didn't quite feel correct to do so."

He smiled, sitting in turn. "Yes, I wouldn't have appreciated it then."

"Nor would I have had any more insight for you. I'd never seen a Negater's aura and could not have identified it." She folded her hands. "So I'm to understand you have some medical knowledge?"

"Huh? Um, no."

"Oh?" Dark, delicately sculpted eyebrows rose. "My Guides informed me you knew a few basics."

"Well, just rudimentary first aid, I suppose." Jathen shrugged. "To be honest, I don't really think I'd be much of a healer. I really, *really* don't have the temperament for it." Images of Petalith smacking him across the back of the head surfaced. "Well, er, maybe."

She chuckled. "The path of a healer is a difficult one—more than most fathom, really. Ours are the unsung heroes. There's no fanfare but lots of rewards. It can be hard. We must do no harm but also follow the First Law. And what are we to do when our patient disagrees with our diagnosis? Or chooses a treatment we know to be harmful? Or denies treatment entirely? It is a narrow path we walk, full of briars most don't realize. It is not for everyone."

"Well, I appreciate you taking the time to send me the letter, then." Jathen shifted uncomfortably in his chair, his fingers suddenly drawn to toy with Ass'shiri's bolt against his chest. "Though I must inquire why you sent it in the first place. *Is* there some aspect of negation that I can learn from Desmoulein's Way?"

"I do not believe so, no." Shaking her head, she spread her fingers, holding her lavender palms out. "To be honest, I wanted to speak with you about keeping us in mind if you *do* master your Ability.

Not all of Desmoulein's healing deals with physical ailments. As a Negater, you would be able to diffuse *spells* put on others by force—curses—without needing to go through the normal, and often taxing, methods. If you'd ever be willing to volunteer your time to such an endeavor, we'd be appreciative beyond words."

"I'll consider it." He chuckled, thinking again of Petalith. "Hell, I'll probably be badgered into it—though not completely unwilling-ly, of course."

"Of course." She smiled back, but then her brow furrowed. "May I also make an alternative suggestion for your use of our Way?"

Ceasing his fidgeting, Jathen cocked his head. "What?"

"As said, not all of Desmoulein's healing is healing of the body. It is also tied into healing of the soul. Are you familiar with the concept of chakras?"

"I, ah, think so. In a rudimentary sense. They are energy points on the body, correct?" Dredging up memories of Petalith lecturing on metaphysical biology, Jathen tapped his forehead. "I know there's one here and another in the chest. I think they go from the crown of the head down to the groin, yes?"

"Correct. There are seven." Like Jathen, she tapped each place on her body as she named them, moving up the meridian of her body. "Base, sacral, solar plexus, heart, throat, third eye, and crown. Each of these, when open and healthy, indicates positive attributes flow-ing naturally for an individual. For example, a bright and open solar plexus chakra indicates creativity and intellect. But when blocked or sickly, it indicates both physical and emotional issues."

Jathen leaned back in his chair, realizing the real reason he'd been encouraged to come to here. "You're telling me I have a blocked chakra."

"Yes. In your case, my concern is for your heart chakra." Leaning across her desk, she tapped his chest. "This is the green chakra, the chakra of Desmoulein. It represents healing, empathy, balance, acceptance, and love. When blocked, it can manifest as a fear to love, to trust, or to feel worthy of love and trust. It affects your sense of self-worth, leaving you with many doubts as to whether or not you are of any value in the eyes of others."

He couldn't contain a snort. "Sounds like a good portion of my life so far."

A begrudging smile threatened on her lips as she stood, though she also nodded. "Most chakra imbalances manifest after many years of facing the same issues without finding resolutions. But you are not merely imbalanced." Walking around behind him, she placed her fingers lightly on the space between his shoulder blades. The touch made him shiver slightly. "I noticed when first I saw you—you are leaking."

"*Leaking*?" Alarmed, Jathen turned around in the chair. "What does that mean?"

"It means, as a Walker of Desmoulein, while I can put your chakras back into balance, I cannot do so until this hole is mended," she said with great brevity. "And to mend it, you will need a Beleskie Walker."

Jathen sighed long. "Is it the only way?"

"A chakra leak is a rare occurrence, usually caused by a deep, deep trauma. For a trauma of the heart, it is best a Beleskie Walker see you and help to diagnose. Once I know the depth of the cause, I'll have a better road map to fixing it."

"And what if I just leave it?" Jathen chewed lightly on his lower lip, recalling what he could about chakras. "Can't I just fix it on my own by working through my issues?"

"You can. If you want to do it the exceptionally hard way." Making a light *tsk*, she put her hands into her green sleeves. "As I said before, it is merely a suggestion. I hope you do take advantage of what the Way has to offer. You don't have to do everything on your own now, Prince Jathen. You can have help, and we are more than willing to give it, as well as the Beleskie Walkers. Trust me, it will be an easier path if you allow us to assist."

Leaning back in the chair, Jathen found his signet ring, fiddling again as he debated. *It could be a side effect of the Grand Artifact living in there, in which case I don't want anyone tampering with it.* Inside his chest, the Artifact buzzed, sounding indignant. *Then again, the hearts of Bree and Bron probably wouldn't cause me any physical or spiritual harm. And those damn symptoms sound like they've been going on since before I had it in my chest. You have any input, Artifact?*

It hummed lightly, this time with a smug air.

Measuring her stoic face, Jathen arched an eyebrow. "What, exactly, would this entail?"

"Well, for the moment, it would involve walking down to Volaille's office and getting her opinion," she replied readily. "After that, it would very much depend upon what she sees."

"So we'd go now?"

"I'd already spoken to her earlier about the possibility of us dropping in, so yes." She smiled kindly. "You have a great deal many choices to make for yourself now, Highness. I consider it doing my duty as a Walker of Desmoulein to see you make those choices with a healthy mind, body, and soul."

"Very well." Though his stomach twitched at the memory of that Red-awful scent included in the Beleskie Walker's letter, he rose to follow. "I'll speak with her and see."

Sitting with Zhìliáo in Volaille's office did not soothe Jathen's disquiet. More than a few erotic woodblock prints hung on the walls, and the shelf behind her desk was lined with seductively titled books and an occasional carved rose-quartz phallus or two serving as bookends. Jathen had come to expect such from the Way, but High Walker Volaille was *not* what he'd envisioned.

Northern human and in her late fifties, she wore every crease and wrinkle proudly on her face, with no makeup to smooth or spoil what Spirit had crafted. Her hair was a mass of pure-white curls, the effect almost halolike against her bright-pink robes. Slender as a whip, she had an air of authority both commanding and comforting—a trait oddly reminiscent of his mother.

Volaille looked him up and down with a pair of doe-brown eyes then hissed through her teeth. "Zhìliáo, you didn't tell me it was a *betrayal*. And one of a lover, at that!"

The High Walker opened her mouth then sighed. "I wasn't certain."

"What *happened*?" Volaille asked Jathen, sounding appalled on his behalf.

Jathen pursed his lips then offered the simplest version of Ishane he could muster. "She was Red. I didn't know. She murdered my friends." He shivered, as the memory of lying in Ass'shiri's blood was not likely to ever leave him. "One right in front of me."

"Spirit in Heaven." She shook her head, white curls bouncing. "May I?" When Jathen nodded, she circled him, prodding lightly at his back and chest. "To be honest, this actually looks much worse than it is. There's already been some start of a healing at the core of the chakra." Stopping, she regarded him with a cocked head. "You actually forgave this girl in a small way, did you?"

The memory of the first night on Jhyarn's ship sprang to mind, when he'd asked the Artifact to help her find some leniency in death. Her warning from beyond death had prompted it, and he didn't regret the prayer. "I'm not certain *forgiveness* is the correct word. I just... empathized in a way."

"Extraordinary." Clicking her tongue, she stepped back next to Zhìliáo. "I know full-grown old souls who'd have held onto that hate for decades—or even lifetimes—before ever considering revisiting the memory, let *alone* treading so near forgiveness. You're an exceptional young man, Jathen Monortith, negation Ability aside."

"Thank you." He touched his chest. "Does this mean I don't have to get this fixed?"

"I would still recommend some basic adjustments, *especially* since you're working on training and expanding your Ability," Zhìliáo replied. "Science is still uncertain if clogged chakras affect the physical body to the point of illness, but everyone agrees they do make working one's Ability more like sloshing through mud than flowing naturally."

"I concur." Volaille nodded. "Besides, it's not some puffed-up ritual. At its core, it's a bath and a massage. I can't imagine that would be so undesirable."

"It's a bit more complicated than that—"

"I said 'at its core,' Zhìliáo. I'm trying to put him at ease. Bedside manner, remember?"

Zhìliáo sighed slightly, giving Jathen the impression this was an argument hashed out many times before.

He asked, "So what will this do, exactly? Zhìliáo said blocked chakras develop over years, that the doubts in my internal monologue are a symptom of it. Are those thoughts just going to suddenly... go away?"

"Hopefully," Volaille replied but then shushed him before he could inquire further. "But it's neither here nor there at the moment. We'll need... what, Zhìliáo, two days to prepare?"

"That should be sufficient."

"Good. Let's not do it here, though. Too many eyes about." She swept over to her desk, where she scribbled on a scrap of paper then handed it to Jathen. "This is one of our training spaces on the Temple Citadel perimeter. Bit more private. We also do empathy training there with the loi path, so if anyone asks who you don't want to know, tell them that's what you're there for."

Jathen couldn't keep from smiling. "Thank you for that consideration."

"Gossipmongers know how best to avoid having gossip spread about them, dear. Remember that." She winked. "And we'll see you in two days."

Chapter 4

C hewing, Jathen listened.

"It was maybe two weeks into my first semester." Seren casually gestured with her knife while she spoke. She'd met him for lunch at the same Republic Quarter café they'd visited the day of Ass'shiri's mourning ritual, though they were sitting inside due to snow this time. "Heart chakra *and* throat chakra—though mine were just blocked, not leaking. And I didn't have the distinction of two High Walkers setting it up."

She returned to cutting her meal, a tenderized meat dish slathered in a heavy cream sauce. It looked delectable, and Jathen regretted ordering the crunchy pastry he'd chosen, but Volaille and Zhìliáo had warned him to eat light for the ritual.

"But yes, it really is just a massage, at heart. I'd not worry."

Jathen swallowed. "I didn't say I was worried. I said I was *uncertain* about it. It seems a lot to promise on the simple act of a rubdown." He waved his half-eaten pastry in her direction. "Though if it played any part in your massive personality change, I suppose I'm more willing to believe."

"Perhaps they should check which chakra dictates humor and cleanse that out for you." She stuck another bite into her mouth then shrugged, chewing. "It wasn't overnight. But yes, I think it had a hand in it. If only to mark a change in how I thought about myself."

Jathen sighed, pushing the half-eaten pastry about his plate. "It just seems so very difficult to silence that voice inside my head. The one that tells me I'm unworthy. That I'm weak, with no claws or wings. That whispers no one truly gives a slaga's ass about the lowly moot." He stifled a sudden welling of tears he'd thought long cried out. *That I'm ugly.*

Seren put her silverware down, blue eyes holding his. "We don't start down a journey like that by silencing that voice. We start by telling it, '*No. I am worthy. I am strong. I am loved.*'" Delicately, she lifted a few stray hairs from his eyes, and he got a couple of light sparks for it.

He adjusted his hair, trying to quell the strange sensation and the rising heat in his face. "And that works?"

"Eventually." Drumming her dark claws across the table, she confessed, "At first, you feel silly. Then it becomes habit. Then you begin to feel strong. And then one day, the voice that said hurtful things is gone, replaced by your own. It takes time and more than just words, but actions too. But it does change."

"Is your hurtful voice gone?"

"No," she admitted after a moment. "But it's softer. And it knows its place."

"Well, perhaps there's hope for me, then."

"No." She shook her head, sarcastic. "You're eternally hopeless, Jathen Monortith."

He reached across the table, stabbed a piece of her delicately cut meat dish with his fork, and popped it into his mouth. Toe-curlingly good, the taste left him chewing without regret even as Seren threw her napkin at him.

"See? Hopeless."

An hour later, Seren ran off to study for her final exams, and Jathen went to the lobby of the Beleskie Way's training center after a slight detour, having ducked away from some Third-Tier Walker acolytes who were probably following him. Salmon-pink walls fitted with white moldings made it bright and a bit sickly sweet, but the smell of the incense captivated him completely.

"What *is* that scent?" he asked of Volaille when she arrived.

"It's a mix meant for the heart chakra." Leading him down a hallway, she winked. "Lotus, lavender, jasmine, and a few other things. I'm not surprised you enjoy it so: our bodies tend to be drawn to the things we need."

"I could come up with a few examples of the exact opposite of that."

"That's because sometimes we crave conflict—and that can be confused with need." She chuckled. "Just don't tell the Balori I said that."

They entered a large room with dark-pink fabric draped upon the walls and across the windows, filtering the light down to a muted glow. White ceramic tiles covered the floor, and three shallow sunken tubs of water lay lined up in the center. The space was very warm, and a cloud of steam and more incense further filtered the light. Two friendly-looking young women waited before the pools, but Jathen found himself hiding slightly behind Volaille.

"This is Celina." Volaille motioned to the girl with long blond hair and blue eyes, clad in pink robes edged in green. She pointed at the other, who had short brown hair, chestnut skin, and brown eyes and wore robes in green edged in pink. "And this is Devon. They are going to take care of you from here on in."

His heart skipping a beat or two, Jathen somehow managed to ask without squeaking, "You mean you aren't doing it?"

White curls bounced as she shook her head. "Zhìliáo and I prepared a good deal of the herbs and oils, and I briefed the girls on what is needed, but no." She put a hand on his shoulder. "Trust me. I'll be nearby, and we can speak when you're done. Until then, I leave you in very capable hands." With that, she left, shutting the door.

"Come," said the girl in green, Devon, speaking in Tazu. A perfect accent marked her as native to the Nation. "We start with a basic cleansing. There is a curtain for you to change behind, a hook for your clothes, and a robe to don."

"When you're ready, come out, and we'll get started," Celina added, also in Tazu but with a musical accent Jathen couldn't place.

Not entirely at ease with the idea of being nude in front of two pretty human Walkers, Jathen slipped behind the curtain and complied. The robe was deep green, the color of moss in the Furōrin-Iki, and felt just as thick and soft too. When he exited, he found they'd set up a chair next to the first pool. Devon held a towel and a dark glass bottle, while Celina cradled a ceramic bowl of water and another towel.

"Sit," Devon said. "We start by preparing your skin."

Hesitant and filled with merciless awkwardness, Jathen steeled himself and sat, not willing to be cowed by a pair of girls and some odd-smelling cream. Devon slathered the stuff heavily upon his arms and legs. Celina placed the bowl of water on the floor then walked around behind him.

Jathen sniffed, the scent of the cream biting inside his nostrils. "What *is* that anyway?"

"Hair removal," Devon explained. "It's gentler on the skin than a razor."

Before Jathen could reply, a cold, sharp sensation scraped across the back of his head.

"What are you doing?" Horrified, he spun around. Celina held a thin blade and a large chunk of feathery gold hair she'd apparently sheared away from the back of his head.

"It is part of the cleansing," she explained calmly. "You've lain with one who betrayed you. Part of the purification is to remove all physical traits to have come into contact with said person."

"But my *hair*?"

"Yes. Upper *and* lower," she informed him, pointing at both parts with the blade.

Eyes grown wide, Jathen crossed his legs. "You are *not* going down there with that thing."

She smirked slightly. "It is a matter of trust. The hair must be removed and burned to free your heart chakra. You must trust me to do this."

Jathen turned to Devon for some help. "And if I don't?"

"Then your issues with trust become painfully more apparent," she replied. "Though I can use the cream if you prefer."

Jathen opened his mouth to summon another protest but then snapped it shut. "Fine," he said meekly. "If it gets it over with."

Afterward, he ran his hands over his shaved scalp, the thin layer of peach fuzz soft but strange under his fingers. Memories of Ishane playing with the gold tresses made him suddenly glad for the loss. Still sticky with a film of cream, his crotch and underarms itched unmercifully, and he exerted a good deal of willpower to not scratch like a madman in front of the Walkers. Given their small crooked smiles, he imagined they probably knew of his discomfort anyway.

"First pool," Celina said, pointing.

Jathen dropped his robe and rushed into the water as quickly as possible. The temperature was perfect, warm and comforting. The girls followed him in, still wearing their thin robes. He squeaked a protest but ultimately let them descend upon him with coarse-looking sponges clutched in each hand. They scrubbed and *scrubbed*, the polishing press of the rough loofahs so strong that Jathen was certain he lost a layer of skin in the process. Pink and slightly raw, he was dragged from the first tub to the next, this one full of harsh-smelling herbs that stung hard against what skin he had left.

"Just rest in there for a bit." Celina wrung out her long blond hair with a few good twists. "While we change and set up the massage table."

"And don't forget to dunk your head under," Devon advised.

This isn't very relaxing. After sinking down to his nose, he blew some frustrated bubbles before clenching his eyes shut and submerging. Colder than the first tub, the fresh water had his raw skin sprouting goose bumps everywhere, including his scalp. *Seren should have warned me.*

The oils they poured on him once he lay on the massage table were sweet smelling and cool on his tarnished hide. Kneading fingers made their way up his spine, digging deep into even the minutest of knots and kinks. *I've been so long in a state of stress I didn't realize how much of it I've carried with me in my very muscles.* He hadn't relaxed, truly relaxed, since he'd been in the Republic. *I've not felt safe. Not even for a moment, until now.* Trickles of wetness surprised him as they gently leaked from his eyes.

"It's normal," Devon said, wiping them away with oil-infused fingers. "There're a lot of emotions that get dredged up, and your body just wants to let them out."

Jathen nodded and let them flow. It was a steady stream, accompanied by not sadness or despair but release. On that table, in that room, Jathen let go of a great many things.

When finally finished, Devon returned his robe while Celina fetched something from behind another curtain.

"Good?" she asked.

"I do feel better," he admitted with a chuckle. He made to run his hand through his hair but then stopped when he encountered nothing but scalp. "Though I think I shall make quite the statement if I ever get back to the Tazu court."

"Oh no, we won't leave you like that." Devon chuckled, leading him back to the chair.

Once he had settled, Celina emerged with a pair of scissors and a hairbrush. "It's a master-charm," she explained. "The bristles, when applied to a scalp, stimulate hair growth and health. It can be accelerated greatly if a Talent also adds their energy to it. Did you have a preferred length in mind?"

"I suppose about shoulder length? Or maybe mid back?"

"I can do that. It will take around a quarter of an hour—perhaps less if you focus on allowing the spell and not negating it."

"I will try my best."

Jathen had forgotten Jephue had loosely followed Beleskie, and the last of his doubts and trepidations with the Way dissipated with each stroke of that brush and his lengthening hair. Giggles bubbled out of him until he shook with laughter and tears. The Walkers only shook their heads, probably assuming he was either unhinged or suffering some strange side effect of the cleansing ritual.

"Would you like a Tazu braid?" Devon asked when Celina finished.

"Yes, please."

He thanked them both profusely when done, going so far as to hug them. Entering Volaille's little office, Jathen felt far more whole than he'd felt in ages. "Thank you." Delightfully warm in front of her crackling fireplace, he happily toyed with the end of his clean new braid. "Honestly, that helped more than I'd believed it would."

"I'm glad, though there is one last part." Picking up a hand-sized sachet from her desk, she offered it to him. "The hair. You need to burn it. To let the last of it go."

Taking it, he felt the rough cheesecloth for a moment before he tossed it unremorsefully into the fire. Snapping and popping, it charred quickly, the bits of hair and oils leaving a bitter smell in the air. Some incense must have been in the mix as well, for the odor didn't linger, replaced instead by the scent he'd adored from earlier.

Goodbye, Ishane. He watched the packet grow black then crumble entirely. *And goodbye to all my other insecurities. I hope.*

Volaille let him meditate in silence for some time before saying, "I can help you beyond the Way, you know. What we do... It is not all romance and psychoanalysis."

Still feeling languid, he slowly turned toward her. "You mean intrigue."

"I mean being able to tell when a man lies. You don't need to see energy transference and aura fluctuations. There are tics: a glance to the left instead of the right, a subtle wetting of the lips, a quick intake of breath at the wrong moment. We can teach you this, to watch for it."

"You can fool a Talent if you are a Talent. But you can't fool a liar when you aren't one," Jathen quoted the air-mage bandit who'd inadvertently sent him to Dodbyen. *I wonder what happened to him after we disappeared.*

"Precisely." Volaille grinned. "Negaters don't actually negate any of what you pick up as an emotional empathic, so it might prove wise of you to learn how to process excess emotions coming at you. It can be a brutal thing to sort on your own. Think on it, if you would."

"I will."

"Good." She leaned back in the dark, pink-tufted chair she occupied. "I'd also like to offer another bit of help, if I may. Though to be honest, it's a bit more like you helping me."

Intrigue stirred him out of his cozy state of mind, and he sat up, shifting his good leg up underneath himself. The bad one he stretched. The massage had done it good, though—it tweaked in pain far less in Tar'citadel than Dodbyen.

"Oh?"

"I was deeply disturbed and mildly intrigued by the circumstances regarding your betrayal. So forgive me, but as I've been a long-standing friend of Annakki Rheadani, I took the liberty of asking her if there was anything more I could do to help." She raised a hand as Jathen opened his mouth. "This was also done at the bequest of my angel guides, my dear, so do not assume I was acting in any way to invade your privacy. All Annakki told me of your situation was that she believed said Red follower was dead and that she had been an acting Way Walker of Beleskie, a mei. Is this true?"

"Yes."

"Then might I respectfully ask her name? I do so only out of a desire to discover if she was, indeed, registered with Tar'citadel as an active Walker." Her brown eyes narrowed sharply. "If so, I wish to see if she'd influenced anyone else."

Jathen leaned back in his chair, uncertain. "I can see your reasoning, but I don't want to start some wild Red hunt, chasing down everyone she'd ever known and interrogating them as possible Red followers. Especially since most were drowned in the Republic tsunami after the earthquake."

"I can assure you that isn't what I intend." She folded her hands in her lap. "Truthfully, we know so little about what makes people turn Red. The basics are there—selfishness, ego, desire for power—but the actual choice of turning is different for each person. If I know who she was, if I can learn who influenced her, I might be able to formulate a reason why this one mei turned evil... and perhaps understand how, exactly, we as a Way failed her. Do you understand?"

"The other side of Beleskie is the understanding of self and, from it, understanding relationships as a whole," Jathen said, nodding. "I knew her as Ishane. I've assumed all this time it was her real name, but I'm not as certain now, listening to you."

"It's possible she changed it, yes. Do you happen to recall in which city and which meison she lived in the Republic?"

"Ca'june and, I think, Verydik? Verdick?"

"Véridique?"

"Yes."

She nodded, solemn. "I know it. We've had a few refugees come home from Ca'june. I'll start with them. Thank you."

Once he returned to Annakki's home, Jathen immediately sought her out. In the drawing room, she and Dor'rhean were playing with his blocks again. The toddler's bright-lavender eyes lit up at the sight of Jathen, and bobbing over on unsteady legs, he handed Jathen a block. Jathen ruffled the boy's hair and sat, putting his block down as a cornerstone for a new structure.

"You didn't tell me you were friends with Master Volaille."

Annakki's eyelids fluttered in the ever-so-subtle movement indicating amusement. "I trust it went well, then?"

"Yes, though if you'd said from the beginning you two were friends, I'd have been far more inclined to speak to her on my own."

She added her own brick to her son's tower. "My apologies. Some Clan habits are hard to extinguish. More so when your father was patron of all spies."

Jathen snickered. "Yes, I suppose you have a better excuse than most."

"I admit I've also been concerned about you since the incident with... *him*. I felt if I mentioned my friendship with her, it might taint your experience." A spark of vulnerability shone in her beautiful tourmaline eyes. "I also hoped this would be a bit of a peace offering, a show of trust, since the... unpleasantness with *him*."

Jathen scratched an itch on his eyelid then his nose, stalling while debating whether or not to mention Na'vosh's suspicions and, admittedly, his own. Her reasoning seemed sound, her words genuine, but even the words themselves were suspect in light of what the other child of Rhean had put forth. *A "peace offering." Does she think, then, that I suspect her as her brother does? Or is she acknowledging that she truly forgives me for having saved the man who murdered her world?* Spirit, he felt as if he were walking a tightrope with Annakki and De'contes on the right, his unknown birth and rumors of being an Aspect on the left, Mikkal and Sister behind him, and fire and rals beneath.

Finally, he ventured, "I've wrestled with what I've done, Annakki, with what Ra'vien asked of me. I don't know if it was the *right* thing, other than knowing once told to act, I *couldn't* ignore it—couldn't be the judge and jury of that man and simply let him die when I could intervene. Yet I can't condemn whoever tried it for trying. I *can't*. Not after all he's done. But I also know Hatori reached out to him for my sake. So perhaps there is something to be said for that, if he saw something redeemable there."

Her eyes hardened again. "I will hate *him* until the day I die—and perhaps beyond, Jathen. He is not redeemable in my eyes. But you... you are. Despite this thing."

Annakki offered him her hand, and he took it. Her skin was cool, smooth, and delicate as porcelain. *Yet if I squeezed with all my might, I'd not harm her, but she could break my hand with a simple twist.* "For all the rage that has colored my childhood, I do not fully understand this particular shade of hate, Annakki. I don't know what it has been like, to have that fury inside for so long, to continue to be put face-to-face with the one who hurt you so much. Ishane died too soon for me to know that horror. But as I don't have that rage, I cannot judge you for feeling it either. We might not agree, but truly, I do trust you have my best interests in mind."

"Thank you." Her fingers tightened just slightly on his, warming them for a moment. "And may you never have reason to feel such lingering hate as this." She released his hand. "Sometimes, I do wonder if it will drive me mad. It had started to, before Ass'shiri came. He pulled me back. Now I struggle on... for Dor'rhean." She smiled brightly at her son, who squealed in delight as his tower fell. "Despite it all, I think I like having the excuse of you, Jathen. To be another... conscience in the room."

Jathen smiled thinly back at her while briefly wondering if he'd just made peace with a coiled ral who was just waiting for a more opportune time before striking yet again.

And as she is truly a child of Rhean, she'll most likely not miss a second time.

OVER THE NEXT TWO DAYS, Jathen made more appointments to see the other heads of Ways, spreading them out over the course of the next few weeks. He also took Master Volaille's advice and sat with her to train his emotional empathy Ability. She showed him simple exercises best practiced with a partner. Since Annakki was both too difficult to read and, frankly, made Jathen absurdly nervous, he recruited Seren for the project.

"*I* could have showed you these," she huffed.

They'd borrowed a few of Annakki's servants and lined them up in the dining room and had each one tell a story without revealing if the tale was true or not. Jathen would watch for the physical cues—difficult in a Clan household of humans trained to keep their faces neutral—while also trying to sense the emotions coming from each.

"I *should* have showed you these," Seren said with a sigh after he got another correct—a tricky one, as parts of the story had been true but others not. "I'm actually quite cross with myself for not thinking of it sooner."

"We weren't really focusing on empathic Ability at the time," Jathen said in consolation. "And you're starting to sound like Thee, pouting that you can't help me all the time. You've done plenty, Seren, really."

"I suppose." Listening as the next servant began his story, she put her chin in one hand, looking pouty.

A strange emotion flowed off her—something Jathen had noticed before and could only describe as a wobble. Strong, it felt as if it couldn't decide what emotion it wanted to be and came out as a mix instead.

When it got too distracting, he finally asked, "What *is* that?" He shooed the servants off with a gesture while she blinked at him, perplexed.

Straightening, she smoothed out a few wrinkles in her Tazu-cut silver top. "What is what?"

"That emotional hodgepodge that seeps off you every once in a while. Are you all right?"

"I'm... fine." She shrugged, the jumble replaced by honest surprise. "Perhaps you're sensing I'm an emotional empathic as well. Sometimes, I feel random things from whoever is in the room. Or the city, if it's strong enough."

Jathen nodded, thinking back to the heavy veil of fear that had permeated the last days of Dodbyen. "So it's like getting hit with a cluster of everything all at once?"

"Yes. It happens more often if I'm tired or not focusing on keeping my personal wards up."

"You mean you have to concentrate all the time to keep that *out*?"

While Jathen balked, she nodded solemnly, and he suddenly felt supremely respectful of what she'd managed to overcome.

"No wonder you never spoke before, if that's what you're keeping at bay."

"Oh, it's not that dire," she said, rolling her eyes. She did smile, though. "You're just not used to it."

He snorted. "I don't think I'd want to be."

"Master Jathen?" A younger manservant returned to the room, a letter in hand. "Chūjitsun just brought in the post."

Upon taking it, Jathen thanked the boy then opened it. "Marcasith is due in tomorrow!" He stood, nearly knocking over his chair as eagerness and relief made the Grand Artifact hum.

Sweeping her bangs behind an ear, Seren frowned. "Don't you have an appointment with the High Walker of Feator, though?"

"In the morning. Marcasith isn't due in until later in the afternoon." Jathen scanned the letter, growing more disappointed. "Your father says Marcasith's coming in with an 'entourage' but hasn't elaborated on *who*." He drummed his fingers across the table. "I've been as patient as I can, but I'm worried about Izzy."

"I'm sure she's fine," Seren replied with a certain ring of rehearsal in her tone. She *had* been assuring him for weeks and probably had reason to be tired of it. "You said she was practically holding onto Marcasith's tail when you last saw her. If he made it, I'm certain she did. Are they going to be at the embassy?"

"Yes."

Jathen didn't need physical cues to feel the cold blast of sarcasm running over Seren's words as she blurted, "Oh, how delightful. You get to meet my mother."

"Do you want to come along?" he offered, hoping to ease some of her sullenness. Jathen well understood how quickly the mention of certain Tazu family members could sour a mood. "Meet Marc and the others? Perhaps protect me from the wicked Chertith?"

She flung a squinty-eyed glare and a wave of annoyance in his direction, but she agreed.

Jathen smiled, eager to see all his friends in one place. "Tomorrow, then."

Chapter 5

"Let me look."

Anorna, High Walker of Feator, had deep-brown eyes reminiscent of the Drannic Jathen had met in Zo'den. Though not speckled with stardust, they seemed to see beyond him, beyond her tiny wood-paneled office in the citadel, beyond time itself. She held his face in her youthful hands, her three center fingers resting lightly on his cheekbones. "You are not an old soul," she said softly, her thin nose wrinkling slightly. "Not brand new, either. Perhaps a dozen times you've tried your hand at life. This is the first you've chosen to do something so very different." She dropped her hands with a delicate sigh, long bronze-colored sleeves fluttering like leaves.

Leaning back against her closest bookshelf, Jathen scratched at the base of his neck under his braid. "Is that bad?"

"Despite what some will tell you, karma is neither good nor bad. It just is." She had a thin but pretty smile and the bearing of someone on age with Annakki, though the Kinawa-looking human couldn't have been more than thirty. "I had hoped I might be useful to you because you'd chosen in another lifetime to be a Negater and would thus hold in your life ladder the memories of that lifetime's training. But because this is the first time your soul has chosen this particular set of circumstances—"

"I don't have any memories to help me relearn how to be a Negater," Jathen finished.

"Precisely."

Exhaling, Jathen dropped his hand. "Do I have any past lives that *would* be helpful?"

She smiled again, this time with a certain doting quality. "All memories can be helpful. They are our lessons. They hold within them the reasons we chose to have the circumstances we have in our current incarnations." She made a sweeping gesture with a hand. "One just has to cultivate them."

Jathen followed the hand motion with his eyes, taking in the many books and tapestries about the circular office—all were ancient, cracking or threadbare, and covered in what he assumed were obscure runes of power and dead languages. "And how does someone go about doing that?"

"Some do it naturally as part of their spiritual evolution. Others need more help to uncover it. Meditation, regression... time, mostly." With a delicate, measured touch, she put an errant strand of her dark-brown hair back into place with the others behind one ear. "In the end, it is up to you and your life's contract how much you uncover. Some are born to this life with the explicit terms that they are *not* to uncover certain memories, for those would most likely interfere with their current journey."

Jathen swallowed. "Can you tell if I have anything like that?"

"It would be easier with your written life ladder to examine, but..." She touched his face again, peering with her timeless eyes. "I don't believe so. Your lives are a very clear 'stepladder.' I believe you've been working toward this current lifetime for quite a few cycles of life and death."

"Nice to know I've had *some* sort of a plan up until now." Jathen rolled his eyes then smirked at her penetrating look. "In all seriousness, though, I wouldn't mind trying, if that's all right. I mean, I don't think I'd go making Feator my whole Way. It's just that—"

"You're curious," she finished. "Most are. And we're happy to accommodate. If you like, we can do a test run now to see how malleable you are for delving down into the past."

"Now?"

"Why not?" She performed an uncharacteristic shrug. "You are here now. Unless you have something more pressing to head off to."

Jathen's eyes darted to the clock sitting on her desk. He had several hours before Marcasith was due to arrive. "No, you're right. I'm here and have the spare time. What's involved?"

"It is not invasive." She gestured for him to make himself comfortable at a low couch placed at an angle beside her desk while she crossed behind it and opened and closed various drawers. "Some incense and a little hypnosis to bring you into a light meditative state. I just wish to gauge how easily you can slip into the mental plane needed to view past lives. If you have a great deal of difficulty, it will, of course, require more structured training efforts."

Jathen nodded as he sat. "So my negation Ability shouldn't affect it?"

She placed a small brazier atop her desk then lit it with a wave of her hand before dropping the powdered incense on top. "It will most likely keep me from viewing anything you see, as your mind is blocked from me, but otherwise no." As a sweet yet barky scent wafted between them, she sat and leaned close to him from beside her desk. "Now lie back, close your eyes, and just breathe... in and out, following the sound of my voice."

"Right."

Admittedly, Jathen felt a little silly, controlling his breathing at her direction and listening to her soothing voice tell him about how his body parts were relaxing while he imagined being bathed in different-colored lights. However, he could not deny the calm spreading over him, a thing far deeper than even the heart-chakra massage.

"That's good." She sounded oddly far away, but Jathen felt far too cozy to care. "Now, I want you to imagine yourself in a room with many doors, all in a row."

Jathen easily conjured an image of the arched arcade that ran through the center of Kidwellith Palace, though he added shiny gold doors where, really, only open archways sat.

"Are you there?"

"Yes."

"Good. Now, I want you to pick a door. Focus on finding one that will be helpful to you. Pick it and open it, but don't walk through. We just wish to peek."

Taking an imaginary step toward the doors, Jathen suddenly felt sick, and his heart lurched, stopping his progress with a jerk. *Something's here.* He felt it before he saw it, a shadow darting across the corners of the moldings, just out of sight. "Something is stopping me," he whispered, his own voice sounding tiny.

"A barrier?" She sounded surprised.

"No. A... *thing.*"

"Describe it."

"I can't. A shadow." Jathen swallowed, as the words took a great deal of effort to get out, for some reason. He could *feel* it though, lurking, making a kind of growling purr. "It wants something."

"To prevent you from moving forward? From seeing the past?"

"No." Jathen couldn't explain how he knew, but this thing wasn't of the past. It *was* old, he understood that, but it wanted nothing to do with his past—though it felt familiar somehow. *It's been watching me... for a long time.* It darted through the suddenly darkening hall, leading him away from the doors, back toward what would have been the main palace. "It... needs me to... follow."

Mildly aware of Anorna's fading voice as he headed after the shadow, Jathen got only a few heartbeats farther before the landscape around him changed, rushing, almost as if he'd stepped upon a moving platform and was speeding forward, faster and faster. Images hit him as he went, brief glimpses of blood, of fire, of clashing swords and bubbling magic, armies marching across the continent, all cumulating into pure devastation—utter carnage. What he saw was akin only to the vision of the end of the Old World he'd seen up on the summit with Mikkal. This desolation did not end in fire, however—this was quaking, shaking, the splitting of the earth in twain, followed by a great rushing of water. Yanked backward as if on a tether, Jathen saw all of it unfold a second time, but in reverse.

Jerking to a stop, he found himself in a room filled with mirrors—dozens of them, all reflecting himself but none of them alike except for one pivotal premise.

In all the mirrors around him, Jathen watched himself die.

Each scene was unique and brief and played in a loop, over and over.

One version of him, blond hair clipped short and wearing an orange uniform trimmed in black, met a horrific end as a hand axe was implanted into his neck. He went down, blood gushing from his jugular and eyes rolled upward into his ashen head.

Clad in violet robes trimmed in black, Jathen watched himself clutching at his throat as either poison or some unseen spell cut off his air. His face turned blue, and he fell, lips curled back away from his teeth, leaving an eerie, mummified mockery of a grin as he lay dead on the floor.

A blue-robed Jathen with a violet vest went hurtling off a cliff, screaming.

A large, red-skinned Annarite missing two fingers sat on his chest and choked the life out of him as he wore silver robes with blue trim.

Wearing a tighter black uniform with orange trim, Jathen was clutching at his stomach, trying to hold in his own entrails before a shard of ice pierced him through the heart from behind.

At least three versions of himself were burning alive, the colors of those robes hard to discern amid the flames.

Black and violet, black and orange, blue and silver, silver and blue, violet and orange, violet and blue, black and pink, gold and black—too many, so much blood, so many implications, he couldn't process them all. Yet through the haze of bombarding emotions, one theme prevailed across the death scenes, one thread that held them all together—he'd failed in one of his Abilities. He hadn't seen an attack, hadn't known how to block, hadn't sensed an empathic wave, or some aspect of his negation simply didn't *work*. This menagerie of terror was all based on a single choice he knew he'd soon make: *Whichever Way wins the Negater wins the prize.*

And the price of a wrong choice is my death.

No, a familiar voice hissed in Jathen's ear. *It is worse than one death.*

With another soul-wrenching jerk, Jathen was torn from the room illustrating his possible demise in a hundred different manners. Filled with despair and panic, he caught sight of a single form off in the distance. Unlike the other versions of himself, that distant Jathen stood alone, older, with a straight back and glasses, unmarred by the myriad of possible futures. Jathen had a strange sense that this future version somehow *saw* him when the others did not—much like his vision with Jörŏ in Dodbyen. Desperate for hope, he reached out, trying to catch the survivor's eye, trying to find out what he'd done differently to live, which Way had led him safely through the mire. It was a useless gesture, for Jathen was again caught in the current of the vision and torn from his older self, and he couldn't even make out the color of the robes worn by the one who had survived before he was merely a smear of light at the end of a long, dark tunnel.

Jathen again felt time racing in reverse amid flashes of devastation—a repeat of the destruction he'd already seen. Then, a new vision appeared, clear as day. Ice and snow, a mountainside's worth of it, was cascading toward Tar'citadel in an avalanche worthy of nightmares.

It all begins with the fall.

Jathen jolted forward, wide awake and sputtering. Seated beside him, Anorna steadied him, keeping him from launching off the couch.

He shivered, suddenly cold. "Why am I wet?"

"You wouldn't wake, so I teleported the contents of the closest snow-filled outdoor basin onto your head." Delicately, she brushed a few flakes from his head and face. "My apologies. None of that was typical of a regression."

"I can imagine not." Straightening then crossing his legs, he swallowed. "What in the Pit was that?"

"I am honestly uncertain." She frowned, those deep eyes of hers perplexed and slightly worried. "I was not privy to anything you felt or saw due to our lack of a telepathic link."

"Right. Negater." Jathen shivered again, trying to process. "Nothing like that has ever happened before?"

"Well, I can hypothesize somewhat upon its origins, though it is nothing definite." When Jathen nodded, she continued, "That wasn't a regression or a block. You weren't deep enough. I do not believe it was demonic in nature because it didn't have a telling signature of *taint*—though that doesn't mean it was a well-meaning spirit, either."

"It was trying to warn me." He swallowed, feeling lightheaded. *It begins with the fall.* "I don't suppose avalanches are common in Tar'citadel?"

She arched an eyebrow but replied calmly, "Actually, a great deal of magic and city planning goes into such concerns. There is a layer to the wards around the city proper that defuses snowfall, hence why the blizzards up here are not nearly as devastating as outside the city. Truthfully, the city could not function without both. In the case of an avalanche off one of the Sentinel Mountains—and they have been known to happen—the barrier would take the brunt of it, while the tar'ka-besh and any available mages would then assist in clearing the rest of the snow off the barrier and probably into the rivers that empty into the Cathiny."

"So it wouldn't be devastating? The snow ward couldn't... fail or something?"

"No." She shook her head but then asked, "Did you *see* it fail?"

"No. Just snow and ice rushing towards the city. Amongst a great deal of other things." He rubbed his eyes, trying to recall all the different versions and colors he'd seen brief flashes of himself dying in. *A lot of violet—best stay away from Rosin, then. Suppose my distaste of Jiāojīn wasn't unfounded. A few Kubesh and definitely more than a few Rheanic black. So many combinations.* The apocalypse he'd seen beyond the mirrored room prodded at him as well, earth cracking and water drowning what was left. He swallowed again. *Spirit, what am I to do?*

"Have *you* experienced something like this before?" Anorna asked.

"Yes." Eyes still closed, Jathen remembered the sound of that voice, the warning shadow in the center of the fire, on the summit with Mikkal. *Deaths and betrayals come in threes.* "It—whatever it is—warned me of danger once before. But not like *this*." He opened his eyes and blinked at her, still unnerved. "But a ghost I was close to told me it had gone. Left me."

"Perhaps it had, but allowing yourself to fall back into a relaxed state of mind opened up your subconscious once more to hear its warning."

Jathen nodded. "That might make sense. I'd been asleep—or at least partially asleep—when it spoke to me before." He sighed. "But what *is* it? And how can I trust what it showed me?"

"Well, was the previous warning sound?"

Jathen bit his lower lip. "Yes, and... no. I can't explain it, but it feels both familiar and yet... frightening. But I can't discern if I'm afraid of it because I don't know what it is, because it's powerful, or... because it's *evil*." *Then again, it warns of evils, so perhaps that's all I've felt.* He closed his eyes again, missing Ass'shiri desperately. "I just wish I knew what it was."

"Unfortunately, stray spirits or ghosts aren't my field of expertise—not in any life." She patted his knee. "Perhaps you should seek out a member of the Turinics. Master Utför is head of the shandi path."

"We've met," Jathen replied.

Though she arched an eyebrow again at his clipped tone, she didn't protest when he stood.

"Thank you for trying to help me, High Walker Anorna. Though it wasn't as intended, this session has been... *enlightening*. But I should go."

"Yes. Process what you've seen. What's happened today is a reminder that not all answers can be found in the past. The other half of our Way, Feator's Aspect, directs us to look at the choices we make in the current life, in the present moment. You must seek both lest you court... *problems*."

The serendipity of such advice in light of his recent vision was not lost on him. "I'll keep that in mind."

"Do." Standing, she took his hand and patted it. "And our Way. If you need help resolving a memory from *this* life, we do that as well."

"I will make use of it if I need it." He forced a small smile as she released his hand. "Thank you. I truly appreciate it."

Despite having more dire visions of doom to mull over, Jathen found relief in the shortness of the visit with the High Walker, for it gave him plenty of time to meet with Seren then head over to the Tazu Nation embassy.

"You're downright exuberant," Seren observed as they walked. "You're practically skipping in the snow."

"I'm *hurrying*, not skipping." As he shoved his cold hands into his pockets, Jathen's heart pounded, the Artifact pulsing along as well.

He wanted to bring up the insane vision if only to *talk* to someone about it, but he found himself holding his tongue anyway. Marcasith and Izzy mattered more, and he needed time to process what he'd seen. Also, he didn't want to worry Seren out of hand. She still had final tests she needed to take, and Spirit knew he'd disrupted her life enough without adding on the distraction of the possible end of the world. As dire as everything he'd seen had been, none of those events were going to come about before the next semester. *At least, I hope not.* So he shoved the new vision back, praying it'd keep somewhere deep and away from Seren until he was ready.

"I've been worried for weeks," he said. "I want to see Marcasith and pat his shoulders and know he's alive and, well—*all* of them."

Coming into the Tazu embassy after having avoided it for so long felt strange. The welling of homesickness hit Jathen the moment he crossed the threshold, greeted by the massive pulled-glass chandelier dominating the ceiling of the grand foyer. A menagerie of colors and forms, it looked almost alive, with curling spirals of glass resembling tentacles. He stood under it in abject awe for several minutes while Seren stood by, shaking her head.

"You're early." A Tazu who could only be Seren's mother walked up, clad in silver robes trimmed in gold and purple, representing truth as well as the Monortith house colors. "I thought for certain you'd delay some more before arriving on our doorstep."

Jathen opened and closed his mouth a few times, completely uncertain if she was being sarcastic or not. Serendibiss Iolith Chertith resembled Seren in facial structure and basic coloring, though her scales were a good two tones darker—more a velvety indigo than the shiny sapphire of her daughter's. She towered over them both by nearly a head, above average for a Tazu female. Her hair was a blond so pale that it was nearly white and picked up the color of her scales, which gave it an oddly pretty blue sheen even when it was wound in a twist tight against her head. Completely unreadable from expression to empathic sense, the hundred-some-year-old Tazu left Jathen slightly staggered in her wake.

"Oh, Mother." Seren rolled her eyes. "Jathen had his reasons—"

"Yes, I've heard the 'reasons' all from your father," she replied sternly. "And you'd best thank Ulic I had that warning first from him. Do you have any idea how embarrassing it's been for me to hear not only that our prince had been in the city for weeks on end but that my own daughter was harboring him? And then, even after the world hears of his resurrection, he *still* hasn't checked in with me?" Crossing her arms and tapping a foot on the exquisite marble inlay of the Tazu Nation flag on the floor, she glared at them both. "Did either of you even consider the ramifications of my career in any of your reasoning and wonderings?"

"With all due respect, Ambassador Chertith, if you've heard my reasons, then you cannot deny that *your* family's continuous reception of me *alone* would have easily been enough to make any fear I had for my general safety more than valid, considering Skaniss's attempt on my life," Jathen retorted, slightly disgusted.

Her brow ridge softened at his words, dispersing Jathen's ire somewhat. "Sadly, your Highness, yes, I can understand that." She sighed and uncrossed her arms. "But if you trusted Seren truly, you could have trusted me. Rhodonith and I might not have seen each other as much as I'd have preferred over the years, but your grandmother Iridosmine and I were very close. As well as your granduncle Cornetith. Spirit knows, I would *not* allow anything to happen to another heir."

Jathen's eyebrows shot up. *She called me heir, unprompted.* "Well, I apologize for any personal ramifications my indecision might have caused you. It was based more in my paranoia than anything else. If needs be, I can speak to my mother on your behalf if the damage to your position here is truly that dire."

Her lips twitched in the slightest hint of a smile. "It is not so dire that I cannot handle it, Highness. Though I do appreciate the consideration."

"Good," Seren broke in. "Now that's settled, can we see Jathen's friends? Or are you going to berate us on our choices of wardrobe next?"

"Seren, truly, I know you've enjoyed your time here, but that doesn't mean you can just throw out all your lessons learned on proper court etiquette. If you are on these grounds, you are as if at court back home, please. *Jathen* is speaking properly. You can as well." Ambassador Chertith sighed again as Jathen stifled his surprise at the sideways compliment from a high-blood Chertith. "Regardless, as I stated, you're actually early. They've not quite arrived yet. Some bungling with the teleportation. Spirit only knows why your father puts up with those lesser-trained mages from the outer provinces."

"Not everyone can be Tar'citadel trained, Mother."

"It's not about training so much as it's about basic scheduling. There's one Great Gate. You can only teleport to it on every hour, half hour, and quarter hour. You have a set time assigned to you to prevent accidents. What is so difficult about being punctual?" She waved a hand, dismissive. "In any regard, come. We've set up rooms for most of them in the guest quarters and barracks, but Marcasith has been granted use of the royal suite. You can wait in its lounging room."

Well, your mother is certainly... interesting, Jathen thought in Seren's general direction.

She stifled a giggle, which earned her a demeaning glare from her mother. *Limit the telepathy, Jath. She can't read your mind, but she can ruddy well read mine if she wants to. She's a very potent telepath!*

Noted.

A replica of the circular royal bedrooms back home, the royal suite had only four bays, with a lounging area set up in the center concourse. Jathen flopped onto one of the purple-clothed chaises, instantly and completely at home.

Ambassador Chertith watched him with a bemused expression. "And you are certain you don't wish to make use of the embassy's hospitality and stay here?"

The beautiful gold-flecked white marble of the floor and pillars, as well as the gold and glass dome, were very tempting, but Jathen ultimately shook his head. "Let Marc have it all to himself. I'm content where I am." *And I still need to watch Annakki. I want to trust her, but just in case, I'd rather stay close.*

"Very well." She turned to her daughter. "With me, Seren."

She stopped halfway to the couch across from Jathen. "But Mother—"

"You are not his nursemaid. He does not need you hovering," she said, hands on her hips.

"I'm not hovering! I wanted to meet Marcasith and the survivors too! Jathen said we have relatives in the mix—descendants of Spinelith, as well as Spin himself."

"You can do that later. For now, it's been ages since we've had tea, and I've a free hour."

Seren groaned, giving Jathen a please-help-me look. He shrugged, unable to conjure up any viable protests. She shot him a you're-useless glare then, with an exaggerated huff, strode off after her mother. Jathen snickered as the door closed. *Mothers are truly universal.* Servants entered shortly after to set up a table that they then slowly piled high with exquisite-smelling food and drink from home. Unable to resist, Jathen fixed himself a plate. He had a full mouth when the door opened again.

"Nephew!"

"Marc!" Jathen choked then swallowed, getting up.

Marcasith looked better than Jathen had hoped for. His splotchy, shale-colored scales were sleeker, with a hint of their old silver shine coming back through. He'd put on a touch of weight, and the white hair of his braid seemed heavier, fuller. Clean and clothed in new Tazu leather tunic and pants in royal purple and gold, Marcasith appeared a good fifty years younger. He swept Jathen up into a hug then set him down, patted him across the shoulders, called him crazy, and hugged and patted him all over again. A bit of shimmer threatened in his golden Monortith eyes when he cupped the sides of Jathen's face.

"You scared me there, Nephew."

"You had me worried too, Uncle." Before he could say more, a bit of blue caught Jathen's eye, and Orne's bag suddenly plopped down at his feet.

Still wearing her same dark-blue cloak, Izzy stood at Marcasith's shoulder, the bright-blue tattoos on her forehead scrunched into a tight frown. "Do you have any idea how hard it was to get *him* through customs?"

"Izzy!" Grinning from ear to ear, Jathen grabbed up the leanly muscled fauni into the kind of bear hug he used to get from Esop. "I was so worried about you!"

She didn't return the hug, instead bopping his shoulder with a fist. "I thought you were *dead*."

He released her, enduring a stern glare from her dark-brown eyes. "I'm sorry, Izzy. It was the Artifact! I didn't know it was going to teleport me here—"

"You didn't know it was going to teleport you at *all* when you jumped off the ruddy bridge! I saw your face, Prince. You *meant* to die for us!" Izzy shook her head, setting her many black braids to slapping about her shoulders. Giving him one last glare of disgust, she then relented, hugging him properly. "I'm glad you landed safely, my prince."

"The same for you, my friend." Letting go, he turned to Marcasith. "But I do hope you didn't come here just for me. Surely teleporting directly home to Kidwellith would have been better."

"Ugh. No, it was shaping up to be a ruddy long trip." The big Tazu flopped himself down upon the chaise and proceeded to pick up Jathen's plate of food and nibble on bits between words. "There're a lot of us and only so many Talents to teleport us. This was closer, and to be honest, I owe my people some rest and decent food. Walkers are also recommending the injured don't teleport longer distances—some rot about things not mending right the farther you have to go—not my expertise. And here, everyone will also get a little bit more of the world before heading home." He pointed at the buffet, where Spinnek—whom Jathen had yet to notice—was sniffing at the various cheeses. "Though this one said he saw you standing between three towers of glass, so we were already figuring on coming here to find you even before your Rosinic friend brought us your message."

Measuring the stark difference a bath and proper clothes had made on the boy, Jathen had to smile at the sight of Spinnek's still completely unruly brown hair and lack of shoes. *He'll probably never use a comb, no matter how much anyone cleans him up.* "You really saw that, Spinnek?"

A glint of amusement shone in his walnut eyes as he puffed up at the praise. "I *did*. Dream I did."

"Yes, our little Spinnek is already garnering a following." Finding herself a seat, Izzy lowered her blue hood. "I think just about every Walker who has come into contact with him wants him in their Way."

Spinnek huffed, blowing a few strands of hair up off his forehead as he tugged absentmindedly at the hem of his tan-colored shirt. "Feel weird. All people talking, but beneath, they *want*."

"I know the feeling," Jathen admitted with a light, nervous laugh. *More than I'd ever wanted to.*

The boy grinned mischievously, drumming his toes across the floor as he rocked on the balls of his feet. "Tell white Walker want join Red. Leave Spinnek alone."

Jathen's eyes widened. "He did *not* tell an Anganite he wanted to join the Red."

"He did!" Marcasith confirmed with a laugh.

Izzy nodded, looking less amused. "Took us the better part of an hour to explain Spinnek thought that was funny."

"Was funny."

Jathen chuckled then sat and turned back to Marcasith, serious. "How did you two survive, clutching the charm-engine? Didn't it explode?"

"Yes, but we'd jumped off of it after you when you slipped off the back," Marcasith explained. "We weren't so far up we couldn't breathe, so I ended up spreading my wings in open air."

"You *flew* down? With your ripped wing membrane?"

"No, there was a slew of debris when the engine blew, and I just grabbed onto a dangling cable. We got tumbled about like a kite but held on for most of the ride down until it came to a hover about a length from the ground, then we just hopped off. Would have been funny under the circumstances—as it was, we scared the Red out of a bunch of farmers."

Izzy shivered even as she put her feet up on Orne's bag. "Not a fun ride down. My fingers were blistered for weeks."

Jathen took a deep breath, afraid to hear but needing to ask. "Did everyone make it?"

After the two exchanged glances, Marcasith hung his head. "No. Rhyo's betrayal cost us. The sanbarna fought our people the whole way down, Jath, attacking the new encampment as well as the teams that set out to deactivate the charm-engines. Altaiss, Evansith,

Spinelith, Verdigriss, and Mal—all gone. Plus another two dozen others."

Jathen held his breath a moment, staggered. Memories of each of them flooded him, precious and all too brief. Mal giving him his tea and rubbing his leg when it cramped at night, keeping him company with her longing to see the outside world. Altaiss, bone-white face contorted as he spouted something cynical, though he'd eventually put his faith in Jathen all the same. And Evansith, whose by-chance whistle had led Jathen to the Grand Artifact's reaction to musical vibration, providing a key point that had saved them all.

I'll never get to introduce Mal to Petalith. And Evan will never hear a piano. And Altaiss will never meet a real Okten. Their loss hit Jathen hard, and he had to blink repeatedly to keep tears from spilling. "And Rhyo and Bengal? And Amtmann himself?"

"Bengal broke the leg on the side of his bad hip, so he's being carried here a bit slower, along with the rest of our injured. As said, teleporting with broken bits or internal injuries isn't healthy. Rhyo's amid them—Spinnek made certain he made it, but that egg is badly battered. It breaks my old heart, to tell the truth." Marcasith closed his eyes, suddenly looking the full of his three-hundred-some years again. "He's a good egg, but he did wrong, and he knows it. He might punish himself the rest of his life for it, more so than any sentence we could level upon him." He sighed sadly. "And I ended up having to kill Amtmann not long after we landed. It was the only way to make it stop."

"I'm so sorry, Marc." Grief and guilt knotted in his stomach. "If I'd have planned better, if I'd paid more attention to Rhyo—"

"Don't you dare, Nephew. You got us out. And soon, we'll be home." He leaned back slowly on the chaise as if uncertain of his weight on it. "And then we'll see if we can live in this world we spent so much time reaching for."

"Speaking of that," Jathen asked, "what are Kinawa and Tar'citadel going to do with the sanbarna and feral Okten?"

"A lot of the feral natives died in the descent," Izzy explained. "The whole of west sector was blown apart. Some of them managed to crawl from the rubble and make it into the wilds. Spirit only knows if the Walkers will bother rounding them up or not. The rest, I think they said, were going to get shipped to the zoo facilities here, to see if they can be brought back to a more 'civilized state.'" As Marcasith huffed, she nodded in agreement. "I admit I'll be shocked if they do."

"I think Alt would be pleased they even tried." Jathen drummed his fingers on the chaise, melancholy. "You find out what happened to him, exactly?"

"I'll call him a hero until I die, if what Rhyo says is true." Marcasith bobbed his head, his eyes sad. "He got the third drop to happen before the sanbarna overwhelmed him. We did find him, though, in the mess. Had a proper pyre."

"Good." Jathen wiped away a tear. Altaiss might not have been his favorite member of Dodbyen, but he'd deserved to see the outside world, and it broke Jathen's heart that he wouldn't. *Too many dead. And yet the world calls it a success.* "And the sanbarna? What happens to them, now that their home is rubble and their every belief has been ripped asunder?"

"Assimilation and then a choice, so the Tar'citadel Walkers tell us." Marcasith smirked. "They'll be taught all of our Ways and cultures and given a choice of where they wish to settle. Kinawa has already offered them sanctuary. Rumor has it Nor'wah might as well... and the Solkies. Once they decide, they can believe what they wish so long as they abide by the country's laws. Oddly comforting, that."

"And the 'bad presence' Spinnek warned of?" Jathen felt some of the flashes in his recent vision might be connected to the evil presence that had once occupied the Red room of Dodbyen—not his deaths but rather the cataclysmic events. Something about the fighting, the armies and swords, just had a feeling behind it eerily similar to the Red madness Marcasith had described in the city after they'd been cut off from the ground. *He will find you in time.* "The presence Jörð said would get free—were you able to find it, contain it?"

"We relayed the tale to the Tar'citadel crew, but as far as any of them could sense, whatever it is was long gone by the time they got there. It didn't help matters that the 'wicked room' was nearly at ground zero for the charm-engine explosion. Most of it was rubble by the time they got in there." Marcasith pointed a claw at Spinnek. "I'm still shocked this one and Rhyo weathered it."

"You didn't see the ward he maintained as we ran the deep tunnels," Izzy said. "We'd have died down there if not for Spinnek."

"I keep friend safe," Spinnek declared, puffing up his chest and using full volume despite speaking around a full mouth. He swallowed then popped another creampuff into his mouth. "Pro-fe-ct goomd."

"Maybe you should be a Rheanic after all," Jathen said with morbid humor. "Spirit knows you did better at it than I."

Marcasith put his empty plate down. "I'm sorry, Jath."

"I am too." He frowned, stoic in the wake of so much sad news, in addition to the vision of his multiple deaths and a coming avalanche still nipping at the edge of his mind. "I hate to think even with the lives we did manage to save that we've inadvertently released something terrible into the world."

"At least the Red room was destroyed," Izzy offered. "That is some small victory in all this, is it not?"

"I suppose," Jathen muttered. *And that's the second room from the Old World destroyed via my actions.* Touching his chest, he considered, *Is that your game, then, strange Grand Artifact? To destroy these rooms from the past? Did we truly destroy Prothidian's Laboratory? And if so, are you done with me, and that's why you revealed yourself to everyone?* The Grand Artifact hummed lowly, noncommittal.

But then why did I just see what I saw? Why did the voice speak to me again? Are the two of you connected, or no?

"You know, your friend the Rosinic had a theory about the bad aura after talking to Spinnek and me a bit," Marcasith said, rising from the chaise and adding more food to his plate.

"Oh?" Jathen tore his eyes away from Spinnek, who'd taken to stuffing as many of the pastries into his mouth as he could fit, then coughing up powdered sugar for his efforts.

"Yes," Izzy replied. "He said the tube-cage thing we'd seen fits the description of similar ones Talents used back before energy manipulators made so much progress under Desmoulein's Way. A kind of healing chamber, where the subject would sleep for long periods to recover more quickly from illnesses. They stopped using them because of efficiency issues and muscle atrophy, but he was of the mind that Raudur might have been the one in there when Spinnek first found the room."

"That *does* make sense." Jathen leaned back, eager to consider the new theory. "We'd already been thinking Raudur was the one to cut that original hole in the wall. If he'd just crawled back through there, all burned and weak, then sealed himself in the chamber for a few decades, it might explain why he managed to survive."

"And when Spinnek wandered in, he woke him again," Marcasith surmised, coming back to sit with a full plate. "Dazed and confused, he didn't remember the hole but tore the door off instead."

"And was just wandering the ruins all that time, looking for anyone to Feed from. It does make sense," Jathen repeated. *But the warning Jörŏ gave me—"He will find you in time." Did he mean Raudur? But why tell me I'd already defeated Raudur once? Perhaps he meant when Marcasith had fought him? It fits, yet not.* Jathen bit his lip, remembering the voice's warning. *It all begins at the fall. Bah, I wish I knew if those two visions are connected!*

"In all honesty, Nephew, I've had enough of talking about Raudur *and* Dodbyen for my lifetime." Marcasith stretched then let out a growling yawn. "I mean to make use of that bed. Now, that ambassador, a Chertith, yes? She said you're not staying here?"

"Ambassador Serendibiss Chertith," Jathen replied, gladdened by Marcasith's interruption of his thoughts. So much supposition had taken a toll, and his head was starting to ache lightly. "And no. I was worried about the guard captain that had tried to kill me in the Republic, so I stayed first with her daughter Seren and now with Annakki Rheadani. I'm content there."

Izzy blinked repeatedly at him, her brow tattoos scrunched up in befuddlement. "Two Seren Chertiths?"

"Yes. The younger one actually gave me the Artifact half, if you can believe it." Jathen sighed softly, bothered by the reminder of yet another mystery. "She doesn't know who sent it to *her*, though."

Izzy bit her lip, tattoos scrunching again. She started to take a breath, perhaps to speak, but Marcasith cut her off. "Well, I can't do scrap about Grand Artifacts, but I'll mention the guard captain to my brother when we speak. You certain I can't lure you into staying?"

"No, truly," Jathen said. "I've all these Ways badgering me, and Annakki's home keeps them out. They'd be able to conjure too many excuses to come knocking on the embassy door to 'accidentally' bump into me."

"Maybe we should send Spinnek with you, then," Izzy joked, though the emotion coming from her told Jathen she wasn't fully kidding.

"Spinnek stay." The boy lay droopy-eyed under the buffet table, face covered in sugar and stomach distended. Within moments, he started snoring.

"He has the right idea." Marcasith stood, putting aside his plate, empty once again. "Izzy, you and Orne are welcome to any of the couches, but the bed is mine." He nodded at Jathen. "Night, Nephew."

"I could ask Annakki, if you'd like a room at the townhouse," Jathen offered Izzy. "It would be quieter." *And I'd have another buffer to help me perhaps to see if Annakki really is behind De'contes's attack.*

Izzy hesitated a moment then nodded. "Perhaps not tonight, but tomorrow, yes."

"Why the wait? I'm sure I could get you there today."

She shook her head, braids flapping. "Honestly? I've been too long away from home. This might be my only chance to revel in Tazu luxury, and I'm of a mind to take it. Besides, Spinnek needs watching. He is too much a handful for Marcasith alone and needs more tutelage in Tar'cil and Tazu. I'd like to arrange that."

Jathen smiled fondly at the still-snoring human. "I suppose we should keep him from starting any international incidents."

She laughed. "Precisely. If I'm to be your bodyguard, I'll have to find someone who he'll accept to watch him."

"I don't know if I need an actual bodyguard, Izzy—"

"Yes, you do. Tar'citadel is safer, yes, but as you said, Walkers will likely approach you randomly on the street, and the ignorant will try to take your Grand Artifact. They will fail, because Orne and I shall be there to bar them from even trying." Her dark-brown eyes narrowed, the blue tattoos on her forehead glimmering slightly. A touch of Orne's deeper tone mixed with her voice as she said, "This is not negotiable, Jathen."

He stood with a long sigh. "Very well."

She was correct. Roaming about on his own in the city had already led to one abrupt teleportation followed by more paranoia than he'd felt since before Dodbyen. Izzy would be a blessing, an extra set of eyes to watch his back. *And maybe having her with me will stave off some of those nastier versions of my death. I was alone in most of them.* "I want to be here when the rest of our people from Dodbyen arrive. Do you know when they're due in?"

Izzy nodded, standing with him. "Of course. The seriously injured actually left before us via airship, so a few waves should be coming in tomorrow, in fact."

"Thank you. I'll be here."

No amount of time could erase the debt he felt for the people he'd led in Dodbyen. They were his responsibility, and he would see to it they were settled, no matter what other concerns prodded at him.

"You can resume escorting me tomorrow, Izzy."

Placing a closed fist over her heart, she bowed the traditional bow of the Kidwellith palace guard—something Jathen had rarely seen directed at himself. It was both oddly gratifying and deeply unsettling coming from Izzy, and Jathen couldn't help but suspect her knowledge of it came from Orne's influence. *He was a high-blood.*

"Until tomorrow, then, my prince."

On his way out, Jathen caught sight of Seren hurrying across the foyer without him. "Seren!"

She glanced over her shoulder, shook her head, and kept walking. Confusion hit him at first, then he felt a warble of sorrow, shame, and despair seeping off her, emotions he knew all too well. An angry knot formed in his chest, and he raced after her, the Grand Artifact buzzing agitatedly.

"Seren!"

She walked faster, but he overtook her and caught her wrist.

"Jathen, I *can't*," she whispered, twisting away. "She said—"

"No," he said firmly, unmoving. Too much had happened in the span of a single day, and he would not abide any more—not when he could confront something head-on. Catching her wrist again, he pulled her back toward the offices, ignoring the panicked jolts of energy dancing up his arm. Seren protested and squirmed a bit but ultimately gave up and directed him toward her mother's office once it was clear he wasn't going to let this discrimination slide.

Ambassador Chertith looked outright startled when Jathen burst in, dragging her daughter behind him. "Seren is my friend," he announced, trying to use his ire to be authoritative and not venomous. "If you *ever* tell her she can't be seen with me again, I'll make every effort in my power to make your position here a nightmare before I have my mother revoke it. Do you understand me?"

After a moment's hesitation, her shocked expression gave way to a surprising mix of sadness and respect rather than anger. "Of course, Your Highness," the ambassador whispered. "I merely preached prudence. Any friendship will cause talk, both good and ill. I apologize if my words were misinterpreted."

"I very much doubt any word falling from your lips would be so poorly sculpted as to be misinterpreted," he replied, still fuming. When she flinched hard, he immediately regretted his retort. Taking a breath, he smoothed the sleeves of his coat, calming himself. "My own apologies, Ambassador. Grief at those lost in Dodbyen has shortened my fuse, and I find I have no tolerance left in me for prejudice, not even supposedly kinder doses of it meant to protect."

"I do not regret any choice I have made in my life," she replied, eyes flicking toward Seren. "But I know the hardships those choices have placed upon my child. Please understand, it is my only desire to see her not make choices which... *compound* those hardships."

Being a half-blood doesn't have to be a hardship, Jathen nearly spat out, but Seren put a hand on his upper arm, allaying a more vicious verbal battle.

"They are my choices to make, Mother," she whispered. "It's as Jathen said. I'm his friend. Would you really deny either of us a friend?"

"No, of course not."

She didn't say more, but Jathen sensed her unspoken words in the way her gaze fell to Seren's hand on his arm. *Not a friendship—but anything more would be ruination.*

Unwilling to press further, Jathen bade her good day and left with Seren.

"Thank you," the pretty half-blood whispered once they were halfway to the University Citadel. "I don't think there are words to express how much that meant to me."

"I only did what I imagined someone else would do for me at least a dozen times a week, growing up." Jathen chuckled despairingly. "But you're welcome. Though keep in mind I did it for myself as well. No matter what I decide about my throne, in the end, if I go home, I am *not* going to let them tell me what to do and who to be around anymore. *Ever.*"

"Good." The wind caught her scarf, flapping it across her shoulder. "Then maybe I'll have the courage to do so as well."

Chapter 6

"**Y**ou've convinced me."

Annakki stood from the edge of the sumptuous four-poster bed dominating Jathen's guest room, smoothing her black silk dress back into place after her declaration. Looking up at her from where he and Dor'rhean were playing on the lush Lubreean wool carpet, Jathen couldn't help but feel mildly skeptical. "To let both of them stay. You're certain?"

"Were you not the one making the case? Yet you balk?" She arched an eyebrow. "I thought our trust had grown thicker than that."

"It has," Jathen insisted, perhaps too strongly. *Damn her. I hate never knowing what she's thinking, making comments like that.* He softened his face, trying to make use of what Volaille had been teaching him. "But given your concerns about keeping Dor'rhean safe, I honestly thought you'd take more time to think it over before allowing two strangers into your home."

"Aside from your judgment, which I do consider to be in good standing, I fear not for the fauni, as you do require a bodyguard, and such Walkers are known for their discretion, if not their Ability to keep telepaths out of their heads. That can be remedied with a simple mind-shielding spell or an equivalent master-charm. I do have connections to obtain either if necessary."

Jathen swallowed, not wanting to think about her "connections" and powerful master-charms—specifically soul-sever blades or Yvette Ashton's master-charms.

"As for your Exemplary Talent," she continued, "I assume you asked if I might assist in his tutoring out of a desire to see me occupied as much as to have him quelled."

Jathen wrinkled his nose, sheepish in his transparency. *Spirit, I need to get better at intrigue. Volaille is doing her best, but maybe I dismissed the Rheanics out of hand too soon.* Then he swallowed again, remembering the myriad of black-clad Jathens fallen in death. *Or not.*

"You did say you were enjoying the distraction of me," he said, doing his best to smooth over his slip. "But truly, I do believe you'll have better luck with him, given your Rheanic bent. He told an Anganite he wanted to join the Red as a joke to get the Walker to leave him alone, Annakki. Spinnek's either going to end up a Rheanic or a Balori, and I'd far prefer the former."

Lips tightening, she nodded. "And the Balori will not knock on this door to woo the boy."

Jathen's shoulders relaxed—he did know one of her buttons to push, at least. "Precisely."

"As said, you've convinced me. If the child is as Talented as you say, then I fear not for his Ability to shield thoughts and keep knowledge of Dor'rhean's existence from being spread." Gazing lovingly at her son, Annakki also had a sadness in her tourmaline-colored eyes. "Though Spirit knows I shall not be able to hide him forever."

"Perhaps that isn't a bad thing." He grinned as the boy scooted along on his butt then rocked forward onto Jathen's knee and stood himself up with wide, violet-eyed wonderment. *He'll be running soon. Talking too. I'd like to see that.* "I know I dreaded being found out, but so far, it's proved less detrimental than I'd imagined." *Random teleports aside, that is.*

"Thus far, yes. You have my sincerest hope it continues to be so."

Jathen bit his lower lip. Her words sounded sincere, but he sensed something else, a light undercurrent that could be construed as a threat. He closed his eyes, trying to feign tiredness. That wasn't difficult, considering the indecision weighing on his soul. *I should be more eager to get Izzy a charm to block her thoughts. I never bothered to find out what kind of Talent Annakki is, and I can't share my concerns with Izzy if she's not protected.*

Dor'rhean reached up for his mother, cooing. Smiling, she obliged him, and he squeaked happily as she picked him up.

"You best be off then," she said as Jathen stood and she turned to go. "It's nearly midday. Your refugees should be arriving soon."

"Yes, thank you."

She nodded once more then left him alone in the guest room.

Admittedly, staying with Annakki wasn't all moral quandaries broken up by sweet moments with Dor'rhean—having a touch of true privacy had proved a blessing. Seren's company hadn't been terrible, but her dorm room had been cramped and dull. Jathen's room here held all the subtle elegance he'd come to appreciate in Republic-style townhouses, with dark, hand-carved tooth molding, a bright tin ceiling, and a bed and mattress large and long enough to fit a full-grown Tazu. *And there's a view.* Jathen smiled fondly at the city skyline out his window as he headed out, Hatori's sword cane in hand.

Arriving at the embassy, Jathen met Izzy outside on the steps. A particular large bag was absent from its usual place slung across her back.

"Where's Orne?" Jathen asked.

"Here," she said with a grin, patting a dark-blue satchel attached to her belt. About the width of her thigh, it had flaps on both top and bottom, which could be unlatched with a single click of a metal clasp. "It's a spatial bag, similar to what the ka'moya wear. I can load him into the top then release the bottom later for him to just fall right out. Gwydion Trahern helped me acquire it."

Jathen whistled, legitimately impressed. "Seren's father is an odd one, but he is very helpful."

"Considering I'm going to be following you about the city, I thought it would be more discreet. And lighter. And quicker. And, well... better."

"Well done, Izzy. I'm sure Orne approves."

The smile on her face didn't quite make it to her eyes. "Jathen, about Orne... about what we need to discover back home—"

"I haven't forgotten." He clasped her shoulder. "I've gotten a bit sidetracked, but I will help you find his murderers even if I have to do it from here. I *promised*, and I mean to keep it." The fauni nodded, but the way she chewed slightly on the inside of her cheek made him think she wasn't completely mollified. *I don't blame her. I have a lot on my plate I've not even told her about yet. But I'll just have to prove it to her.* He patted Izzy's shoulder once more. "Oh, and I got Annakki Rheadani to agree to tutor Spinnek and let him stay on with us. You can both come tonight, provided you're willing to wear a thought-shielding master-charm."

"Is that all?" She seemed genuinely impressed. "A small price for a room in a Clan household, I suppose. But good, that's a relief. Spinnek already managed to climb up onto the glass chandelier and completely infuriate the ambassador and rattle all the guards. If not for Marcasith, I think they'd have called in half the tar'ka-besh to contain him."

"Did he come down?"

She shook her head. "Still up there when I walked out."

Jathen knocked Hatori's sword cane against the cobblestones with a smile. *Nice to know some things manage to stay predictable, even if it's in their unpredictability.*

The guards announced the refugees' arrival. They came in waves, clusters within a longer line that seemed far too sparse. Around fifty Tazu and humans had been among Marcasith's people before—now fewer than thirty if Marcasith's numbers were accurate. Jathen was moved by a mix of joy at seeing people finally freed along with sorrow over the blatant absence of certain faces in the crowd. A part of Jathen wished Seren was there as well, but she had a final exam, and despite his bravado, he preferred not to flaunt his friendship with her in front of the Tazu embassy so soon after her mother's admonishments. *Choices, indeed.*

Marcasith did join them, of course, greeting each of his people as soon as they stepped up on the stairs. Their faces lit up when they saw him, and he had a way of putting them at ease in this strange city with a pat, a handshake, and a smile. He had been, after all, the singular figurehead of surviving Dodbyen throughout their lives, now only one of two who'd been there since the beginning. Some had even known him for generations, reared on stories of the great Monortith prince who'd been sealed away from the world.

Jathen, though, they approached differently, clutching his hands and staring into his eyes with a reverence strong enough to make his knees quake.

"Thank you," one half-blood whispered, his little claws grasping Jathen's hands as if he might dissipate before the child. "Thank you for my life."

The exchange left Jathen's head spinning from emotion, his breath thick in his throat.

"Let's have you step away a moment until the next wave," Izzy said as an aside to him and Marcasith. "You look overwhelmed."

Jathen shook his head, trying to clear it. "I'll be fine."

"No, you won't, Nephew. I've seen that look." Marcasith shooed away the guards, who were eyeing them worriedly. "Empathic overload. You *should* go inside and lie down for the rest of the day, but I'll settle for you standing over to the side for a bit." His glare deepened when Jathen opened his mouth to protest again. "This is an order, Nephew. I don't pull it often, but I *do* outrank you. Don't make me get the guards to drag you off."

Jathen smirked at his uncle. "You wouldn't. But I'll not call your bluff. Come, Izzy, let's just walk from one side of the embassy fence to the other."

The arrival of the survivors of Dodbyen had drawn a crowd, and tar'ka-besh as well as Way Walkers mingled near the fence to keep the curious in check. Jathen and Izzy strolled slowly along the side of the building, the gold of the Tazu embassy's massive dome glimmering in the afternoon sun on their left, the dark iron bars of the fence on their right.

Jathen breathed in through his nose and out through his mouth, as Izzy had taught him in Dodbyen and High Walker Volaille insisted he do more often. Slowly, he felt less dizzy, and the tightness around his throat loosened. "I thought I'd been getting better at this."

"Dozens of people whose lives you saved, mixed in with feelings of remorse and sorrow all coming up and *touching* you?" Izzy made the noise Jathen had long ago identified as Orne's laugh leaking through into her own chuckle. "Any empathic would need to pace themselves if facing this."

Behind them, a few Tazu embassy guards ran up, looking flustered. "Ah, Walker," one said to Izzy, "your presence has been requested inside."

"Why?" Jathen asked, concerned.

The guards exchanged glances, looking embarrassed. "His Highness Prince Marcasith's guest... the boy—"

Izzy groaned. "We told you to just leave Spinnek be. He'll come down when he pleases."

"We realize this, but he's now throwing things at the welcoming party of Walkers. Prince Marcasith bade us to bid *you* to speak to him."

Izzy shot Jathen a pained look. "Go on." He nodded in the direction of the tar'ka-besh on the other side of the fence. "I doubt anyone will attempt to harm me here."

"Harm, no. Bother? Yes," she said, arching her chin in the direction of a few Walkers doing their best to pretend they weren't watching the Negater by the fence. One, the closest, Jathen immediately recognized.

"I'll manage. Go." Deciding he'd better face this particular pest head on, Jathen turned and made distinct eye contact with Master Utför as Izzy hurried away.

The head of the shandi path took it for what it was and walked over, blue robes swishing as he regarded Jathen from between the thick iron bars.

"I'll make this quick for you," Jathen said, tucking the sword cane up under his right armpit and crossing his arms. If the clear memory of himself dressed in blue, throat cut and blood gushing out as his eyes rolled up into the back of his head weren't enough, he also simply didn't trust the Walker. "I have *no* desire to join Turin's Way."

Master Utför had the audacity to look surprised. "Oh? I noticed your friend. It's uncommon to see a fauni in Tar'citadel. I had also heard tell you were indeed a True Medium, from Master Arika. She seemed disappointed you'd not taken to Rosin, and I had assumed your choice was due to your preference lying perhaps with another Way—as a medium, I'd hoped."

"Partially true." Releasing one arm, he kept the other tucked against his chest, slowly spinning the handle of the sword cane. "High Walker Jiāojīn and I seem to have a difference in philosophy, not necessarily I and the Way of Rosin."

"This, I believe. Jiāojīn can be abrasive." His tone turned genuinely probative as he asked, "But if you are not interested in Turin as a True Medium, then what brings you into the company of a fauni, young Negater?"

Jathen chewed lightly at the end of his tongue. This wasn't a man he would confess his vision to. Luckily, he had other good reason to dislike him. "Do you honestly think I'll explain anything more than I have after you tried to have the Grand Artifact taken from me?"

"I'm not supposed to suggest prudence with regards to items of immense power?" He cocked his head, allowing the buttons clasping his cloak together at his neck to catch the light. The color of old cream, they looked carved of bone, making Jathen shiver. "Us Turinics are taught more than any Way just how dangerous Artifacts can be. As with soul-sever blades, their use can be deadly. Or did you forget Artifacts are made of the body parts of Avatars and Aspects and call on not just the skills of Charm Masters, but also the knowledge of fauni?"

Jathen stilled, pursing his lips. "I actually didn't know about the fauni."

"I was uncertain if you did. Fauni are a rare sect of our Way, trained only by the Solki. Some claim that Yvette Ashton herself gleaned her skills to create Grand Artifacts from Solki knowledge blended with charm making." Hands clasped behind his back, he rocked on his heels a moment. "For what it is worth, I do apologize if I offended you—though were I to do it over, I'd do the same. If you truly are worthy of that incredibly unique and powerful item, you will understand my concerns."

Begrudgingly, Jathen nodded. "More people than I can tell you have died in the pursuit of this. I do understand. More than I can say."

Master Utför turned his head, gazing out over the crowd. "And yet rumor has it the Grand Artifact played a large part in all these people being saved. Perhaps it seeks penance too."

The idea surprised Jathen, though he did a passing good job of hiding his eyebrow twitch. "Perhaps."

"Well, I am sorry to have troubled you, Prince Jathen. I shall take my leave."

It all begins at the fall.

"Hold a moment."

Pausing, Master Utför regarded him.

I don't have to tell him everything, but I can't risk not asking anything. "I have a question that relates to your Way, and since you're here, I thought perhaps you might save me *immeasurable* time shuffling through *innumerable* tomes to find an answer."

"Ask away, then."

"I lost someone," Jathen began, "a few someones at this point, but in particular, my friend Ass'shiri."

"My condolences."

Jathen nodded, uncertain if the man's words were sincere, given how rehearsed they sounded. He certainly didn't *feel* commiseration coming from Utför, but then again, all empathy was suspect as of late. "It was Ass'shiri who first talked to me from the near-side of the Veil—at least, so I thought. Before, there had been another... *thing* that warned me, scared me, and Ass'shiri later confessed he'd seen it as well, but it had left me by then. He said it had an aura and didn't seem like a demon. Or a ghost or spirit. I remember its voice—it sounded, no, *felt* familiar. Like something I'd heard and talked with in a dream. Now, I've heard its voice again while in a light hypnotic state." He swallowed, hopeful and yet afraid. "Do you have any idea what such a thing could have been?"

Master Utför widened his stance, his brow furrowed and hands deep inside his sleeves. "Unfortunately, it's not an incredibly detailed description you've provided me. Did your ghost-friend happen to mention if the 'thing' had a visual aura or an emotional aura?"

"No. He just said, 'an aura.' And that dead things don't have auras unless they are angels."

He shook his head. "It's a misconception that only living things have *visual* auras. Angels can have them, as well as arch demons. And then just about everything else can have an emotional aura. Without knowing which he was talking about, it can be hard to determine."

"I was afraid you'd say that." Jathen squirmed a little while resisting the urge to grind his teeth in frustration. "Why is it I never seem to find the full answers to anything?" he said, half to himself. "Am I doomed to always be left wanting?"

"We've come a long way as a civilization, in understanding the works of Spirit and what happens to us after death," the Way Walker answered. "Further even than the one that proceeded us in the Great Fall, if our nearly nine thousand years of history holds true. But there's much we have lost from that time. And even more we've found and lost in our own. Simply summarized, we don't know everything." He chuckled. "Personally, as recent events have once more proven, I've found the more I learn, the more I realize how little I truly know."

"I do believe I empathize." Jathen sighed, suddenly feeling a little more thoroughly that emptiness where Ass'shiri's presence had once been. "Thank you for your time, at least."

"You are quite welcome." Master Utför inclined his head in a bow then took his leave just as Izzy came walking back.

Her eyes followed the retreating Turinic. "Problem?"

"No." After untucking the sword cane, Jathen put his weight on it. "Just more attempts to recruit me, compounded by more lack of answers to questions."

"That explains the mix of frustration and disgust on your face." Izzy smirked slightly. "That's good, though. You'd make a terrible Turinic."

Jathen cocked his head at her, suddenly wondering if she could somehow lend a concrete credence to his visions of death in Turinic robes. "And why is that?"

"Other than the battered cliché that you care too much for the living?" She sighed long. "There's a certain amount of acceptance amid the Turinics. Acceptance of death, of fate, of the 'natural order.' It's healthy in small doses, but many of them swallow much larger pills. You'd never just *accept* your lot in life, Jathen. You never have. That's partly, I think, why you've struggled for so long—against the world, against yourself. You've always known you should have a hand in your own destiny, even as Spirit makes up the rest."

"I think you just described yourself as well, Izzy." Jathen smiled to himself when she didn't deny it. "Did you know the fauni had a hand in the creation of Grand Artifacts?"

"No, but it follows logically. Soul-sever blades are made by a joint effort between fauni and shandi with Solki supervision."

"You ever see a soul-sever made?"

"No."

The unsettling thought of Annakki acquiring the one to try to assassinate De'contes went through his mind again. He swallowed, uneasy yet again. Eyeing him cautiously, Izzy asked, "Feeling better?"

"Mostly," he lied. "But just in case, I think I'll refrain from shaking any more hands."

"Wise."

Taking a chance, Jathen took a breath and quietly relayed what he'd just told Utför about the voice and a brief recounting of the recent vision and the specter on the summit, as well as what Ass'shiri had said about the aura. "Do *you* have any idea what that could be?"

"Give me a moment. That was a lot." Blinking repeatedly, she sucked a short inhalation between her teeth while crossing her arms. "Well, vision aside, as we can't deal with that until we have reason to trust it, and to do that, we must assess the shadow-voice-thing. That being said, if the familiar sense you felt is the most prominent emotion, the 'thing' could be a spirit or angel guide. In which case, there is a great deal of credibility you should put toward the vision itself."

"Would either of those Guides have an aura?"

Izzy cocked her head. "Possibly. Granted, neither of those would *leave* you either, but given Ass'shiri's confused state, he might simply have been mistaken. And given your recent strengthening of Abilities, it would be logical that your Guides would start to make contact."

"That makes a decent amount of sense." Jathen snorted, pointing his chin in the direction Master Utför had walked off. "What are the odds the head of the shandi wouldn't think of it?"

"Low," she admitted then turned to meet his eyes. "I think someone wants you to keep asking him for help."

De'contes did something similar. "I'm beginning to hate being the prize everyone's vying for, Izzy." Jathen sighed long. "Especially when my life and the fate of the whole world might all be tied to what Way I pick."

"Let us return to the coming wave of refugees for now," she suggested. "At least those emotions are genuine. The rest will keep for the moment."

"How did you contain Spinnek, anyway?" he asked as they walked back.

"I told him the truth—that we're going to be living with you. He came down to go gather up his things."

"Spinnek has *things*?"

"Oh yes." Izzy's eyes widened as she spread her hands. "Big pile of salvage from Dodbyen. Mostly storage quartz."

Jathen chuckled, sadistically amused by how much a huge drake-style nest piled into one of the townhouse guest quarters would probably irritate Chūjitsun.

"Teal!" His heart waxed glad at the sight of the black-scaled Tazu standing beside Marcasith. Scmit and Citra were there as well, and Jathen grinned, waving. Each had been on the teams to disable the charm-engines in Dodbyen. Though, for the life of him, he couldn't remember which of the two females the full-blood was and which was the half-blood, he did recall Citra had peach scales and pale-yellow hair, while Scmit had the gray scales and white hair. "I'm happy to see you three," Jathen said, joining them.

"Happy to have made it," Tealanithiss said with a smile, but then his dark-blue eyes turned more serious. "Jathen, if you would, we've been thinking a lot about what we want to do now that we're in the world. And Marcasith here mentioned that you don't have a proper honor guard back in Kidwellith. Is that correct?"

Glancing curiously at Marcasith, Jathen nodded. "I'm not certain who he heard that from, but yes, I suppose I don't." He'd had a tendency to get his honor guards dismissed or transferred due to his petulance in eluding them to gallivant about the city proper. *That and I'd now imagine Skaniss took measures to make my life miserable too.*

"Well, if you'd like us to, we"—Teal gestured to himself, Scmit, and Citra—"and probably a few others would like to fill that void."

Jathen stood in stunned silence a moment before managing to stutter, "A-are you sure?"

"What His Royal Awkwardness means," Marcasith said, saving him, "is that it's rather dangerous, guard duty. And you'd be dedicating your lives to a great deal of discipline—even death at the hands of an assassin—to serve the crown. After a life practically imprisoned, what you're asking to do can grow to have suffocating restrictions of its own. Are you sure you want to trade one set of walls for another?"

"Exactly," Jathen said. "You can do anything, my friends. Are you sure you want to use that freedom bothering with me?"

As a unit, the three grinned. "We've already learned that our options are not as unlimited as you make them sound." Citra flicked a strand of her muted-yellow hair out of her pale-green eyes with a brown claw. "But yes, we've thought hard about this. We wouldn't be here if not for you. We owe you, and we know you'll treat us well."

"And from what we've already seen from *some* Tazu, that's not a guarantee," Scmit added with a snort.

Jathen wasn't sure if she was speaking about Tazu they'd met on the ground or perhaps Rhyo, but a spark of anger flashed in her deep-blue eyes.

"Marcasith also tells us they might not allow you to be king," Teal explained, his voice low. "That would be a travesty, Jathen. You're a leader and a good one. We've all seen that. That's worth protecting."

"You all feel this way?"

They nodded, scaled faces bobbing.

Jathen took a breath then let it out as a confused laugh. "All right, if you're set to it. Um, report to Ambassador Chertith and tell her I said to put you in with the guards here at the embassy. They'll see to it you get trained. But keep in mind I still haven't actually decided if I *want* to be the king yet. If I decide not to try for it, you'd just be guarding a glorified prince and nothing more."

"Jathen, it's not about guarding a king. It's about guarding *you*," Teal said with a grin. "But we'll take our chances."

"You're honestly surprised, aren't you?" Izzy observed to Jathen as the trio headed inside and Marcasith returned to greeting refugees.

"Well, yes." Watching them, their heads held high, looking for all the world as if they'd struck gold, Jathen grasped for the right words. "I got them on the ground, Izzy, but I also let dozens of them get killed. I mean, I understand some gratitude... but *loyalty*? The kind that might come with them laying their lives down for mine?" He closed his eyes, wondering how many of his friends would have had to fall to get him to so many of those deaths in the vision. "I just... I worry they don't fully understand."

"I think they do. After all, they've already done it, Jathen. And *you* did it—for them—the moment you jumped off that catwalk toward that charm-engine. To lay down your own life for a man who you know will lay down his own for the greater good—that's something worth doing." Her lips twitched in a morbid smirk. "It's what *I'm* doing."

"That's different, though. I'm going to help you with Orne." He raised an eyebrow at her. "Or are you saying you'd protect me even without that?"

Izzy's expression hardened, fixed on Marcasith shaking hands with the refugees still coming in. "Before Dodbyen, I'd say perhaps not, Jathen. Orne influences much of what I do, and I do believe the hand of fate put you in my path so that I might find his answers, yes. But after you jumped..." She shook her head. "Yes, my prince. If you stripped away all of me that's tangled up with Orne, I'd still follow you, believe in you." She met his eyes again. "There's a lot of muck in our country, Jathen. More than you even know yet. I truly believe you have the capacity to change things."

He laughed nervously. "Well, that doesn't add any undue pressure, Izzy."

She softened, crossing her arms and smiling. "After saving a whole city and so many lives, I think making some major social changes should be relatively easy, my prince."

"Fair enough. I just have to live that long." He sighed, desperate to change the subject. "But do you have to keep calling me 'your prince'? I was quite content with Jathen. Or Jath."

"I don't call you 'your prince.' I call you '*my* prince,' Jath." Grinning wider at his sour expression, she added, "And yes, I do have to. It was only for subterfuge's sake I abstained before. You are royalty, the heir to the king's throne of the Tazu Nation. How will Kyanith ever admit to that fact if you do not?"

"Again, I shall remind you I've not decided yet if I'm going to try to claim it. Or if I'll even *get* to sit on it." His stomach rumbled as he thought about the visions again. "Kyanith might still outlive me."

"It may come down not to whether or not you actually want to rule but to whether or not you want to make them *admit* they should *let* you. An important distinction, and something perhaps worth fighting for in that little country of ours."

Jathen held his breath a moment, pondering, realizing Izzy might very well be right. "Perhaps," he admitted, turning his attention back to the refugees. "Perhaps."

Next came those too injured to walk, borne in on litters carried by Way Walkers and tar'ka-besh. Amid them was Zebradorith Bengaliss, one of the last to be brought in. The eyelid over Bengal's bad eye drooped considerably, and even the good mossy-green one had a long, tired gaze. Propped up on pillows, he had one leg wrapped in a splint. Beneath one tan-spotted arm, he cradled a medium-sized opaque jar—perhaps some of the unique plant life from Dodbyen he'd been intent on salvaging.

"We're home, old friend," Marcasith said, his somberness clear as he patted the deep-brown-scaled Tazu. "At least, Tar'citadel's corner of it."

"I'll celebrate when I see the old dome." He squeezed Marcasith's hand then smiled softly at Jathen. "Hear tell you've had more adventures without us, little highness."

"Nothing so noble." Despite his fear of emotional backlash, he found Bengal's hand and squeezed it. He felt the press of sadness, but as it matched his own, it didn't weigh him down too much. "How are you healing?"

"The hip was already terrible, and now there's still talk of taking the leg off if I want to decrease the amount of daily agony I'm in. Not as lucky as you." He tapped Jathen's right leg with his cane. "No more pain?"

"Not everyone has the benefit of the finest of Tazu field medics." Jathen smiled as Bengal chuckled lightly. "It's good. A few twinges here and there, but really, I owe you."

"I'm paid in full, Jath. I'm alive and here, bad leg or no." Bengal patted the container, his moss-green eye awash in pain that had nothing to do with sore legs. "Mal's ashes."

"Oh, Bengal." Jathen put his hand on it as well, trying to hold back tears.

A flash filled his vision, and he saw Mal stepping in front of a sanbarna warrior's spear while Bengal lay prone behind her. Then the old Tazu clutching his great-granddaughter, her green eyes vacantly staring up at the domed ceiling as Bengal wailed, covered in blood.

Jerking his hand back, Jathen didn't wipe away the tears trickling down his cheeks as the vision faded. "I am so sorry." His voice came out thick. "She deserved to be in the world. I'm so sorry I failed her."

"'Twasn't your failure, young prince. The sanbarna—"

"Should have never known we were doing what we did."

"But that wasn't *your* fault," Bengal said with a tight clip of finality. The words he didn't say were palpable: *It was Rhyo's.* He tightened his grip on the urn, sighing. "I mean to spread them once we're home. Off the top of Montage's temple there. Or perhaps the old dome."

"Or in the atrium," Jathen suggested. "She'd have liked that."

The old Tazu nodded. "Good idea. For once we're home."

"I'll be there when you do," Jathen promised.

Bengal smiled a little, and the guards lifted the litter, carrying him up the steps and into the embassy. Misery wafted off Marcasith as Jathen watched the Tazu, further breaking his heart.

"I'm sorry," he whispered to his uncle. "His sorrow is hard to bear."

"Aye, but mine is too," Marcasith whispered back. "After a certain point, I gave up imagining I'd be standing here. Spin and Verde, my own wife and son, and so, so many others over the years... They deserved to be here more than I. Survivor's guilt can be tough to rectify. I imagine we'll all wrestle with it for a time. Perhaps the rest of our lives."

Guilt tugged hard on Jathen then too as he recalled the sanbarna boy he'd killed in self-defense in the wake of being attacked by Raudur. He didn't feel guilty about having done it but about the fact that he *didn't* feel bad about it at all. *I don't think of it. I barely spare a thought for having taken a life. I wonder if that makes me coldhearted. Or just numb.* Again, he wished for Seren to read his morbid thoughts and tell him he was being absurdly hard on himself. *I need to quell that. Seren won't always be here. Like Ass'shiri, I cannot afford to lean too hard on anyone anymore. Not her, not Izzy, not Marc.*

I must stand on my own... and make my own choices.

"Where is Rhyo?" he quietly inquired of Marcasith. "I didn't see him come in."

"We agreed to house him in the Temple Hospital along with a few others. His injuries are still bad, and he's not eating enough." The great Tazu adjusted his weight, suddenly projecting uncomfortable emotions that felt like worms in Jathen's stomach. "That and I decided it was better he not be housed with the rest of our people. There've been... *threats.*"

"Not from Bengal?"

"No, don't be silly. But a lot of ours aren't happy with him. Calling him a traitor. Telling me they want justice, that he should be tried and sentenced for what he did. Thought it better he recovers away from the rest."

"*Will* you try him?"

"The Elders were judge and jury in Dodbyen. Bengal and I discussed it. The egg's only actual crime was foolishness. Deep, deep foolishness with a heavy cost. I'll not begrudge him his life—not after all this death. But I won't force his presence on the rest of my people." He sighed long, claws twitching around where the straps in his armor would have lain. "Once recovered, he'll have to make his own way in this new world."

Jathen nodded then turned to Izzy. "Go gather Spinnek. The three of us are going over to the Temple Hospital."

"Jath—" Marcasith began, but Jathen stayed his protest with a wave of his hand.

"I promised to greet all the survivors today. I intend to do it."

"There is a feast and celebration scheduled," Izzy reminded him. "I do not think Ambassador Chertith, nor those attending, will appreciate your absence, my prince."

"Marc said Rhyo's not eating, Izzy," Jathen replied, whispering among the three of them. "It would be a tragedy for one of the imprisoned of Dodbyen to waste away to death after reaching the ground. As Marc said, too many have died. No more."

"I'll convey your sympathies to those in attendance," Marcasith said. "And I'll tell the Chertith you do this at my request."

Jathen smiled slightly, relieved that he understood. Rhyo's foolish disobeying of orders was his own, but Jathen and Marcasith both bore the brunt of having ignored the Tazu's concerns about the sanbarna's safety. If they'd have listened, he'd not have felt the urge to warn their enemies of the descent, or they would have been better prepared for their response when Rhyo did what he did. Rhyo also risked his life—crawling in insurmountable pain through the ruins to warn Jathen and save Marcasith—when a *true* traitor would have simply fled, hidden, or at least given up. Theirs was a strange bond, but the two Monortith princes shared a responsibility for Rhyo, and what Marcasith couldn't provide Jathen needed to.

"Thank you," Jathen said.

Ambassador Chertith's ire seemed completely mollified by the fact that Jathen and Izzy were relieving her of Spinnek and made no fuss when the three departed before the party had even begun.

Spinnek, however, made the short walk far longer by constantly diverging to examine everything, usually by climbing on top of it.

"My patience is at its end, little spider!" Hands on her hips, Izzy glared up at Spinnek from where he'd perched himself, hanging off a second-story ledge to examine a winter-resistant rose planted in the window box. "If you do not come down this instant, I shall send Orne up there to retrieve you!"

Ignoring the thorns, Spinnek sat on the window box between the lavender-tinted roses, grinning as he wiggled his still-bare toes at them. "Like Orne. Do send."

"Spinnek," Jathen called as Izzy huffed. He didn't like the look of a few tough-looking Balori clad in red and black, whose long glances had been drawn by their friend's antics. "Come along. We're going to see Rhyo. Don't you want to see him?" When the boy shrugged, Jathen hardened his tone. "Or perhaps you are too unruly to have at Annakki's home. Perhaps you don't wish to stay with me and Izzy after all, and I should tell the Tazu Embassy to just do away with your things since you are too wild to stay anywhere."

Heaving a long sigh that said he didn't believe Jathen's threat but was deciding of his own accord to comply anyway, Spinnek leapt down, landing without even a thud despite the two-story drop.

"Show-off," Jathen commented, earning him another grin from the Exemplary Talent.

"Ho there."

Beside him, Izzy stiffened as Jathen turned around to face the speaker. Three Balori men, one human, one Clan, and one Annarite, had crossed the street, peering at Jathen with their three vastly different sets of eyes. The human's were icy and eerily devoid of emotion, while their owner had a hook nose and a very pointy chin. A series of burn scars ran from left to right across the Clansman's face, giving Jathen an unbidden chill, as it invoked memories of Raudur, though these wounds weren't nearly as extensive. Luckily, this Clansman's eyes were intact, shining a soft bluish violet. The third, the Annarite, had garnet-colored eyes similar to those of A'ron De'contes, though not anywhere near as deep or intelligent.

The last nibbled upon his ebony-colored bottom lip a moment then asked, "You're the Negater, aren't you?"

Jathen swallowed, trying to channel Spinnek's curious, head-cocked expression instead of Izzy's frozen, battle-ready stoicism. "Yes..."

He measured Jathen for what felt like a long time, with little emotion coming off him and no facial expression to indicate his intent. Finally, with a flick of white hair, he nodded, simply saying, "Thank you." When Jathen arched an eyebrow, the Balori clarified softly, "For the Prophet's life."

Jathen held his breath. The Prophet was the title some Balori had bestowed on A'ron De'contes, something to do with a prophecy about the Red. Jathen's stomach rolled as he just stood there, dumbly unable to decide how he felt in the wake of being thanked for A'ron, let alone what to *say* in response. *"You're welcome" doesn't quite fit this.* Finally, he conjured enough wherewithal to nod then asked, "Is Nannazen recovering?"

The trio blinked, clearly surprised that he would inquire after the girl.

"Well enough," the human in the back replied. "We were just at the hospital, checking in on her."

Jathen furrowed his brow, exchanging a troubled glance with Izzy. "Still? It's been weeks. I hadn't thought her injuries were so severe."

"Whatever scum replaced her had done it on and off for weeks—maybe months—learning, spying, waiting," the Annarite explained. "She'd had memory-removal spells, telepathic probing, and all sorts of manipulations done to her. Mind is a scrambled mess."

"I'm genuinely sorry she had to suffer that." Jathen sighed long, for whatever his thoughts on De'contes, the teenage Annarite hadn't deserved to become a pawn in the attempted assassination of her leader. "I—"

A pair of black-and-silver-clad humans crashed between him, Izzy, and the Balori, paying no mind to his toes or the Balori Annarite's shoulder.

"Hey!" Jathen said.

"Thick crowds do not excuse thick-headed maneuvering, gentlemen," Izzy called to them, her voice stern as she kept one hand on Spinnek's chest. "Common courtesy to your fellow pedestrians on the avenues is not difficult."

The two probable Talents turned, both making smug, superior faces in the direction of the three Balori. One, who had black hair and Lubreean features, spread his hands, sneering as he replied to Izzy, "My apologies, lady, for you and your toes, but as you were standing so near refuse, I thought perhaps you might have been rendered immobile from the stench."

"You ruddy little shit," the Clansman Balori growled, taking a step toward the other Talents while wrapping a hand around the hilt of his sword.

"What was that?" The obnoxious Talent cupped a hand around his ear while his friend snickered beside him. "Did the garbage fart?"

When the other two Balori both took steps forward, Jathen closed the gap between himself and the Annarite, pitching his voice as low as possible to say, "You and I both know A'ron wouldn't want violence. Not this close to your vote."

The Ways had delayed the vote after the attack on De'contes but were reconvening soon. It was only a vote to decide if they would vote on letting the Balori into the Temple as a Way, but violence on the Balori's part wouldn't help. Not really throwing his hat in the ring with De'contes and the Balori, Jathen just wanted to keep himself and his friends out of the way of more violence in general.

"Please, just let it go," he said.

Pressing his lips together hard enough to turn them from ebony to gray, the Balori nodded, though Jathen didn't miss the rhythmic throbbing of the man's temple or the rage burning in his eyes. "Come, my brothers." He jerked his chin in the direction of the two obnoxious Talents. "We'll not play the part of stand-in for their internal conflicts." With that surprisingly deep analogy, the trio stepped off the curb and crossed the street, not bothering to look back.

Jathen's sigh of relief seemed to ebb out from the depths of his soul. "Come on, then," he told his friends. Izzy nodded, delivering the pouty Talents a glare worthy of Hatori Chann before ushering Spinnek forward. The boy, however, eyed the retreating Balori, and Jathen could practically hear the gears of curiosity clicking away inside his brain.

Jathen's own mind whirled, thinking on Nannazen. *Could Annakki have been replacing the girl, waiting it out? It seems a very Rheanic thing to do. Damn it, I wish I'd been closer to her beforehand, as I have no way to track Annakki's movements before having lived with her. Even if I questioned Nannazen and she could remember when she'd been replaced, I'd never be able to substantiate it.* He rubbed his eyes, tired. *I don't even know why I bother. It's not as if I would do anything if I knew the truth.* He bit his lip. *Would I?*

"You seem rattled, and not just by the rattling of sabers," Izzy observed.

"I was just thinking on the Balori," he said, eyeing the scatted clusters of red-and-black forms walking the streets. "I can understand the threat some perceive them as. There are a lot more of them in the city than I originally realized."

"And more of them are Talented than not. Many Way Walkers are targeted by Red followers to fall to the Red, and then they have few to no options of returning to their Ways should they throw off the Red's influence." The fauni cocked her head, catching his eye from under her dark hood. "Though that's hardly enough to warrant the face you were making."

Jathen chuckled sadly at his transparency. "I'll talk to you about it once you've gotten that nice mind-shielding charm from Annakki. My visions are one thing. This is, sadly, another."

Izzy nodded, her eyes turning back once more to track a skipping Spinnek. "Fair enough."

The Temple Hospital sat in the shadow of the Great Temple, a large, orderly-looking building shaped like a capital *T*. They soon found a Daughter of Desmoulein in charge of the Dodbyen survivors, and she was happy to admit Jathen to see them. They greeted him with more awe and joy and shaking hands, which Jathen bore stiffly but genuinely.

"It really gives them a real joy and thrill to see their prince cares, doesn't it?" he murmured softly to Izzy while they walked the aisles between beds.

"Yes." She smiled softly at him. "Again, you seem surprised."

"Not surprised. Humbled. And a little frightened by it. It's a lot to live up to, this image I've become in their eyes."

"Good," she said, surprising him. "If you feel that, there's hope yet for you."

"Hope for what?"

"That you'll truly be a good king."

Jathen held his tongue, uncertain of how to react.

The Daughter of Desmoulein took them to Rhyo last. "To be honest, I'm glad you asked to see him," said the Ki'ra in green as they walked the hallways, her foxlike ears pressed back into her dark-brown hair. "I hated having to separate him from the others."

Jathen frowned. "Marcasith said there were threats."

She nodded, her lips a grim line. "I know. Nothing too dire, but I didn't want to risk anyone's well-being." Stopping at a door, she first shooed away Spinnek, who'd gotten underfoot while examining the lock. She waved a hand, opening it with Ability.

Inside, a mottled green-and-brown Tazu lay on a bed, motionless but for shallow breathing. He still looked bad, even so many weeks into healing. His bruises had turned yellow, and he looked thin—thinner even than the normal waiflike build of most from Dodbyen. Seeing Jathen, his smoky-quartz-colored eyes grew wide, then they narrowed as Rhyo retreated into his own thoughts. He rolled over, putting his back toward them. Seeing Rhyo bandaged and bruised, Jathen remembered just how bad the slashes on the young Tazu had been.

"Will he fly again?" Jathen whispered.

"The wing membranes were slashed when he was tyrn, yes, but he's young and mending well regardless. He should gain most if not full movement once he's healed," the Daughter of Desmoulein told him then sighed. "I'm more concerned with his state of mind, honestly. He's not eating nearly what he should. Nor talking. He's not so much as cried since the descent, from what I've been told. It's worrisome."

Torn, Jathen tried to decide what he felt. Since the young Tazu was responsible for what had happened, Jathen still *wanted* to be angry at Rhyo for betraying them to the sanbarna. Then perhaps Rhyo's injuries would be some vindication, justice for those who'd died thanks to his meddling. Instead, Jathen felt nothing but overwhelming pity and a touch of relief at the diagnosis. *No matter how deep Rhyo's sins, no Tazu should ever lose the capacity to fly.* Taking a deep breath, Jathen walked across the room to stand beside Rhyo's bed and deliver the message he'd intended to.

"You need to eat."

Rhyo didn't move, didn't even acknowledge Jathen had spoken. The scene was quite familiar—the way he huddled, the deep sorrow clinging to Rhyo like the bandages around his wounds. It transported Jathen back in time to Ca'june, in the wake of the Republic's earthquake and Hatori's and Jephue's deaths, followed all too soon by Ishane's betrayal and Ass'shiri's murder.

Leaning close, Jathen whispered just over the younger Tazu's ear. "My first friend, my *only* friend, died because I made the wrong choice. I walk around with that pain every day. But I do *walk* around, Rhyo." Cupping the Tazu's yellowed shoulder in his hand, Jathen squeezed ever so lightly, careful not to hurt him. "Please get yourself well. I don't want another death on my conscience."

Rhyo remained still, and Jathen walked away, not knowing if he'd had an effect.

Spinnek scuttled past him, creeping up to Rhyo's bedside. He said nothing but deposited one of the pastries from the feast on Rhyo's pillow. Jathen smiled despite noticing a bite had already been taken out of it—or perhaps because of it.

"Come on, Spinnek," he told the boy once he saw Rhyo still wasn't budging. "He'll have it when he's ready."

"Don't let stale," Spinnek said in Tazu before leaving.

Outside, Izzy stared with poignant eyes but said nothing. Jathen took a deep breath, enjoying the crisp winter air in his lungs and feeling tired enough to climb into his four-poster bed at Annakki's and never wake.

"This day has been full of far too many ups and downs," Izzy whispered.

"Go now?" Spinnek asked. "New home?"

"Not home," Jathen answered. "Just the place to lay our heads. For now."

Chapter 7
Seeker

Celina's pupils dilated.

"You're lying," Jathen declared with a certain amount of triumph, narrowing his eyes at the Beleskie follower. Sitting across from her, back in the Beleskie loi path's training building, Jathen had been practicing Volaille's exercises for over an hour. "At least about that last part involving the ferret."

Celina grinned wide, perfect teeth shining almost as bright as her blue eyes. "You caught me. And on a tough one too. It was actually an ermine, not a ferret," she whispered with a wink.

Leaning forward toward her in his chair in the High Walker's office, Jathen grinned back. "That was also a lie."

"*Very* good," Volaille said, looking up from the papers she was organizing on her desk. "What gave her away on that one? I wasn't watching."

Jathen shrugged, settling back in his chair. "Lucky guess."

"Stop that," the High Walker scolded. "You might have only agreed to learning physical cues from us, but when you use Ability, don't disregard it. You're a Talent now—you don't get to be agnostic on the fundamentals, no matter the lesson plan."

"Just on which Way I pick?"

"Indeed." She smiled slightly.

Jathen regretted not having shared his vision of deaths with her. He couldn't quite explain it, but he had a *sense* that the fewer people knew about it, the better.

"So what *did* you feel that tipped you off?"

"I have no idea. I just... knew."

"Good," Celina said. "Believe it or not, that means your Abilities are sharpening."

Crossing his legs, he fiddled with the end of his braid. "I'd feel better if I knew *exactly* how I knew, though."

"Ability can be subtle, Jathen," Volaille told him, her doe eyes serious. "Not knowing specifically why you're certain of something oftentimes means your mind is *better* processing the empathic information you're receiving. Think of it as... instead of being given a long, detailed letter describing a painting, you are just simply *given* the painting to look at."

"But how do I tell the difference between Ability-based knowing and me just being stubborn? Or honestly guessing? Or, I don't know..." His mind skittered toward Mikkal. "Delusional?"

"Simply the fact that you're concerned about it at all is a good sign. You must master balance, to trust and learn when to believe in your Ability and when to be conservative. It honestly isn't easy, Jathen. We—all Talents—must always struggle with the fine line between ego and Ability, imagination and providence. You've been progressing quite well—impressively even, considering how recently your chakra began healing. You mustn't press."

"I know. And I am pleased, truly." Jathen sighed, thinking once again of the Rosinics trying to Awaken him and the Balori stopping him on the street. *Not to mention navigating Annakki.* "But I need *more*, Volaille. I need to not *feel* like a Negater when walking down the street. Is that even possible?"

"It is," Celina said, nodding. "Most empathics work on putting up wards, protective barriers to keep you from feeling so much when you don't want to."

"Yes, Seren mentioned doing that," Jathen replied. "To be honest, given how much I've been sensing lately, I'd like to do the same, if possible."

"I said before, we can teach you." Behind her desk, Volaille leaned back, looking thoughtful. "It's honestly some of the most basic of Ability training taught, as most people are empathic to some extent, Talented or not. As a Negater, though, you'll need to also work into your protective wards a certain amount of... deception, as it were."

"Deception?"

"Instead of a ward, you'd actually be projecting your emotional aura *out* in order to fool people into thinking you're *not* a Negater."

Jathen exchanged an intrigued glance with Celina. "That sounds... interesting."

"It's not as unusual as you'd think," Celina explained. "Many powerful telepaths and empathics will put forth something similar in order to fool others into believing they're less Talented than they are. Some will even allow an invading telepathic to romp around in their mind for a bit, compartmentalizing things in such a way that they seem to have nothing to hide. This is a necessary addition to any empathic's training, Jathen."

The High Walker nodded when he glanced back her way. "I've been meaning to start nudging you in this direction but didn't want to stress you."

Jathen squirmed slightly in his seat. "Why would it stress me?"

"Well, as previously mentioned, as a Negater, you don't *quite* negate emotional energy, and thus it could still be used to do you harm under certain circumstances. An empathic Talent can bring a person to their knees with a well-placed burst of misery directed at a subject. You are not immune to this, but I didn't want you to rush forward into training it out of fear—especially so soon after your heart-chakra cleansing."

"Well, do you think I've enough of a foundation to try?"

She pursed her lips. "Building a proper base for empathy is a tough and often delicate process. I'd be happier if you were processing what you're receiving better—or at least learning to throw up proper wards. Once that's established, we can move onward to you projecting what emotions you want to be read, then to manipulating others' emotions, and then, perhaps, the true subterfuge of allowing someone into your head. But for that, we need to counteract your natural Negater tendencies."

"You said I don't *quite* negate emotions—and 'under certain circumstances.' Do you know *exactly* what my variants are?"

Her shoulders slumped as she smiled begrudgingly. "All right, you caught me. No, I do not. Sometimes, emotional bursts register to you. Sometimes, they don't. I was hoping I'd be able to better sort the pattern behind what you're doing based on more observation. But"—she leaned forward—"please don't take this as a setback. Yes, we'll fumble a bit together while we try to sort what you do, but we can start on the building of the wards. I do feel confident I can at least continue helping you to build your foundation, Jathen."

"No, I agree, that sounds reasonable. Slow but reasonable." He chuckled. "Spirit knows I am an enigma—at least here, we've only a few mysteries about how I do what I do."

"Ah, now," Celina said with another infectious smile, "but unraveling mysteries can be part of the fun."

Jathen smiled thinly at her. He liked the Beleskie Walker, but dual threads of her personality reminded Jathen of both Mal and Ishane—a fact that soured his mood for two very different reasons. He imagined he was one of very few who didn't respond overly warmly to her flirting. "Speaking of mysteries and empathy and telepathy," he said, redirecting back to Volaille, "I have noticed something odd on occasion, and I've been so distracted that I keep forgetting to mention it."

"Oh?"

"I have a friend. I'm not certain why, but my normal Negater's telepathic block doesn't seem to work on her. She's able to hear my thoughts regardless of what either of us are doing, and I recently started hearing her as well."

Weaving her fingers together, Volaille arched an eyebrow. "Are there any other symptoms?"

"Yes, but it's... *weird*." He chuckled nervously, not sure how to describe the phenomenon. "There's a tingling, like sparks, every now and again. Only when we touch, usually skin contact, but not always."

Beside him, Celina absolutely burst into a fit of hysterical giggling. He turned in his chair to catch sight of her sitting bug-eyed, hands clasped over her mouth as she tried in vain to stem the tide of laughter. Baffled, he could only stare a moment then ask, "What is it?"

She made a squeak-snort giggling sound, shaking her head and waving him away with one hand while clasping her mouth with the other. The High Walker was also covering her mouth and chuckling, though hers was far more demure and subdued.

"I am clearly missing something." Jathen had become used to elusive and even unhelpful or upsetting answers, but being laughed at was truly unexpected. "Do either of you care to enlighten me?"

Volaille dropped her hand, though by the tightness in her cheeks, she was still holding in her snickers. "Sadly, Jathen, while I do know the source of this particular phenomenon, it is honestly in your very best interests if you do *not* know right away what it is."

"What? Why?"

"I can assure you it is nothing dire and certainly not attached to your Negater Abilities." She shook her head, white curls bouncing as a smile spread across her face. "But past that, it'd be unwise to elaborate."

"That is incredibly unhelpful."

"Please, trust me. You'll be happier with me later if you don't get an answer now."

"If you insist." He slumped in his chair, irritated by Celina's continued sniggering. "I suppose this won't affect my other training?"

"No, indeed. Let us get started and put this out of our heads. Celina"—her voice ebbed stern once more—"let's work on showing Jathen the breathing techniques we use to build up a mental ward, shall we?"

Composing herself—finally—Celina straightened and turned back to face Jathen. "Thoughts are energy," she started.

"And we're all a piece of Spirit, and our thoughts have the power to manifest, depending on our level of Ability." Jathen rolled his eyes, still feeling slighted. "I know."

Celina stuck her tongue out at him then continued, "Then this should be easy. To control our Abilities long term requires visualizations, structures for our conscious mind to direct our Abilities to do as we desire. Over the long term, our subconscious will do some of this automatically, but that takes time."

"So what do I need to visualize to make a ward?"

"Honestly, it can be anything you wish." Celina brought her legs up and crossed them, tucking her feet under her knees on the chair. "The key is *breathing* and *consistency*. Now, I see auras as well—since you're a Negater, you might never get to be a visual medium—but as I do, I like to imagine the actual lights of the aura doing things." She closed her eyes, taking in a deep breath. "As I exhale, I imagine all the things I don't want—other people's feelings, any outside influences, et cetera—I see them all as a dark slime just seeping down out of me and back into the earth. Then, once I'm cleared of anything that's not *mine*, I imagine a white light made completely of Spirit's energy coming down, covering me, and protecting my aura like the shell of an egg. I do this every morning. Then, throughout the day, I can do basic maintenance, just imagining the lights of my aura doing what I wish of them." She opened her eyes. "Your turn."

Jathen pursed his lips as he tucked his legs as she'd done, trying to sort out how in Spirit's name imagining happy lights and slime was going to work. It just seemed... *silly*. Indeed, he couldn't keep a straight face as he tried to breathe in and exhale, instead snickering at the thought of pretty lights shooting out of his many orifices. "I'm sorry, but I'm going to need a different set of images."

"Pick something that is already part of your internal monologue, as Celina has with her lights," Volaille said, not looking up from her papers. "Empathic Kubeshians imagine shields and armor, Ulic Walkers and Featorians will imagine book covers and locked bookcases, while Bree Walkers have been known to imagine anything from layers of paint to walls covered in murals."

Jathen's eyebrows shot up in interest. "So I could think of a building?"

"Yes. It's a good base. Considering you eventually want to put forth different facades, perhaps even to let some into your mind, visualizing in terms of many rooms or floors might prove beneficial."

Jathen smirked, settling into his seat and closing his eyes again. "Buildings, I can imagine." Clearing out the muck was easy—sunlight through windows, brightness chasing away shadows throughout what he imagined as the dusty, unkempt halls of his mind and body. Then came the ward itself—one part the parapets surrounding Kidwellith palace with its spikes and towers and one part the dome around Dodbyen, crisscrossing and menacing, with a distinct overture of *stay out*.

"Oh!" Celina gasped softly.

Jathen opened his eyes, startled. "What?"

"That was *good*," Celina told him, her blue eyes wide. "Though you dropped it when you opened your eyes."

"Damn," Jathen muttered, annoyed.

"Don't start that again," Volaille chided. "That was *excellent* for a first try. And everyone drops their first ward attempt. You need to practice every morning, putting it up and maintaining the thoughts throughout the day before your subconscious decides to maintain it even a little bit long term."

"So I'm going to have to constantly be thinking about buildings for the rest of my life?" Jathen sighed. "Nice as that sounds, it seems limiting."

"As said, over time, it will build up until you'll only have to spare them a thought on occasion to maintain them." She waved her hand at them. "Try again. You'll see."

They did try, again and again, for another hour, before Jathen managed to maintain his empathic ward for a few minutes, according to Celina and Volaille. "Very good," the High Walker said again. "Though remember this won't completely keep you from sensing or feeling other emotions, mind. It will simply keep them from overwhelming you."

"Like viewing an invading army from a parapet versus standing in the middle of a field, waiting for it to overtake you."

Volaille and Celina both grinned.

"Never let it be said you're not a creative boy, Jathen Monortith." The High Walker checked the timepiece sitting above the fireplace. "Though I believe our time is up for today. Work on your wards as prescribed, and I'll see you next week."

Thanking her and Celina as he rose, Jathen then picked up Hatori's sword cane before taking his leave. Back down the incense-laden hall, he found Izzy where he'd left her, waiting in one of the little sitting rooms that took up some of the square footage at the front of the building. While she sat calmly in one of the overstuffed dark-pink velvet chairs, Spinnek sat at her feet, folding the portion of the *Tar'citadel Tribune* Izzy wasn't reading into three-dimensional shapes. Since he, too, had been garnering attention from Ways as an Exemplary Talent, they'd brought him along to see if Spinnek might take an interest in any of Beleskie's Way paths.

Lowering and folding her paper once she noticed Jathen, Izzy inquired, "So how did training go today?"

"Spinnek made a Walker throw up!" the boy announced before Jathen could reply.

Izzy moaned as Jathen turned a curious gaze upon her. "He did," she admitted, tapping an arm of her chair with her rolled-up paper. "They were trying to gauge his empathic skills, to see if he'd benefit from training here as well. He hit a loi with full power and sent him to the hospital."

"Spinnek!" Jathen exclaimed, horrified.

The boy just shrugged. "He ask Spinnek to. I warn—he no listen."

"He's not wrong," Izzy explained, shaking her head. "And the Walker's fine, just ego bruised and a bit dehydrated. They brought word a little bit ago." She smirked, leveling a mildly fond glance at Spinnek as she stood. "I hate to say it, but I think they were impressed."

Jathen shook his head, repressing a grin as they began to leave. "Well, while Spinnek is decimating Walkers, I'm still working on building up emotional wards."

"That's good." She nodded at Spinnek, who followed along, still looking smug even as he "hid" his newly folded paper dragon behind his back. "You don't want to be on the bad side of an Exemplary someday."

"*Pfft.* I no hurt Jathen," he said as if it were the most obvious thing in the world.

"Thanks, Spinnek," Jathen said with a chuckle. Outside again, he was caught off guard by the wind whipping down from the mountains, and he yanked up his collar and hood to brace against the cold. "That's comforting, since, other than starting wards and getting giggled at by Beleskie followers, I'm not progressing much."

"You're progressing fine, considering you've only had most of your Abilities develop in the last few months and only known about the negation for half that time. Less, even," Izzy replied tartly. "And shame on them for ridiculing you if you aren't progressing at the speed of light."

"No, they weren't laughing at me for *that*." He eyed the fauni hopefully. "Do you know what would cause telepathy to exist where it normally wouldn't, along with little sparks when you touch a person?"

Izzy froze in her tracks, indigo robes fluttering in the wind. "This happens with a *single* person?"

"Yes. With Seren."

Izzy didn't laugh, but her eyes grew wide, and she shook her head. "I suspect I do, and I assume they held their tongues for the same reason I shall—you're better sorting it out on your own."

Jathen slumped his shoulders, righteously indignant. "You're going to delve into the depths of conspiracy as well—really?"

"I mean it, Jathen. Don't go poking about looking for answers on that one. And especially do *not* mention the phenomenon to any of the high-bloods at the embassy." She toyed with the new mastercharm about her neck, tiny hematite stones set around a miniature mirror on a short silver chain to shield her thoughts from probing telepaths. "It'd be... bad."

Jathen snorted, turning to Spinnek. "I don't suppose you know and can tell me?"

The boy shook his head, sporting a befuddled expression.

After inhaling deeply, he let it out in one long, shuddering exhalation, thinking about walls and wards as he did. "Ruddy hell, I'm so tired of secrets."

"Exactly. You've enough to occupy yourself without fussing over this," Izzy said.

The way her tattoos furrowed on her brow made Jathen uneasy. He was reminded of the expression Rhodonith wore when she was calculating damage control in her head after a political mishap.

"Focus on the rest of your training, and this will eventually be clear."

"So far, the 'rest of my training' is limited to my empathy Ability and maybe, at some point, telepathy—helpful, but not the entirety of what I require to become a competent Talent." He kicked at a random pebble, sending it off into the street. "I *need* the negation under control." *Not to mention this ruddy Artifact.* Yet again, the terrifying memory of his multiple deaths splayed out across the landscape of his mind. Still, he held onto the one image of him alive and well, his one shred of hope that he had a chance to make the correct choice. *I just wish I knew what robes* that *me wore. There must be a balance amid the Ways or a trainer to be found. There must.*

"You're only just getting started, Jathen," Izzy continued over his internal concerns. "You've got that appointment with the Kubeshians later in the week on New Year's Eve morning. There're still options. We'll find a solution."

Hands in his pockets, Jathen shrugged noncommittally at the advice. He hated to admit it, but a part of him actually missed the strange sense of purpose he'd managed to carve out for himself in Dodbyen—one objective, one goal—to get *out*. Since he'd landed back in the world, nothing had been as simple as that mad rush toward survival. *Perhaps the structure of a Way* would *be helpful, though I can't imagine how much the Kubeshians know about training Negaters.* He withheld a snort. *Spirit knows the Rosinics wouldn't endorse them for it.* He closed his eyes, remembering with a shiver the orange-and-black-uniformed him going down in a bloody heap in his vision. *And probably with good reason.*

"There's something else you should know, too," Izzy added, "regarding our discussion last night."

Jathen arched a concerned eyebrow at the fauni. Izzy had been presented with her new master-charm, so he'd finally spoken to her about Na'vosh's suspicions of Annakki's hand in the attempt on De'contes. Izzy had been rightfully worried, though she seemed more preoccupied with the political ramifications should Annakki be found out than afraid Annakki would hurt Jathen.

"What is it?" he asked.

"The vote was last night. They put it through, Jathen." She took a step closer, her voice delving lower. "The High Walkers *will* be voting on if the Balori should be sanctioned as an official Way. It's on the docket for the end of the first quarter next year."

"What?" Inside his chest, Jathen's heart skittered alongside the Artifact's buzzing. "Annakki's going to be furious."

"Hence my concern." Izzy pursed her lips. "To read between the lines of the articles in the papers, you can tell the High Walkers decided to at least allow the vote to occur mainly *because* of the incident with the assassination. 'It is logical to go forward with the vote to reduce the disturbance and chaos caused by the uncertainty of the Balori's position' is what they quoted."

"In other words, it's causing so much trouble for everyone that it's better to just move the issue forward and get it over with." Jathen closed his eyes. "And that's my fault. Since I saved him, he now has this chance."

"It could be interpreted that way, yes." Izzy's brown eyes were hard. "Are you certain you wish to remain at the townhouse? Things might genuinely be safer at the embassy—and less politically prickly, at least in this aspect."

Jathen shook his head. "No. I'm honestly more concerned she'll try again than I am about being physically hurt or once more getting caught in the crossfire. I *need* to remain there to keep an eye on her more than anything else. Ass'shiri would *not* want her to destroy herself for her hate. I know it." He sighed. "Besides, as you were quick to point out last night, it's circumstantial evidence at best. We still don't *know* she was behind anything."

"And I do still agree with that assessment. My priority, however, is your safety, and—" She stopped, eyes growing wide. "Spinnek, give that back!"

Jathen stiffened, turning forward to find Spinnek holding something behind his back and looking innocent. A very sour-faced Way Walker clad in bronze, green, and silver robes stood nearby, his side satchel hanging conspicuously open.

"Ruddy hell, Spinnek." Mimicking both Izzy and the poor Ulic Walker whose satchel contents were scattered about the snow-spotted street, Jathen put his hand on his hips. "What did you do?"

"He nicked one of my papers, and poorly," the Walker grumbled then tried to settle the contents of his bag.

Spewing apologies, Izzy sprang forward to help the man, picking sheets up off the street and leaving Jathen to deal with Spinnek.

Jathen put a hand out expectantly. "Give it here."

Spinnek rocked back and forth on his heels then drummed his bare toes across the cobbles. "He no use. Why I not use?"

"Because it's not *yours*," Jathen said with an exasperated sigh. "This isn't Dodbyen, where everything is salvageable. You wouldn't like it if someone came and took *your* quartz, would you?"

Spinnek sighed long then gave up the paper with an overdramatic show of reluctance. Taking it, Jathen glanced briefly at its contents—a detailed chart cataloging the maximum drilling depths of the various mines around Tar'citadel. Jathen shook his head, unable to imagine what Spinnek even wanted such a thing for.

"Like pattern," Spinnek explained as Jathen handed it back to the Walker. "When fold, look as dragon scales."

"Spinnek, we can *buy* you patterned paper for you to fold if you like," Jathen told him while Izzy offered more apologies to the Walker. "It'd even be colored."

Spinnek's eyebrows arched in interest, and Jathen turned to say his own apology to the Walker.

An energy bolt slammed into his back.

Jathen heard Spinnek squeak and Izzy yell his name right before the Grand Artifact buzzed happily then whisked him away.

FEELING SLIGHTLY DIZZY, Jathen sat up slowly, only to bang his head. "Red take the Rosinics," he muttered, glaring at the pattern of the light oaken desk he'd arrived under. Rubbing his sore forehead, he crawled out from between a few chairs and glanced around.

A smaller study than the library he'd been taken to the last time, the new room was windowless, illuminated with strange blue lights bobbing near the ceiling. *Reminds me of the light spell the Interpreter cast on the summit.* Seeing someone perusing the shelves next to a thin maple-wood desk across from him, Jathen stood then tentatively cleared his throat until the man looked up.

"What's this now?" Pale of hair, he had the lighter, creamy-pink skin tone of perhaps Kinawa or Nor'wah, though he lacked either accent. He wore the gold outer robe of a Montage Walker but sported the bright-pink-and-amber vest of a Beleskie loi over a mint-green shirt, a strange pair of black-and-silver pinstripe pants, fencing shoes, and a scarf made of an overly fuzzy yarn in a rainbow pattern. He adjusted a pair of square, rimless spectacles, peering at Jathen over them with ice-blue eyes. "Where did you pop in from?"

"Out on the street," Jathen explained, tentative. "I'm hoping this is still Tar'citadel but just another spatial room?"

"Well, technically, this is an office that exists on the second vibrational level removed from the physical plane, so it's part of the nearside of the Veil, though its particular location is parallel to rooms in Tar'citadel, yes."

Jathen's heart sank. "So you're saying there's no doorway anchor to this room, as it doesn't actually exist in the physical plane?"

"Quite right." He adjusted his glasses again, looking more intrigued than cross. "Rather ingenious of you to get into it without the teleportation password."

Jathen huffed a laugh. "I've quite the talent for that."

"Talent?" He cocked his head, the fuzzy scarf falling slightly off his left shoulder. "Ah, you're Jathen Monortith, then."

He nodded. "The Negater."

Righting his scarf, the probable Montage Walker chuckled. "I have it on good authority you've a bit more to you than a single title, Prince Jathen." He smiled kindly. "However, no large inconvenience. I'll give you a jolt, then just tell your Artifact where you want to go."

"Wait, what—" Jathen exclaimed too late.

A burst of energy crackled between the Walker's fingers then hit Jathen in the chest. He felt the growling *roar* of him negating the energy, followed by the buzz of the Artifact. *Oh, um, back to Izzy!* Jathen managed to think just as the world went fuzzy.

Jathen landed in the street.

Dropping directly onto his feet, he felt a sharp jolt in his ankles right before they went out from under him. Tilting sideways, he collapsed onto Izzy, who managed to steady him and keep them both upright despite her surprised yelp.

"Told come back," Spinnek declared. Sitting cross-legged in the middle of the road between two tar'ka-besh, the boy nonchalantly picked at a dry patch of skin between his toes.

"Apparently," one of the tar'ka-besh replied with a sneer in his tone.

Jathen recognized him immediately, even as Izzy helped Jathen sit on an obliging bench.

He was Burjiro Tan, Ass'shiri's brother. He looked the same—black hair, hard amethyst eyes, and a sour expression. "This fauni claimed you were... assaulted?"

"I'm fine," Jathen said, though his head was swirling a little. *I must have been unconscious in that study for a bit if Izzy had time to call for the tar'ka-besh. Might need to get checked later.* "It was another set of damn Rosinics."

"This has happened *before*?" Izzy demanded, hands immediately going to her hips. "Why didn't you inform me? How can I protect you if I'm not aware of all the dangers, Jathen?"

Burjiro arched an eyebrow at her outburst then nodded in agreement.

His partner, Dredona, also bobbed her head and said, "You should have informed the tar'ka-besh as well, Prince Jathen. We might be precognitive, but there are tens of thousands of people and *other* precognitives in this city whose choices alter that pattern in an eyeblink—to the point that precognition can be almost irrelevant in Tar'citadel. And it's *much* harder preventing things we don't know to watch for."

"I didn't mention it because I was told it was harmless and had assumed those doing it had been told to stop." *So much for trusting random retired Rosinics I run across.* Jathen rubbed the back of his head. *Though precognition being unreliable here is interesting... Perhaps my visions of death have more outs than I think...*

"How is an assault harmless?" Izzy demanded.

"It's a prank," he said, skirting the Aspect issue. He didn't revel in the idea of spreading that rumor any further than necessary, and their little group was already drawing a few curious bystanders from the normal street crowd. *I've been having far, far too many public incidents on the streets of Tar'citadel lately.* "Some Rosinic acolytes from the university are just seeing what happens when they energy whack the Negater."

Burjiro snorted, wrinkling his nose in a way that said he doubted Jathen was even a Talent, let alone a Negater. "Can you describe these 'Rosinic pranksters,' then?"

"No." Irritated, Jathen sighed while Izzy also shook her head. "I didn't get a good look last time, and this time I literally got slammed in the back."

"One had green lights," Spinnek offered, still absorbed with picking at his feet. "Other orange and white lights."

"An aura description is, sadly, not very helpful," Dredona told him, though she did look impressed that he'd mentioned it. "Unless we catch a suspect that you can later identify."

Finally releasing his foot and stretching out his legs, Spinnek shrugged then yawned. Jathen resisted the urge to place his head in his hands and groan aloud.

"Well, since the... *prince* didn't see anything else, I doubt that," Burjiro proclaimed. "So we best just file a simple report and be done with this... complaint."

Dredona narrowed her eyes at him but didn't argue.

Izzy looked ready to spit nails into his eyes, but Jathen stayed her with a hand on her elbow.

"That's fine," he said, ignoring Burjiro and speaking to Dredona. "Just inform Commander Na'vosh of it, if you would? I'm certain he'll speak to whomever on my behalf, to put an end to this."

"Of course," she said with a proper bow, fist clenched over her heart.

Burjiro huffed softly, teleporting out without another word.

Straightening, Dredona leveled an apologetic look at the trio before teleporting away herself.

Izzy groaned, pinching the bridge of her nose. "Before we return to the townhouse, is there anything *else* I should know, Jathen?"

"Yes." He grinned, pleased with at least one aspect of his little misadventure. "I truly *can* direct the Grand Artifact to where *I* want to go."

Chapter 8

"**D**istract him!"

"Jathen?" The confused panic on Izzy's face might have been comical under other circumstances, but as Jathen desperately tried to duck into the nearest unlocked door, he couldn't spare a moment to find it so.

"Really—Izzy, keep him busy," he whispered firmly.

"What, who, why?" She grabbed the edge of the door, not allowing him to close it fully. "I thought I was escorting you back here to speak to the queen, not run interference against random high-bloods stalking the embassy's hallways."

"Izzy, please." Jathen stole a glance, hoping beyond hope he'd not been spotted.

No, Bertrandith Larsenitiss was still speaking with Ambassador Chertith, his back to the pair.

Swallowing his panic, Jathen pleaded softly, "Just station yourself outside this door, then. Don't let them in."

"Jathen—"

"That's an *order*," he barked then wrenched the door closed. He leaned back against it a moment, feeling childishly idiotic. *What is wrong with me? Then again, can my luck be any worse? Scheduled to ask my mother about my father, and who shows up but the very Tazu that Skaniss implied is my father just before he tried to kill me?* Jathen rubbed his temples with two fingers, breathing to try to calm himself

144

while imagining his empathic fortress around himself. *I'm beginning to hate being an empathic more than being a moot. At least that never made me act irrationally.* Then again, he wondered if perhaps it had. For years, he'd become a ball of rage at the mere mention of his condition. *I did punch a mirror once. Seems so long ago now.*

Events in his life had been moving very quickly since he'd saved De'contes and discovered he himself was a Negater. He'd been neglecting the exercises Master Volaille had taught him, using them only when he noticed a problem and not first thing in the morning as she'd instructed. This left him with a nearly irrational sense of not progressing quickly enough, thanks to a vision of doom that he hadn't yet been able to interpret. The wave of all those disasters played across his memory again—all starting with an avalanche. *Spirit, what exactly is it I'm racing toward? Or can it be as Dredona suggested—that precognition in Tar'citadel is almost irrelevant? What if I do all this and it doesn't even matter? Maybe I'm better off just acting as if I'd never been shown the ruddy thing.*

His heart finally slowing, Jathen heard Marcasith's voice then his uncle laughing. Opening his eyes, he straightened away from the door and walked through the little sitting room toward the arch on the other side.

"I had a damn bath!" Marcasith bellowed.

Turning the corner, Jathen caught sight of his uncle's profile, sitting in a chair and facing one of those charm-viewers set up on an easel.

"I tell you, when I get home, I am going to bathe at least twice a day, if not all day, morning to night, after what I've been through!"

From the other side of the viewer, Jathen heard a low-throated chuckle. *Is that... is that Kyanith laughing?* The sound so boggled him that he missed Kyanith's response, only snapping back to attention when Marcasith grew quieter.

"'The moot.'" Marcasith's gold eyes flicked upward, catching sight of Jathen. Acknowledging him, he nodded slightly but otherwise kept on with his conversation. "Listen to you, brother, sounding like a prejudiced old lizard. Is there really that little love between you two?"

"Things are more complicated than they appear, Marcasith."

"I figured as much. I couldn't imagine you quite as cold as the egg describes. And there're always two sides to every tale. Got to hear both to sort the truth." He adjusted himself in the chair, one hand moving to tighten the straps on the old Tazu armor he used to wear. Finding nothing, he grimaced at himself then scratched his side instead. "Still, he's a good egg, Kyan. He's got the blood. I don't know if he's got the gumption to rule, and Spirit only knows what the politics will support, but he *can* lead, Brother. And well."

"He can't rule, Marc," Kyanith said, stern.

"That's a little gruff, even for you." Marcasith put his hands on his knees, frowning. "Why not?"

"I'd prefer to explain over less impersonal channels. But trust me, it's no small thing."

"I do trust you, Kyan. But trust me too—the egg's a Monortith in his heart. And a damn fine one at that."

"That's precisely what I'm concerned about, Brother." Kyanith actually sounded tired and perhaps a little sad. "As said, I'll confide better in person."

"Fair enough."

"I've sent my youngest up to collect you—and Jathen, for that matter. We'll speak when you're home."

"Good. Though it will be a few weeks more, at least." Yawning, Marcasith leaned back in his seat. "The Walkers say we can't teleport the injured, and I've a mind to let my people heal up a bit more before taking them on the road again. That, and I've got a few half-blood females 'bout ready to hit their first heats, and the last thing any of them needs is to jump into the political mire of court romances before they've had half a chance to decide what they want to do with their lives."

"Can't blame you. I'm quite set in my vocation, and I can barely abide court romances," Kyanith replied with a dry humor Jathen had rarely heard from the monarch. "For the injured... They'll heal better in the Tazu south than that bitter Tar'citadel winter, but do what you must to keep them comfortable."

"Trust me, this is a tropical paradise compared to where I've spent the last three centuries." His eyes darted back to Jathen for a moment then returned to the charm-viewer. "Oh, the egg's letter, it got to his sister all right? You're handling that craziness with the guard captain?"

"Yes." A low rumble on the other end of the viewer told Jathen Kyanith wasn't at all pleased about the situation. "As you said earlier, both sides of a thing must be heard before the truth is decided. But Skaniss will not be leaving Kidwellith for the foreseeable future."

"Truer words were never spoken." Marcasith smiled. "It will be good to see you again, Brother."

"Likewise."

"That"—Marcasith nodded to the dim viewer as Jathen walked over—"was the Kyanith I am accustomed to. Quite a bit older, bit gruffer, but still honest, cautious, and honorable."

Jathen nodded, wanting it to be true but unable to ignore the tightness in his throat. "But what did he mean: 'He can't rule'?"

"You know as much as I do, Nephew. I'll admit he seemed more guarded than I recall. But near-on three hundred years is a long time, even for Tazu. Much has changed." He shrugged, sighing. "I might simply not know him as I once did."

"Thank you, though, for sticking up for me. Few have."

His eye ridges arched, Marcasith regarded him with genuine and deep surprise. "By Montage, Nephew, I'd follow you into the ruddy *Pit* after what you've done for me and mine."

"I appreciate that." Jathen smiled thinly. "But my plan is to let you grow fat and lazy in Kidwellith, Uncle. You deserve that after everything."

He laughed. "Oh, that I do."

"Here you are!" Gwydion Trahern turned the corner, looking flustered but relieved. "Wandered everywhere looking for you, and then your fauni tells me you're in the correct place." He walked up to the viewer to exchange its crystals. "I'll have your mother up on here in a moment."

"That's my cue to exit, then." Marcasith stood, moving considerably more slowly than usual. "You enjoy your mother."

"I will." Jathen hesitated a moment then added, "Please apologize to Izzy for me on your way out. I was... gruff."

Marcasith snorted. "She's got a thick skin, Nephew. I'd not worry. But I'll convey the message."

Jathen sat, and within moments, his mother was in the crystal-viewer—pink scaled and black striped, wearing the Monortith colors. Gwydion Trahern took his leave, slipping away after Marcasith with little sound.

"*Jathen.*" Her voice brimming full with too many emotions to count, Rhodonith put her hand upon the glass, her golden eyes begging to reach through and hold him.

Jathen matched the movement, and though the glass's image shimmered coldly under his fingers, he found comfort in the illusion of a mother's touch.

"Oh, my darling, darling little egg." Tears shimmered in her eyes.

Soon, Jathen's throat constricted. "I'm well, Mother," he said when he finally found his voice. "I'm so very, very sorry I made you worry."

"I'll always worry, love, no matter what." She smiled through the tears. "I'm just so glad you're safe. I'd come up, love, but—"

"What?"

She turned hesitant. "We thought you lost. I had taken the season off, but losing you... I couldn't. I just couldn't be alone, and he was there just to be there without agenda—"

Mild surprise filled Jathen. "You've gotten another egg."

Similar to shifting, teleporting early on would lead to a guaranteed miscarriage—for not just Tazu but any woman.

She nodded, seemingly shy. "Please, don't think I was trying to replace you. It was never my intention to get an egg out of season. I just—"

"Oh, Mother, that would never cross my mind," he exclaimed, horrified. "You needed someone. If I get another little brother or sister out of it, it's only a blessing." He smiled at her long sigh of relief. "So who's the new mate? Someone that's got Kyanith grumbling, I hope?"

She pursed her lips, and Jathen knew. Before she even spoke, he knew.

"Now, please don't be—"

"Bertran."

She eyed him sadly. "Yes."

Suddenly, he couldn't ask her. He needed to know, needed to ask about his father, but couldn't—not across such a distance and not with Bertran standing out in the hallway. The words just weren't there, and some things couldn't be asked if not in person, where he would be able to touch, to hold if necessary.

"I know you two haven't gotten along," Rhodonith continued, obviously misinterpreting whatever bizarre expression he was sporting. "But as I said, he was there. No questions. No agendas. For me and only for me."

Jathen nodded, feeling an unexpected stab of longing and loss for those who'd once been such for him. "You don't have many people in your life like that. If you find it, hold onto it, Mother."

"So you actually approve?"

"I approve of your happiness—from wherever or whomever it stems. As far as Bertran..." He let the words hang a moment. *Perhaps I should have a chat or two with him. Either bury the hatchet or uncover it. I can't duck into doorways forever.* "I will try."

"Thank you." A smile managed to curl upon her lips. "So how are you, now a Negater and guardian of a Grand Artifact, with all these Ways currying your favor?"

"Horridly insecure," he admitted. *She must be talking with the ambassador. Seems I shall have to keep my secrets from Mother as well. Though Spirit knows she doesn't need to worry about the many ways I can die any more than she already does.* "I think I actually hate it."

Rhodonith laughed. "You'll be fine, my little egg. Remember, good teachers fill your head with tactics and facts. Great teachers provide you with a compass. Heed the compass bearers."

"I will." *Ruddy good advice. Sometimes, I forget she's a Talent in her own right.* He shifted in his seat, wanting to get off the subject. "Speaking of compasses, is Thee there? I think she'll be amused by the fact I still have that atlas Kyanith gave me."

Rhodonith plastered a slightly too-stiff smile on her face. "Thee is indisposed at the moment. I'm certain we can arrange another chat like this soon."

A pang of worry and sadness hit his chest. "Thee didn't want to see me, did she?"

"You are getting more observant of people, aren't you?" The queen's expression softened into that of a torn mother in her surprise. "Jathen, your sister loves you very much. But she's still very young. She doesn't understand that a sister's love... It's just not enough. Not enough to make you content at home, not enough to bring you home now. It's hard for her."

"She believes too strongly in Beleskie at times, I think. The silly notion that love can conquer all if you just *feel* it enough." He sighed, thinking on Ishane. "Love provides no bandages if you are bleeding, no balm if the wound's infected."

"But it does help, my love."

He nodded. "Tell her that for me?" Memories surfaced of being tied to a chair as Ishane offered him the chance to become Red in exchange for his life, sharp in their painful clarity. *I knew Thee would hate me, so I said no.* "That I thought of her, and living for her and you helped to get me through? It's true. It might offer some solace."

"I'll see that she hears such."

They talked for a great deal longer, on life back home in court, upon Kyanith's surprising gratitude at Marcasith's rescue, and of time spent in Dodbyen and Tar'citadel. Jathen didn't know how long the conversation went, but the relief he felt in talking without worrying for at least a brief moment about all his troubles was something he wished he could hold onto and stretch out as long as he could. Finally, they had to be cut off when Seren's father returned.

"The charm-loop on that is going to wind down soon," Gwydion Trahern explained. "I'll need at least a few hours to infuse it again."

"We'll see if we can arrange another chat," Rhodonith promised. "Charm-viewers are rare, as well as the Talents to work the crystals. We've only one on our end, and he'll be almost a week to recharge ours. Until then, we'll write. Give any letters to the ambassador, my love. She'll see they get home."

Jathen promised and said goodbye, then Seren's father removed the crystal, and the mirror dimmed.

"Did you find your answers?" he asked.

"I didn't ask yet." Probably looking pathetic, he smiled nevertheless. "She's my mother. It's not easy."

"You and Seren could probably pen a tome about the complexity of mothers."

Jathen laughed but, realizing the man wasn't joking, stifled his smile. *Perhaps I can still prove to myself I'm not a coward and get some answers in the process.* "Do you think you can point me in the direction of Bertran Larsenitiss? He and I need to have a chat."

"I believe his suite is adjacent to Marcasith's."

"Thank you." After leaving him, Jathen found Izzy still obediently guarding the door, though the emotions coming from her were mildly grumpy.

"I took the liberty of allowing Gwydion Trahern in, as I assumed you'd want to see him."

"Thank you, Izzy. I did. And I am sorry."

She nodded, though her lips were still pressed thin. "You can't expect to hide like that in the Tazu court, my prince."

"I agree. A momentary weakness, which I intend to remedy. Come, you can escort me to Bertran Larsenitiss's room."

"So the Tazu you were avoiding we are now seeking out?"

"Yes."

She smirked, a spark of Orne's snide humor in her brown eyes. "Well then, let us away."

They found the room easily enough, occupied by the Larsenitiss heir alone, luckily. Izzy took up guardianship of the door once more, waiting outside while Jathen entered. Bertran looked the same, boasting handsome dual-toned silver scales, dark-brown hair, and the latest Tazu fashion in pale green.

"Jathen." Surprised, the Tazu stood up from the desk he'd occupied, the silver ribbons woven into his braid catching the light as he crossed through it. "I'm glad to see you're well," he said, formal but slightly shaken. "I had searched for—"

"I know." Jathen closed the door, remaining in the little foyer section of the four-bayed room. "I had been hiding at Lady Nosalia's after the incident with Skaniss... uncertain whom to trust." Though he knew this wasn't the case, according to his life ladder, Jathen bluntly asked, "Are you my father?"

Jathen couldn't quite quantify the expression on Bertran's face. He paled slightly, and his pupils shook, denoting surprise, but the rest was hard to read, even with Ability—a bit of worry, horror that Jathen had asked outrightly, fear, and some longing as well, at least that was what Jathen thought he sensed.

Or perhaps it's hope I sense.

Recovering, Bertran formally replied, "I think that would be a question better suited to your mother."

"I couldn't. Not just yet, at least." He paused. "In the Republic, when bent on killing me, Skaniss claimed that, while he could not touch my father, he would see him suffer from my death. I ask again: Are you my father, Bertran? And if not, how does Skaniss claim to know when I do not?"

Bertran winced, his bright moonstone-colored eyes hurt. "I arrested Skaniss personally the day your letter reached Thee's hands. The look in his eyes... I suspected he's always believed it, how he's acted with you, but to actually go so far—" He cut himself off, shaking his head then holding Jathen's gaze. "Jathen, your mother and I... Yes, years ago. She asked to keep it quiet, and I agreed, as the first heir, the politics at the time..." He waved a hand dismissively. "Inconsequential now. When you hatched, I made to claim you, but she wouldn't allow it. For months, we argued the point in secret, as I believed she was doing it to protect my status."

"Was she? Protecting you?"

"I thought so, but as I told her many times, my status could only *help* your position—not to mention lessen Kyanith's ire." He was more deadly stoic than Jathen had ever seen the Tazu. "I would have gladly claimed any egg of mine, no matter their appearance. Please believe that."

Measuring him, Jathen sensed his burning desire to have done so, as well as a long-latent thing, a desperate longing to connect, to love a child he thought his own. "Then why didn't you?"

"Please don't think less of Rhodonith for this, but after months of my badgering, one night, she finally confessed to me that I was *not* your father. There was another, she said, but she refused to tell me more."

"You didn't think she was just saying that to end the argument?"

"I considered it. Tried to pursue it, but in the end..." He sputtered half a chuckle. "You know how stubborn Rhod is. Ultimately, I believed even if she was lying, her reasons for wanting the matter ended had to be greater than my understanding of the situation." A pained set of lines furrowed his forehead. "Forgive me, Jathen? I tried. I tried so hard to be as kind as I could while respecting your mother's wishes. I tried to soften Kyanith and keep Skaniss in line, but I am all too aware of how it was just... not enough."

For a moment, Jathen suddenly saw what the past twenty-one years would have been like through Bertran Larsenitiss's eyes, and his heart broke. To have seen Jathen every day, growing, struggling, hurting... but never able to truly help. Being torn apart by the knowledge that he didn't really, truly know if the poor little moot was his son or not. Added to that, the hurt of loving Rhodonith, of losing her and never knowing if that loss had really been to another Tazu male or not—to have seemingly lost Jathen and, in his and Rhod's grief, to have found her again.

What kinds of guilt and sorrow have hidden so long behind your moonstone eyes, Bertran? I truly was a fool, as Seren and Skaniss said, to have never seen it.

"I'm sorry too," he whispered. "There was a great deal I just never saw."

"You were a child through most of it, Jathen. It wasn't your responsibility to see."

He smiled thinly, oddly gratified. "If I might offer some solace or at least a portion of an answer... What I am about to tell you, I say in the utmost and strictest of confidences, and it cannot be repeated—not to my mother, not to Kyanith, not to anyone. Am I clear?"

"Yes. I never meant for Kyanith to do what he did, that once. And I certainly never meant to betray your trust."

"I know. It's been a childish grudge."

Jathen had wanted to build skywalks between the temples in the temple complex so that he wouldn't have to walk up and down so many stairs or hitch a ride on an obliging Tazu. Bertran had shown genuine interest in the idea for the sake of human parishioners, or so Jathen had thought. Bertran had presented the proposal in open court, planning to then reveal it was Jathen's, but Kyanith had known already and shot it down rather viciously, citing the instability of earthquakes as a negative. "I'd come to expect better from you, Bertran," he said while looking right at Jathen. "I can only imagine such fancies weren't spawned in your head." That still stood out as one of the more cuttingly humiliating moments of Jathen's childhood.

He buried the memory, determined to move past it. Finally stepping down into the center bay where Bertran and his desk stood, Jathen confessed, "I have had my life ladder drafted in secret here. I will not say much more except there is an... *abnormality* with regards to my father's addition to it."

Crossing his arms, Bertran drew his head back a touch. "Abnormality?"

"I cannot say more." Jathen shook his head. "But for what it's worth, I do not believe my mother lied to you. Given your story, and given what the life ladder revealed, I don't believe you are my father."

"I find myself more disappointed than relieved." Leaning against his desk, he sighed, bright eyes looking inward. "I've a very intelligent nephew, a bright and promising niece, and three daughters, but never a son. In an odd way, you always represented a strange sort of hope for me, Jathen. I never knew, and in not knowing, there was always that hope, small as it was, that you were mine. I've watched you grow, wanted and waited from afar, and seeing you now, your potential as a man and as a king, I had hoped I could be part of it. Part of your life."

An image popped into Jathen's head of a little Tazu boy, bright-silver scaled with black stripes and golden Monortith eyes. Perhaps six or seven, he had a regal arch to his neck, as if to say, "I would be a king," but wisdom shone as well in his bullion eyes, as if to add, "I'd also be a good one."

"I have the feeling your unborn egg will be a boy," Jathen said once the vision faded. "As none of us know what Kyanith has in store for my trials once I go home, nor the actual extent of my or the king's lifetimes, perhaps you will get your chance to raise a king after all."

Bertran's brow ridge arched. "You do mean if Dolomith chooses to abdicate as well? Any son of mine and Rhodonith would only be king if both you and Dol were passed over."

A strange shiver ran down Jathen's spine, and he shifted uncomfortably from foot to foot. "Yes, you're right. For some reason, I forgot about Dol." *Spirit, that was strange. It felt... precognitive, yet not.* "How is Dol's health?"

"Quite well, since your rescue of him. Started talking in small portions." His eyes narrowed. "Should I be concerned, Jathen?"

"I'm not sure." Jathen scratched the back of his neck. "I'd had a vision of Dol's funeral before, which is what prompted me to be watchful of him in the first place. Just now, I had an image of your son and this feeling that if I were not king, he would be. Dol didn't even come into my mind."

"As you said, there are many factors to consider between now and then. Dolomith is weaker and more soft-spoken than others his age. It's not inconceivable that he might choose to forego the throne if offered it." He worried at his bottom lip a moment. "Still, I would mention this to your mother if that is well with you."

"Perfectly fine. Regardless of the additional ambiguity of precognition while in Tar'citadel, I will take no risks when it comes to my little brother's health." Jathen smirked. "Either of them."

Bertran smiled back. "And parentage of kings aside, Jathen, if you'd allow me, I'd like to help you beat those trials."

Jathen's eyebrows shot up. "Really?"

"I've stayed neutral between Rhodonith and my father on the issue of you for far too long. My uncle Tourmalith Larsenitiss has been bucking hard at the yoke of Chertith and Grandidieriss politics and would see a change. He would see me do more for my birth house and line than my father's."

"Are you actually telling me I have *allies* at court?"

The silver ribbons braided into Bertrandith's hair glimmered again as he nodded. "They are not as united or as strong as those who would keep you from the throne, but yes, Jathen, you do." He frowned. "And to be honest, a great deal more enemies than we thought as well."

"You don't believe Kyanith put Skaniss up to murdering me, do you?"

"No." The Tazu actually laughed. "My father might be many things you don't always understand—indeed, neither of us understand—but he'd never do that. Not to family. By Rhean, not even to enemies. Assassination is so underhanded. He'd sooner clip his own wings."

"But you don't believe Skaniss was acting alone, either."

"I don't believe someone put a dagger in his hand and said, 'Go kill the moot prince.' But someone must have fanned the flames of his hate, putting just the right word in his ear at just the right moment. Such as 'Wouldn't Bertran be devastated if his moot son were to never come home' or something like."

Jathen nodded, imagining. "He had recruited someone, another Tazu that I'd gotten into a confrontation with on the way to Zo'den. I never knew his name, but he had a scar on his eye, sergeant rank from..." Jathen racked his brain for a few moments. "Bronzith province. He'd been soliciting bribes from travelers, and I broke a chair over his head. He died in the Republic when Skaniss tried to murder me. Perhaps there is a connection. Bronzith is a decent way from Kidwellith, so I don't think those two could have just happened upon each other in a tavern."

Bertran drummed his claws across the top of the desk, considering. "Faustith Bustamiss rules Bronzith province. Bustamiss bloods haven't been to court in quite some time, so I'm not as familiar with their politics."

Jathen frowned, thinking on the theory Seren's father had put to them a few weeks back. "Gwydion Trahern had speculated that killing me and making it look as if Kyanith were responsible would easily start a civil war between the king and queen's seats in the Nation. Do you think there's any weight to that?"

Bertran's eyes grew wide even as he shivered. "That's a bold play but a conceivable one," he murmured. "I'll see what I can discover—discreetly, of course."

"Thank you." Jathen offered him his hand. "For all the things I never knew."

"Ditto." His moonstone eyes glassy, Bertran took Jathen's hand and shook it.

Chapter 9

"You seem frustrated."

Jathen nearly jumped across the elevator, slamming into Izzy, who yelped. Na'vosh eyed them quizzically, as if the Clansman had been standing there the entire time instead of having just miraculously appeared.

"You're liable to make my heart stop," Jathen said, punctuating the sentence with a shaky breath. He put one hand on the elevator wall and the other on Izzy's shoulder to calm her. "Couldn't you have just walked up and asked instead of teleporting in?"

The Clansman smiled. "Apologies. In actuality, I was here when you two happened in. I occasionally find it wise to patrol while cloaked in a light-bending spell... so I know what goes on when my soldiers don't think I'm here."

Izzy straightened, taking her hand off the lower clasp on Orne's satchel. "And commendations to the ones who can spot you, I suppose."

"That is one benefit." He cocked his head slightly. "You've an appointment with High Walker Kriger's representative today, correct?"

"Kubesh, Way of the Warrior, yes." His heart slowing, Jathen straightened his shirt. "The High Walker is off playing general somewhere in the Middle Lands, so I hear, so I'm meeting with Master Enillydd."

"That frustration I mentioned is in your tone again."

Ignoring Izzy's smirk, Jathen nodded begrudgingly. "I've met with most of the Ways at this point. None but Rosin really offered any kind of *help* regarding training me as a Negater. And I didn't like the terms Jiāojīn put forth." *Nor the damn vision's implications.* He frowned, thinking on the rash of unfruitful visits. He'd hoped to have found some sort of sign or additional vision—or perhaps the clouds parting and angels singing or some rot to tell him what path wouldn't lead him to death by the new year—but with it happening tomorrow, and only Kubesh left, he didn't think his chances good.

The urgency I felt in my vision still haunts me. And there's some connection, some truth I'm missing. Like when I sensed the Grand Artifact as well as Ishane's and Mikkal's true natures. I kept dreaming the pieces but not the connection. Now, it's only a feeling. I don't even dream anymore. He sighed, thinking again on what Dredona had said about precognition being difficult in Tar'citadel. *Perhaps that's it. Not a hopeful bit of information, though.*

Turning back to Na'vosh, he confessed, "I feel the worst is happening. I'm going to be left floundering on my own with no training to temper this negation Ability. I've learned so much but am still left so wanting."

"Have you spoken to Plajă yet?"

"Who?"

"High Walker of Bree."

Jathen blinked, trying to recall any amber-colored robe combinations in his vision. *There might have been, but none jump to mind.* "I... I don't think he sent me a missive."

"Considering the rumors of Grand Artifacts, I'd assume he expected you'd eventually go to him." Na'vosh chuckled as the elevator came to the Kubeshian floor. "I'll put in word that you'd like to speak with him."

Jathen could only shake his head at his own stupidity. "Thank you."

"Welcome."

Memories of the avalanche in his vision suddenly became overwhelming, and Jathen caught the elevator door just before it closed. "Na'vosh, one more thing. I don't suppose there's any way you could prevent an avalanche from happening, is there?"

Though Izzy stared at Jathen as if his head had just fallen off, Na'vosh only raised an eyebrow. "I assume this is a precognitive question?" When Jathen nodded, the Clansman frowned, tucking his hands behind his back. "Well, I can set a few of my own precognitives to scan for it, see if there's any merit to the vision. But with natural disasters, the smallest change in snowfall or air pressure could contribute to it happening or not happening. If it's any comfort, such things actually occur regularly, and we do have procedures and quite a few preventive measures in place. A natural avalanche is unlikely to cause any true damage to the city."

Jathen nodded, as the High Walker of Feator had said as much. "And what about an unnatural event?"

Those bottle-green eyes of his squinted slightly. "You have reason to believe that?"

"Nothing concrete, even in my head. Just a feeling."

Na'vosh smiled ironically. "My mother had 'just a feeling' for nearly ten years before the coup. Never discount them." Sighing lightly, he crossed his arms. "I will take what precautions I can. If a mage wants to cause an explosion to trigger an avalanche up on one of the Three Sentinels to bury the city, it'd be nearly impossible to head it off without direct knowledge of where they intend to cause it—even *with* precognitives. However, I can bring this up to the tar'ka-besh order and have more of us checking on the snow wards and the melting stations. Also increase some of the patrols of the outer city towers on the Blackwatch Sentinel between us and the Middle Lands."

"Melting stations?"

Na'vosh nodded. "We can't just magic away all the snow that comes off the mountain faces. It has to *go* somewhere. Tar'citadel's solution was to craft a long line of melting stations that sends the bulk of the snow on Copperwatch into the Dragon's Tongue tributary river *before* it hits the snow wards in the city. It's not perfect, but even a Red Mage would be hard-pressed to get past all the wards to affect anything on Blackwatch, let alone all the way across the plateau to the Copperwatch Sentinel on the Casfeild side to bother the melting stations. As said, I will put in a word to make certain they are working properly and guarded sufficiently."

A deep relief filled Jathen, and the Grand Artifact hummed soothingly in his chest. "Thank you."

The tar'ka-besh shrugged slightly. "No need. I'm pleased you told me. You'd be surprised how many precognitives keep their visions to themselves, even seasoned ones who've been proven correct many times."

"Why would they do that?"

"Because most likely, what you saw will not occur. Precognitives—especially the more powerful ones—have more *not* happen than happen because they are able to see more *possible* futures, not *definite* ones." He chuckled. "That, and sometimes *saying* something will actually be the catalyst in *causing* what was seen to happen—though unlikely in this case, I think."

Jathen shivered, remembering an incident with his mother and a foreseen miscarriage from when he'd been much younger, while Izzy nodded beside him. "Your tar'ka-besh Dredona had said as much—it's difficult to sense things precognitively in Tar'citadel because of all the Talents counterbalancing each other's futures."

"Exactly. To be honest, we are incapable of following up on every single precognitive lead generated by even our own tar'ka-besh. There're simply too many. But to take reasonable precautions against a probable threat... That we can almost always do, and should. So again, thank you."

"You are quite welcome, though I admit I do so more for my own peace of mind. I'd not be able to live with myself if something happened and I'd said nothing." He sighed. "Though I know what speaking can lead to as well."

"I think you chose best in this case. Follow your instincts. It's all we can do, really," Na'vosh said, smiling warmly as Jathen let go of the doors. "Oh, and don't forget Master Galduran. He heads Montage," he added. Jathen nodded just before the doors closed, but his heart wasn't in it.

"Not going to try for Montage?" Izzy asked softly, following.

He raised an eyebrow but abstained from asking—Izzy had been around him long enough to know his moods. *Though you'd better tell me if you've started being able to read my mind like Seren does.* When she didn't respond to his mental probing, he said, "I've had enough of Montage from home, I think. That, and I'm fairly certain I saw at least one gold-robed me die in that mirrored room inside my head." *Though Spirit knows I'd love to chat with Hausmannith and try to sort out my options.* Thoughts of asking his mother if he could speak to the High Walker in Kidwellith went through his head as he made his way down the orange-and-black-decked hallway toward the waiting Walker with Izzy a step behind. *Worth a try—though I have a feeling he'd just tell me to go to Montage as well.*

Chain mail clad, Master Enillydd wore over the metal a tabard in a deep burnt orange. A brighter citrine Kubeshian dragon outlined in black stitching sat in the center of it. A crisp, sun-bleached tan weathered her skin and made her appear perhaps in her fifties, but the straightness of her back and the bounce in her step made Jathen wonder if she was closer to forty.

"You aren't quite what I expected," he admitted after a swift introduction and tight handshake.

She had thick calluses on her palms, and even Izzy flinched when the woman shook her hand. The laugh that burst from Master Enillydd reminded Jathen of the Ki'ra Esop. *Perhaps she isn't so far off from a typical Kubeshian.*

"We aren't all big brutes wielding axes and screaming for battle," she said, followed by another boisterous cackle. "Come." Her auburn-colored braid flicked over her shoulder as she strode farther down the hall. "I wanna show you something."

Jathen and Izzy caught up after a few paces. Whatever her age, the Kubeshian training had made her fit. Her boots looked as if they must be her favorites, for unlike the rest of her gear, they were well-worn, the russet leather cracking at the ankles.

"What path are you, if I might ask?" Jathen called.

"Tesgree. Masters of—"

"The bastard sword, I know." Jathen smiled back at her toothy grin. "I know a Clansman that's of your path. Setsuken Daten. Do you know him?"

"Sounds familiar, but more likely, he was before my time. 'Tis the way with Clan in Kubesh. We don't have too many of them clogging up the ranks. 'Sides, the Rheanics already have enough of them, and too many immortals in a Way based on living in the moment can get binding."

"I can imagine."

"Not to say we don't love our Clansman brothers-in-arms, mind," she clarified, grinning at Izzy. "Or that we'd bar them from joining or gaining higher positions. They just seem to prefer taking their lessons learned back to their homeland armies or striking out on their own 'cross the continent. Honestly, I tend to think they just get bored of us after a fashion."

She led them to a round vestibule flagged in orange-and-white-banded granite. It looked like a secondary shrine room, complete with a small, incense-laden altar and a bronze statue of a woman.

Clad similarly to Enillydd, she was cast with a very youthful face, un-lined by the rigors of battle. A sword was raised high in her right hand, pointing to the distance as if directing troops.

Or perhaps challenging an enemy, Jathen thought. *Though her expression is so serene I wonder if she's even in a fight or is just posing for posterity.*

"This is Kubesh's Aspect, Ta'ekni." Pride glowed from Master Enillydd's face. "I know you're a Montage baby, so I'm not sure what you know of the Aspects."

"More every day, but not enough at the moment," Jathen admitted. "I'm afraid I don't know anything about her."

When he glanced at Izzy, she shook her head. "I barely know anything about *Turin*'s Aspect. She's not spoken of much among the Solki, at least. Far as I know, she rarely incarnates."

"'Tis why I asked." Master Enillydd explained, "Some think Aspects are the exact opposites of their Child, but I find it's usually not the case. Most are a complement, even in extreme cases. With Kubesh and Ta'ekni, he is the warrior, the fight, the action, the physical power and adrenaline. She is the calculation, the timing, the thought behind move and countermove. She is *strategy*." She gestured dramatically to the statue. "That's what my Way offers to you, Jathen Monortith. I'm not going to lie—looking at you, you are built more for Rheanic fighting styles: ducking, slipping, sneaking. You're not going to wield an axe or sword and come crashing into battle with a mighty roar, as much as I love to fantasize about a True Negater bashing through a wall of Red Mages, screaming Kubesh's name. No. But we can teach you when to push the front line, where to strike when the enemy's troops are pressing. We can teach you *where* to cut so that one stroke can kill. Even if you don't become a Way Walker, I think those skills are worth being taught to a prince who might still someday be a king."

Jathen held his breath a moment, honestly taken aback, as what she was offering specifically didn't involve him in a Kubeshian orange uniform, thus leading to his death. "That... is a much better argument than the Rosinics led me to believe you'd make."

Her belly laugh echoed off the walls. "Oh, even if you say no, boy, that made my day!"

Jathen could only grin back. "Can I think about it?"

"Of course." She shrugged. "Though remember, I'm not going to throw you into drills the second you agree or anything. Fact is, you'll mostly learn just from me and a few others. You're a Negater; you need to learn to fight *smart* no matter what you choose to do."

He nibbled lightly on his lip. "So it'd be more like secondary path training?"

"Oh, of course, unless you developed a knack for it or the desire to improve till you can master the full Way, though I'd honestly be surprised if you did."

"Why's that?"

"Because of what I said before about you not being a traditional warrior. Being a Negater is just an added benefit for this Way, which means we won't treat you much different for it. If you decide you want to push to be a Kubeshian, we'll teach you and try to get you there, but we'll not throw you into the ranks if you can't take it, either."

"Fair enough."

After leaving Enillydd with a smile, Jathen wasn't surprised when Izzy shared her thoughts again in the hallway.

"Is there a reason you're just 'thinking about' that offer? That truly seemed as if it were worth pursuing unless there's an aspect to your vision I missed out on understanding."

"No, you are correct. What she offers sidesteps the destiny of death I saw. But her training is also only relevant *if* I want to be king, Izzy. I don't plan on leading armies if I'm not."

"You didn't plan on using your knowledge of charm making or architecture to save hundreds in a stranded floating city, either," she pointed out. "And the offer to learn to fight is going to be useful if you're a king or not, doomed by a vision or not. You managed well enough in Dodbyen—better than I ever thought you would have untrained—but sooner or later, you need to be prepared to defend yourself from a foe that's been trained to fight. Orne and I might not always be able to protect you."

"True. But I've had another offer before you got here. As much as it pains me to admit, Master Enillydd pointed out something very true—I'm built to fight like a Rheanic. If that's the case, it might make sense to learn from them directly. And now that Enillydd has put it in my head that I can learn without being a Walker for Kubesh, I'm betting it might also be safe to make a similar deal with the Rheanics." He bit the inside of one cheek, his fingers finding the lump beneath his shirt where hung the Monortith signet ring and Ass'shiri's crossbow bolt. "I just have to decide if it's worth putting up with their more... *annoying* tendencies."

"Another mark in the favor of the Kubeshians, then."

Jathen chuckled begrudgingly as they approached the elevator, memories of Setsu, Esop, and the rest of the crew brimming in his mind. *I can almost hear their voices.* After three cries and Izzy tapping on his shoulder, he finally realized he *did* hear someone calling him.

"Jath!"

Holding his breath, Jathen spun around. They *were* there, the big kilt-clad bear-like Ki'ra, his massive axe still strapped across his back. The dark-haired tesgree Clansman wore his tough leather armor and an orange Kubeshian tabard similar to Master Enillydd's.

"Ha! I told you it was him, Set!" Esop bounded over and immediately grasped Jathen's braid with his padded paw. "Went and changed the hair now that he's a famous Negater, but I know that moot-smell!" After releasing Jathen's braid, Ki'ra plucked him up into a stifling hug. "Not even a day home, and we find ya on the Kubeshian floor! Montage *does* like you, kid."

"Esop!" Jathen coughed a laugh, surprised and happy even as his legs flopped about like a rag doll's. Nose pressed into thick fur, Jathen was assaulted by the smell of wet dog and vanilla soap. "It's good to see you, but I can hardly breathe!"

"Aw, sorry." He put Jathen down gently then hooked a claw at Setsu. "I'm used to hugging this one. Clansman can't feel it 'less you crack their spine a bit."

Looking at the much more subdued tesgree Walker, Jathen suddenly found he had no words for Ass'shiri's original travel companions. His stomach quaking, the memory of Ass'shiri's last moments assaulted him, of him exsanguinating mere feet away while Jathen lay in the blood, helplessly tied to a chair. Jathen tried to form words, but no sound came out. Izzy braced a hand on his upper arm, and he realized he'd started to shake.

"We know." Setsu spoke softly, pale-green eyes calm as he spared Jathen the pain of explaining. "He came to see Hkym."

Hurt and relief both scored a hole in Jathen's stomach. He swallowed, strength returning to his legs. "He fought like a tiger."

Setsu clasped him on the shoulder opposite where Izzy was holding him. Esop sniffed away a tear. "We don't mourn the dead with tears. It's not right."

Izzy let Jathen go then turned to Esop, asking, "Ki'ra have feasting nights, correct?"

"Aye, lass. The Turinics know. Death isn't tragedy. It's rebirth. A warrior gets to return to train again."

Setsu squeezed Jathen's shoulder once more before letting go. "Have a drink with us? We'd not been planning to gather for Ass'shiri, but we are meeting up with Cy'shā and Hkym now for the new year. I'm sure they'd like to see you and have a round in Ass'shiri's name."

Jathen couldn't quite claim Ass'shiri's death a thing worth celebrating, but seeing the others, perhaps speaking a bit on the man they'd all known, sounded good. "Yes, I'd love that." He smiled softly at Izzy. "We've a few hours to spare before the party at the Tazu Embassy, correct?"

"Yes. But even if we didn't, we can afford to be late, for this," she said.

The group talked sparingly as they went, Jathen formally introducing Izzy and covering the topic of their stint in Dodbyen, as well as Setsu and Esop's recent part in it.

"We've been escorting survivors for weeks between the crash site and the capital," Setsu explained. "Finally got all those strange sanbarna humans settled and took an offer of teleport to ride out the rest of the winter here."

"*Pifft*, soft southern boy you are, Set." Esop leaned in to whisper loudly to Izzy, "Kinawa winter is no worse than Nor'wah."

"You should try a blizzard in the Solkies," she replied.

"And you weren't complaining when we got here." Setsu punched Esop playfully in the shoulder. "But all the same, I've had enough of hunting down those feral Okten things for a lifetime."

"Try being caught in a massive cage with them," Jathen murmured.

"Then you understand."

Glancing at the Clansman, Jathen found he had forgotten how much he liked the tesgree who'd led them through most of Zo'den and the Furōrin-Iki. Ass'shiri had always spoken of him with pride and admiration, and Jathen found himself relaxing in his presence. Something about Setsuken Daten was *steady*, with his pale-green eyes, tesgree tattoo on his elbow, and bastard sword strapped across his back.

"Your dirigible-captain friend is in town, too, you know," Setsu said.

"Pallotos? Really?"

"Yes, he brought the injured survivors from Kinawa on his ship. Weathering the winter here, too, so I hear."

Though Jathen was gladdened to hear Pallo was nearby, he was also surprised his friend had not come to see him. *I guess I'll have to seek him out on my own, then.*

The tavern was in the Nor'wah district, a large building made of wood and stone. It stuck out in Tar'citadel, but in a warming way, the lights from the windows throwing gold across the snow in the late afternoon of an overcast day. The inside smelled of meat, garlic, and beer, and not a single table lacked at least one Kubeshian Walker or Ki'ra on its stools.

"Cy'shā!" Esop bellowed across the room. "Look what we found!"

"Hkym may not speak, but we both can still *hear*, Ki'ra," Cy'shā scolded once the group crossed the room to the table she was sharing with her Tyr'sat husband.

Nodding reverently, Hkym remained seated, his ever-changing legs hidden beneath baggy pants and loose-fitting shoes.

Cy'shā did rise, a soft smile on her cinnamon-stick skin—the hardened hide inherited from her Msāfryan bloodline. She'd dressed more warmly here, clad in yellow tunic over a white shirt and baggy pants similar to Hkym's. "It good seeing your face, Jathen."

"You too," he replied, hugging her. "I'm sorry I couldn't keep Ass'shiri safe."

"He kept *you* safe." She released him, patting his upper arms. "Hkym told us Ass'shiri's words. It enough for him that you live."

They joined them at the table, everyone ordering except for Izzy, who took a seat and lowered her hood. "No disrespect, but alcohol affects my connection to my golem. Most fauni go without."

"At least get some meat, lass, or you'll be mistaken for bones too!" Esop pounded the table, laughing uproariously.

Around them, other Ki'ra and Kubeshians echoed the banging, though they had no knowledge of the joke. Jathen chuckled at Izzy's arched eyebrows. She relented and ordered cider and food, which came, steaming, along with the rest of their dinners not too long after their drinks. It put a much-needed warmth in his soul for Jathen to reminisce of better times on the road, of Hatori and Jephue and, of course, Ass'shiri.

"He ever tell you 'bout the time he lost his crossbow?" Esop finished off his second pint with a single swig, slamming it down atop the table.

"No." Jathen lowered his mug, incredulous. "He didn't."

"He did!" Wiping his mouth clean with his furry arm, Esop then patted his big fuzzy belly with a laugh. "What was it, Setsu, the first week out?"

"Something like that," Setsu managed to say around a mouthful of Kubeshian sausages and wild rice. He finished chewing before continuing. "Ass'shiri claimed he'd been out hunting and camping with his brothers in Tan'cha lands a lot before Tar'citadel, and I wanted to see what he knew. We just got over the Casfeild border, and I let him pitch his own tent—which he did well—but he put it right in the migration path of a bunch of itazura."

Jathen scrunched his nose at the unfamiliar word. "Itazura?"

Esop chewed around his toothpick a bit, thinking. "They are these little... I'm not sure how to describe them. A little like a spider monkey but no fur, with amphibianlike skin. Big ears, big cat eyes, big mouths, sharp little teeth, and little claws. In Nor'wah, we call them ellyll, and ours are a bit dumber, but the breed does the same all around. Mischief makers. Kind of like Native Near-Siders, but in body."

"But they no return what taken," Cy'shā added. "Itazura use for nests."

"They're in the Solkies too." Izzy sipped her spiced cider delicately. "More active in cold weather. They'll steal horseshoes right off the animals if not stabled."

"So they stole his crossbow?"

"And Ass'shiri!" Esop guffawed, losing his toothpick to the ground. "There he is, sound asleep in his bedroll with about ten of these little bastards carrying him out of his tent, with another five or so following behind with the crossbow. I ruddy near pissed myself laughing before he woke up, and then I did piss myself."

"We couldn't tear our eyes away or help laughing," Setsu said. "He beat about six of them into submission with his pillow before we were finally able to catch our breath and rescue him."

"Oh, ruddy hell," Jathen managed to cackle out between bouts of laughter.

They continued to chat well into the afternoon and, indeed, the early evening, Jathen sharing a few stories of his own—like the first time Ass'shiri let him try the crossbow and he'd ended up on his back—much to everyone's enjoyment. *I'll have to mention that one to Annakki and Dor'rhean.* It hurt not to mention Ass'shiri's son to this group, but considering he'd already had to push to have Annakki trust Izzy and Spinnek, he knew he had to forgo it. *Though maybe someday, when he's older and better able to defend himself, he'll be able to meet them.* Esop laughed and ate so much that he eventually fell asleep, slumped right over the table, his large pink tongue lolling about as he snored, openmouthed and drooling.

"It's getting late," Setsu finally said, sparing an affectionate gaze at the Ki'ra as he stood. "I best get this silly kit back to the barracks before the tar'ka-besh start blocking off the streets for fireworks."

"You two aren't staying here with Cy'shā and Hkym?" Jathen inquired.

"Nineteen months together," Cy'shā explained as Setsu prodded Esop awake. "Time for separate space." She grinned at her husband. "Much love for boys, but more for Hkym. Prefer express alone."

"Plus, we two are still registered Walkers if not working directly for the Way at the moment," Setsu said over Esop's grumpy mutterings. "So we're allowed space in the Kubeshian barracks for a minimal fee."

"Far cheaper a bed, but far inferior food." Eyes hooded, Esop yawned loudly then hiccupped, scratching his chest. He began to stand then swayed, landing back in his chair hard enough to make the table shake.

"We'll walk with you part of the way if that's agreeable," Izzy offered, standing. "Enough time for him to sober a bit before we head for the Tazu Embassy."

Setsuken nodded. "Appreciated."

"Be safe!" Cy'shā called to the four of them as they headed out. "Avoid side roads if you can!"

"Will do." Jathen waved goodbye to the fellow precognitive.

Outside, they headed northwest toward the Temple Citadel and the Lu'shun Republic district. Esop hummed as he walked, swaying with the tune. Setsu and Izzy strode silent and stoic, while Jathen bobbed his head along with Esop, feeling full and content, if not particularly happy after having thought so long on Ass'shiri. *I miss him.*

A few blocks into their trek, the great bear staggered a bit, crashing into Setsu with an inebriated grunt. The Clansman bore the weight without flinching, and Jathen felt a sudden wave of gratitude that he'd not been the target of Esop's body. "I see why you keep Setsu around, Esop," he said with a smile. "You need a Clansman to pick you up when you fall."

"I'm sure a tall Tazu would do," Setsu retorted. "I just have to convince one he's worth the trouble."

"I don't understand Tazu," Esop declared, surly. "You're a good boy, Jath! What's it matter what you look like? Ki'ra kits get born with no fur and claws all the ruddy time! We call 'em Ki'ra-kin and throw 'em right in with their pack mates and tell 'em ta bite and kick all the same. I mean, ya got to watch 'em sometimes 'cause they *don't* have the claws, but the point is they are *loved* the same, and the lot of it's stupid. The Tazu, I mean. They're stupid, and I don't understand them." Staggering a step away from Setsu, he called to a random Tazu male dressed in expensive robes who happened to be passing on the other side of the street. "Where is your tail? Where does it go when you change? Is that the thing that's shoved up your scaly arse?"

"My apologies, please!" Jathen yelled to the confused Tazu in their native tongue while trying to choke down laughter as Setsu pulled Esop further down the street. "He's drunk."

"And Kubeshian!" Izzy yelled as well.

Jathen had a good giggle until he collided with a young girl. She'd darted out from around a corner and slammed right into him, knocking herself to her knees.

"Oh, Spirit, are you all right?" Jathen offered her his hand.

The frail slip of a human had wide pale-blue eyes and sharp features. Brown hair a windswept mess, she stayed prone at his feet, staring at him with her mouth slightly open. "Negater," she whispered in the same moment he noticed her black-and-red clothes. The Balori suddenly grabbed at Jathen's wrists, trying to pull his hands to her head. "Thank you for the Prophet! He will lead all the wicked back—you'll see!"

Jathen did his best to untangle himself from the still prostrate teenager. "No, really, it's fine. You don't need to—"

"Author of new magic shall fall—a sacrifice to the Red—shall be born anew the Prophet, to return the Red-mad to the world!"

"All right, little love, that's enough. Spout your Annarite prophecies elsewhere." Setsu plucked the girl up under her arm, letting Esop sit down on the curb with a plop. He managed to remove her from Jathen, though she was still very vocal, shrieking on about wanting Jathen to bless her.

The whole of it drew attention, of course, more so than even Esop's drunken ranting.

Mortified by the strange looks, Jathen turned to Izzy. "I think there's a side street just over here. I'd really prefer to duck down there."

"I think it wise." Turning, she called in Setsu's direction, "Join us once you've deposited and collected, Sir Daten!"

The Clansman waved an affirmative, and Jathen and Izzy ventured off the main boulevard. Mindful of Cy'shā's warning, Jathen scanned the street extensively but saw no one suspicious. In fact, an abundance of Walkers were about, so he felt safe enough to relax.

"What *was* that child going on about?" Izzy muttered once they'd put in some decent distance.

"I'm not entirely sure. She was obviously Balori and happy I'd saved De'contes, but the rest..." He took a breath, recalling. "De'contes himself mentioned a prophecy some of the Balori believe in, and I've heard a few of them call him 'Prophet.' He said it was something about bringing the Red back to the Ways."

"'Returning the Red-mad to the world' sounds more like freeing the Red from the Pit when the Red Star rises rather than bringing him back to the Ways."

Jathen nodded. He'd been raised on the old nursery rhymes as well. *Unknown Red, wicked dread! Trapped, can only whisper lies 'til the dawning of the Red Star's rise!* "Like with all prophecies, perhaps it's open to interpretation."

"Damn, they are following us. Don't look. Keep walking."

Jathen stiffened, whispering, "I thought you wanted Setsu to follow?"

"I did, mostly because of the looks the three behind us were giving you. But Setsu's still farther back."

"Ruddy Red," Jathen muttered. He tightened his grip on Hatori's sword cane, glad he'd taken to carrying it again.

Despite Izzy's urging, he managed a covert peek behind them in one of the windows on the opposite street. Milky and distorted somewhat in the glass, the three looked like the ghosts that'd chased them throughout the final battle of Dodbyen. They did appear human, which was slightly encouraging.

"It's probably just more students trying to prank the Negater again—and there're only three of them, Izzy. You and I both know Orne can handle more than that."

"Regular thugs and minor Talents, yes. But those uniforms aren't those of some Rosinic Way Walker acolytes out to laugh at your expense. They're Pearl Paladins in training, to be specific."

Memories of Master Mağrur freezing everything, down to the bits of falling plaster within the collapsing Balori townhouses, made Jathen curse mentally. He might be immune as a Negater, but Izzy and Orne most certainly wouldn't be. "Perhaps they're just making certain we don't do anything 'wicked' or 'impure.'"

"You two! Halt!"

Feeling the weight of Izzy's so-much-for-that-idea glance, Jathen turned to face the men. Not dressed as elaborately as Master Mağrur in full plate mail, each of the three still wore a shiny breastplate and heavy padding, as well as chain mail on their legs. They looked cut from the same cloth, too, with identical tightly cropped hair and equally disdainful expressions on their faces. Two of the three looked enough alike that Jathen imagined they were probably siblings—both with skin tones a shade darker than the third. None of them had the same type of long sword as Master Mağrur did. Instead, they had a shorter version strapped to their hips, and each clasped his hilt tightly with a gloved hand.

Jathen cleared his throat. "Is there a problem, sirs?"

The tallest of the bunch, one of the siblings, responded, "You're the one who saved the Red traitor, then? The Negater."

"Not entirely by choice—"

"There's *always* a choice," the non-sibling one said, cutting him off. "And you chose to allow evil to linger still in this world. And not a small bit of it, but the head of a snake. Do you honestly expect good men to stand by and let that go unavenged?"

"I expect you to hold to your training and common sense and not harass a Tazu prince unprovoked in the middle of the street," Izzy replied, authoritative. She pulled aside her blue cloak, revealing Orne's satchel. Her hand on the clasp, she stood poised and threatening.

The three hesitated, looking as a group like they'd suddenly gotten a whiff of something foul smelling. *Probably their combined bullshit,* Jathen thought. He must have smirked noticeably, because the non-sibling of the three glowered more deeply. The acolyte's fingers flexed against his sword's hilt, but Jathen relaxed slightly as Setsu and Esop walked up behind the trio.

"And what seems to be going on here, gentlemen?" Setsu spoke calmly, one hand on Esop's elbow while guiding the Ki'ra.

The three Anganites separated their ranks for the two Kubeshians, so the group now stood in a strange circle in the street.

"It's a bit late for heated discussions," Setsu continued.

"I'm sure any of our differences in philosophy can be discussed at another time," Jathen offered. "In a more civil setting."

The non-sibling spat in the street. "Civility toward the Tainted leads to ruination and death. Only a blade can cut out a cancer."

"Listen to these sad little unplucked pearls!" Esop suddenly yelled, reaching to swing his axe off his back. "Ya want a fight, you ruddy well will have it with *me*, ya prudish little virgins of battle!"

With that uncouth declaration, swords were drawn. Jathen couldn't help cursing both Kubesh and Angani unremorsefully in his head. Two of the Pearls flung their stasis spells, one encompassing Esop and the other, Izzy. Setsuken dodged the third spell, rolling through the street and knocking down the shorter sibling acolyte.

Remembering his encounter with De'contes, Jathen slammed into Izzy, releasing her from the stasis but knocking her sideways. *Don't you dare do anything!* Jathen screeched inside his head at the Grand Artifact. Seemingly amused, the Artifact hummed, allowing the diffused energy to go undirected. Instead, the negated spell turned back into a whirlwind, lifting Jathen and Izzy off the ground. When it dissipated, they dropped into a tangled mess at the feet of the non-sibling.

Sword held high, the Pearl kicked a stunned Izzy in the face. Furious, Jathen launched up and tackled the bastard around the waist. Slamming his cheek hard into the breastplate, Jathen gasped, and his ears rang as they landed in a heap. Splayed out beneath Jathen, the acolyte lost his grip on his sword. He formed a fist and slammed it into Jathen's already-sore cheek. A second blow landed, and Jathen's world blurred. A third hit was followed by the sensation of rolling.

Through the haze, Jathen caught sight of Izzy, bloody and holding Hatori's sword cane. With a disciplined thrust, she deflected the taller sibling's stab. Then, slipping down onto one knee, she punched upward, catching a spot on the man's inner thigh where he lacked chain mail.

A nerve cluster, Jathen disjointedly recalled from Setsu's teachings. The non-sibling yelled, staggering sideways and dropping his sword. Jathen tried rising, but the world tilted, and something slammed into him from behind.

Then... blackness.

Chapter 10

Jathen's head pounded.

The intense swelling pain expanded and contracted with every ragged breath. Covered with something, his face felt cold and numb. Reaching, he tried to remove the object, but a hand intercepted his, gently pushing his fingers away.

"Don't remove the ice pack, please," a female murmured. She sounded familiar, but he couldn't quite place her. "You could very well have a concussion, so I'm trying to do some energy work to avoid long-term effects." Fingertips lightly touched his temples. "However, you seem to keep negating my efforts," she said, sighing.

Jathen groaned, feeling a wave of nausea. He gripped the edge of the bed he lay on. "I'll try to direct it to helping. No promises, though. I feel wretched."

"To be expected. Your cheek is fractured and your nose broken. I've already set your nose and cleaned your face."

Slowly, Jathen felt the soft tickling energy envelop his head. *Be better, be better,* he chanted silently.

"That's it. Just keep doing what you are doing, Prince Jathen."

He lay there, allowing the soft tickles to course across his body. "Where am I?"

"Tar'citadel's Temple hospital."

"And is Izzy all right? And my other friends?"

"They are well and injuries treated, currently giving their statements to the tar'ka-besh."

The tingling slowed, and the nausea in his stomach waned, along with the pounding of his head.

"There you are, Highness. You may sit up... slowly. There's only so much one treatment of energy work can do."

"Thank you." His face still sore, Jathen didn't feel dizzy, at least. He sat up with her assistance, crossing his legs. Keeping the ice pack on the throbbing side of his face, he did manage to open one eye, revealing the brown-haired, chestnut-skinned Devon from his heart-chakra ritual. "I'd say nice to see you again, but this isn't exactly pleasant."

She grinned sympathetically. "I didn't think volunteering at the hospice tonight would lead to such a meeting either, Highness. I'd say happy New Year, but somehow I don't think this moment is exactly happy."

"Yes, I really hope this isn't some sign as to how the rest of 8960 is going to go." *Not that 8959 was much better.*

Jathen glanced around slowly, finding his accommodations a fairly comfortable hospital bed surrounded by a green curtain. It pulled aside, and Master Zhìliáo entered, gracefully dragging the curtain closed behind her.

"I'm glad to see you are finally accepting some energy work," she said, untucking her violet hands from her billowy green sleeves. Coming to his side, she bade him lower the ice pack then delicately felt across his eye and cheekbone with a medical touch. "Inform those waiting that he's awake, please," she said to Devon. The ache in his cheek lessened considerably as she worked. "But no visitors until I say so."

"Yes, Master Zhìliáo."

"I must be truly injured to warrant the attention of the High Walker of Desmoulein," he said, smirking as Devon scurried out through the curtain.

"A Negater's physiology can be complicated when energy healing. Manipulating another person's organics is difficult enough without your efforts reverting to Spirit energy—which, when negated, can manifest as just about anything. According to Devon, you kept having the most spectacular light show of silent fireworks exploding over your head for the last hour." Zhìliáo returned the smirk with moderate irony. "Aside from that, I am actually here to stent the surge. You've quite an entourage out there, waiting. I'm honestly not certain who to allow in."

Jathen raised his eyebrows in surprise and immediately regretted the action. He adjusted the ice pack back onto his face, where it dulled the remaining pain. "Aside from the three I came in with, who's out there?"

"Lady Annakki, her bodyguards, Prince Marcasith, the Tazu Ambassador Serendibiss Chertith, and her daughter are still waiting, while High Chancellor Dàshī Jidoja and Master Mağrur were here and then gone, but both left word to be informed when you'd awakened."

"Ruddy Red, how long was I unconscious?"

"You were in and out for approximately half an hour before arriving, and then we put you into a deep healing state for about two hours with medical herbs to put your subconscious into a mindset that would accept even a *little* energy work." She raised an eyebrow, her dark void eye shimmering. "Remember, too, you are a prince, Highness. An assault on you can be construed as an international incident. And this is twice now, in almost as many months."

"I'm surprised my mother didn't fly up here," he muttered.

"Don't be smarmy." She tapped his leg, apparently finished. "I'll send in your uncle. Family has priority. The others will understand."

Jathen hesitated then shook his head. "No, they won't." He slid off the bed. "I'll come out."

"I really can't recommend—"

"Am I in any danger of dying, truly?"

"No, but you look a sight, and it might not be best to have so many people who care about you suddenly all flustered at once for seeing it."

He removed the ice pack, squinting at her through his swollen eye. "Are you telling me that my being a Negater means even *you* can't completely fix this?"

"Of *course* I can, but that's not the *point*." She crossed her arms. "As I've explained to *many* a Rosinic over the years, prolonged use of energy manipulation to heal tissue results in the decline of the body to repair itself on its own. Severe cases have led to the point of developing hemophilia, organ failure, chemical deficiency, rapid malignant cell growth, and much more, which will all inevitably lead to death—"

"All right, I comprehend." He returned the pack to his eye. "But I'm still leaving if you don't intend to do anything more for me."

She shook her head, sighing. "Very well. Just sit here for a few more minutes, please? After that, you are ordered to rest. And return in a few days for a follow-up for more energy work on the concussion. You do *not* want months of dizziness."

"Yes, High Walker Zhìliáo." He reluctantly slid back onto the bed. "Just let everyone out there know, and they'll *all* make certain I do."

As she exited, the curtain swished back farther, revealing Izzy. Stripped of her hooded cloak and Orne's satchel, she looked more vulnerable in her blue-and-black robe, the front of which was still covered in a large stain of dried blood. Her battered face supplemented the sentiment, both eyes purpled and her upper lip puffed. "Thought I heard you up."

"Izzy." Jathen lowered his ice pack reflexively, a wave of guilt punching him in the stomach. "Oh, I'm so sorry. I tried, but that damn—"

"I'm fine, my prince." She stepped in, closing the curtain behind her. "You did well, dispelling the stasis."

"But not well enough to do anything useful with the negated energy." His fingers tightened around the ice pack, skin pinching from the cold. "That stupid whirlwind nearly got both of us killed."

Izzy said nothing, simply patting him on the knee.

The curtain swished open again, revealing a wide-eyed Seren, with Marcasith close behind. Her pretty eyes traced his battered face with concern and mild horror then came to rest on Izzy's hand on his knee.

"Seren!" Jathen exclaimed. When a wave of unexpected embarrassment hit, he shrugged off Izzy's hand. "I thought the High Walker was only letting family in."

"I vouched for her," Marcasith explained with a wink. "I'm not stupid, Nephew. Pretty Tazu looking worried—I know who you'd prefer to see."

Jathen's embarrassment deepened, and he felt a sudden gratitude for his ice pack to hide any inconvenient flush.

"We're just friends," Seren asserted stiffly.

Marcasith crossed his arms, snorting. "Then I'm an Okten."

"Regardless"—Seren quickly rerouted to Jathen—"you're still better off if we check you over then mollify the others. My mother and Annakki Rheadani are fighting a contest over who is the most furious right now."

"Let them know I'm sorry," Jathen begged. "I tried—"

"Not at *you*, Jath." Seren clucked her tongue. "They're both furious at the Anganite idiots who did this, as well as the Pearl Paladin order, the tar'ka-besh for not patrolling properly, the tar'ka-besh for not arriving soon enough... It's a veritable blame storm out there."

"As I said, you should not blame yourself, my prince. You did well," Izzy said.

"He has a habit of that," Seren said, looking her up and down. "You must be Iridosmine, Jathen's fauni friend." She clucked her tongue again, sliding her blond bangs behind one ear as Izzy nodded. "Those bastards certainly made a mess of you too."

"And they *shall* be paying for it," Marcasith said, his tone rumbling toward a growl.

Are you really all right? Seren asked over Izzy lecturing Marcasith on the benefits of prudence.

Jathen started. Some time had passed since she'd popped into his head, and Izzy's knowing glare had him on edge for some reason. Also, he would've preferred that Seren not suddenly become privy to his visions of death, given the current circumstances. *Honestly, I am fine,* he told her, hoping to get her out of his mind sooner than later. *A little sore, but not even that mad—at least not over my wounds.*

What? They could have severely hurt you!

Yes, but they were backing off until Esop decided to go drunk Ki'ra all over them. He shrugged. *Really, Seren, I'm fine. There doesn't need to be a "blame storm" over this.*

Tell that to my mother and Annakki.

I intend to. He slid off the bed again. "Shall we? I'd really prefer to spend the night in my bed, not one of the hospital's."

Out in the waiting room, he discovered Bertran and Setsu were also amid those lingering, though they were calmer than Ambassador Chertith or Annakki. The two women contained enough rage that Jathen actually saw it—a distortion hanging above their heads like the rippling heat over a fire. Both were flanked by their personal guards, the ambassador's gold-and-purple-clad Tazu a stark contrast to the black-hooded men beside Annakki. Abstractly, Jathen wondered where those two went off to when Annakki wasn't using them.

They were never in the house and only appeared when she left, which wasn't often. *Like shadows cast by a torch.*

"Is Esop all right?" Jathen managed to ask Setsu before the storm of anger broke.

"Big bear's fine—sleeping off his hangover. He's too heavy for anyone here to move, and I didn't feel like dragging him back to the barracks." He put a hand on his chest, the brown glove lying over the Kubeshian dragon on the tunic. "I'm sorry, Jath, for both of us. We were a sad excuse for professional fighters out there."

"Well, you two weren't exactly under contract," Jathen replied. "I don't think I ever saw Esop drink so heavily when we were on the road. Thank you, but really, this wasn't your fault either. It was just a cluster of bad choices that happened to collide."

"That doesn't mean responsibility is annulled, Highness," Ambassador Chertith interjected. "Those who started the incursion need to be held responsible."

Jathen sighed, covering a desire to flinch. Just *looking* in her direction made him tremble, and he was having little luck maintaining a decent imaginary wall ward while his head still throbbed. "But it was just words until Esop swung, and I'd prefer to keep my friend *out* of trouble."

"Jathen, truly, those three were searching for an excuse," Setsu said. "A fight was inevitable."

"Agreed," Izzy said. "If anything, Esop bought us time, surprising them as he did."

"I'd still just prefer—"

"Perhaps excessive stimulation is unproductive," Annakki spoke, her tone carrying that eerie rhythm that managed to sound quite soft yet carry such massive, unbendable authority. The empathic punch was practically an anvil to Jathen's face, and he had to shake his head to clear it. "We all agree Jathen requires rest. That is not accomplished squabbling in a waiting room."

One hand laid across her chest, Ambassador Chertith recovered from the Ability onslaught first, frowning. "And as *I'd* said earlier, I'd been hoping Jathen would reconsider staying at the embassy."

"I'm fine at Annakki's," Jathen replied, earning him a sour look from the ambassador and disappointment waves from Bertran and Marcasith. All the clashing emotions in the place were making him dizzy—though that could still have been from the head wound.

Seren must have sensed it, because she caught his elbow, bracing him. "Mother, please, squabble later."

"Yes, Seri, crown prince or not, Jathen's an adult," Bertran spoke up. "His mind is set on where he's staying, so let us agree to take this incident up with the High Chancellor tomorrow."

"Agreed," Marcasith said. "That High Mage has a good deal of sense in him."

Though relieved to be freed, Jathen couldn't shake the feeling that he'd failed—not just in the fight but in dealing with the emotional empathy too. *I have got to find a better means to control all these Abilities.*

JATHEN WOKE WITH AN *ooof.* "Spirit, Spinnek," he wheezed with underinflated lungs at the boy crouching on his chest. "I can't breathe."

Grinning like a maniacal harlequin, Spinnek held an arm out, a mushy mess in his hand. "Bring Jathen cheese."

"Um, thank you?" Jathen attempted to take it, but it wound up a clumpy smear across his hand. "I'm sure it's very good."

The boy grinned wider then slipped off Jathen and the bed, licking his fingers. Jathen groaned as he sat up, shaking off the remains of an odd dream involving a blue landscape. He remembered hearing the voice from his vision prattling on in it but couldn't recall what had been said. *Maybe just my subconscious worried about it.*

Despite the rude awakening from disconcerting dreams, he felt better, his head nowhere near as pained as it had been two days before, after the attack. The Chancellor had been spoken to, with Ambassador Chertith mollified by the promise that the three acolytes would be sternly disciplined. *Though the whole thing doesn't fix my shortcomings,* Jathen brooded as he dressed—after having visited the bathroom to wash off the offending cheese. *I need proper training.*

Downstairs, he found the hour quite late, Spinnek and Annakki having already adjourned from breakfast to the library for their lessons. The pair was sitting studiously at the long walnut table, flipping through a thick tome covering continental history. Spinnek had taken better to the Clanswoman than any Walker who'd tried to teach him, seemingly fascinated by her teeth, Clan grace, and the fact she was of the same breed as Raudur.

Interesting logic, but I can't complain as long as he's contained. Jathen smiled slightly at the sight of them. He suspected Spinnek also preferred Annakki because she didn't pressure him into a Way and allowed him to pick his subjects. *Wish she knew how to teach a Negater—then all my problems would be solved. Mostly.*

Annakki glanced up. "Good, you've risen. Thank you, Spinnek."

Jathen swallowed the slice of bread he'd plucked from the kitchen. "Oh, so there was reason for my unceremonious awakening?"

When Annakki gave Spinnek a sharp glare, he only grinned more widely. "Say wake. Not say how."

"Part of civility is interoperating with propriety. With great intellect and Ability comes great demand for one's attentions, but it does not excuse one from common foolery. If you wish to continue our lessons, you will not feign ignorance for the sake of humor only *you* find amusing," she admonished in her Ability-fueled tone.

Surprisingly, Spinnek straightened in his seat, looking sheepish.

"Thank you." She turned back to Jathen. "And yes, my brother writes that he's acquired an appointment with High Walker Plajă of Bree for you. Eleven Morning, if you are so inclined to attend."

Jathen immediately brightened. "Oh, yes."

"Then you best fetch Izzy and be on your way. You've less than a half an hour." Returning her attentions to Spinnek, she bade him begin conjugating some of the more complex verbs from Tar'cil before she would return to the history lesson.

Despite his eagerness to go, Jathen hesitated, watching Annakki. They'd not yet discussed her reaction to the Balori's "vote to vote" having passed, nor Jathen's part in causing it. Her silence during the past week worried him. Granted, they'd been distracted by the attack on Jathen, but she was still acting as if the vote's passing had never even occurred.

"Annakki..." he ventured softly, and her head darted back up, eyes and face neutral. Jathen swallowed, uncertain what to say. "The vote... I just..." Words failed him, and he stood there, floundering and feeling idiotic for opening a jar of demons he couldn't close. "I'm sorry."

The continued neutrality in her face was more frightening to him than rage. "You best hurry, or you'll be late," she said then turned back to Spinnek.

Jathen frowned, staring sadly once more at the two of them before heading out.

"WOULD I BE REMISS IN my guardianship if I waited down here for you?" Izzy asked, kicking snow off her boots.

Jathen raised an eyebrow, halting in the Temple Citadel's main concourse. "Why? Afraid I'm going to get you trounced again?"

"Nothing like that." She yawned deeply. Her wounds much improved, she still sported a few yellow spots around her eyes, adding to her tired countenance. "Spinnek and Annakki are night owls, and I was drawn into letting them use Orne as a sparring partner for Spinnek last night until very late. I thought I was alert enough, but I think it'd be better if I meditate at Turin's shrine for a bit. You're in little danger here, what with Na'vosh hovering about, but I want my mind sharp for the walk back."

He nodded, brushing a few flakes of wayward snow from his shoulders. "Fair enough."

When the elevator doors opened on the Bree floor, Jathen found another circular foyer and an unexpected crowd. Wading slowly into the mix of Walkers and general bystanders, Jathen furrowed his brow. The focus of the attention involved half a dozen Bree Walkers crouching around a colorful rug. *What are they sprinkling onto it? Is that... sand? Why would they...? Oh.* It was not a rug. They were crafting a dizzyingly elaborate sand painting across the floor itself, a mandala.

Entranced, Jathen stood with the crowd, watching. The process looked tedious, sprinkling the sand just so to form the correct lines, but the Walkers' faces were serene.

"It's beautiful," Jathen murmured. Though it was only two heads in diameter, he was astonished by the intricacy of the geometric design. "I wonder how long they've worked."

"They are just starting it," a Walker beside him said. He was tall for a human, about a scale and a half more than Jathen, wearing long, exquisitely embroidered robes in varying shades of amber and gold. His head was shaved and oiled, the deep, dark skin of his scalp reflecting the light and highlighting the geometric and draconic tattoos on the sides of his head.

"You must be High Walker Plajă," Jathen said.

He smiled, an infectious thing reminding Jathen of Pallo. "Yes. I meant to meet you at the doors but got caught up in watching." Bells attached to several bracelets he wore jingled as he gestured over the mandala and the artists. "They mimic the ones done by the Msāfryan in Zo'den. They start the mandala when they all arrive in *Antqāl Mdynh*, work on it until the season is over, and then it is destroyed when the city is packed up to return north. The ones we make here start in winter and are destroyed in summer. It will fill the room once done."

Jathen raised an eyebrow, impressed. Even if they left two heads of space around the circumference of the room to walk, the mandala would easily be eighteen heads in diameter. "I think I remember seeing the Msāfryan doing something up in the collapsible pavilion they use for their Bree Temple." Because Hatori had been too obsessed with the party "getting a move on" for Jathen to get a closer look, he mourned the loss of the experience. "So the mandala is never kept?"

"No."

"Why not?"

"We honor the act of creativity versus the object created. Pure creativity is what we believe raises our vibrations, not the thing left behind. It is a seasonal reminder that Bree's teachings are more about the path walked, not the result."

More the path walked, not the result. A memory tugged at Jathen's heartstrings, some comment about observation made by Ahalteke, the half-Tazu, half-Msāfryan trader they'd ridden with through the Nation and part of Zo'den. *"Most, they look at our homes and see a hut. You... you see brilliance. Creativity is in seeing too."*

Maybe this is *where I belong.*

"Come," High Walker Plajă said after they'd stood watching for a few more minutes. "I have some music for you."

"Music?" Jathen followed, the crowd parting for the High Walker. "Why?"

"You'll see."

Inside Plajä's office, Jathen found dozens of musical instruments, from horns to woodwinds to string instruments to a full harpsichord, tucked back against the wall and covered in turn by more drums. Instead of desks or chairs, large cylindrical cushions made of silk dotted the room. Plajä placed one of them beside a very large drum and bade Jathen sit.

"I hope you don't want me to make the music," Jathen said, trying to find a comfortable position on the odd seat. "Because it won't be pleasant."

Standing before a shelf that went to the ceiling, High Walker Plajä laughed deeply, shaking his head. "I would not subject you to that, no." He shuffled through a multitude of small drawstring bags made of more silk. "Ah!" he exclaimed, plucking a green one with gold strings. "This is it."

He grabbed a crystal player from a windowsill and placed it atop the large drum. The iungo plants in the charm-device immediately snaked away from Jathen, but the High Walker either didn't notice or didn't mind. Instead, he removed a storage quartz from the pouch and placed it into the crystal player.

The music started simply, a single violin weaving a slow, soulful melody. It continued for several measures, next adding in another, lower string instrument Jathen didn't know. Gradually, more instruments joined, the tempo increasing each time they did. Then the song crested, the music becoming transcendent as all the ribbons of sound clinking and playing off each other collided in an explosion of rapture.

The Artifact in Jathen's chest swelled with the music, not activating but pulsing along to the beat, almost excited. *"I know this!"* it seemed to say.

"What... what is this?" Jathen asked. Not since his time in the Republic before all that death had he felt so still, so calm. A single tear of relief and release trailed down his cheek as the melody spun on.

"The Endless Opus, by... well, I'm not entirely certain how many Avatars and Incarnations of Bree and Bron have contributed to it. It's been quite a few."

With a sudden upswing in the tempo, the Artifact couldn't seem to contain its buzzing and burst from Jathen's chest to float above the crystal player, its rings spinning in time to the song.

"Ah," Plajă exclaimed, holding his hands up in achievement. "I knew if something would draw it out, it would be the Opus."

Jathen laughed, wiping his eyes. "You could have just asked me."

"Yes, but then I'd not know for certain if this *is* Bree's Grand Artifact. D'ilinde, as the Msāfryan called it."

Jathen blinked, surprised. "It has a name?"

"Yes. D'ilinde—'within.'"

"Find what has never been found, hidden within what was never hidden. Interesting, with all that, its name focuses on the 'within' portion." Jathen eyed him hopefully. "I don't suppose this means you know how it works?"

"Not a clue!" He laughed again, and the Grand Artifact—D'ilinde—flitted back into Jathen's chest as the music slowed. "Honestly, I just wanted to see it but didn't wish to pester you."

Jathen breathed in sharply, both alarmed and confused. "So, you... you're not going to try to convince me to join the Way? Or that you'd be able to train a Negater?"

He grinned widely again. "You are a very imaginative and creative boy, Jathen Monortith, who has been honored as a keeper of a Grand Artifact of Bree and Bron. I would think it is *obvious* you belong to the Way of Creativity or, at the very least, are personally favored by our Child." He shrugged, holding his hands up in a pitying manner. "But as it stands, I don't really see any of the practical Way

Paths of Bree being able to train a Negater. But we—and Bree—will always be here for you. That's the power of creativity, truly. It seeps into every Way and is found in bursts and spurts in every path. We *are* your Way, if only as an undercurrent to the rest of what you do. I do not feel a need to convince or compete for that fact. It simply is."

Jathen let out a long, sad sigh that migrated into a disbelieving laugh. "I... Spirit in Heaven, that's the most sense I think any of you have made in quite a while."

It didn't save him from his vision, though—only explained it. *No wonder there were no amber robes to be clad in; there's no official Way path for me here.* Still, Plajă's words were kind, and knowing the Grand Artifact had a name seemed useful.

"Thank you," Jathen said.

"You are very much welcome. Please, as I said, if you need anything, feel free to ask."

Jathen debated mentioning he'd actually *seen* Bron in Dodbyen, but fear of being asked if he'd seen any *other* Aspects worried him. As nice as Plajă seemed in the moment, De'contes was a controversial figure, and letting any High Walker know that Ra'vien had urged Jathen to save the head of the Balori seemed treading far too close to internal Tar'citadel politics for his taste. *I'm enough of a target for their attentions already. I can't bear more, not with everything else rolling about inside my head.*

"Do you at least know of anyone who might know about how the Grand..." Jathen corrected himself, "D'ilinde works? Some expert within the Way who might have some insights?"

"Sadly, I did make a few inquiries before our meeting, and while I have a slew of charm-masters who'd compose sonnets to your glory for the rest of their days just to glimpse D'ilinde, I do not have anyone who'd be able to offer insight on its actual workings. To be honest, you probably know more than anyone about D'ilinde at this juncture."

Jathen's heart sank. *Yet another dead end. Spirit, I wish I knew where this damn thing is leading me—and if it is to the same place as the voice in the vision.* Seemingly privy to his thoughts, the Artifact hummed eagerly.

He smirked, interpreting the sound. "Is there any chance of getting a copy of that music?"

"Of course. I'll compile you something right away." As Jathen listened for a few moments, the High Walker imprinted a second storage quartz with the song.

"Thank you again," Jathen said after Plajă handed the crystal, held in a golden silk bag, to him.

"And welcome again." He grinned once as Jathen turned to go. "Oh, and do say hello to Hausmannith for me when you return to Kidwellith. And tell him I'm in his debt for sending that ebanna tea. It's quite lovely."

Jathen stopped at the door, mind reeling. "You know Hausmannith?"

"Oh, yes. Haus is a friend." He cocked his head to one side, the shaved skin catching the light again. It made the dragon tattoo on the left side of his head look like it winked. "Don't despair, Jathen. Some of us work more subtly than others. We trust our intuitions and listen to a music only a few can hear. You're not abandoned. When the time is correct, your correct teacher will find you."

Jathen shivered, surprised and relieved by the insight Plajă offered. *Mind the compass bearers.* He nodded, grateful, then took his leave back toward the elevator. Moving slowly through the crowd, he at least felt better, though he still didn't have much to go on. *Could it be just that simple? Wait, and a teacher will show? Or has one already showed, and I just dismissed them?*

The sense he'd gotten in his vision didn't quite seem to indicate he'd dismissed a teacher and thus caused his own fate, but then again, he didn't know if he needed to keep looking, either. *Perhaps I'm just supposed to remain alert for one I'd not have accepted if not for the vision, as opposed to just picking a Way and going through the training.* He bit his lip. *But I'd already decided before the vision that I didn't want to be a Way Walker, so why would the shadow voice show me those possibilities if they'd already been mitigated by fate?* Jathen sighed, trying to remember the colors of his outfits from all those deaths. *Some of them might not have been Way colors at all. And if that's the case, I'm in even more trouble than I thought.*

Still pondering inside the elevator, Jathen glanced up momentarily when the doors opened on another floor. A few Turinics stepped on, nodding quietly. Jathen stepped to one side to make room for them and caught sight of the clear line of a familiar cheekbone and braided hair in the hallway.

Izzy. I wonder what she's doing here. She's always said fauni business can't be found in Tar'citadel. Then again, maybe there're still things she can discuss with a fellow Turinic. Slipping through the doors before they closed, Jathen moved to intercept her. *I'll just—*

The thought halted along with Jathen's legs as the Walker she was speaking to came into view. It wasn't Master Utför or even another blue-robed member of the Way. No, it was Anorna, the High Walker of Feator. *What on the continent?* Ducking back behind a turn in the corridor, Jathen strained to listen but couldn't quite catch the conversation, so he set to watching body language instead.

Master Anorna looked calm and collected, though Jathen figured she would have the same stoic expression even if a Red Mage burst in and set the building aflame. Conversely, Izzy made jerky hand motions while she spoke. Jathen couldn't see her facial expressions but could detect a *sense* from her.

Deep concern and a little fear, he concluded. *My empathy is getting better, but not strong enough to know what she's so concerned about. Should I just ask or leave it be? Maybe she's trying to see if she can find out more about my vision from the Walker. Or perhaps she's trying to see if she was somehow connected to Orne in a past life. Yes, I bet that's what it is. It would explain why she's doing what she's doing for a Tazu she's not met in this lifetime. Still, do I ask or no?*

He drummed his fingers on the wall, careful not to make a sound. *Would I want her to ask if it were me? Probably not.* Putting his back to them, he headed once more toward the elevator. *If she wants to talk about it, I'll let her come to me. Spirit knows I have no right to press anyone about their secrets when I keep so many.*

The ride down was a quiet one, and he didn't like the thoughts his mind conjured while alone in that tiny moving room. He liked Izzy and trusted her with the same fervent loyalty he gave Marcasith or Seren. The Interpreter himself had put her in Jathen's path, most likely to protect him. But he had doubts—little things, seemingly inconsequential, but added together... well, they could add up to anything. That was how it had been with Mikkal, with Ishane—subtle cues that ultimately added up to betrayal. *Even with Rhyo. With Annakki.*

When the elevator stopped, he closed his eyes and took a great deep breath, exhaling it when he exited into the great foyer. *I am so sick of secrets, of conjecture and lies. Both mine and the world's.*

A breath close to his ear made Jathen start, spinning right, but his eyes found nothing. His heart pounding as he scanned the room, straining, searching, he just caught the sound of a giggle beside his left ear. Turning, again he found empty space. *The ruddy hell...?*

What felt like hands pressing into his shoulder shoved him sideways, and the crackling burst of another energy wave crashed into his back before he teleported once again.

"RUDDY, BLOODY *Red*!" Jathen screamed, kicking at air and not very much caring if he busted some random tome on a shelf. In the second study again, the Montage Walker with the eclectic fashion sense blinked at Jathen repeatedly from over his rimless glasses.

"Now, now... No need for such dramatics." Clad in another wild ensemble, he had a Rosinic's deep-violet shirt, a silver vest heavily embroidered with neat lines of runes, gradient white-to-black pants, a Montage-gold overrobe, and the fuzzy multicolored scarf as a belt over it all. "I believe this can be resolved easily again."

"I'm sorry, and I appreciated your help last time, more than you know," Jathen said, clipped. His fist tightened around the little silk bag Plajă had given him. "But I'm sick of this! I'm not some novelty Talent to toss about on the whims of Children and Grand Artifacts!"

A chair creaked noticeably to their right, and Jathen whipped his head toward the noise. A young woman was sitting low in a chair at the table he'd originally arrived under, a large tome covering her face in what was a clear attempt to hide herself.

Jathen felt a stab of pity for frightening her until his host said, "All right, Raleigh, he's clearly not an Aspect and clearly becoming severely agitated. I think it's about time you put a stop to these attacks."

"*You* are behind this?" Jathen squawked, caught somewhere between wanting to throw the bag at her and scuttling away to hide.

"Galduran!" She slapped the book down, glaring at the Walker with narrowed, mismatched eyes. One was an amethyst so dark it was nearly black, the other a brilliant clear blue that seemed nearly translucent. "You're *ruining* it!"

She was pretty, Jathen's tormenter, and he vaguely recalled having seen her briefly during his first attack. Perhaps half-Muilan with pale skin sporting purple shadows, she dressed even more eclectically than the now-named Galduran. Her university uniform was Kubeshian orange with violet trim, but she also wore a mage's overrobe in Montage gold like a coat. Her hair was a deep brown in the center, while the sides of her head were shaved close to the scalp and dyed in a Walker color-wheel pattern. She also sported numerous necklaces and at least two dozen rings, with multiple stones adorning each and every finger—a veritable jeweler's tray worth of gems splayed across her hands.

Galduran put his hands on his hips and glared at her over his rimless glasses. "I ruin nothing, my dear. You are in denial. Go see for yourself—he is not the Aspect of Rosin."

With an angry huff, she pushed aside the giant tome and dragged herself out of the chair.

"I should have the tar'ka-besh arrest you for assault!" Jathen threatened, fuming even as she stalked up to him, the rainbow-colored knee-high socks sticking out from the top of her leather military marching boots somehow matching the gleeful mockery in her eyes. Still, he gave way to her, backing up against the bookshelf as she raised a hand then extended a finger. "Don't you *dare* cast something at me again!"

She poked him—right on the crown chakra, in the center of his forehead. She held her finger there a moment, her lips turned into a smug little smile as she pressed Jathen's head back with her index finger. Then her face fell, the smugness melting into surprise and, strangely, hurt. "No," she murmured as, clearly, whatever she'd expected didn't happen.

"All right, that's enough!" Jathen batted her hand away, not having felt even the smallest transfer of energy negated. Rubbing his forehead as she stared at him with little trickles of angry disbelief rolling off her, Jathen demanded, "Are you finished with this farce now, whoever you are?"

"No," she repeated, shoulders slumping. "It can't be! A True Negater toting about a ruddy Grand Artifact? You can't *not* be!"

"Raleigh," Galduran explained softly, "I told you before he's not in possession of Rosin's Aspect's Artifact. He has Bree and Bron's."

Tears threatened in her eyes, but she closed them with a frustrated cry before promptly teleporting out.

Abandoned, Jathen could only gape at Galduran. "The ruddy hell was that all about?"

He sighed slightly, seeming a touch embarrassed. "My apologies, truly. She believed in all honesty that you were the Aspect of Rosin. That you are not... honestly never crossed her mind."

"Is she unhinged?"

A smile started to spread across his lips, but he repressed it. "No, just an aspiring High Mage stuck in Third-Tier who was terribly disappointed."

Jathen rubbed his forehead again, as if to wipe away the bizarreness of the encounter. "Well, I'm sorry my lack of being an Aspect ruined some random Montage acolyte's academic aspirations."

Galduran shrugged sadly. "It is honestly a bit more complicated than that. But as she's not chosen to bring you into her confidence, I am unable to elaborate. Still, after your last arrival, I thought it best she be confronted with the truth."

"Thank you." Jathen sighed. "And for before too. You inadvertently taught me something important about D'ilinde—my Artifact. I really did appreciate the help."

"Ah well," he said with a smile, taking off his glasses and polishing them with his fuzzy scarf-belt. "Things, perhaps, weren't as inadvertent as they appeared, hum?"

Jathen frowned, mildly puzzled. "What do you mean?"

"Just that I think your Artifact, and thusly Bree and Bron, work in your favor more than you know."

Jathen nodded. "It did help me in Dodbyen. And brought me to Tar'citadel."

"Then perhaps you should trust it more." With that, he threw another little energy ball at Jathen, who, startled again, simply let D'ilinde pick his path. He appeared where he'd been attacked, back in the lobby of the Temple Citadel. Jathen grinned as no one around him even commented on what had probably looked like another Talent teleporting about. *Inadvertent, indeed. This may well prove useful—if only for small distances.* He smirked as D'ilinde buzzed happily. *I guess I am going to start trusting you more.*

Chapter 11

The bell rang.

Jathen ignored the sound, along with the growl of his stomach, identifying the dinner hour. Instead, he continued climbing up one of the shelves in Annakki's library. Spinnek was sitting at the top, Hatori's sword cane in his grasp and his tongue sticking out between his lips as he tried to discern how to unclip the sword from the cane's sheath.

"It's important to you, thus it's important to him," Izzy explained from below.

"I understand that," Jathen replied, tone curt.

Relieved as he'd been to find some balance with D'ilinde and seeing an end to the random attacks, he'd been moody toward Izzy, since she hadn't offered an explanation as to where she'd been earlier at the temple nor noticed his latest attack and disappearance. Jathen knew he needed to quell his frustration with her lest she suspect he'd seen her with Anorna, but so many secrets from all sides had him on edge in general.

"You need to give it back, Spinnek!" Gripping the narrow shelf more tightly, he extended a hand to the boy.

Spinnek ignored the gesture.

Jathen turned back to Izzy. "Get Annakki."

"Annakki out," Spinnek declared. Legs hanging over the edge, he kicked them nonchalantly, unconcerned about his bare toes' proximity to Jathen's face.

Jathen scowled, prepared to unleash his hatched-blood climbing skills to dash up there, but the sound of Chūjitsun clearing his throat waylaid him. Relaxing slightly, Jathen turned away from Spinnek's kicking feet to see the manservant standing beside a brooding Master Mağrur and a sheepish Izzy.

"Master Mağrur to see you, sir," Chūjitsun said.

"So I gathered." Jathen's mood darkened.

White robes had also been absent from his vision, but nothing Mağrur or any other Anganite Walker could say would make him join the Way of Purity—*especially* after the assault on him and his friends. He climbed down off the shelf as the Pearl Paladin walked into the room and Chūjitsun left.

Spinnek leapt to the floor, landing in a perfect crouch. Straightening, the boy looked the taller Angani Walker up and down then made a face as if he'd tried some old cheese. "Not like whites." He handed the cane back to Jathen then strolled out as if nothing had happened.

"Interesting child," Mağrur noted.

"An understatement when it comes to Spinnek," Jathen muttered, slipping the sword cane back through a loop on his belt. "So why are you here, exactly?"

"Annakki Rheadani, Ambassador Serendibiss, and High Chancellor Jidoja all bade me to conceive of a suitable punishment for the three acolytes of my order who were involved in your... scuffle. I am here to deliver word of that verdict."

Jathen crossed his arms. "Well, Annakki is not here."

The man pursed his lips then said, "Surely, you can relay the message and thus keep me from returning."

Jathen huffed. Mağrur's energy made it seem as if even the white dragon on the man's tabard disapproved of Jathen.

"Fine," Jathen said. "What did they get?"

"They've been summarily dismissed from the order."

Flabbergasted rather than relieved, Jathen exchanged an alarmed look with Izzy before responding, "You completely severed them? With all due respect, Master Mağrur, they were in the wrong, but I'm not certain tossing away three men who'd dedicated their lives to the Way over one incident is the wisest course. I can't imagine it will brew anything less than bitterness in them. Shouldn't Angani be preaching forgiveness and whatnot?"

A single thin eyebrow arched on the man's otherwise stoic face. "I didn't expect such from an agnostic."

Jathen chewed on the inside of a cheek. *He certainly doesn't mince words, this one.* "Well, at the very least, it is just about fairness. They did use poor judgment in stopping me on the street, but the actual fight was started by my very drunk Kubeshian friend, Esop. The three of them might have chosen to back down if he'd not drawn his weapon."

"But as you said, they chose to follow you, *stalk* you, with the intention of confronting you. That is a great deal of Red-like thinking." He sighed lightly. "But if it is of any condolence, this is not the first such incident with these three but rather a final salvo after years of aberrant behavior. The Pearls lose very little losing them."

"Oh." Awkward in the silence hanging between them, Jathen suddenly felt a very clear *sense* coming off Mağrur. The familiar feeling was one Jathen regretted knowing so well.

Betrayal.

A smaller dose than the bitter tonic Jathen had drunk, it probably accompanied Mağrur's thoughts on all the years spent on traitorous students. Either way, Jathen decided to bid the Pearl Paladin good evening, and Izzy showed him out.

The whole encounter—coupled with the lack of progress in finding a teacher to train a Negater, Izzy's strange detour, and Annakki's
oddly detached behavior—left Jathen seeking solace in the quiet of
the slowly darkening drawing room after dinner. Curled up in a chair
and wrapped in a blanket, he pondered the portrait of Annakki's
Rheadani family, all dead save for her and her brother Na'vosh. A bit
of dwindling sunset lay across the canvas, catching the green eyes of
Bolynne des Rheadani. *Ra'vien. Who helped me live through Dodbyen
and bade me save the man who murdered her.*

Jathen sighed, tired to the marrow of his bones of the same questions.

A lamp bloomed to light, then another. Though most buildings
had electric lights via the charm generators located under the city,
Annakki kept oil lamps in her townhouse. Jathen had wondered if
that had anything to do with her having been raised in Clana-Ca'sta,
the first city, but he hadn't gotten around to asking. Looking over, he
saw who was lighting them, and his stomach.

Chūjitsun.

"Can't you just leave me to the dark?" Jathen pulled the blanket
more tightly around his shoulders. He had no heart for dealing with
the servant's judgmental eyes.

"Lady Annakki has ordered it. She wishes to teach the boy later."

Jathen scowled. Like Mağrur, no matter how neutral Chūjitsun
made his voice, he still sounded disapproving.

"Then can someone *else* do it?"

"No." The straight-backed human gazed with dark eyes that
looked black in the dim light. "I am the master servant of this house.
I shall be here long after you depart. I shall not cower and hide
from your displeasure just to provide you a comfort in your supposed
moral superiority."

"My moral..." Turning, Jathen could barely get the words out.
"You walk around here glaring at me as if I'm the scum you'd prefer

scraped off the bottom of your shoe, and you lecture *me* on moral superiority?"

"A lack of courtesy, a lack of formality, implies a lack of *discipline*. There is incredible strength in being able to hold onto the civility of nobility, a quality you lack, not out of ignorance, as you were born to it, but out of *laziness*." The frown lines at the corners of his mouth deepened. "Now please, you are just as capable of brooding over your easy choices in the light as in the dark, so leave me to my task."

Jathen snorted. "I don't brood over easy choices."

"Are you implying they are difficult ones?" Chūjitsun didn't scoff, though Jathen swore he heard one echo in his head. "You've made no hard choices in your life, prince. You've taken risks, gambled with lives, and won despite your losses. But you've yet to stare deep into the pit of your soul and choose between two impossibilities. It's easy to self-sacrifice for those you care for, easy to choose between the Red and the rest, easy to place the value of a thousand lives above one. But to die without fanfare, without love, unremembered for a cause that might yet falter, all without ever knowing your name—to die knowing the one you care for most in the world will probably die as well, along with everything you live for, all in the hope for a greater good... *That* is hard."

Jathen's eyes narrowed even as his heart softened. "You made a choice like that once?"

He hesitated a moment then nodded ever so slightly. "Yes. One I did not expect to come back from. I also suspected I'd be found out and, thusly, lose even the one I valued." He lit another lamp, the light blazing across his face then dimming as he adjusted it. "I was prepared to end everything I have of value—my life, my home, and my mistress—all because I was asked to... was made to believe it necessary."

"But you survived—came back despite the odds."

"Only because I failed," he whispered.

Not knowing what else to say, Jathen murmured, "I'm sorry."

Chūjitsun raised an eyebrow but otherwise continued to light the lamps. As he worked, one sleeve slid up slightly away from his spotless white gloves.

Jathen stared at the gap, unable to look away from the burn marks there. *Pink skin, scarred skin—from being betrayed, Annakki said. The flash, the day of the assassination, Nannazen's black skin turned pink and scarred.* Jathen froze in his chair, a chill running through him, along with the truth. He remembered Nannazen marching up to him, clear as day. *"You! I know you,"* she said. *It was Chūjitsun then, with her face, telling me to leave.* "Annakki—"

"It seems the young prince has noticed my scars, Lady," Chūjitsun broke in, his tone dispassionate.

"I see," Annakki said, her cool, sad voice tearing Jathen's eyes from Chūjitsun to where she stood in the doorway, hands folded in front of her. "That will be all for today, my friend. See to your wounds, will you? I know you're still pained, despite the brave front you put forth."

"Very well, Lady." Chūjitsun shuffled off slowly, a subtle limp still visible from where Master Akira had clipped him with her attack spell. Had he not been looking for it, Jathen would never have noticed it.

All this time, I thought it was her, but I should have known it had to have been him. He turned back to Annakki, doing his best to keep his horror and sadness in check. "You *did* order it."

She stepped down into the room, tourmaline eyes holding his. "You don't sound terribly surprised."

"Na'vosh outright asked me if you had." Jathen managed to push the words out past the thickness in his throat. He didn't know what to feel—sadness, anger, regret, betrayal, suspicion—too much. "Why? Why do it? Why bring me here to stay? Only to cover your tracks? Or to keep me close, freeing yourself to plot for another attack?"

"As said, Jathen, I'd be a hypocrite if I had condemned you, but you are here for many reasons, the foremost being Ass'shiri loved you." Her eyes hardened. "But as for *him*, he's been making too much progress, pressing this vote to allow the Balori into the Great Temple as a recognized Way. I fear for my son, for the whole of the continent. And I *hate* him, as said, more than words can express. My blood boils at the idea he is a step closer." Her voice shaking, she wrapped her arms about herself, turning her eyes to the painting of her mostly dead family. "But my mother, she *is* vengeance. The Black Phoenix, the Punisher, the Aspect of Rhean. If any hand but hers had stayed you, I'd not have accepted it. But she... she sees more than I." Glancing back his way, she cocked her head, as if looking for some small approval. "Is it really so surprising, what I've done? Did you not do the same to she who murdered Ass'shiri?"

"Ishane was self-defense. And a bit of an accident. Or fate." Looking at her, Jathen saw no longer the imperial princess, the star-crossed lover, or the prim exile being strong for her son. Annakki was a lost and vulnerable child duped into treachery and torn from her parents to live a life of obscurity. He felt nothing but pity and a strange sense of comradery. Had the story of his life taken a few different turns, he could have been her. His rage had certainly been as strong. *But I chose to extinguish that flame. And now, I don't know if I'd order a man's death. No matter what he'd done. And if she's plotting another attack, it will be the end of her. And Dor'rhean.* "You have to promise me you aren't going to do this again, Annakki. Or I will tell Na'vosh or the Chancellor."

A flash of heat lit up her eyes. "You'd put conditions on me?"

Sitting very still, as if facing a predator in the wild, Jathen said, "To protect you from yourself, yes."

She turned toward the painting again, her eyes seeming to hover on her father. When she looked back, she smiled lightly. "On my honor as a Rheadani, so long as you are under my roof, I shall not reach out to scratch De'contes. As I am already considered a suspect in this, it would prove unwise. Though in the spirit of being truthful, I admit it was part of why I wished you to stay here, yes."

Jathen closed his eyes, feeling mildly ill. "As your brother said, people will suspect you less of his attempted murder if the man who saved him resides happily under your roof."

She nodded when he opened his eyes again. "I am sorry to use you this way, Jathen. Know that these were plans set into place long before you came to my door, long before I knew Ass'shiri had passed. I fear De'contes *that much*. For your sake, I will stay my hand while you reside here, but beyond that, I will make no such promises." Her brows knit together. "I know he must have seemed charming and even remorseful, Jathen—perhaps even holding your answers in his grasp. But you cannot trust him. He is a monster, as villainous as any other Red Mage—or even Prothidian Altar. Remember that."

Then why did your mother ask me to save him? And not just her but D'ilinde as well? Jathen sighed long before he stood, his limbs feeling heavy. Walking out, he paused but a moment beside her. "I will remember all of this, Annakki," he whispered then walked out.

If Hatori were here, he'd probably lecture me about how this is part of the price we must pay for alliances and politics. Jathen closed his eyes as he slowly trekked up the stairs, uncertain how to feel. *Still, she promised on her honor, on her father's name. Clan take such things seriously, so I suppose I must trust her for now.* The memory of his many deaths swam in his mind again, foreboding. *But what has that trust brought me? For her sake, I've kept away from De'contes, though he is the one who had Hatori's letters, who knew first what a Negater was. And for what? She has helped me, yes, but what if in her helping, she's also hindered me unwittingly? There were no red-and-black-robed versions of me dying in my vision.* He bit the inside of one cheek, suddenly full of purpose, though the idea itself churned his stomach. *What if there was always another meaning behind saving him?*

No more brooding over easy choices.

Upstairs, he first checked in on Izzy, who was quietly reading in her room. "Do you need anything?" she asked.

"No, just letting you know I'm turning in for the night."

"It's very early." She put her book down, those brow tattoos crinkling. "What are you up to?"

"Must I be up to something? Can't I just be tired?" Jathen squirmed as she glared at him, unmoving. He sighed, giving in. "Nothing I need a bodyguard for."

"That is *precisely* when you need one the most. Or have you decided you like getting teleported randomly or assaulted in the streets?"

Jathen bit his lip then conjured the best lie he could. "I wanted to slip away and see Seren, all right?" He felt himself blushing even as he said it, convenient for the lie.

"So you don't want a fauni tagging along as a third wheel." Izzy snorted slightly. "I do understand. But I can still escort you to where you're meeting her."

"I'm just going to a café a few blocks up." A good lie—even if she insisted on coming, he could send her back on the pretense of not letting Seren see her. "It's really very close, and I really can go alone, Izzy. Please? I just need some breathing room after all this smothering."

"No." Closing her book, she stood and reached for her cloak. "If anything happened to you right now, the Nation would throw a fit. This isn't just about you, Jathen. I'm coming. I'll keep my distance, but I will sit and wait for you as well."

Damn it. "Ugh, fine," he groaned, pretending to fold. "Put down your cloak. I still need to bathe and dress."

Leaving her, he headed to his room and locked the door behind himself. He stuffed his boots and sword into his pack then left it by the open window, along with his coat. After grabbing a towel, he removed his pants and wrapped them in it then donned a robe over his shirt. He then headed down the hallway past Izzy's room to the bathroom, barefoot and looking ready to wash. Once inside, he locked that door and ran the water in the tub while he redressed. He opened the window then turned off the water before slipping outside. His bare feet protested the cold of the snow-covered roof, but the trek back to his room's window to retrieve his pack and boots was short. With coat and shoes on, pack on his back, and sword cane in hand, Jathen easily shimmied down the gutter to the ground.

Probably gained about a half an hour. He slipped through the main iron gate, making his way down the well-known path toward the Great Temple. *Best make the most of it.*

"JATHEN MONORTITH, WHAT a pleasure to have you drop by for a visit."

A sickening knot of anxiety sank through Jathen at the sound of A'ron De'contes's voice. Tightening his hands into fists inside his coat pockets, Jathen stepped inside the little makeshift office De'contes currently called home, a single cot and chair blocked off from the rest of the Balori by hastily hung blankets. Theirs was a single long room amid the Angani buildings just outside the Temple Citadel, depressingly bare and akin to a barracks with its rows of sparse cots. The place smelled of body odor, staleness, and despair.

The red-eyed Clansman pulled closed the thin, sweat-stained blanket behind him, cutting off the gazes of the few Balori who were in attendance. He had that sloppy smile on his face, the one that looked like he was attempting to smirk, but the grin came out genuine instead. *False arrogance, meant to disarm. Spirit, this man is strange.* Jathen swallowed hard, not willing to let the Clansman assume too much with this visit. *Then again, do I even know the full of why I'm here?* But Jathen did know—among all those versions of himself, he'd seen no red and black. *One bit of hope, to avoid barreling toward doom if I don't find a teacher.*

"Have your ranks thinned since the attack?" Jathen asked, regarding the fairly empty room he'd just passed through. "Or are they just about the city, causing havoc in celebration for winning your vote and trying to get me to bless them for saving their 'prophet'?"

"Hardly. Most of my people are independent and thus come and go as they please. Though most at this hour are merely receiving a free dinner, courtesy of Angani mercy and restaurant leftovers." Not wearing a coat, De'contes smoothed the front of his red-and-black robes, the odd smile fading into a pandering pout. "Though I do admit I've been remiss. I heard of your little... incident with Mağrur's Pearls and how one of mine sparked it. She was spoken to, of course, and sends her apologies. I'd also have come to you, to extend my own thanks for saving me, young Monortith, but I've been barred from doing so properly due to your... current accommodations."

The way he said it, Jathen knew he knew the truth about Annakki or at least highly suspected. *And what's more, he* wants *me to know he knows.* "No thanks necessary, really."

A true smirk danced on his lips, as well as a light in his eyes. "So Annakki did call for my death, then?"

His fingers turning cold, Jathen faced him fully, so furious that, for a moment, he forgot he was dealing with a Clansman Red Mage. "If you murmur *one word* against Annakki—"

"Oh please." He waved a hand dismissively then, with a ruffle of robes, sat down in his sad little chair, crossing one leg over the other. "I've gained enough inadvertent notoriety from that fiasco—indeed, it gained me my vote—I don't need to go turning her in to fulfill some warped sense of justice."

"Anything she would do to you *is* justice, A'ron," Jathen practically spat back, though his heart wasn't fully committed to the words.

"Annakki Rheadani can have my head on a platter if she would but ask for it," he replied seriously.

Jathen blinked rapidly, shocked. He *meant* it. *Or at least seems as if he does.*

De'contes steepled his fingers, eyeing him with those bright-red orbs of his. "Why are you here, Jathen Monortith?"

Suddenly becoming overly interested in the stains on the hanging blankets, Jathen didn't meet his eyes. "You named me for what I was first. I suspect you knew even when you were blustering in your office when we first met. But I don't like the Rosinics—don't trust they'll give me what I need."

"'And what is that?"

"Training on how to be a Negater."

De'contes dropped his hands and arched an eyebrow. "You'd risk Annakki's wrath to seek *my* training?"

Slowly, Jathen nodded. "Hard choices. I'm asking for your silence in training me in return for my own."

"Your own silence?"

"Yes. I don't plan on telling Annakki about this." He shifted from foot to foot, still uncertain about what he was attempting. *I don't plan on wearing black-and-red robes. I can only hope it's enough to circumvent the vision.* "Or anyone else, for that matter."

"*Tsk tsk*, Jathen." De'contes wagged a finger at him. "Of course you'd never speak up, for fear of Annakki finding retribution. If we are to do tit for tat, I'd want something more substantial in return."

Jathen crossed his arms. "You didn't seem interested in a 'tit for tat' when you offered to help me before."

"Despite what you might think, I *wasn't* certain about you being a Negater then. And I had no idea about your Grand Artifact, though, given certain things Lady Nosalia said, I'd also suspected its presence. When we first met, you were in hiding, and the act of discovery, the desire of mine to gain knowledge, was, in itself, its own reward. But now..." He spread his fingers. "Now, we know. And I have no benefit from helping you other than the act itself. I might be cut from a different shade of red, Jathen, but it is still my Way. I do not help for helping's sake."

"What do you want from me, then? Haven't I done enough, saving you? Torn myself to pieces enough over coming here, all desperately trying to see some *sense* behind saving you?"

That was the heart of it, really, the true reason Jathen had come. Ra'vien had bade Jathen save De'contes so that he could be *trained* by De'contes and thus avert the coming darkness he'd seen in his vision. *"The plan laid will bend to suit his life or his death. But you must choose, for you are the one who can act," she said.* Of course, Jathen couldn't very well tell a Red Mage that.

"Yes, you have done all that. But it's not what I need now." De'contes dropped his pretenses, his pale face softening into something far more vulnerable as he leaned back in his chair. "I suffer, Jathen. Far more than I will ever tell most. The Balori is the only scrap of sanity I can find in this world," he whispered. "What I want from you is merely *why*. I suspect you lied about having a premonition, yet you came back with purpose that day, specifically to save *me*. Why?" Those red eyes darted about his face, searching, pleading. "Why am I still here, Jathen?"

Jathen shuddered. He'd not known what he'd been expecting, but De'contes's plea hadn't been it. "You really need to know if you're damned or not, don't you?"

"It would be nice to know." Glancing away, he chuckled sadly. "There is a famous quote, attributed to Marin Manna, that goes, 'If I be damned—'"

"'Let me then make use of my damnation,'" Jathen finished. "I know it. Hatori. He also told me Marin screamed that at the top of his lungs in the middle of a pack of humans who wanted the Originals dead."

"That Marin did. And from that chaos, Rhean in a spurt of inspiration came up with the Life's Pact." He chuckled, holding up a finger again. "All from conflict. Let me put forth this to you, Jathen. Considering your systematic rejection of every single Way thus far, I'm also inclined to believe you've left yourself with only one option, hence the deeper meaning to why you are here tonight. One I can see is tugging at you despite your denials."

Jathen scowled, taking a step back—vision or not, some things he couldn't abide. "I am *not* Red."

De'contes smiled grimly. "You do not need to be a Red follower to evolve in his Way. If I may provide a theory based on past behaviors, rather than offering ideals for future endeavors?" When Jathen just stared at him, he continued, "In your childhood, much as today, you forsook all the Ways, claimed none of them fit you, yet here you are, a True Negater, whose powers are needed, *required* even by the Twelve. How was your potential supposed to bloom? How could you unlock it if all you ever did was lie in stagnation? When you pushed all eleven of the good Children into a corner, there was only one Way you *could* have trod."

"Conflict." A numb sort of understanding filled Jathen as he realized just how far into the past the head of the Balori was delving for his example. "You're saying all the death, the misery and sorrow I've experienced until now—it was all just to kickstart my Ability?"

"Yes and no. It's never that simple, never so clean-cut. We can create conflict, and then sometimes conflict is inflicted upon us—all in the name of evolution." He leaned forward, whispering, "I *believed*. I held the Red in my heart because that was what I'd been raised in, fed and Fed upon, breathed in and swallowed in heady gulps. I sowed conflict with a deft hand, but Spirit save me, I never *experienced* it. It was easy, effortless, to be evil incarnate all for the Red. I *always* won.

I didn't know what conflict *was* until I Awakened with the blood of my true Child on my hands."

Straightening, he sighed, looking troubled even as Jathen tried to make sense of this strange confession—was De'contes truly using the rumor that he was Marin Manna reincarnated to keep his sanctuary in Tar'citadel, or was it possible it was true? *And if it is, by Spirit, what does that mean for the motives of this man before me?*

Or the motives of Ra'vien, for that matter.

"I like to think all things happen for a reason," De'contes continued, "that those horrific choices were still somehow part of a plan I cannot fully grasp."

Jathen nodded sadly, empathizing all too well. "That their deaths were not senseless."

"That it was all *for* something, yes." He clutched his robes, gathering slack in the place above his heart. "This is what it means, truly means, to be Balori—the true Red. We see the evolution, the necessity in conflict, no matter how horrific the actual acts were. We accept them with stoic reverence and try our damnedest to learn from them so that we may *not* repeat them."

Suddenly, Jathen understood. He saw why this Clansman had gained dozens of followers who called him Prophet and believed he'd lead the Red back to the Ways. And why he was begging answers from Jathen, hoping to receive a confirmation from one of the Twelve that what he so desperately believed was true. *He is right—at least about conflict evolving.* D'ilinde hummed happily, agreeing. *Sometimes you must want what is given to you. That, too, is a choice.* The Drannic's words echoed in Jathen's head, feeling hollow.

Hard choices.

"I am not Red, not even the Balori's particular shade of it," Jathen managed to say, though his voice came out thick. He wanted to flee but held his feet still, willing himself to see this through. "Are you capable of assisting me in training my Ability without me being a Balori member or no?"

De'contes leaned back in his chair, measuring Jathen with fingers resting lightly on his chin. "Are you willing to tell me what made you come back that day?"

Measuring him, seeing his want, Jathen wondered for a brief second if any harm would be caused, but then he shook his head. That secret wasn't merely his. It belonged also to Annakki, to Na'vosh—Ra'vien was their mother, and Jathen might be wrong, and she might have just done it to save her daughter from ruin. De'contes didn't deserve to gain absolution at the cost of Annakki's. "No. I cannot."

"Then I would require some formal acknowledgment from you, that you are under my instruction. You'd be coming here anyway. There'd still be talk. You don't have to be fully Balori, but I would wish the world to know you trust me to help you."

The words of the Rosinic in the library flitted through Jathen's mind, clear in their cutting truth. *Whoever wins the Negater wins the prize.* He would not, under any circumstances, give De'contes reasons or tools to solidify his claim of legitimacy for the Balori or sway the impending vote. That was too much, too large a pool for Jathen to just dip a toe in and pray he didn't make ripples that would land tsunamis on distant shores. *But then coming here was for naught—my instincts were wrong. Or I'm just condemning myself to death.* "I don't think I can do that either."

"Well, those are my two prices. One for myself, the other for my cause, my people." He shrugged. "Think on it. I'll be here, should you choose to change your mind."

Jathen nodded then fled as quickly as propriety would allow.

Chapter 12

Jathen was lost.

After wandering the streets with abandon, Jathen had no idea what corner of Tar'citadel he was treading through. His mind and heart were still a cluster of swirling conflict, unable to make sense of what he should do, let alone what he wanted.

If it was simply a matter of need, I'd go to the Rosinics. Even the thought of them turned his stomach as much as De'contes's "prices" had, more so when he played in his head his many deaths in those violet robes. D'ilinde buzzed slightly, agreeing with his dismissal, which relieved him as much as worried him.

I've gained some foothold over the emotional empathy with Beleskie and Volaille, and even Desmoulein and Zhìliáo, but they don't have much to teach with the other Abilities—which explains the deaths while in any of their robes. Utför would be the one for the medium Ability, but I'm honestly using that the least now, and Izzy probably knows enough to get me through there—plus again, the prominent deaths in blue robes. Once more, the Artifact hummed, agreeing.

Ulic, Truth? I've not even seen them, and I don't remember any silver-robed deaths, but I don't want to be a scholar, and they don't strike me as having a path to train a Negater. Same for the Featorians. The Rheanics, maybe, since they won't put me in the robes? Perhaps for the fighting, but I don't know if I can stomach their subterfuge and hidden tactics—though, Spirit help me, I might need their knowledge against

Annakki. Though Annakki warned me not to get any more tangled up in the ruddy Shadow Court than I have to—and they must have members in their ranks.

Despite himself, his thoughts returned to A'ron De'contes.

He knows about Negaters. Even the Chancellor said he'd forgotten more about nontraditional Talents than most of the Rosinics know now. Your teacher will find you—but then why do I feel like I'm running out of time if I don't do something?

Spirit, what if the Balori really is the Way to save my life? What if I saved him, not to preserve Annakki, but because the man is honestly right? What if this is what Ra'vien truly wants of me—to bring the Red back into the Ways and save myself in the process?

The very idea of it made Jathen's head spin and his stomach twist into knots. Touching his chest, he turned to the one thing he was reasonably certain would lead him in the right directions, odd though they seemed. *Please,* he begged of D'ilinde. *I need help.* He bit his lip. *I need to be trained. I think you and I both know I'm going to need these skills, though I don't know for what, much beyond survival and that avalanche. I believe you might. Please, if I truly need this, then I need you to help show me the way.*

D'ilinde became very quiet, almost eerily still—perhaps reverent. Jathen stopped in the street when he saw a shadow, a glimmer of movement out of the corner of his eye. Turning, Jathen saw someone there, down the boulevard, standing just before a haze of sewer mist rising from the vents.

Bron.

A small, humble smile spread to Jathen's lips—the first feeling of hope he'd had in days. He walked toward the specter, expecting it to disappear, but instead, the amber-eyed, brown-haired human pointed to the right when Jathen reached him. Glancing in that direction, Jathen saw a new Bron farther down, his outline barely visible against the darkness of an alley. The first image was gone. So Jathen moved on to the next then the next, following the Aspect of Bree through the streets in a deliberate chase to find an answer.

Jathen turned a corner to find Bron standing not in the street but above, gazing serenely down at him from a rooftop. About four stories tall, the building for public training sat in the shadow of the University Citadel. Surveying the street, Jathen saw no one around save for the watching Bron. Grabbing the closest ledge, he lifted himself up then began the short climb up the face of the marble. Admittedly, he'd missed the feel of the wind on his back and the sensation of gaining height bit by bit, hand over hand.

Reaching the top quickly, Jathen was greeted not by another image of Bron but the soft sound of crying. Padding across the roof, he followed the muffled sobs until he found a girl sitting on the ledge on the other side. She turned when she heard him, her expression a mix of deep torment and righteous indignation at being interrupted.

"*You*," Jathen said with a gasp.

D'ilinde had led him to Raleigh, the Third-Tier student who'd put him through a gauntlet of attacks for the sake of Awakening something that wasn't within him. Sniffing, she wiped tears from her mismatched eyes with balled fists, looking about ready to swing the ring-laden things in his direction.

"The ruddy hell do you want?" she practically spat.

Floundering, as she'd been the last person he'd expected, Jathen simply said, "For the moment, I'll start with why you're crying."

"Oh, as if you have to ask." Getting her feet under herself, she stood then hopped down off the ledge to stand with him on the roof. "You were *there*."

Jathen pursed his lips, suddenly feeling guilty for having ranted at her, despite all she'd done. "Listen, just because you were wrong about me being an Aspect doesn't mean all your chances for advancement in"—he eyed her eclectic clothes—"whatever Way you're in are for naught."

She scoffed, glaring daggers at him as she ran a hand over the colorful shaved portion of her scalp. "Only you would think this was about something as *petty* as academia."

"Well, you want to enlighten me as to what it *is* about?"

"No."

"You know..." Breathing through his teeth for a moment as the last of his patience and pity died, Jathen pinched the bridge of his nose. "I'm not having a very good night either, here. And you caused me a decent amount of undue trouble, spreading rumors and technically putting me in danger, so unless you want the High Chancellor and Tazu Embassy breathing down your throat, I think a little cursory explanation or at least a *ruddy apology* is in order!"

"Uck, I am so *sick* of you young souls, always demanding, always thinking you are entitled to your answers and clarifications, begging to have things *explained*." She glared at him, lip curling up in disgust. "I don't owe you a ruddy thing, Jathen Monortith. If anything, you owe me, for getting my hopes up and dashing them."

"Dashing *your* hopes? What the ruddy hell about *my* hopes?" He stomped a foot, close to crying in frustration himself. "I've got the full dozen Ways all trying to curry my favor, and while some are helpful, none of the ones who'd actually know about how to train a Negater really give a damn about that aspect of it and are only interested in me because they want ruddy political accolades from being the lucky Way to claim me as a prize! And I've got a ruddy voice from Spirit-knows-where showing me all the different ways I can die from choosing the wrong training path, which may or may not lead to the whole ruddy world ending! Meanwhile, I got the Grand Artifact that uses its home in my chest to lead me to someone who'd help me, and it brought me here, to you, and your sobbing little riddles."

At a loss, Jathen raised his arms only to flop them back to his sides. *What in the ruddy Pit were you thinking, Bron, bringing me to this insane person?* "So unless you know how to train a Negater, 'Miss

Old Soul,' I think you're being quite the intolerable brat all on your own."

Clearing the last of the tears from her face, she coughed a pathetic laugh. "Actually, I *do* know how to train a Negater, but I don't want to train *you*."

Jathen gaped at her. Everything Volaille had ever taught him said this bratty little acolyte was telling the truth—she *did* know how to train a Negater, probably gleaned from memories of a past life. Perhaps she'd even *been* one. *Spirit, that would make a good deal of sense.* "But... *why*? I need help! If you could—"

"Oh please." Twisting one of the rings on her index finger, she pretended to be more occupied with its deep-pink stone than him. "Don't go falling into that morbid young-soul thinking that there's only a single person on which your destiny hangs. Even your precious Artifact would tell you that if you'd listen."

"Bron *led* me to *you*."

She scoffed. "*Bron* didn't lead you anywhere. He doesn't *live* in it. D'ilinde merely used the image of his energy to direct you. It's like a dowsing rod that just led you to the closest body of water. It'd lead you to the Red if it loosely fit the terms of your intended request when you asked."

Jathen crossed his arms. "You also seem to know a hell of a lot about a Grand Artifact that no one else in the city seems to know a thing about."

Flicking the longer dark-brown portion of her hair, she measured him with a contempt sharp enough that he could practically feel a blade pressed against his neck. "You're clearly not a complete incompetent. Why don't you do as thousands of unschooled Talents before you have done and ruddy well sort it out for *yourself*?"

"You think I haven't tried that? That I'm not flailing around with my arms held out wide, desperate to sort out whatever the hell is going on inside me?"

"No, I don't," she proclaimed. Putting her hands on her hips, she closed the gap between them and raised her voice. "I think you're being a spoiled brat and a prince. I think you're whining, wanting someone to walk up and just hand you an answer rather than putting forth any tangible amount of ruddy *effort*!"

Jathen bit his lip, shaking. That was the second time this night someone had pressed him, saying he hadn't grown much beyond that sad little moot he'd been. *But I have! I know I have. It was just—*

Suddenly, Jathen's internal turmoil drained, and the external factor came into focus. Raleigh was watching with her mismatched eyes, breath held, *waiting*. "Ruddy hell," he whispered in a disgusted awe. "You're *still* trying to Awaken me."

Dropping her hands, she closed her eyes with a sigh then shrugged. "It was worth a try. I suppose you truly aren't, then. *He* would have instinctually known how to use his Ability and wouldn't be so damn set on finding a teacher." Looking away, she muttered, "Unless, of course, he was instinctually trying to find Rosin, but that's neither here nor there."

He blinked at her, not knowing what to think. "Who *are* you?"

"Someone who wants nothing to do with you, as long as you are *not* the Aspect of Rosin." Rolling her eyes, she seemed to finally take pity on him. "There are plenty of people who can teach a Negater. Go pick one of *them* and leave *me* alone."

"I don't *know* who to pick! Everyone who could teach a Negater that's attached to the Ways gets me killed—and on top of that, I don't *want* to be taught by De'contes or Jiāojīn!"

"Jiāo—" This time, she burst out laughing. "Oh, Spirit in Heaven, no! Stay away from *her*, for Spirit's sake, unless you want to be smothered in rules that don't apply to Negaters or anyone else who thinks outside the standard manifestation." She actually giggle-snorted. "No wonder you're having visions of getting yourself killed if she's who you've been contemplating."

"It's not just her. As I said, in every single Way that could teach a Negater, I've seen myself dead. I'm drowning in the blood of negative possibilities."

She arched an eyebrow. "Even the Balori?"

Jathen bit his lip, unwilling to commit.

Raleigh held her stomach, shaking her head in disbelief. "*Fine.* Since you seem unwilling to leave me be until I bestow some grand tidbit of knowledge, go on and bother Marin. He *is* your best bet. He's trained more Negaters than I have. Hell, he trained the *first* one."

"Marin? Marin *Manna*? He's... dead."

"Ugh, De'contes, then! Same ruddy person." She huffed, pulling her overrobe further closed over her Kubeshian uniform. "I *hate* young souls."

Jathen swallowed, feeling ill again, and not just at the prospect that De'contes wasn't lying about being a reincarnated Original. "If I choose him, I may lose from my life someone I desperately don't wish to. Not to mention giving him fuel to legitimize the Balori—not a political step I'm willing to make."

She laughed again, ignoring the wetness in his eyes. "Then don't *tell* anyone. Spirit, you make things so much more complicated than they need to be."

"And living my life on a pile of lies atop everything else is *less* complicated?"

She shrugged again. "I do it." When he just glared at her, she raised and dropped a hand, sighing. "What do you want me to say, Jathen Monortith? You don't like the way things are being presented to you? Well, you've got *the* Artifact of creativity in your chest—get creative."

Jathen gasped as, inside his chest, D'ilinde buzzed heavily, clearly laughing. Swallowing, he glanced back up, only to find her gone. Rubbing his chest, he frowned, considering. *Get creative?*

Jathen's heart tweaked as he stared up at the University Citadel less than a block away, confronted yet again with something he wanted but couldn't have. With a low sigh, he headed down off his perch, deciding he could at least seek an opinion he trusted over the mildly insane ramblings of a stranger. *Besides, I can't go back to Annakki's feeling like this.*

"WELL, HELLO." SEREN let him in after he'd journeyed up to her room and knocked. Clad in her nightclothes with a fuzzy white robe thrown over the top, a mild annoyance wafted off her. "I thought you were avoiding me."

"I'm not—" He cut himself off. He *had* been avoiding her. He didn't want to admit it, but for all his bravado, for all his determination in the face of her mother, the old prejudices had still gotten to him. Jathen also knew the feeling prodding him, but he didn't want to face it, even less so when she could so easily read his mind and *know.* If he stayed away, he could imagine she already knew and agreed why certain things couldn't be. But face to face with her, no, she might just force him to try again.

And he wasn't ready.

For all the strides he'd made, for all the heart-chakra healing and confidence building, Ishane was still a ghost in his head, whispering, giggling. *And nothing about tonight has been helpful in quelling that particular insecurity. Not to mention I just can't bring myself to tell her my odds of dying are so much higher than I'd ever imagined.*

Shielding his thoughts with an image of the greenhouse back home—clear, seemingly revealing glass but with shady plants hiding more sensitive thoughts—he told Seren, "I'm sorry. You're right. I've been avoiding you. Not completely, as I honestly have been busy as well, but yes. You had finals, and I didn't want to add the stress of your mother being, well, a ruddy *Chertith* on top of it."

Putting a hand on her hip, she sighed, claws toying with the tie on her robe. "While I do appreciate that, I will also point out this very behavior is exactly what we were trying to cull from ourselves."

Jathen shrugged, too tired to argue. "I'm here now, aren't I?"

"At nearly eleven at night." As her pretty eyes darted back from checking her dresser's clock, she crossed her arms and raised an eye ridge. "Which makes me question if this visit is for your benefit or mine?"

"Um, mutual?"

"You are still a terrible liar." She huffed, rolling her eyes and pushing her bangs behind an ear as she finally closed the door. "Fine. Sit. Please regale me with whatever dark thing is torturing your soul."

He bit his lip. "Am I projecting that much?"

"Empathically, telepathically, no, but your face is terrible. You *really* need to sort controlling all of those at the same time."

Jathen relaxed, relieved she didn't seem to have noticed his more personal internal debate regarding her. *Just the more surface one. At least my wards seem to be working somewhat.*

Settling on the chair beside her bed, he took a deep breath and began with the vision of doom. After getting a very dark glare from Seren and a mental thrashing regarding why on the continent he hadn't told her sooner, he then explained the events since Mağrur's visit, his disastrous revelations about Annakki, the disturbing prices De'contes had put upon him if he wanted training, and the strange meeting with Raleigh. He told her everything, knowing she'd understand *and* keep her tongue.

"So let me see if I follow your logic," she said when he finished. "It sounds as if you're considering somehow convincing A'ron to be your teacher based on an unhinged student who was behind your little 'prove he's an Aspect' attacks?" Twisting a strand of her hair between her fingers, Seren arched a brow ridge again. "Why do you think this is a good idea?"

"Because I *didn't* see a red-and-black death in my vision. And she's not unhinged." Reconsidering his words based on the look on Seren's face, he amended the statement. "At least, not totally. I'm fairly certain she's an old soul—perhaps was a High Mage in another lifetime—maybe a Negater herself. She said she *trained* Negaters, and it wasn't posturing, Seren. I think that was her whole reasoning for bothering me. She desired to be the one who'd train the Aspect of Rosin in his current lifetime."

"Like the ultimate feather in her cap." Seren nodded begrudgingly. "Admittedly, I've heard of stranger motivations from old souls."

"I just don't know what to *do*, though. She said, 'Be creative,' but all roads seem to lead to De'contes." He held his hands up, as uncertain what to do with them as with the rest of his life. "He makes sense if I follow the signs, but the cost of him... not to mention I don't think I can suffer actually *being* Balori, no matter how much it might actually fit my tormented soul." He rubbed his eyes with his fingers. "Or save my life, and Spirit knows how many others."

"Prophecies of doom aside, I think"—she drummed her fingers against the mattress's side—"De'contes's idea of seeing good in the bad, it's a Montage concept, Jath. Perhaps they got it from the Red originally, but it's there. It's understood as a part of the Way of All Ways. What De'contes says, it's not *new*, but he takes it to another place. A place that, to be honest, I don't think fully fits you but, well, probably fits a lot of other people out there. People that are... *broken*."

He shot her an incredulous look. "I'm not broken?"

"No." She smiled slightly. "You're wounded, Jathen, deeply, but you aren't broken. You still have hope. You still have a lot of things. Don't mistake me—I know you've had a lot taken from you, but you still have a lot left. *One* of you survived what is to come. You saw it. There are some out there that believe their very souls are gone, their every choice doomed to condemn them to the Pit. No, you aren't broken."

"So you think it's best I just ignore De'contes's points, as well as that crazy old soul's advice, and just clench my teeth and work with the Rosinics, despite the danger of wearing violet robes?"

"I didn't say that." She scooted down to sit nearer him. "I think, Jath, after all of this—going and listening to these other Ways make their cases—none of them sound as if they fit you, not the whole of you. And the vision seems to point you in that direction as well. At least, that's what you seem to be saying."

"Lovely." *I was afraid of that.* "They finally all want me, but I still don't fit. And even if I did fit, I'd be dead."

"I didn't say you didn't fit. I said they don't fit *you*." She prodded him with a foot, irony playing on her lips. "And what Way does one follow when none of the others fit? What Way is the only Way that bends to suit the follower?"

He snorted at the blatant obviousness of it. "Montage."

"You could do worse." She shrugged, patting his knee. "Have you gone to see Montage's High Walker yet?"

"No." He squirmed a little on the chair, her touch sending tiny zaps up his leg again. "He's not invited me directly, and I've not tried, because I'm fairly certain I saw a gold robe amid the dying."

Seren's brow ridge rose. "Jathen, you are a Monortith prince. A gold robe doesn't necessarily mean a Montage Walker for you."

He closed his eyes, feeling sick again. "I wondered about that possibility as well."

"Spirit, Jathen, you can't spend your time flopping about like a fish out of water, afraid to make a move in this. Making *no* choice is just as devastating as actually making the *wrong* choice." She sighed at his forlorn expression. "Maybe you should seek out the High Walker of Montage. Or not. It's up to you, Jath. As rambling as your old soul was, she had one point right—you can be creative and sort things yourself. You don't *have* to pick a Way. In fact, that might *be* the safest course."

Longing hit him hard as he realized that really, truly was what he wanted: to not have to choose a Way at all, if only to avoid all this mess of politicking surrounding being a Negater. *Is that even possible? "Your correct teacher will find you." If that is true, then it can't be De'contes or Raleigh or Jiāojīn, as I sought them all out myself. But then again, were Plajă's words prophecy or merely advice?* Jathen rubbed his eyes again, tired from everything. "If I want to sort how to be a Negater, I'm going to need help, though."

She sat back, folding her hands into her lap. "To that I do agree—you *should* get some help, but no matter what they tell you, none of them can *make* you join. They'll say it's better, they'll say it's wiser, but in the end, you're a Negater, Jathen. Nontraditional Talent. They'll be happy—and lucky—to have helped you in your journey at all. You said that Rosinic pointed out whoever gets the Negater gets the prize—well, maybe the best way to level the field is if they can *all* 'get you.' That way, you gathering skills from De'contes, while suspect and not exactly the most reputable thing, won't at least be seen as blatant favoritism." She smirked. "*And* you avoid all robe color combinations, hopefully preventing your prophecy."

"That might actually work *if* I can get Annakki to agree to it." He bit his lip, pondering. "You have an inordinate flair for saying the right thing, you know that, Seren?"

She laughed hard, combing her hair with her claws. "Well, I suppose it comes from listening in on your mother and Thee. Spirit, there were times I'd felt as if I was your invisible second sister."

Jathen chuckled softly, thinking back to days when he thought she was younger than Thee and he couldn't remember her name. It seemed... *stupid* in retrospect. "You were never completely invisible, Seren," he admitted. He'd always found her eyes lovely. "Just mute."

"Be nice." She flicked his ear, giving him a minor zap.

"Oh, please, no more electric bolts." Jathen rubbed it feverishly to hide his rising blush. "Did you ever sort why that happens, by the way? I asked around but got nothing but riddling and giggling."

"Riddling and giggling?" She wrinkled her nose, clearly also bewildered. "No, I hadn't. I tried looking it up under properties of Negaters, but there is literally no mention of 'little sparks.' I was going to broaden the search, but I had finals." She nibbled absently on a thumb claw. "It might be a variation of Negation on emotional empathy, in which case I can probably redirect my research's direction or perhaps just ask some of the empathic masters around here. A lot of them are on leave for the break, so it might be a bit before I can—"

"Don't bother. I was promised it had nothing to do with Negation."

"Oh?" Her shoulders slumped a moment, then she continued, "Well, if that's the case, I'd need to redirect the search entirely—"

"Seren, it's all right, really." He held up his hands in mock surrender. "You don't need to spend what little time you've left on your winter break researching my odder Abilities just because I can't pick a Way."

"Jathen, don't you understand? What else am I *possibly* to do? I have no social life outside of researching the oddity that is you."

He opened and closed his mouth a few times. "I... I'm not certain if you're joking or not."

She pinched her claws together until only a small space lay between. "Only a little, which is so tragic."

He chuckled then crossed his legs, dark thoughts still prodding. "And Annakki? Chūjitsun?"

"What about them?" She drummed her claws across her knees as he gave her a punitive look. "I don't know what more you *can* do. De'contes is hated. Venomously by some. There are those who'd support what those two have attempted. And bringing them to light would only reinforce that hate, that righteous desire—even *De'contes* seems to understand that and isn't using it for his own ends. Besides, from what I've seen and what you've said, I think Annakki has been quelled."

"For now. I'm fairly certain she caved to me simply because she believes she'll have another chance to finish it." He sighed long. "And that vote *is* coming."

"And you've seen to it she won't as long as you're around. And let's be honest, it was a pathetic attempt—sending one Talent against a *Red Mage*? Even if she'd given him a soul-sever blade for every pocket in an alchemist's vest, the man would have had an insane task. There's more merit in Na'vosh's theory that Ra'vien had you stop it for Annakki's sake than De'contes's. Even *if* he's some piece to the puzzle of you getting trained." She sighed when his expression didn't shift. "Jathen, you can't fix people. You can only apply some balm and hope they heal on their own."

"That your proven methodology for me?"

"No, I just zap you until you remove your head from your—"

"Fine, I get it." *Hard choices.* "But I still have to find my own way."

"Isn't that what you've always done? Be creative, right?"

Staring at her, he suddenly knew what to do. "You're right. I have."

IZZY WAS WAITING FOR him when he finally returned to the townhouse, sitting stiffly in a chair dragged into the foyer.

"I'm sorry," Jathen said while giving his coat to a manservant who was *not* Chūjitsun, thankfully.

"You lied to me." Her flat tone had an undercurrent of Orne's voice in it. "You endangered yourself, and for what? I went to the café. You were not there."

"I did go see Seren later, but it wasn't what you think," he whispered. "Just... please trust me, Izzy. I had to do it alone."

She stood quickly, braids flapping up. "You want me to trust you, but you can't trust me with what you were about?"

"You want to tell me what you were sneaking around talking to the Featorian High Walker for? Because you didn't seem upset about me getting attacked and teleported again while you were wandering off."

He hadn't meant to bring that up, but the evening had been far too stressful, and the words just exploded from him. She was hurt—he could feel a wave of sorrow and shame as she flinched hard.

"You saw A'ron De'contes again."

Jathen and Izzy both started at Annakki's voice. She was standing just past the light of the foyer, so a shadow draped across her face. Her watermelon-tourmaline eyes seemed to glow, accusatory.

"How did you..." Jathen stopped, knowing better. "Clan, you know everything. Yes, I saw him."

"*Why?*"

"Because I need answers, Annakki—and because you *lied* to me!" Trembling, Jathen bit his bottom lip a moment, catching both his thoughts and his breath. *Get creative. You can do this.* "I need training. I cannot continue to flounder as I have, or people *will* get hurt by my misaction. I told you before, Hatori had been writing to him. The letters were destroyed when that Rosinic deconstructed the townhouses. I need to know if De'contes remembers his questions and has those answers as Hatori once hoped he did."

"There are other trainers, other masters—"

"Where, Annakki?" Jathen held his arms wide, stretching into empty space. "All I've been given aren't going to help me without fueling their own agendas." *Or getting me killed,* he thought but did not say. He wasn't certain Annakki deserved that truth from him just yet.

"And you think *De'contes* won't?"

"I think I know *exactly* what his agenda is," he countered. "He asked me tonight, gave me a choice of two prices to pay for his help, but I know a way, a way around it so I won't pay either."

Her eyes narrowed, shimmering with what seemed to be tears. "How?"

"Tonight, he told me Annakki Rheadani could have his head on a plate if she but asked for it. He *meant* it, Annakki. I will go to him, and I will tell him he will train me, or..." He paused, measuring her face. "I will get you to ask."

Annakki shook her head, letting out a shaking breath. "Jathen, no, you don't understand what kind of evil he is. He'll never follow through with such a claim, or he has some dire plot to better his cause for it. You can't trust him. Not with the vote coming up..."

"Annakki, please, listen to me." He took a step toward her, heart pounding. "You hate him, I know. But that hate clouds you, keeps you from seeing the weaknesses of the person inside the monster. I don't *really* think he wants to be a martyr. Not truly. But I think if pushed, he *would* for his cause. But the Balori wouldn't survive without him—not yet, at least, not without some foothold in the rest of the Ways. So let's just give this time. The vote is coming, yes, but we've a few months at least. Let me try this, Annakki. And if it fails, I will stand at your shoulder when you ask him for his head."

"Jathen, no—" Her voice came out choked, her eyes not meeting his. "You can*not*."

"Spirit in Heaven, Annakki, I do this only out of true *need*. My soul is torn over this, given who he is and what he did and who he claims to have been. I have no soft feelings for the man, *especially* given what he did to you." He stomped on the foyer's parquet, frustrated.

Beside him, Izzy stood stock-still as if afraid any movement would drag her into the argument.

"Have I not proven that enough for you the last few weeks?" he asked.

"You don't understand," Annakki said, her breath catching quick at the end, nearly a gasp. "There's been another offer—one you can*not* refuse."

Scanning her face, Jathen recognized something he'd previously overlooked—Annakki was *afraid*. His heart pounded, unsure. "What are you talking about?"

"You asked me some time ago to make inquiries about the Grand Artifact." Putting a hand on her chest, she walked forward, and the shadow cloaking her retreated. "When it became known you were a Negater and the other Ways seemed to hold no firm answers for you, I expanded that inquiry."

Jathen's first instinct was to take the petite Clanswoman by the shoulders and shake her, but instead he rolled his hands into tight fists. "Why the ruddy hell didn't you *tell me*?"

"Because I had no idea if the search would glean any fruit. And given how much I know you'd prefer a nonpartisan trainer, I did not wish to sour you to a Way Walker teacher on the hope of something I might prove unable to provide." She closed her eyes, shivering. "Tell me this pact you are fancying with *him* isn't finalized?"

"No, it isn't." He exchanged a glance with Izzy, feeling as if he was scraping the very bottom of his barrel of energy for the day. "Despite what you might think of me, I came here first. I'd not have done it without your agreement."

She sighed long, the waves of relief that rolled from her enough to slow Jathen's heart rate as well. "I received the missive with the offer this very hour. A word and a day, and you will have the answers you seek."

Feverish hope sprang up inside him, but he pressed it down, concerned still by all the secrets that'd been kept—and, perhaps, others still hidden. "And what makes you think I'll just take some Clansperson you throw at me? You said I couldn't refuse"—memories of his vision still hung close to him—"but what if I need to?"

"You must at least listen to this one, Jathen. That is all that is being asked."

"And if they don't suit?" he asked gently.

He didn't like the haunted look in her bright eyes. "Desperation makes for strange bedfellows," she whispered. "This I know. I've meditated for many nights since your act of rescue, trying to understand, *begging* my mother to offer me some reasoning. Nothing. Except now, the word has spread, and this offer has come forth. So perhaps there is reason there. We shall just have to see." With that, she retreated, slipping back into the interior.

"Jathen—" Izzy began, but he cut her off with a wave.

"Not now, Izzy, please. I've spent the whole night in what now seems like a ruddy snipe hunt. I'm in no mood for more talk."

"I only wish to apologize... for my silence. For lying about the Featorians." She swayed back and forth, fingers toying with the clasp on Orne's pouch. "I just—"

"It's fine, Izzy," he insisted. "You don't need to tell me. It's just been a long day. I'm grumpy. I'm mean. You don't deserve it, but I'm grateful you put up with me."

"I've certainly dealt with worse," she admitted, voice leaning toward playful. Then she sobered. "It's not that I don't want to tell you, Jathen. I just... *can't* yet." She continued to fidget with the clasp, popping the top one open and closed with little snaps. "Though if your choice to exclude me tonight had to do with my silence—"

"No! Honestly, Izzy, I meant it when I said I needed to do it alone. I didn't want Annakki finding out—though I realize now that was a fool's errand."

After staring sadly at him, she nodded.

Jathen sighed long, exhausted and frustrated. "I'm going to bed."

Chapter 13

S he sliced.

Pale hands moved deftly across the cutting board as Jathen sat nearby, watching his prospective tutor work. Dressed simply, she wore a servant's black dress, though hers lacked the formal white ruffles or green apron. She didn't look Clan, her features tending toward more Nor'wah or Kinawa humans, albeit far paler. While he had once described Annakki as *stony*, this new Clanswoman who'd bade him meet her in, of all places, Annakki's kitchen had a manner that made him think of a mirror—as if all his flaws were reflected back at him from her bullion eyes. Though that gave him a deep shiver, he tried to assess what he could from the mysterious noble.

Her gold eyes have shades of burnt sienna in their depths.

"You're a Manna," Jathen said plainly, trying to decide how he felt. He carried some of Hatori's prejudice of the supposedly "twisted" Clan bloodline because of his encounters with Mikkal, who had been a cousin of sorts. Then again, so had Nosalia, and the sweet albeit "unofficial" Manna, as she had put it, had been patron to Hatori and of great assistance to Jathen.

From very crimson lips came her controlled reply, "Only by marriage." Her long, unbound hair shone a bright and taboo color somewhere between burgundy and a brownish black—striking, if somewhat reminiscent of the Balori's colors.

"But you have the eyes."

"Not every Clansperson with gold eyes is a Manna by birth." Continuing her task, she displayed the knife skills of a master carver, flaying the whitish flesh of the fruit the way an experienced butcher would carve up a rabbit or bird in a clear act of intimidation. Jathen could easily imagine his own flesh in place of the purple-skinned fruit. The image irritated more than frightened him, though, and he sighed, slightly exasperated.

"Are you going to introduce yourself and perhaps speak on training me or continue to cut your fat fruits?"

"It is more commonly recognized as a vegetable, not a fruit. When one reaches my age, young Tazu, one does not rush in any task—even when one *can*."

"All well and good for a Clanswoman of countless age," Jathen replied, undaunted and vexed. He'd heard enough of Hatori's bluster over the years to be immune to Clan intimidations, and her "young Tazu" comment reminded him too much of Raleigh. "But I've a human's years to measure with and nowhere near that much time."

"An appropriate, if not terribly original, answer." She turned those blazing eyes back on him, still cutting. "I've yet to decide if I shall be training you, young Tazu."

Drumming his fingers across the old wood of the kitchen table, Jathen resisted the urge to purse his lips. "So you're trying to gauge me. In true Clan cloak-and-dagger fashion."

"In a sense."

Jathen rolled his eyes, exasperated by the prospect of continuing with what was essentially another Rheanic bent on riddle spinning their mysticism around a core of intrigue. "I'm beginning to think I might have preferred A'ron De'contes," he muttered.

The temperature dropped.

Goose bumps broke out across his skin as the heat was literally sucked out of the room. Energy congealed around the petite woman, leaving Jathen totally aware that he was sitting in the presence of a

Clanswoman Talent of unknown age and origin who could probably swat him the same way Hatori used to pin flies to the wall with etching tools.

"I'm sorry if I offended," he managed to squeak out.

"Nothing to forgive," she said without emotion, and the sense of doom snapped back as if on a sling, and the temperature returned to normal. "I have merely become accustomed to having those around me who censor that name. It has been a long time since I have heard it uttered in my presence."

"I shall refrain, then." He squirmed in his chair, heart slowing from its sudden upswing. "And for what it's worth, I empathize. Both Hatori and Annakki have felt the sting of his crimes, and their pain causes me pain."

"A pair of traitors' pains cause you pain in the face of a traitor." Lifting the cutting board, she deposited her diced vegetable into an awaiting bowl then fetched another without skipping a beat. "Interesting."

Jathen scowled. "I do not know the full of Annakki's history, but I know for a fact that Hatori was innocent."

"Of what, exactly?" She stabbed the blade through a slice of purple vegetable and into the cutting board, where it stayed upright. "Of treason or aiding in the murder of his emperor and countless others by providing a Red Mage with soul-sever blades? He may have been unaware, but he was still guilty. Do not forget that."

Jathen stared hard and long at this woman he was certain could kill him as easily as blinking. What was more, he needed her to be the one to help him find a way to save himself. *But there are some things I will not abide.* "I don't think I want to be trained by you."

"You seem to be saying that to a lot of people as of late."

He swallowed, stomach rumbling even as D'ilinde buzzed agitatedly in his chest. "I meant it every time, but yours is a personal pinch."

Those crimson lips smirked slightly. "And when you attempt to take your throne, you expect to work and smile and sup, reclining at Tazu tables only with those with whom you approve?"

"No, I don't." He bit his lip, debating bringing up his vision, but then decided against it, managing instead to say, "But that's all the more reason I cling to it now. This part of my life is mine to choose and mine to discern. I've lived enough of my days in discomfort from those around me, so in this, I would choose a teacher whom I at least *like*."

"So you claim you *liked* the head of the Balori?" When Jathen did no more but squirm in his chair again, she continued, "Or do you believe that because you liked Hatori, then he would have been the most capable of training you? If that were so, why did he defer to others, writing letters to a man he supposedly despised?"

"I'm not going to bother asking a Clanswoman how she knows that," Jathen replied, though he suspected Annakki. "You have a point, but so do I. So far, the only Ways that have treated me like an equal were the ones that hold nothing for me as a Negater—and the ones I could learn from acted as if I was a tiny hatchling to be whacked on the tail should I think in a manner against their choosing. You are correct—I don't need to like my trainer—but I will ruddy well demand some respect, which I *did* get from the 'head of the Balori' despite his other massive drawbacks. But if I will not have respect, I will be content *not* being trained." He swallowed, hoping he could take such a gamble in the wake of the vision's deaths still hovering over his destiny, just out of sight.

She cocked her head, long red hair catching the light, and Jathen suspected she already knew he was posturing. "Do you know what it means to be a Negater, child?"

"I suppose you are going to tell me."

"I cannot, for I am not one. But I have known four—one of which was as you are, a True Negater and Exemplary. No one else alive can make such a claim. I also do not hold any affiliation with any Way—never have. I will not teach you doctrine. I will simply teach you how *you* work. I won't even be here often enough to be repressive. I have responsibilities at home I cannot shirk and so shall simply alight back to you, give you lessons to practice with sparring partners I shall arrange, and then return to check in on your progress and teach you anew. As far as respect, you will have it as you earn it. But on the flip of the coin, so shall I. I have lived long enough to know that age and rank do not earn us automatic respect. It is in how we act, how we treat others. We will bend to each other, you and I."

Crossing his arms, he leaned back in his chair. "You talk as if you already know what I'll decide."

"I merely have seen the possibilities, yes. But as to the final outcome, that is and always shall be your choice, Jathen Monortith."

Jathen pursed his lips, a begrudging hope springing up that made D'ilinde buzz. "You're precognitive as well."

"Yes, an Exemplary. Technically, a nontraditional Talent as well, though my Ability does not flow quite the same as a Negater."

"May I ask what type?"

She smirked again. "Storm Mage."

Jathen felt himself pale as waves of chills crossed his body, and he straightened in his seat. He'd read up on the other types of nontraditional Talents while working with Seren to uncover his own Ability, and a Storm Mage was *not* a person to be trifled with. They weren't born nontraditional Talents as Negaters or Ice Mages but instead learned their craft over the course of hundreds to thousands of years, mastering their Ability until they could wield multiple elements at the same time: wind, water, and lightning. It was a self-taught practice, mastered by only a handful of High Mages and only *one* Clanswoman.

Erin Manna—Marin Manna's widow and one of the Clan's eight Originals.

Left literally speechless, Jathen just sat there, numb with awe. Her red lips twitched, knowing. "You're dismissed, young Tazu. Think on my offer. Discuss it with Annakki, your fauni, and your half-blood friend. I shall be here."

Relieved to be released, Jathen exited slowly from the kitchen, afraid to put his back to her until he was up the short flight of steps to the main floor and out of sight. Then he bolted through the house in a kind of half-dazed escape. He immediately sought out Annakki, holed up in the solarium with Dor'rhean.

"You brought me *Erin Manna*?"

Surrounded by lazy ferns and seated upon a thick Lubreean rug, Annakki did not look up. Instead, she played with Dor'rhean, rocking his hands back and forth to his gleeful cries. "My inquiries for you were never directed at her specifically, Jathen. She asked after *you*, not the other way around."

"It didn't seem—"

"She's an Original. Without a Walking Avatar on the continent, she and Orrick Ashton are the most powerful beings alive. Not even the High Mages would dare challenge them. I *brought* you nothing. She is Erin Manna: she ordered—I *obeyed*."

"You're afraid of her," he said softly. "I saw it the moment you told me about the missive."

"Terrified," Annakki admitted, her lovely eyes finally rising to meet his. "You must understand. Your ancestors... They *die*. You are connected to them, but when they cross the Veil and their bodies return to ash, they take their biological ties with them to the pyre. With us, it is not the same. Every one of us is descended from the Eight in one way or another. Our very *blood* obeys them. You do *not* speak back. You do *not* disobey. There is no other option."

"There is always the option, Annakki—"

"No." Her dark hair whipped back and forth as she shook her head. "Not when they can invoke *sangui mandat*."

"I... What? Are those even Clan words?"

"Old Clan. 'Blood command.' An Original can *literally* compel us to obey, Jathen. It's more powerful if their target is a direct descendant, but it works for us all."

"Spirit," Jathen whispered, the word coming out like a breath. "Doesn't that violate the First Law?"

"Yes. That's why they don't use it. But the threat of it..." She shook her head. "My father, he had sangui mandat as well. Any Avatar of Rhean or Ra'vien born of Clan blood can invoke it. He used it *once* in all his long reign, but once was all he ever needed."

"Well, I guess I should feel honored, then, as she *did* give me the option."

"Yes." She bowed her head low. "You should."

Adrenaline abating, Jathen sat down beside her, ready to think. "She said to discuss it with you, Izzy, and Seren." He bit his lip. "Had you told her, or is she that precognitive?"

"I told her nothing aside from the fact you were a Negater in search of a teacher." Pursing her lips very slightly, Annakki shook her head. "My father once said Erin Manna can flay your soul as easily as she flays a side of beef. My mother said she always preferred Erin's chicken dishes."

Jathen coughed a laugh despite himself. "They certainly were an interesting pair."

"They had their moments. Sadly, though, I am uncertain if I can advise you well on this. I would *never* be able to turn down Erin Manna. And since I could only make one choice, I cannot imagine I'd be much help in weighing yours." She gazed at him sadly. "Though you know my thoughts on your other... *option*. I'd only ask you not to put us all through that. Though—" She cut herself off, preoccupied with bouncing Dor'rhean.

"What is it, Annakki?"

"I am uncertain as to the Lady Manna's motivations, but her precognition is beyond repute, and she rarely *acts*. When she does, I have seen her respond with razorlike precision, usually based on knowledge only she can see. If she is here to train you, there *is* a reason—probably a very good one."

Jathen smirked, knowing Annakki too well. "You think she stepped in to be my trainer to prevent me from going to De'contes."

She gazed at him steadily with her tourmaline eyes. "Given the timing, it would be hard to speculate upon such a conclusion."

"I know," he whispered. Time spent away from De'contes had sobered Jathen's thoughts toward the Clansman, and he was less inclined to chase the Red Mage on Raleigh's advice and a slim possibility that his single surviving self wore red-and-black robes in the future. It seemed... *reckless* now to pin his survival on a possible interpretation of one aspect of a very complex vision. However, the idea that his excursion, romping about the other night, might have sent Erin Manna some precognitive vision of *his* need was a bit humbling. *But sadly, not out of the realm of possibility if my own visions prove to be true.* Jathen leaned back, putting his weight on his hands. "So I must decide, then. Interestingly, I think I can already tell you exactly what the other two will think. Seren will tell me I'm being a ruddy moron if I tell her no after whining on for so long about wanting a nonpartisan teacher."

"And Izzy?"

"She'll just nod along stoically with Seren and then say in her cool tone, 'I knew I liked you, half-blood' or somewhat similar. Not to mention, she'd probably agree outright with your theory. Izzy and I met under similar circumstances, to be honest."

Annakki slipped Dor'rhean into her lap, smiling at her son, the relief flowing from her palpable. "I think your answer is found, then."

Jathen sighed long, sat forward again, and ran his hands through his hair. *But why did D'ilinde lead me to Raleigh the other night? Is it really as she said, just acting as a dowsing rod? Or was there some greater providence to it—like sending Erin here?* "It doesn't quite solve everything, though, does it? Training my Negater Abilities, yes, but what about the rest? Combat and past lives, and I was torn on if I wanted to learn strategy from the Kubeshians or try the Rheanics for hand to hand. Not to mention, I'm already working with Walker Volaille—"

"Jathen." Annakki interrupted him with a hand on his shoulder. "Erin Manna is nearly nine thousand years old and has had students before. She's also the High Judge for the highest court in the Clan lands—should it be needed, she alone has the authority to try an emperor. I'm certain she's capable of overseeing your schedule to incorporate what you need." She removed her hand, suddenly looking mildly indignant. "But as far as martial combat, Jathen, I'm surprised. You need look no further than me if you wish to be taught."

"Truly?" Genuinely surprised, he knit his eyebrows together.

Annakki had a sort of resilient daintiness to her—similar to a diamond, pretty but able to cut steel—but it didn't invoke a fighter's image. Honestly, he'd thought of her as more of an operative in league with assassins than as a trainer of martial combat. *Then again, Izzy had mentioned she'd been teaching Spinnek a few things.*

Her tourmaline eyes were pitying even as Dor'rhean blew bubbles at Jathen from his perch in her arms. "My *father* taught me."

Blinking repeatedly at her, Jathen took a moment to register the enormity and equally embarrassing obviousness of that fact before he burst out laughing. "Oh, Annakki, yes. Of course he did. I'm ruddy obtuse still, I swear it." He grinned, pleased to see she sported a small smile as well. Suddenly, in that moment, the tension that'd been building between them for so long broke, and Jathen could swear he heard Ass'shiri heave a long sigh of relief somewhere in the distant recesses of his mind. "Of course. I'd love for you to teach me. As well as the Lady Manna. You were right—this is perfect."

From the doorway, Chūjitsun cleared his throat, and Jathen cringed. He'd not seen hide or hair of the master servant since discovering he'd been the man behind the master-charm trying to kill De'contes. Still, he'd just made peace with Annakki—and Chūjitsun himself had stated why he'd done what he'd done. Annakki had asked it of him, and loyalty of that level was something Jathen could not fault.

He and Annakki turned toward the servant, who, for the first time ever, looked mildly concerned. "My deepest apologies, my Lady, but there are two tar'ka-besh at the door."

"Not my brother?" Annakki asked. Her tone was even, but an unsettled concern flowed off her.

Jathen's own throat pinched. Now would be an absurdly unfair time for Tar'citadel to decide to investigate the attempt on De'contes's life.

"No, my Lady. Two of his subordinates." Chūjitsun cleared his throat again. "They have our Mr. Spinnek in tow."

Annakki arched her eyebrows and made to stand, which made Dor'rhean whine, unhappy to be removed from his mother's lap.

Jathen sprang to his feet. "I'll handle it. Spirit knows Spinnek is more my responsibility than yours."

She nodded in the direction of the front door. "He certainly has his moments."

Jathen chuckled in agreement, following Chūjitsun out into the foyer. A glowering Burjiro and his fellow tar'ka-besh Dredona stood on the stoop, with Burjiro clutching a sheepish-looking Spinnek by his collar.

"*This*"—the scowling tar'ka-besh said with a growl, thrusting the collared boy over the threshold—"is supposedly yours."

Spinnek fell forward into a roll, rising to his feet within a moment and unharmed. He did scuttle around behind Jathen, though, where he made a rude gesture at Burjiro.

"Spinnek!" Jathen stayed the boy's hands, mortified as well as mildly curious as to where the boy had learned such a thing. "What did you do?"

The boy grinned widely, brazenly ambiguous.

"He was attempting to remove some very valuable and heavily imprinted storage quartz from the High Temple's public library," Dredona explained, her tone slightly less venomous than Burjiro's but still stern. "He snuck into the restricted sections and stuffed his pockets. Ultimately harmless, as all such quartz can be lent out if using the proper channels, but obviously very frowned upon. Commander Na'vosh bade us deliver him to you rather than provide sterner punishment. Though with the warning and understanding that another incident will *not* be as lightly tolerated."

"I'll deal with him. Thank you."

They left with a curt set of nods.

While Chūjitsun closed the door, Jathen rounded on the boy, doing his best to sound like an admonishing Hatori. "I told you before. You can't just take things anymore, Spinnek. This isn't Dodbyen. There are rules you have to abide by."

"Why?" Still grinning, he tumbled through Jathen's legs, flipping on the other side to lounge on the floor like a reclining Tazu at dinner.

"Don't be a wiseass with me, Spinnek. You and I both know you're smart enough to comprehend why there are rules and why you should obey them." Jathen crossed his arms, glaring at the smirking teenager. "My question is: Why are you breaking them? You know if you wanted any of those books, you could have just asked me or Izzy or any number of people to help you. Speaking of such, *why* are you out without Izzy?"

His expression meandering back toward resignation, Spinnek shrugged. "You do."

Jathen sighed, irritated his behavior so easily influenced Spinnek for the worst. "I did it for very specific reasons to try to protect Annakki, and I can tell you I regretted it immediately. You, on the other hand, are breaking rules just to see if you *can*, Spinnek. Next time, I will *not* help, and you'll have to deal with the consequences. If that's the only way you'll learn, so be it."

Suddenly, Spinnek's normally mischievous brown eyes went wide, fearfully fixated on something past Jathen's shoulder. He then squeaked and jumped, a fully Ability-fueled leap upward. He landed on the grand crystal chandelier hanging in the foyer, setting the expensive brass fixture swinging dangerously, half its oil-fueled lights flickering and the others going out. Jathen barely got in an angry yelp at the boy before Spinnek jumped again, diving through the air onto the banister at the top of the stairs. Sliding off that, his feet scarcely hit the landing before he bolted around the corner and out of sight.

The chandelier still swinging madly above his head, Jathen turned to find Erin Manna in the foyer. She'd changed into an elaborate rouge-pink-and-yellow robe set with long, billowy sleeves and a thunderbird in gold stitched across the front. *Mannachi crest,* Jathen recalled from Hatori.

A singular reddish eyebrow arched curiously on her forehead even as the odd illumination swayed and reflected off the tin ceiling, sending anomalous lights and shadows across her face. The flickering made her gold eyes crackle like flames. "Might I inquire as to what that little whirlwind was, precisely?"

"That was Spinnek, one of the survivors of Dodbyen. An Exemplary Talent of high intelligence left to his own devices for Spirit-only-knows how long." Jathen sighed long as servants scampered into the foyer, toting long poles to try to right the chandelier and preferably avoid starting a fire. "And, apparently, a book thief."

"Sensible, having grown up in a place with no laws to speak of. Explains his mental wards as well." Avoiding scampering servants, she stepped closer, closing the gap between them. "But the vehement departure?"

"Maybe because you're Clan? But no, he had no fear of Burjiro, nor Annakki. Aura, possibly? Spinnek's shown a sensitivity to them in the past." He flinched slightly—suddenly aware of a wave of warmth coming off her, as well as the large berth the servants were giving her, reminding him he was in the presence of an Original. "I can't imagine yours is, well, *subtle*."

"It can be when I so choose it, but just now, it had a minor bent of flare to it." She smiled very subtly, and the power ebbed. "I heard the raised voices and a Clan accent and thought I might see if my authority were needed."

"No, I have little fear of Ass'shiri's older brother. Burjiro Tan is a blustering ass." Taking a breath, Jathen measured the great, if considerably shorter, lady for a moment. "You're Erin Manna."

"And you are Jathen Monortith." Those brilliant gold eyes met his. "You've decided, then?"

Jathen nodded deeply.

She returned the motion, though far shallower. "Come. These things are best discussed in a setting intended for longer conversations." She took up an armchair in the adjacent sitting room, leaving the servants to finish their work.

Jathen made himself comfortable in the chair across from her, though he wasn't certain he'd ever feel totally at ease in the presence of a Storm Mage Original.

Crossing her legs at the ankles in a very prim movement decidedly akin to a cat, Erin Manna asked, "Were you aware *Jathen* was the name of the First King of the Tazu Nation?"

"I am." Jathen nodded, for Ishane had found him the origin of the name back in the Republic, but he had a feeling the Lady Manna wasn't bringing it up for the sake of idle conversation. "You knew him."

"I spoke of a True Negater before—Jathen was one as well. The first, in fact. There is also a resemblance between you two." Bracing an elbow on the arm of her chair, she rested her chin in her hand, two of her fingers stroking her cheek and her elaborate sleeve draping down over the side. "I thought a reincarnation at first, but I see now it is not so. You seem much more cautious than he, warier. And younger. Your soul isn't brand new, but you're still shaping your fate. His soul was old when so many of us were still young."

"I didn't know that was possible."

"Oh yes. The other Originals, I, the rest of the Children, not all of us were old souls when the world turned. Some were. Montage, for example. Rhean, Ra'vien. Jathen."

"You say I look like him. Was he full-blooded Tazu, able to shift?"

Those red lips twitched, not quite a smile. "No. He was the child of a half-blood and a human."

So Ishane had that right, at least. Jathen measured his words, having so much he wanted to ask and such a rare opportunity to do so. "What was he like?"

"Calm. He had his grandfather's empathic Abilities—specifically the skill to soothe large groups with his mere presence. He did it almost subconsciously and was very useful for it."

Spirit, I really am talking to someone who was there, *nine thousand years ago.* "The Tazu tell tales of him being a great leader but also a warrior. I've always wondered what it must have been like, to take a sword and walk out onto that battlefield to face Prothidian, not knowing if he would live or die."

"Oh, he knew," she said. Her eyes darted sideways, watching the servants leave the stable chandelier and give the two more privacy. "I told them both—he and Jor'don—that they would win and live."

Jathen couldn't help but widen his eyes. "You knew that, for certain?"

"No. I had seen both possibilities. Well, in truth, perhaps about four dozen variants of how the battle could play out. But in that same knowledge, I knew telling them they would survive increased the probability of the favorable outcomes enough that I deemed it necessary. That is a basic tenant of precognition, Jathen. I'm surprised you don't apply it yourself."

"Mine's too random—and, at least until recently, I've never seen more than one outcome to anything—and there was no clear indication of what the choice I made would lead to." He squirmed a bit in his seat, debating how much he wanted to tell her. "It's been... stressful."

"For now. Your Abilities, and your skill to interpret them, will grow."

"Is that a promise or a probability?"

Her lips twitched again. "Both."

Jathen cracked a smile despite himself, but it vanished at the memory of the vision of the charm-store fire that'd claimed Hatori and Jephue's lives, as well as the looming doom of his dozens and dozens of deaths. "I just wish I knew why I see what I see."

"There is always this grand question of 'why'—a search for reason when it comes to precognitive vision—*why* do this versus something else or not at all? To prevent it from occurring, or to bring it about? To drive us mad or serve as warning of what 'might have been'?" She leaned back in the chair as Jathen wondered if she knew just how relevant her words were. "No. The truth is far more mundane and simpler: you see what you see *because* you are precognitive—because you were *able* to see it. It is the very definition of the Ability—to see the possibilities of what *may be*."

He squinted, thinking of the little shadow with the familiar voice that'd led him to his vision. "So it's just random?"

"Yes and no. We choose to be born with it, choose to have it, and choose to use it to peer into the ever-flowing river of infinite choices spilling over each other. It, like everything created for this experiment of a world, is not as random as is how we choose to respond to it. We can chase it or be beaten down by it, uplifted or baffled. We can choose to believe it is all put into the hands of fate, saying nothing written can be unwound, or we can hold the examples in our hands, claiming we can shape and mold this world as we choose, for the visions so often change as our choices do."

Jathen bit his lip, wondering if this somehow made his strange night and his meeting with Raleigh make sense. *Perhaps Bron led me there so that she could make a choice, but not for me. Perhaps it simply happened because it could happen. Then again, why was I shown what I was shown by that voice?* He sighed, leveling very serious and tired eyes on Erin Manna that carried the full weight of all that'd been stirring in his mind for weeks on end. "Does it all always, always come back to choice?"

"Yes." She cocked her head, those bright golden eyes softening slightly. "Would you wish to tell me of the choices you've avoided making thus far, Jathen Monortith?"

Jathen coughed a nervous laugh, and something inside him broke, a floodgate of fear and indecision he'd been holding together with sheer willpower and twine. "High Walker Anorna had wanted to see if I could easily look into my past lives and so put me into a light hypnotic state—"

"This triggered a vision," she concluded.

Jathen nodded, all too aware of the slight warble of his lower lip. He wet it, trying to continue without becoming too emotional. He'd told Izzy and Seren before, but this... this *felt* different. Perhaps that was so because he didn't know the Lady Manna very well, or perhaps it was because he sensed she might be able to actually answer things, which both relieved and frightened him to the verge of tears. Swallowing, he managed to continue, "It wasn't typical. Something... hijacked the vision. I don't know what it was: a spirit or ghost or guide.

No one can seem to tell me for certain. But it warned me before, and this time it showed me—" He swallowed again, his mouth dry.

Erin Manna held a hand out to him. "Would you wish to show me?"

Staring at her outstretched palm almost as if he didn't recognize what it was, Jathen then met her eyes. "I'm a Negater—my mind can't be read."

"Not unless you wish it to be. But you are already aware of that fact." She extended her hand farther. "Relax your mind. Allow me in. I shall not seek more than you wish me to see—and you would rather me view it within a heart's beat than have to speak on it for hours more."

Pursing his lips and holding his breath, Jathen listened to the sound of D'ilinde's *hum* inside his chest. *It's all right,* it seemed to say. *We know her.* Taking a deep breath, he nodded and took her hand.

With a flash of light, Jathen relived the nightmare over again.

The second time through wasn't easier. He focused on new deaths, ones he'd missed the first time. A gray-green Tazu in tyrn form sank his teeth into the back of a Jathen wearing red and black then twisted away, ripping and tearing at Jathen's spine. A Jathen in gold and violet hovered, choking, in midair while an invisible force crushed him from both sides and then from the top and bottom, leaving him a square-shaped mass of bloody pulp and smashed bones. On and on it went, and he wanted to jerk away but couldn't, for the petite Manna had a vise grip that would put adult male Tazu to shame. Then came the cataclysm scenes, violent destruction and the end of the world via water, all racing back toward the avalanche coming at Tar'citadel.

When she finally did release him, Jathen pulled back so quickly he set his chair to rocking, and the back of it knocked against the wall. Righting himself, Jathen let a sob escape his lips while the world spun around him.

"I can appreciate your disquiet," Erin Manna whispered, her tone like a cool, uncaring breeze amid his turmoil. "A vision of this magnitude contained a good deal of information to process."

"You seem to be handling it well enough," Jathen replied between gasps.

"I have seen far worse." Her words quelled his irritation, and she leaned back in her chair, giving him a sense of hope. "You were correct. The voice that brought this to you was trying to warn you."

Jathen swallowed, the spinning of the room finally ebbing. "So it was a Guide of mine?"

"No."

"How can you be certain?"

"Because I have spoken to your Guides, and neither of them sounds like your specter."

"Oh." Leaning back in his own chair, Jathen did his best to catch his breath. "Then what is he?"

"A spirit of some sort—perhaps someone who knew you in another life or a Native Near-Sider who has taken an interest in you." She paused slightly, as if considering something, but then dismissed it. "It is not unusual to have more than one random spiritual guardian aside from your Guides. But they are always worth keeping an eye on. What might serve their motives on one day may not serve yours on another."

"You think it could mean me some harm?"

"Not with this. In this, it absolutely was warning you. In other things... well, my visions at the moment tell me that telling you more would do you more harm than good."

Jathen chuckled a slightly envious laugh. "That's a helpful skill for a precognitive, to know what to say or not to say for any given question of destiny."

"For the fate of the world, yes. For the fate of relationships... not always." She stood. "Come. I've decided the first step in how to train you."

Jathen blinked rapidly. "Wait, you mean you didn't know until now?"

"Possibilities, perceptions, and choices, remember? I had to measure them all before deciding." Motioning with a hand, she bade him rise. "Obtain your coat. We venture out for this."

Standing on slightly unsteady legs, Jathen did as bidden. Mildly alarmed but mostly confused, he scuttled as quickly as possible down the street after the petite Clanswoman. *Spirit, she moves fast.* His longer legs were nothing against her Clan speed. "So where are we going?" he asked between ragged breaths.

They passed through the crowd easily as *everyone* gave way to her, even sets of tar'ka-besh.

"And why are we doing this?"

"Because you've yet to pick a Way."

Jathen's heart pounded, and he almost skidded to a stop in the street. "But I thought *you* were training me. The vision—"

"I am training you how to be a Negater, but this still leaves many things that I cannot teach you." Still walking, she gazed back at him, her face a porcelain mask but with soft eyes. "You claimed you sensed a theme throughout your deaths—a lack of skill. By choosing one Way over another, you were somehow lacking. But choosing a nonpartisan education leaves certain other spiritual aspects weakened as well. You need the Ways' support lest you court dangers of *lack* from that end as well."

He jogged a few paces to try to catch up to her. "So you're going to *make* me pick a Way?"

"I can't *make* you do anything, Jathen Monortith. But I can finally lead you to the end point you've been reaching toward and let you make your choice—which is what we are doing." She stopped so suddenly in the street that he nearly plowed right into her. "Do you trust me, Jathen Monortith?"

"Umm..."

"Good," she replied with another subdued smile. "You shouldn't yet, at least not completely. After this outing, I shall either have all your trust or none of it. To train you properly, I need that trust. Do you not agree?"

"I do agree."

She nodded. "Good. Come."

Luckily, they didn't venture too far, heading for one of the townhome complexes on the perimeter of the Temple Citadel. Still, Jathen was a breathless mess when Erin Manna finally scaled the front porch of her chosen house and knocked daintily. Not waiting for an answer or for Jathen to catch his breath, the Lady Manna turned the knob and walked right in.

"Please tell me you know the owner," Jathen practically wheezed, staggering in afterward.

She did not reply.

A man's voice shouted from the depths of the house, "We're in the den, Erin!"

Jathen shot her a pitiful look, and she paused to let him breathe. When he finally felt as if he wasn't going to black out any second, she proceeded forward down a narrow hallway and into the room farthest back in the house. Jathen discovered a cozy den with dark hardwood floors, a thick Walker's star rug in the center, walls painted pale blue, and an overly large stone fireplace.

Four men sat at a round table centered on the rug, jabbering away as they played cards and completely ignoring their arrival. Jathen immediately recognized the High Chancellor, who was wearing the same crisp silver-and-gold robes. The human sitting on Dàshĭ's right looked native to the Tazu Nation and sat tapping two fingers on the arm of his chair, the ebony digits fluttering like frightened sparrows. Like the Chancellor, his robes were equal parts silver and gold, though his were stained slightly at the cuffs with ink. He looked not at his cards but at the man across from him.

"Will you hurry up and bet, Galduran?" he said in a rich Tar'cil, scratching the back of his shaved head. His was the voice that'd called them back. "Waiting for you to sift through every possible combination of future calamities is positively *boring*."

"I am doing no such thing," responded Galduran, the Walker from the spatial room who'd helped Jathen with Raleigh. Tonight, he wore fingerless gloves in a rainbow pattern that matched his fuzzy scarf, along with his usual Montage gold overrobe. Peering through the pair of rimless spectacles propped on the end of his nose, he kept rearranging his cards while little tufts of multicolored fuzz lifted away from the scarf. "These gatherings of ours might be pivotal, but only because of our conversation, not our betting."

"So then why do you take so ruddy long?"

"Because he likes to annoy you, Ophisa," said the man sitting across from Dàshī.

Jathen breathed in sharply—it was the Rosinic he'd met the day he stumbled into the spatial room for the first time.

"He's got it down to a science," the man went on. "The delayed betting bothers you, and the spectacles bother Dàshī."

"And what does he do that bothers you, Si'hir?" Ophisa asked.

"Nothing, but that's because I'm painfully perfect."

Undaunted by their banter, Galduran turned to Chancellor Dàshī, a look of mild shock glowing in his light-gray eyes above his spectacles. "My glasses bother you?"

"Of course they bother him. They ruddy well bother me as well," Ophisa responded.

"Why on the continent would they bother you?"

"Because you don't need them," Dàshī stated evenly but with a superior undercurrent. "Your eyes were healed years ago, so now gazing through them makes everything a blurry mess, which is why you wear them so low. This translates into everything you attempt to achieve taking forever."

"But I *like* my glasses. I've had them *forever*."

"So wear them around your neck or something," Si'hir suggested. "Like a talisman."

"Oh, Si'hir, that isn't the point—I like how I *look* in them."

"Well then take the ruddy lenses out and place a ruddy bet!" Ophisa yelled.

"They're rimless, Ophisa. You can't take the lenses out." Galduran snorted, took a single coin, and tossed it upon the pile. "There, happy?"

"Exuberant." Ophisa brushed a few of the shedding fuzz bits off the table. "I shall sing the praises of the Twelve from the top of all three citadels."

"I don't understand the fuss. It's not like any of us are pressed for *time*." Galduran sniffed.

Erin Manna finally spoke. "Gentlemen."

"Evening, Lady Manna, Prince Jathen." The High Chancellor waved nonchalantly at them, not turning around. "I had wondered when you would take advantage of our standing invitation, Erin, and come play with us."

"My work in the High Court has been mildly diverting enough to keep me away, though now I have the excuse of a student to bring myself to the city, and thus am I available for diversions such as these." Turning to Jathen, she fielded the more formal introductions. "Might I present Galduran, High Walker of Montage; Ophisa, Headmaster of Tar'citadel University; and you've met the High Chancellor previously."

"And as I told you before, I don't have a title," Si'hir said on his own behalf. "Because having a title means I've come dangerously close to having responsibilities, and that is a direct threat of me having to do *work*."

"Oh, ignore his posturing. He was the High Walker of Rosin for nearly four centuries," Ophisa clarified. "He just got ruddy sick of them and so retired last decade."

"Best Red-be-damned thing I ever did."

"Four hundred years?" Jathen asked, the realization slowly dawning.

"Oh, ho ho, Erin, you sly little vixen. You didn't tell him." Galduran chuckled then winked at Jathen.

Glancing at Dàshī, Jathen suddenly understood. "You're all High Mages."

"That we are, though we used to be five up until a few years back, when Sharhara decided to ascend out," Si'hir said.

"When an immortal has lived long enough and has grown tired of life, they can choose to just 'walk out' of their body and ascend to the far-side of the Veil," Galduran clarified to Jathen's concerned expression. "She'd gone up over a millennium, and I think for her, that was a sufficient amount of life."

"Too many card games, I imagine," Dàshī muttered.

Jathen bit his lip. "She committed suicide?"

"No, it's not so self-destructive as that. It's more akin to having realized she'd learned as much as she could within her current body and was ready to move on to another reincarnation," Galduran said. "The Clan do somewhat similar as well, if I'm not mistaken, yes, Erin?"

"You are correct."

"Thank Rhean they do, or the continent would be crawling with them," Dàshī commented then amended in a more affable tone, "No disrespect to your personage, Erin. Nor Orrick's."

"No offense taken, Chancellor," Erin said with silken smoothness. "I, in all honesty, agree with your sentiment. To be Clan is to be a magnifying glass upon humanity. All we do is of greater glory or disreputable deviltry. The world is far better for having a limited population of my race, lest our failings disrupt too many corners of it."

"Well, then, now that we've established that even Erin Manna dislikes Feron Rheadani's recent stupidities, let us get on with the game," Si'hir said, much to Jathen's mild bafflement. Si'hir smiled at him, making him wonder if the High Mage was aware of his confusion despite attempts to mask his reactions. "Do you play jimble, son?"

"Terribly."

"Well, that's all right, take a seat anyways," Galduran said, scooting his own chair over to make room for two new chairs materializing out of nowhere. "No one can read your mind, so you'll at least not be at a disadvantage as a Negater."

"Certainly not. I've been prodding him telepathically since he came in, and once again, he hasn't so much as flinched," Si'hir declared. "*Impressive.*"

"That is so *rude*!" Galduran gasped, horrified as Jathen made himself comfortable next to Erin Manna.

"Oh, you have no room to judge after you let Raleigh prod at him for weeks," Si'hir retorted.

"He has a point there," Jathen added.

"I apologized for that," Galduran replied, looking legitimately regretful. "But in all fairness, she could have been correct. And if she had been, her actions were viable. But since she wasn't, I put a stop to it."

"Anyone could have just asked me," Dàshī pointed out. "Jathen was very clearly not an Aspect, from where I was sitting."

"You were sitting pretty much in De'contes's *lap* after that damn assassination attempt," Si'hir said with a triumphant sneer.

Dàshī arched an eyebrow but said nothing, staring down the other High Mage with a stony countenance Jathen wagered would make even marble statues flinch if exposed long enough.

Finally, Si'hir shrugged, undaunted. "Fine, fine, I'm certain Jathen here has had far worse as a moot from the Tazu Nation."

"Hear, hear," Ophisa said, dealing the cards. His dark eyes met Jathen's with a depth of understanding. "I grew up with those ruddy lizards. They are *crazy*."

"Vermeilith wasn't too bad," Galduran said. Jathen's memory swirled, recalling the name of Kyanith's uncle, the king who preceded him to the throne.

"Vermeilith Monortith was a good five hundred years *after* my time there." Ophisa sniffed then turned to tell Jathen, "And before you ask or try the math, I don't remember how old I am. Somewhere in the twelve-hundred range, I think."

"You were born in 7829," Lady Manna said, her hands folded neatly beneath the table on her lap. "So, in truth, you are only one thousand one hundred and thirty years old."

"So I rounded up." Ophisa laughed. "How the ruddy hell did you remember that, my Lady Manna?"

"The tenth Avatar of Rhean took the throne that year," Dàshī answered.

"And how do *you* remember *that*?" Ophisa asked.

"Because he's old as sin," Si'hir drawled.

"The tenth Avatar of Rhean was the first one I met," Dàshī clarified. "It was also my first trip to Clana-Ca'sta and my first introduction to Erin." He folded his cards. "And if I am as old as sin, then what does that make our dear Lady Manna? You need to temper your courtesy, Si'hir."

"She knows I meant no offence."

"That doesn't always excuse discourtesy."

The rest of the card game went by without deeper incident—at least, as far as Jathen could follow—full of squabbling, cursing, threats of *real* curses being placed, and accusations of cheating or using precognition, all spouted out in a playful, harmless sort of banter. What Jathen did discover was, for the most part, these were men—powerful, incomprehensible men who'd seen ages he couldn't fathom, but they weren't perfect, timeless beings with boundless Abilities and bottomless wisdom. They were messy and real and not at all as intimidating as he'd once thought. *Or as infallible. If I were immortal, any of these men could just as easily be me at this table.* Jathen swallowed. The thought was both comforting and alarming.

Erin Manna ended up winning the final pot against Ophisa and Dàshī, which, for some reason, got a round of hysterical laughter from Si'hir, who rocked so far back that his chair fell over—though the man disappeared entirely before it clattered onto the floor.

"Well, I suppose that calls it for the night, then," Galduran proclaimed. Standing, he pushed his glasses back up his nose. "My townhome next week, then?"

"Only if you serve those little cake things again," Ophisa replied, still seated as Jathen and the others stood.

"I shall do my best to conjure the recipe from my memory."

"Good. Next week, then." Standing, he waved his hand, and the whole table, chairs, and cards set disappeared, sans Lady Erin's winnings, which remained hovering.

The Lady Manna put a hand up and shook her head. "Put it in the university coffers. I've no need."

"Neither does the university, to be truthful," the headmaster replied with a laugh. The pile of gold and silver disappeared. "I'll find a worthy cause that does."

"Obliged," she said with a nod.

"Next week, gentlemen," Dàshī said. "Lovely to see you as well, Erin. I do hope you can make the time again—though I have a feeling it will be later than sooner."

"Sadly. But I will attend again when in the city."

He nodded then disappeared as well.

"So rude, those two," Galduran muttered. A long coat of tan leather with emerald buttons appeared in his hand, and he pulled it on as he began to exit. "Didn't even bother to see you two to the door."

"It's not their house, Gald," Ophisa replied, following Jathen, Erin Manna, and the other High Mage back to the foyer. He chuckled then patted Jathen on the shoulder. "Putter yourself over to the university sometime this week and sit in on a class or two. My assistant will see you get the schedule for the one-day lectures."

Jathen blinked repeatedly at him then exchanged a curious glance with Erin Manna, who nodded. "Thank you," he replied. "I think I'd like that."

"Thought so. Oh, and please also bring along that little Exemplary Talent I've heard is on your heels. He'd benefit from getting around a few peers, I think."

"I shall. I think Spinnek would actually enjoy it as well."

"Very good." He grinned, waving to them as they stepped off the front step. "Good night!"

Back in the street, Jathen smiled knowingly at High Walker Galduran. "Why didn't you tell me who you were, the first time we met?"

"Well, you didn't ask, firstly." The High Mage and head of Montage shrugged, still buttoning up his coat. "And secondly, I was under the impression you weren't terribly inclined to accept any Way help at the time."

"At the time, no," Jathen admitted with a begrudging chuckle. Glancing at Erin Manna, he had a feeling, a *sense*, that perhaps it was safe now. He'd truly found the correct balance. He turned back to

Galduran. "I suppose you want me to putter by your office as well at some point?"

"If you like." He shrugged again. "To be honest, you've already been there twice, and there isn't a great deal to discuss Way-wise, really. You were raised in Montage. You know the doctrine quite well. Since you are a Negater, I suppose I can work with Erin to schedule you with the other Ways to settle what you'd want to learn from them, but as you've already done most of that on your own, it's really just formality at this point. Though I admit I can probably quell some of the political mumblings if you'd like. Other than that, I can't imagine you want to be a full Walker, so I'd suggest just going along as a typical Montage follower would. We're here if you need us."

Jathen arched an eyebrow, bemused at himself for avoiding Montage for so long. "And that's it?"

He smirked. "If you want fanfare, I could bother Volaille and have her round up a few Beleskie Walkers to throw some sort of party—"

Putting his hands up, Jathen stifled a laugh. "No, no. That's fine, thank you."

"As I thought." He winked. "You have a good night, Jathen. I'll make certain to say hello to Hausmannith for you in my next letter."

Jathen shook his head, only somewhat surprised. "I suppose he sends you tea too?"

"No, just tidbits and updates of the progress of the prince I'd been so concerned about."

Jathen stiffened somewhat despite himself. "And you're not concerned now?"

"Nowhere near as much." He put his hands in his pockets, leaving the thumbs out. "Erin here will tell you better than anyone else in the continent—precognition is not an exact science. Far from it. I see the longer game, always have. I nudge, I whisper, but I don't push. I know too little, see too little, to push."

"Well, for what it's worth, thank you for sending Hausmannith. He was a beacon of comfort and rationality when I needed it." Jathen put his own hands in his pockets. "And admittedly, his has been one of the voices in the back of my head, guiding."

"As he was meant to be. Good night, Jathen." With that, the man teleported out.

"Well." Jathen fell back into step with Erin Manna, who was keeping a slower pace. "That was enlightening."

"As it was meant to be." She seemed pleased, but several things still nagged at Jathen.

Taking a tentative breath, he asked, "Back there, at the beginning, Si'hir mentioned Feron Rheadani doing something so stupid that even you didn't approve. What, then, did he mean?"

Lady Erin remained quiet a moment, her bright eyes focused forward in the night. "The Emperor has been entertaining the idea of moving the capital of the Clan Lands from Clana-Ca'sta to the new city his father had built up on the border of Lubreean. This has not been... well received."

Perhaps fatigue had set in, for it was late, or perhaps all the banter of the evening had worn him out, but Jathen just couldn't fathom the depths of such an idea. All he could grasp was a *sense*, a swirl of emotions and turmoil bubbling up inside his head. *Empathic Ability or precognition? Either way, this seems bad.* "Back when we first left Kidwellith, Hatori had told me that a civil war was brewing in the Clan Lands," he ventured. "Is it... is it really going to come to that?"

"Jathen, I have lost count of how many times I've seen the *possibility* of civil war in my country. Some possibilities will always be there, threatening at the corners of our vision or poised to strike out from the curve of a shadow. All one can do is be as water, malleable and ready. Anything else invites madness. You understand?"

"Don't worry about it until it is actually a problem." He smirked. "Like the vision of my deaths and picking a Way."

"Precisely." Her gold eyes caught the lamplight, sparkling bright in the night. "Besides, I have also learned that for every time the possibility for disaster is there, a hundred alternatives resolve themselves whether we are privy to them or not in visions. Despite what many might claim, the world does follow a pattern, and that is to evolve. Even from its most wicked of falls."

"But then why would Si'hir ask you about it? As a High Mage, wouldn't he already understand such things?"

"Ah. Si'hir fears, as many do, that a civil war in the Clan Lands would affect *all* Clan on the continent, including those living in his homeland of Aralim. There is already a concern that civil war there is an inevitability over the next generation or so. I will not bore you so late with the politics of it, but Clan in Aralim are few and powerful, and if they were to retreat home or take some side in Aralim that they would not have otherwise, it could affect the landscape of that country greatly. His desire tonight was to see if I would divulge some vision of either doom or assurance so some decision might be made. He may be of Rosin, but his tumultuous homeland is not far from his heart, even after so many years."

Jathen's fingers found the ends of his sleeves, fiddling with the little bumps of stitching there. Hatori had many times told him of how Clan could be considered an infestation in other countries, but it somehow disturbed him more to hear one of their Originals admit just how much her people could alter a history. "Why didn't you? Offer him some vision, that is?"

"After all I've told you, you cannot guess?"

"Anything you would have told him would alter the timeline of what might be and thus possibly cause more problems than it solved." He shook his head, smiling lightly. "Or you just don't know. Not with a certainty."

"Yes. Si'hir might be a High Mage, but he is not precognitive. It is a delicate art, hard to explain to even the most knowledgeable Talent."

"As Galduran said." Jathen arched an eyebrow. "Then there is a difference between a 'long view' and a 'short view' with precognition, as he also hinted."

"Of course. Short can mean the difference between blocking left or right in battle, while long views—well, let us just say I am an expert in far-flung futures."

Jathen nodded. He believed that after what she'd done tonight to counter his doom-filled prophecy at last. "But not short."

She did not answer, asking instead, "How would you summarize the events of this first session of my tutelage? And what lessons have you learned?"

"Well..." Jathen pondered the depths of the evening for a moment. "Tonight, you've put me into a position where not only did I finally admit that I follow a Way for the most part, but I also learned a great deal about precognition, my oldest and most turbulent Ability. You put some *sense* to a vision that was tearing my soul apart. And you put me in a room with the most powerful men in the world—showing me that while I'm not anywhere near their equal, I can function amid those far higher than myself with a moderate amount of aptitude—and proved to me that despite the morbid destiny I saw, it really isn't all up to *me* to prevent what I saw, for I'm not the only one seeing the future, and thus everything changes just from the act of seeing. And it also looks as if you've managed to put me in a position where I'm even taking classes at the university without having to formally enroll and become indebted to Tar'citadel, further squelching the circumstances which would lead to my 'deaths.'" He sighed long, impressed. "You were right. That did earn my trust."

Erin Manna smiled the widest he'd seen, her delicate fangs shining bright in the night. "This was only the *first* lesson, Jathen. There is far more to go."

Jathen breathed in the crisp cold of the night air, feeling a loosening of the tension he'd been carrying between his shoulders for the first time since being named a Negater. "I actually find myself looking forward to it."

Epilogue

For the Prophet.

Yala resisted the urge to whisper the words aloud, since managing her tasks was difficult enough, with the way the charm-engineers cast glances her way every other heartbeat. Still, her heart waxed glad as she removed her hand from the slab of ice and nonchalantly slipped her glove from her pocket.

"Girl!"

She started slightly, pulling her brown bangs out of her eyes as she spun around. The head charm-engineer stood in the center hallway of the melting station, his hands on his hips and glaring. The energy manipulator looked older than his forty years. So much time out on the glacier had weathered his skin and bleached his hair, giving him a rosy yet sour mien. He huffed again, breath frosting in a little puff that floated around his fur-lined coat collar like tobacco smoke.

Yala blinked at him a few times. Or'sen had said her youth was her best asset, and making people underestimate her would probably save her life should she get into a tight spot. That had already worked decently on that Negater, so she wasn't going to stop.

"Yes, sir?" she asked innocently.

"What did I tell you about touching the ice?" he barked.

"That even though the melting stations are melting it, it's still cold enough to give you frostbite if you touch it barehanded."

Putting her hands behind her back, she rocked a few times on her feet, playing up the fact that she'd be barely old enough to enroll in the First-Tier of Tar'citadel University if she hadn't had the misfortune of being born first in the Middle Lands. "I'm sorry. But it doesn't hurt my hands." She held the bare one up and stopped rocking, showcasing her unblemished fingers. "See? Ice mages don't get bothered by ice."

Rubbing a gloved hand over his face, the Talent sighed. "Girl, the *only* reason you are being allowed up here is to help us clear the snowbanks using that weird Ability of yours that lets you do it without melting it. Otherwise, this is absolutely no place for a child to be puttering about." He gave her a sharp glare as Yala assumed another comment he'd kept to himself: *"And especially being one of those damn Balori."*

Of course, Yala wasn't officially a Balori, which was why the tar'ka-besh were taking a chance on the wide-eyed twelve-year-old ice mage to help at the melting stations. *But this one suspects,* she thought, imagining shoving ice shards into the man's eyes. *But not enough. You have no idea what I'm capable of, Way Follower.* She worried at the bottom of her lip while twisting the one glove back and forth.

"I'm sorry. I just... I like ice. And I've been waiting here forever. I thought you said you wanted me up on the mountain today." She shrugged. "I can't move the snow if I'm not *at* the snow."

He made a gruff sound in the back of his throat. "Get back to the others, and you'll get teleported up soon. Got to wait for the sun to do the first wave of our work. Protocols are still protocols, no matter what Ability you have. Got it?"

"Yes." She grinned, finally slipping her glove back onto her hand.

Turning around, she could still feel his eyes following her as she walked back toward the observation deck, the gaze as prevalent as the *hum* of the melting charm-engines. Admittedly, Yala admired their glorious work, turning literal tons of snow into a gigantic ice levee meant to protect the city. It was a feat of true engineering brilliance, the likes of which she could never have conceived, not even being as predisposed to ice magic as she was.

It's almost a shame to think of it all demolished. Picking up a tune, she hummed as well, the tones of her song harmonizing with the charm-engines' buzz. *For the Prophet.*

And for Nan.

Author's Note

G ods, this one was hard.

I'm going to first explain that this book, *Tainted Talent*, started off as the middle section of what had originally been intended to be one book, *Broken Cities*, which covered Jathen's time in Dodbyen, Tar'citadel, and the upcoming Tarshishum in Aralim. However, it got too big, and I decided to split it into three books instead. But as things worked out, trying to take a middle section of a book with no direct plot arc except for character development and turn it into a book that must stand on its own is, well, hard. Really hard. Thusly, it took a really, really long time to write, and then it was way too long to publish for my small publisher. So we split Jathen's time in Tar'citadel again. This ragtag adventure of Jathen's is still making its way forward, just at a much jerkier pace than anticipated. All I can say is thank you for reading, thank you for taking a chance, thank you for being patient, and thank you for continuing to hang in here with me. More fun is coming, I promise.

Literally thank you to everyone who has put up with me through this crazy time of working on this while moving, cleaning out houses, selling a house, buying a house, moving again, adopting another cat, losing my doggo Nala, and actually having a baby (almost all at the same time, because why not?). It's been an incredibly stressful and tiresome five years, and I'm just so grateful for the few who have stuck by me through it.

You know who you are. ?
J. Leigh ~ May 2020

Glossary

A **Ability:** term referring to magical or supernatural aptitude, classified formally into five major categories: empathy (emotional or energy), medium (emotional or visual), telepathy, precognition, and energy manipulative.

Akira, Master: Way Walker of Rosin, head of matter deconstruction.

Altaiss: a Tazu of Dodbyen.

Angani: the Child that represents the Way of Purity. Also see **Pearl Dragon**.

Angel Guide: a Guide attached to a mortal soul that has never been born to a physical body itself; they watch their Charge and offer advice and spiritual guidance.

Annarite: the race of the Red and natural inhabitants of the Middle Lands. Known also as "the Tainted."

Annesi: meaning "mother" in Aralic, the title *Anziz* means "one who is so sacred they are beyond reproach" in Aralim culture.

Anorna: High Walker of Feator.

Antqāl Mdynh: "moving city." The native Msāfryan name for the city of Zo'den.

Aralim: the Nation founded by Angani followers. Shares a border with the Tazu Nation.

A'ron De'contes: former Red follower/Red Mage and head of the Balori order of the Red. He is also responsible for the murders of Yvette Ashton; the last Avatar of Rhean, Car'son des Rheadani de la Rhean; and the Aspect of Rhean, Bolynne des Rheadani de la Ra'vien.

Ascended: term referring to an Incarnation of one of the Children that has Awakened and come into their full power.

Aspect: term referring to the "other side" of each of the Twelve Children. They are the Incarnations of the Children's twin-flames.

Ass'shiri Tan: Way Walker, Path of the Kasior, part of Setsu's crew.

Avatar: term referring to the Awakened and Ascended Incarnation of one of the Children—the mortal body of the Child Awakened.

Avenea: the chosen race of Feator and residents of the country Casfeild. They are characterized by an almost turtlelike appearance, with bonelike plates covering their arms and legs and a shell-like plate coving a large portion of their backs.

Awakened: term referring to souls, usually Avatars, who remember more than one lifetime of experiences. An Awakened Avatar usually indicates full memory of all their past lives.

B

Balori: the Balori movement is a divergent Path amid the Red that believes the Red went mad and must be brought back to Spirit.

Bawan: a Beleskie Way Path that specializes in matchmaking.

Beleskie: Rose Quartz Dragon, Child of Love and Relationships.

Bertrandith Larsenitiss: Royal Adviser to the King's Office, heir to the Larsenitiss house, and Kyanith Monortith's youngest son.

Bolynne des Rheadani de la Ra'vien: historical figure of the Clan Lands, the last Awakened Aspect of Rhean. Murdered by A'ron De'contes.

Born, Born Clan: a term referring to Clan that were born vampiric Clan, versus a human that was Changed into Clan.

bound: Tazu unit of measurement, equal to one mile.

Bree: Child of Creativity, the Amber Dragon.

Bron: Aspect of Bree, he who embodies application while Bree embodies inspiration.

C

Car'son des Rheadani de la Rhean: historical figure, the last Avatar of Rhean to Walk and be emperor of the Clan Lands. Murdered by A'ron De'contes.

Casfeild: a country on the southern border of Tar'citadel and home to the Avenea race. Founded by the Avatar of Feator.

Cathiny Mountains: the highest, longest mountain range on the continent.

Cathiny River: river running beside the Cathiny Mountains.

Changed: term describing those who have been changed into Clan. (Humans are the only race able to be Changed.)

Charge: term referring to the soul that Spirit Guides are assigned to watch and look after.

charm: a magical item, usually a crystal or metal, created to hold a certain spell within itself. Usually very small and meant for singular personal use. See also: processer-charm, master-charm, or charm-device.

charm-device: a more complex version of a master-charm. An object that uses a charm spell or multiple charm spells in order to activate a third-party device. It is usually small to medium in size and meant for personal use. See also: charm, processer-charm, or master-charm.

Charm Master: a maker of master-charms.

Children, the: see also **The Twelve**. They represent twelve facets of Spirit and incarnate again and again to teach their different Ways to evolve the souls of mortals to once again become one with Spirit.

Chūjitsun: a manservant in Annakki's household.

Citra: Tazu female born in Dodbyen, peach-scaled with pale-yellow hair and pale-green eyes.

Clan: the vampiric race of the Clan Lands.

Clan Lands: one of the largest countries on the continent and home of both human and Clan. Founded by Rhean.

Clevelandith Freibergith Grandidieriss: Father of Dolomith Monortith.

crystal-recorder: a charm-device usually including a recorder crystal, used to record information. See also: recorder crystal.

Cyaone D. Ja'han: historical figure, author of *Lost in the Landscape*.

Cy'shā: empathic and precognitive Talent for Setsu's crew, wife to Hkym.

D

Dàshī Jidoja: High Mage merged with the element of air. Elected High Chancellor of Tar'citadel.

Daughter of Desmoulein: a Way Path of Desmoulein, healers and doctors.

death marker: also just called a "marker," it indicates, in a life contract, one of the seven times a person might "exit a lifetime" or die.

demon: an incorporeal spirit that feeds on negative emotions. There are hundreds of different types of demons of varying strengths and powers, as well as dozens of different classifications of intelligence.

Desmoulein: the Child whose Way is the Way of the Healer; the Emerald Dragon.

D'ilinde: Msāfryan name for the Grand Artifact of Bree and Bron.

Dodbyen: one of the Kinawan "floating cities," lost during one of the last battles of the War of Truth.

Dolomith Monortith: son of Rhodonith Monortith and Clevelandith Freibergith Grandidieriss. Prince of the blood and possible heir to the King of the Tazu Nation's throne. Baby half brother of Thee and Jathen.

Drannic: a very mysterious race, rarely seen and said to harbor the secrets of the Children. They resemble Tazu but have wings and tails and do not shift into dragons.

Dresden, High Walker: High Walker of Angani in Tar'citadel.

E

elemental empathy: not to be confused with Empathic, elemental empathy falls under the Ability category of Energy Manipulative and refers to an above-average ability to draw in the vibrational energy of a particular element.

empathy, Empathic: a person's sensitivity to the constantly moving energy fields around them, also known as the near-side of the Veil. Occurs in two types: emotional empathy, with which one can sense the emotions of things; and energy empathy, with which one can feel only the shift in the energies. Having both refers to a True Empathic. An Empathic is someone who has one or both types of empathy.

Enillydd, Master: Walker of Kubesh, head of the tesagree Way Path.

Erin Manna: historical figure, one of the eight Originals of the Clan race. She and her husband Marin Manna were the founders of the Mannachi clan.

Esop: a Ki'ra, Walker of Kubesh, part of Setsu's crew.

F

Fallen One: an arch-demon, one of the most powerful spiritual minions of the Red.

Fauni: a Way path of Turin, specializing in the usage of a golem.

Feator: Child whose Way is the Way of History, the Bronze Dragon. He covers not only written history but also past lives.

Feed: Clan term referring to the drinking of blood for sustenance.

Fersmannith Chertith: current head of the Chertith house, son of Halith Chertith and uncle to Serendibiss Chertith.

Furōrin-Iki: from "furora" for "flora," "shinrin" for "forest," and "iki" for "breathers." Name of the country/region where the Nijū-Iki live.

G

Galduran, High Walker: High Mage merged with the element of air. Serves as High Walker of Montage in Tar'citadel.

Galena Torberniss: Lady of the Torberniss bloodline, sister of Arsenopyrith Torberniss.

Genthelvith Proustith Attieth: Thee's paternal grandmother and namesake; Dicinith's mother.

Grays: a group of Clansmen who hunt Red followers in the Clan Lands outside of the Way orders.

Great Fall, the: also the "Fall of the Red" and "War between the Veils." Refers to when the Red whispered in the ear of Prothidian Altar and together destroyed the Old World. It was Rhean who finally threw the Red back into the Pit, and for a thousand years, the survivors hid underground before resettling the new Continent.

Great Gate: One built in each of the twelve countries' capitols, the Great Gates allow for small groups to teleport from their respective capitols into Tar'citadel.

Guide(s): Angel or Spirit Guides that are attached to mortal souls. They are usually in pairs and are spiritual "assistants" to mortal souls while they are in body.

Gwydion Trahern: Serendibiss Chertith's father.

H

Halfling: Clan term referring to a child whose parentage is half Born-Clan and half human.

Halith Chertith: female head of the Chertith house, grandmother to Serendibiss Chertith, and close friend of Genthelvith Proustith Attieth.

Hatori Chann: Clansman Charm Master for the Monortith family.

Hausmannith: High Montage Walker of the Montage Temple in Kidwellith.

Hauyne: a light-blue-scaled, silver-blue-eyed Tazu from Dodbyen. A relative of Spinelith, he took issue with the leniency given to Rhyo.

Havnebyen: sky city to which Sannhet Rørt is beholden in northern Kinawa.

head: Tazu unit of measurement, equal to six scales or one foot.

High Mage: a powerful elemental empathic Talent that has undergone a ritual to fuse themselves forever with their element. This process makes them physically immortal and incapable of becoming "drained" of energy with which to cast.

high magic: magic that is far more complex than typical energy manipulative work; usually it involves multiple elements of ritual and artifacts to supplement the work.

Hkym: Medium for Setsu's crew, husband to Cy'shā.

I

Iki: a shortened term for the word Nijū-Iki.

Incarnation: a Child reborn into a body that has not Awakened or Ascended.

Ishane: Way Walker, Path of the Mei at Véridique Meison.

Ishim: meaning "incarnated souls" or "angels of the material world." A general term referring to any spiritual soul incarnated into a body as a person.

iungo plant: meaning "connector" or "bridge," an empathic, energy-manipulating plant created by Prothidian Altar to bridge the gap between non-Talents and Ability-driven devices. Variations of it also carry power, sound, and a variety of other currents in a manner similar to electrical wire.

Izzy: a fauni from the Tazu Nation.

J

Ja'heir Mountains: the *V*-shaped mountain range of the Clan Lands.

Jathen Cornetith Iridosmine Monortith: prince of the blood and heir to the king of the Tazu Nation's throne.

Jephue: Romantic and business partner to Hatori Chann.

Jiāojīn, High Walker: the head of the Way of Rosin.

Jörŏ: historical figure, one of the supposed Incarnations of Ulic, Child of Truth during the War of Truth.

K

ka'moya: Way Path, Rheanic messengers.

kasior: Way Path of Rhean, crossbow snipers.

Kidwellith: Capital city of the Tazu Nation.

Ki'ra: a race resembling humans mixed with a menagerie of bears, large canines, and large felines. Native to the nation of Nor'wah.

Kriger, High Walker: High Walker of Kubesh in Tar'citadel.

Kubesh: the Citrine Dragon of the Children, Way of the Warrior.

Kyanith Monortith: king of the Tazu Nation.

L

Laws of Heaven: the five laws of Spirit: Do not impede upon the free will of another. Do no harm. Do not deny Spirit. Respect all the Ways and find your place amongst them. Respect all physical forms of Spirit.

length: Tazu unit of measurement, equal to twelve heads, twelve feet.

life('s) contract: the "terms" that each soul agrees to before being born into the world as a person. It supposedly covers everything from birthplace and parents to major life lessons and contains all the possible paths and choices a soul can have presented to them while they are alive.

life ladder: the actual genetic code that maps certain aspects of the life's contract.

Lubreean: country to the southwest of the Clan Lands, home of the Muilan and founded by Rosin.

Lu'shun: Beleskie's chosen race. All of them have bright-blue eyes and hair, but the rest of what they appear to be is dependent on who is looking at them. Whoever looks upon a Lu'shun will see a person of their own race reflected back.

M

mage: more common term referring to an Energy Manipulative Talent, often indicates one not trained as a Way Walker.

Mağrur, Master: Way Walker of Angani, head of the Pearl Paladin order.

Marin Manna: historical figure, one of the Original eight Clan. He and his wife Erin Manna founded the Mannachi clan.

master-charm: created when multiple charm-spells are infused into a singular charm. They are usually more complex and involve more magical and energy work to be created. See also: charm, charm-device, or processer-charm.

Matamir: in Sister's employment, one of several agents of the Shadow Court she brought over to her side.

Mei, Mei Path: a Way Path of Beleskie that focuses on the physical aspect of interpersonal relationships.

meison: temple and home of mei.

Middle Lands: the Land of the Red, it is a province sitting in the middle of the Continent that is not quite an official country.

Mikkal Lan'chi: a member of the Grays in the Clan Lands; powerful Energy Manipulative Talent.

Monortith: the royal family of the Tazu Nation.

Montage: the Gold Dragon of the Children, whose Way tries to merge the teachings of all the Ways in order to create an "Ultimate Way."

moot: Tazu children born looking human and lacking the ability to shift to a dragon form.

Msāfryan: meaning "travelers," proper name for the people that live in the Zo'den territory, encompassing both the human and Tyr'sat populations.

Muilan: Rosin's chosen race, they are a semi-incorporeal people, capable of "phasing" in and out of the physical plane for brief periods.

N

Nai'dol: meaning "to cry sorrow," a new river in the Tazu Nation formed from the earthquake. From "naite," meaning "to cry," and "dolor," meaning "sorrow."

Neek: shaman for the iki settlement.

Nevershen Supai: Clansman and Rheanic Walker in Tar'citadel.

Nijū-Iki: meaning "double breath" or "dual breathers," the plant hybrid race that live in the Furōrin-Iki. See also: Iki.

Nor'wah: the country north of the Clan Lands, home to the Ki'ra race and founded by Kubesh.

Nosalia, Lady: Clanswoman resident of Fauve in the Lu'shun Republic, patron of the arts and historical excavation.

O

Obsidian Dragon: see: Rhean.

old soul: a soul that has incarnated a massive amount of times, not necessarily going the furthest back in history.

Ophisa, High Mage: Headmaster of Tar'citadel University, merged with the element of earth.

Originals, the: the first eight vampires who gave rise to the race known as Clan; four couples who founded the four Great Clans.

Orrick Ashton: a Clan Original, he and his wife Yvette founded the Ashoni clan and the Ashton bloodline.

Or'sen: an Annarite amid the Balori; friend of Nannazen.

P

Pallotos Nuummith: Moot captain of the dirigible *Charmed Wind*.

Path: also "Way Path," one of the different orders and classes under each Way.

Pearl Dragon: Angani, one of the Twelve Children—she represents purity.

Petalith: personal Daughter of Desmoulein for the Monortith family.

Phine, Phine Path: Way Path of Beleskie, focusing on psychological study and counseling services.

Pit, the: banishment place of the Red, a dimension even deeper than Hell. Also the birthplace of all demons.

Plajă, High Walker: Head of the Way of Bree in Tar'citadel.

processer-charm: the most complex of the charmed objects; charm-devices that are used to absorb one type of energy and then put out another type of energy, spell, or information. See also: charm, master-charm, or charm-device.

Prothidian Altar: historical figure, supposedly imprisoned beneath one of the capitals. The first Red Mage, he is responsible for both destroying the world and then reseeding it with his own creations, including many of the current races.

R

ral: Old Clan word for "bad" or "nasty." Ral snakes are black and green and are the deadliest animal on the continent in terms of venom.

Raudur: a Clansman from the sky-city Dodbyen. He was first maimed horribly by Marcasith after murdering Marc's mate and child. He was thought dead but emerged during the descent of Dodbyen and was killed by Jathen.

Ra'vien: formal name of the Aspect of Rhean, known also as "the Punisher" or "Shadow Bird," represented by a dark-feathered phoenix. Hers is the task of dispensing spiritual justice.

recorder crystal: a single charm usually made from a quartz crystal, used to record information. See also: crystal recorder.

Red, the: The Red Dragon, the Fallen One, the disgraced Child. His way represents a Way that turns from Spirit's laws and is commonly known as the Way of Evil.

Red Mage: powerful Talents that have given the Red a piece of their soul; the effect of this actually fuses them with both the elements of fire and air, unlike High Mages, who are fused with only one. Immortal of body and very, very dangerous.

Red Star: the prophesied signal that time is "up" and the Red shall be freed from the Pit if the world is too evil.

Red Tide: historical event where a hundred Red Mages attacked half of the Continent during a search for Prothidian Altar.

Rhe'don: another formal title for the High Walker of Rhean.

Rhean: the Obsidian Dragon of the Children, Way of the Protector.

Rhodonith Monortith: Queen of the Tazu Nation and mother of Jathen and Thee.

Rosin: the Amethyst Dragon, whose Way is the Way of Magic. Also called the "Mistress of Mages."

S

Sacora Rheadani: Hatori's deceased wife.

Sal'mar: an Annarite warrior in Sister's service, uses the *kusarigma* as a weapon of choice.

Sanbarna: the "true children" of Dodbyen.

sangcordis: the organ in Clan bodies that regulates blood intake. It is located in the chest between the lungs and heart, with an attachment to the esophagus.

sangui mandat: "blood command," a powerful Ability of the Originals and Rhean to forcibly compel any Clansperson to follow their orders.

scale: Tazu unit of measurement, equal to two inches.

Scmit: half-blood Tazu female born in Dodbyen, gray scaled and white haired with dark-blue eyes.

second sight: another term for Medium Ability, meaning to see spirits and spiritual beings.

Serendibiss Iolith Chertith: Seren's mother and the Tazu Nation ambassador to Tar'citadel. Nicknamed "Seri."

Serendibiss Spheniss Chertith: Thee's best friend, nicknamed "Seren."

Setsuken Daten: Way Walker, Tesgree Path. Leader of a mercenary group in Zo'den.

Shandi: Way Path of Turin. The meaning of the word is "spirit movers." They are the primary Path of Turin and serve as mediums, performing the majority of funeral rites and assisting the dead in crossing over to the far-side of the Veil.

Si'hir, High Mage: merged with the element of air, served as High Walker of Rosin previous to Jiāojīn. Retired, does his best to do as little as possible.

Simpsoniss Chertith: cousin to Marcasith and Kyanith Monortith, uncle of Fersmannith Chertith.

Skaniss Malachith: Captain of the Monortith Royal Guard.

slaga: pack beast in the Tazu Nation, similar to large salamanders.

slikan: follower of the Path of Ulic, trained to delve into minds and find the truth for the various justice systems of the continent.

Solki: Turin's chosen race, they are sexless and inhumanly strange, feeding only off of the emotional energy of fear and pain.

soul-circle: a group of soul-mates that incarnate together often.

soul-mate: a term used for souls that choose to incarnate together often, sometimes as friends, sometimes as lovers, sometimes as family, and often changing roles.

Spirit: the recognized God of the Way Walkers, the eternal consciousness that all souls return to once evolved enough.

Spirit Guide: a Guide attached to a mortal soul that has been born to physical body itself; it watches its Charge and offers advice and spiritual guidance.

T

Ta'ekni: Aspect of Kubesh, she is the embodiment of strategy.

Taint: the evil influence of the Red that interferes with the soul's evolution, often manifested in large amounts of anger, fear, sorrow, arrogance, or even full-blown psychotic behaviors. To be Tainted is to be under the influence of Taint. Also, "the Tainted" describes the race of the Annarite. Can also manifest in an environment; places where extreme violence has occurred are often Tainted.

Talent: a person with more than one measurable classification of the five Abilities. General Talent describes most empathics or low-level mediums, Classic Talent describes the empathic-telepathic combination, True Talent is reserved for people who have at least three combined Abilities, and Exemplary Talent refers to a Talent with measurable levels of all five Abilities. The term "Nontraditional Talent" refers to those Abilities and combinations that don't readily fit into the typical categories.

Tar'cil: the scholar's tongue and written language of Tar'citadel.

Tar'citadel: the holy city of ice and light, where lies the Great Temple of Spirit, the Tar'citadel University, and the formal meeting place of the twelve nations.

tar'ka-besh: the home-guard of Tar'citadel, they learn all the fighting Paths.

Tarshishum: capital of Aralim.

Tazu: Montage's race, they are shape shifters who can appear humanoid (tazu) or as a full-dragon (tyrn).

Tazu Nation: the country founded by Montage and home of the Tazu.

Tealanithiss: a black-scaled Tazu born in Dodbyen.

telekinetic: also known as Energy Manipulative, an Ability to move/channel energy either about oneself or into oneself to fuel other magical works.

teleportation: the spell to transport one's physical body through time and space; powerful Talents can also move multiple people with them. A physical destination must be in one's head to do it, though, i.e., they would have had to have been in the area once before.

Tesgree: followers of the Kubesh Way Path, masters of the bastard sword.

Tghyyr'sāqyn: meaning "changing legs." Native term for the native race of Zo'den, whose legs shape-shift. Tg'sāqyn is also used commonly as a shortened version of the term.

The Twelve: another name for the Children of Spirit. See also: Children.

The Twelve Ways: the twelve individual Ways taught by the Children; each Way is an aspect of Spirit and aids the soul in evolving to become one with Spirit once more. They are: Ultimate Way, Truth, Protection, Magic, Healing, Warrior, Death, Creativity, Love, Purity, History, and "the Way of Evil," which diverts from the rest and goes against evolution.

Thee (Genthelvith) Monortith: Jathen's half sister, daughter of Rhodonith Monortith and Dicinith Attieth. Princess of the blood, heir to the Queen of the Tazu Nation's throne.

Tourmalith Larsenitiss: Bertran Larsenitiss's uncle and the head of the Larsenitiss line.

tru'suli: followers of a Path under Ulic's Way of Truth; known as "truth seekers," they are academics and lecturers.

Turin: Sapphire Dragon of the Children, Way of Death.

tur'ri: Turin's most powerful Walkers, they merge themselves somewhat with their Child and essentially become Death. They cycle with the moon, aging and growing younger back and forth every month. When they are in the "death cycle," they can kill with a single touch.

twin-flame: term referring to the soul-pairing of each mortal soul, the masculine and feminine aspects. Each twin-flame pairing is romantically linked to each other for eternity.

tyrn: a Tazu who is in dragon form.

Tyr'sat: Tar'cil word for the shifter race of the Zo'den region. From "Tghyyr'sāqyn" and "shifter."

U

Ulic: Silver dragon of the Children, Way of Truth.

Utför, Master: Way Walker, head of the shandi Path.

V

Vas: an acolyte Pearl Paladin.

Veil: term referring to the invisible spiritual barrier that divides the physical world from the spiritual world. There is the distinction between the near- and far-side of the Veil; the near-side refers to spiritual beings that can be sensed and interacted with by physical beings while in physical form. The far-side of the Veil refers to the higher planes and the whole of Spirit, also known as "Heaven."

veil-sliding: the act of raising the vibration of one's body height enough to slide along the barrier between time and space. Unlike teleportation, it is easier to take people along for the ride, and no distinct destination is needed, though it does take longer than teleportation.

Verdigriss: one of the lost five hundred Tazu of Dodbyen.

Vermeilith Monortith: King of the Tazu nation preceding Kyanith, uncle to Kyanith and Marcasith. Stabbed to death by a jilted lover.

Volaille, High Walker: Way Walker, High Walker of Beleskie.

W

ward: a magical protective barrier.

Way: one of the individual Twelve Ways.

Way Walker: a trained disciple of a Way, usually a member of one of the many Paths; essentially, an ordained priest or priestess of an individual Way, as opposed to a "follower," who is not ordained. They are almost always Talents of measurable Ability.

Whydā Shrā: "lonely desert," native name for Zo'den Desert.

Y

Yvette Ashton: Historical figure, deceased. Mistress of Metals, greatest Charm Master to ever live. One of the eight Original Clan who founded the Clan race; wife of Orrick Ashton. Founder of the Ashoni Clan of the Clan Lands. Murdered by A'ron De'contes.

Z

Zhìliáo, High Walker: High Walker of the Way of Desmoulein.

Zo'den: the country as well as two "city sites" of the nomadic Msāfryan and Tghyyr'sāqyn peoples. The country borders the Tazu Nation.

Also by J. Leigh

The Tazu Saga
Way Walkers: Tangled Paths
Way Walkers: Tainted Talent
Way Walkers: Broken City

Watch for more at waywalkersguide.com.

About the Author

J. Leigh wrote her first novel at the tender age of eleven, delving deep into the extensive fantasy world she entitled Way Walkers . Since then, she has never really left, though occasionally does emerge to enjoy the company of friends, family, horror movies and the ever-popular sushi dinner.

She currently lives in southern New Jersey with a chow-chow, several cats and fictional cast of hundreds. Leigh's published works include a "choose your own" interactive novel, Way Walkers: University , with Choice of Games.

Read more at waywalkersguide.com.

About the Publisher

Dear Reader,

We hope you enjoyed this book. Please consider leaving a review on your favorite book site.

Visit https://RedAdeptPublishing.com to see our entire catalogue.

Don't forget to subscribe to our monthly newsletter to be notified of future releases and special sales.

Printed in Great Britain
by Amazon

72460701R00169